MANCHU PALACES

ALSO BY JEANNE LARSEN

FICTION

Bronze Mirror

Silk Road: A Novel of Eighth-Century China

POETRY

James Cook in Search of Terra Incognita

Brocade River Poems: Selected Works of the Tang Dynasty Courtesan Xue Tao (translator)

A John Macrae Book

HENRY HOLT

AND COMPANY

NEW YORK

MANCHU PALACES

A NOVEL

JEANNE LARSEN

Henry Holt and Company, Inc.

Publishers since 1866

115 West 18th Street

New York, New York 10011

Henry Holt® is a registered trademark of Henry Holt and Company, Inc.

Published in Canada by Fitzhenry & Whiteside Ltd.,

195 Allstate Parkway, Markham, Ontario L3R 4T8.

Library of Congress Cataloging-in-Publication Data

Larsen, Jeanne.

Manchu palaces: a novel / Jeanne Larsen.—1st ed.

p.   cm.

1. China—History—Ch'ing dynasty, 1644–1912—Fiction.   I. Title.

PS3562.A735M36   1996   96-21500

813'.54—dc20   CIP

ISBN 0-8050-1111-0

First Edition—1996

Book designed by Claire Naylon Vaccaro

Map by James E. Horgan

Printed in the United States of America

All first editions are printed on acid-free paper. ∞

1   3   5   7   9   10   8   6   4   2

for
Sir Hugh Fitz-Hyffen,
Sean Siobhan,
and
Cosmo Cotswaldo, Ph.D.

"I tip my hat, my hats, I bow my head."

"We at last reached a covered pavilion open on all sides and situated on a summit. . . . I saw everything before me as on an illuminated map, palaces, pagodas, . . . plains and valleys watered by innumerable streams, hills waving with woods."

—GEORGE LORD MACARTNEY (1737–1806)

"All those prospects and pavilions—even the rocks and trees and flowers will seem somehow incomplete without that touch of poetry which only the written word can lend a scene."

—CAO XUEQIN (1715?–1763)

"I meditated on that lost maze: I imagined it inviolate and perfect at the secret crest of a mountain; I imagined it erased by rice fields or beneath the water; I imagined it infinite, no longer composed of octagonal kiosks and returning paths, but of rivers and provinces and kingdoms."

—JORGE LUIS BORGES (1899–1986)

CONTENTS

CONTENTS

ACKNOWLEDGMENTS

The author wishes to thank Hollins College and the Virginia Center for the Creative Arts for making the writing of this book possible. The research was begun during the National Endowment for the Humanities Summer Institute at the University of Michigan, "Reading the Manchu Summer Palace at Chengde"; heartfelt gratitude to the NEH, the organizers and faculty of the institute, and my engaging colleagues there.

PREFACE

For more than two and a half centuries, until the last emperor's abdication in 1912, the Manchus' Qing dynasty ruled China. Descendants of hard-riding invaders from the cold forests and dry scrublands of Manchuria held sway over the Han Chinese and all other peoples "within the passes."

But their empire was not limited to the domain of the defeated Ming dynasty. Beyond the Chinese homeland, the Manchus controlled the northeast tribes and the khanates of the Mongols, the rich oasis city-states around the far west's Tarim basin and the broad verge of the Tibetan plateau. They claimed at different times, with differing success, sovereignty over the Himalayan uplands, and greater swaths of Central Asia and southeast Siberia. They accepted offerings from Korea, Nepal, Vietnam, Kazakhstan, and more—along with eager embassies from Russia, Great Britain, and other exotic lands.

The Manchus did not win and hold such power unaided. Han Chinese as well as Mongols fought beneath their banners. Some by choice, and some in bondage: a clever, lucky man or woman could benefit from being born in thralldom to an emperor. As you will see.

Holder of the dragon throne for most of the eighteenth century, through the years Qing glory reached its greatest heights and began its slow descent, was a son of the Aisin Gioro clan named Hongli: the Qianlong emperor. This strong-willed man desired the building of costly temples, and many palaces. He surrounded himself with grandeur even as he tried to stop the dying of his ancestors' disciplined ways.

In the heart of Beijing, behind the fortifications of the Forbidden City, stately halls and ornate chapels and scarlet-trimmed pavilions in walled-garden compounds were added or replaced at his command. Just outside the capital, regal villas rose among delightful landscapes reserved for the imperial household. And in a green valley one hundred fifty miles to the northeast, a former hunting camp grew to magnificence as a summer retreat. There, elegant mansions, shaded courtyards, and airy lakeside lodges flowered within the spacious circle of its stone wall.

Few subjects of the empire ever set foot in any of these splendid precincts. Yet some must have dreamt of glimpsing the fabulous constructions: Such imagined palaces, at least, you may enter in.

The Qianlong emperor and those close to him also saw another sort of palace, a kind still known to believers in the Tantric Buddhism of the Thunderbolt Way, teachings brought to the Manchus by lamas from Mongolia and Tibet. Open only to those who passed through initiations, who learned the secret practices and took the vows, these *mandalas* were intricate palaces made by human artisans—as dwelling places for the gods.

NOTE ON SPELLING

Different writers have used different systems to spell Chinese words in the roman alphabet; a city may be called "Beijing" by one person and "Peking" or "Pekin" or "Beeijing" or "Pei-ching" by another. Yet each of these represents the same two Chinese characters (meaning "northern capital"), with the same pronunciation.

The writers' choices sometimes reflect political allegiances, sometimes their beliefs about how the sounds of languages work, sometimes the spelling practices of their native tongues, or the tongues of intermediaries. The words we read, after all, are not transparent windowpanes, but lenses, shaped and chosen.

To accord with the most common present usage in the United States, I have used standard *pinyin* romanization to spell historical names. The *q* in such terms as "Qing dynasty" is pronounced much like the English *ch*. But to make pronunciation easier for English speakers, I have generally used a modified version of pinyin, substituting, for example, *ts* (as at the end of *cats*) for the pinyin initial *c*, and *hs* (a slightly hissing "sh") for *x*.

Some sections of the book, however, reflect the romanization practices of writers in earlier times. When "the Qianlong emperor" becomes "the Ch'ien-lung emperor," you may assume that the same historical figure is being pointed to. But you might also imagine yourself to be standing in a portrait gallery, and ask if the man you know from the luminous tempera painting before you is the same as the one in the incisive engraving beside it, or that other depiction in heavy oils.

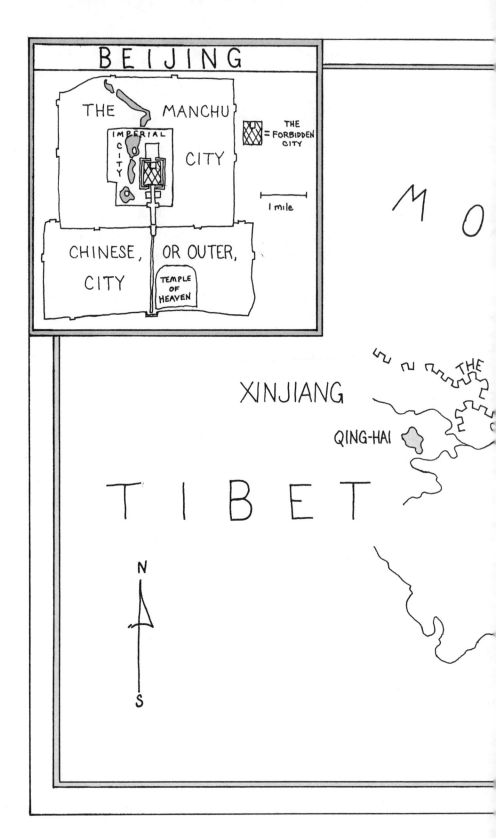

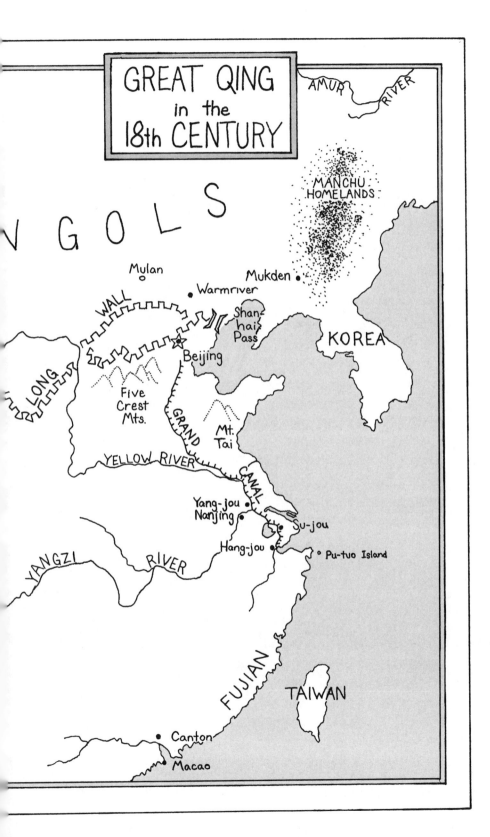

GREAT QING
in the
18th CENTURY

MONGOLS

AMUR RIVER

MANCHU HOMELANDS

Mulan

Mukden

Warmriver

WALL

Shan-hai Pass

KOREA

LONG

Beijing

Five Crest Mts.

GRAND

Mt. Tai

YELLOW RIVER

CANAL

Yang-jou
Nanjing

Su-jou

YANGZI

RIVER

Hang-jou

Pu-tuo Island

FUJIAN

TAIWAN

Canton

Macao

MANCHU PALACES

HOW IT ALL BEGINS

This is no story: today I learned of a secret text. It tells how once upon a time the blessed Guan-yin, who regards our world with love and pity, descended to the underwater palace of the Dragon Monarch. It does not tell all that happened afterward.

How clear and sweet the aura light that must have washed the coral pillars of the Dragon's porticos! How all the eels and seastars in the courtyards, the mackerel courtiers and oysters-in-waiting and Yangzi River dolphins in the throne room must have throbbed with joy!

There, the holy bodhisattva revealed the Mantra-Charm of All Compassion, that grants relief from suffering.

In gratitude for that powerful teaching, the daughter of the Dragon Monarch—in another old text she's said to be a granddaughter—gave Guan-yin a jewel like no other.

I wonder if it was a pearl.

I wonder if it was a story, glistening layers of slick talk around an irksome grain. If so, it could go like this.

In the cool of the Purple Bamboo Grove, Guan-yin sits at royal ease on her island home in the Southern Sea. (Though the bodhisattva takes on many forms, it might as well be "her." It might as well be radiant Mount Potalaka, called in Chinese "Pu-tuo Island," though it could be anywhere.) Rising full out of the ocean, the moon inscribes a halo around Guan-yin's graceful figure, and casts its own reflection on her lotus pond.

But look! A huge, bewhiskered carp shatters the surface of the water. It snaps at a fly, it swirls, it plunges down. Crisscross ripples, all at odds with one another, set the tranquil water rocking, reeling, gone awry. They smash the contemplative mirror moon into ten thousand shards.

Standing now at Guan-yin's side, the Dragon Daughter frowns. The bodhisattva's other attendant—call him Pilgrim Lad—squints his pious eyes. And Guan-yin's white parrot (I saw it flying in a holy picture just today) is so startled that it drops the rosary dangling from its beak.

The string of the rosary snaps. Yet its pearly beads stay in a circle as they fall. One hundred eight small moons gleam and loop and tumble through the air.

A splash resounds. Again within the round reflection of the moon, wavelets spread in rings. But this time they dance in flawless order, sketching a mandala that maps the cosmos breathing outward from its empty core.

The beads sink into the muck beneath the lotus pond.

Dragon Daughter (being new here) worries. She knows too well that dwellers in the human realm need all the help that they can get. Need the help of sacred paintings, statues, mantras, rosaries. With this one lost, will it fare worse now with the world? One hand flies up, adjusts the snaky dragon headdress on her heaped-up hair.

Pilgrim Lad (being the sort he is) turns anxious, vexed. His shaved scalp puckers. His soft earlobes flutter as he shakes his head. How will the scattered be found? How will the broken be made whole?

Even the ruddy carp—who long ago grew fat and strong on Guan-yin's words, then (being the sort *it* is) turned its new powers cruelly on men and women, till the bodhisattva caught it and returned it here—even the ruddy, fleshy carp feels troubled. What will come of its unthinking act?

And perhaps the bodhisattva herself is a little curious about the working-out of things, although she surely knows the story's end. Or perhaps it is to teach her two attendants that she asks what they think happens next, after the beads' fall into the mud from which, sometimes, lotus blossoms grow.

Dragon Daughter says she has an answer. Or she might. Her dark eyes flash green: would the others like to hear the tale, maybe play a part?

Pilgrim Lad nods, thinking of his old home in the world of mortals. Guan-yin smiles her faint inward smile and settles back. The carp swims round and round in a familiar figure eight, smacking its full lips, already savoring tastes and smells and tickles. They listen. You can too.

A LOTUS BLOSSOMS: 1

I can't forget her. I mustn't. I only want to stop remembering for a little while.

Again today, a few flakes of snow mix with the dust on the sharp wind. Nurse complains that spring is coming late this year; she wants me to close the papered window and huddle with her near the charcoal burner. But I sit alone up on the warm brick platform of my bed, pretending to embroider, looking out at the white petals of the early-blooming plum. When the wind tears them off, they scatter, lost on a sweep of air come south from the steppes. And again I wonder, will my father come home soon?

Ten days ago, Aunt Gao told New Year's callers to our household that my father hoped to leave Nanjing at midmonth, returning to Beijing by way of the Grand Canal. Last year, he and Mama both were here to accept the New Year's calls.

But on this same day last year—the fifteenth, beginning of the Lantern Festival—Mama was too sick to look forward to joining in the fun that night, so sick she fainted after we finished the offerings to the family's ancestors in our main hall. Her whole body ached, she said, and her eyes watered as if she were crying and couldn't stop.

Before sunrise the fever rose till she burned like a lantern made of parchment. The doctor arrived at midday. He took her pulses while I peeped from behind a screen; he prescribed a tonic, shook his head. On the evening of eighteenth, they lifted her off the bed so she wouldn't bring a curse down on it, and she lay on a wide, cold plank, her face turned away from us all. In the morning, she was dead.

The loose, ugly stitches I'm making blur. I swallow. If I cry now, Nurse will scold, reminding me one more time how I failed to make a proper daughter's howl of grief after Mama let out her last ragged breath. And when they put her in the coffin. And during the burial procession. She says, Aunt Gao and Grandfather said, even Father told me: because I didn't join the wailing, I'd disgraced the family.

The other girls and women of the household did their duty, Nurse will say, and no use for me to mumble that I kotowed, tore my hair loose, put on mourning clothes, did whatever someone told me to. *You brought shame on every one of us, little missy,* she'll say. *All you would do was sit like a lump, and stare at the altar lamp. How do you think your mother's soul felt then, confused and wandering in the dark? And you too proud or foolish to call to her?*

Not proud. Every time I tried to cry out, my throat closed, thick and tight.

I drop the sash I'm embroidering. I'd cover my ears if it would stop the rest of the words I've heard Nurse say too many times: . . . *her without a living son to make the offerings, and* (her voice always drops here, but I hear it, loud as the funeral drums, piercing as the reedy funeral piping, when I lie awake at night) *your Aunt Gao and First Uncle cutting corners wherever they could, little missy. That cheap coffin! And then rushing the burial to save on guest expenses, skimping on the sutra-chanting nuns and priests and on the Taoist masters, too! Your grandfather so . . . distracted. And your father too proper to cross his older brother. Ai ya!*

Nurse only said that last part once, only once hissed that Father should have paid more honor to a wife who after all did give him a boy, stillborn though it was. But she might as well have chanted her complaint ten thousand times: the words still ring within me like the sutras' drone.

One thing will hold the sadness back. Where is it? I grope behind the bolster at the back of the bed platform, look quietly to make sure Nurse is busy with her own needlework. There. The unpolished base of the small statue digs into my palm when I squeeze it, hard as I can.

Keep this secret, Mama said, when she gave me this image of holy Tara after her fever came. She promised that the goddess would look after me. Its points and edges press into my skin. The dull pain reminds me I'm alive.

Hurry, Lotus, I can't wait much longer!" My cousin Wintersweet grins and tugs at my heavy cape. Her apple-cheeked maid, Happiness, helps her pull me onto the veranda outside my room. In the evening light, Wintersweet's thick pock marks fade a bit, and I see again how beautiful she is, or would have been. Dusk at last, and the fifteenth-day rites for the ancestors are over with. Last year at this hour, my mother had been carried, weak limbed and shaking, to her bed. Now we are going out to walk the city's crowded streets and admire the fancy lanterns hung at every gate, or dangling from scaffoldings set up in the streets.

Of course I'm not allowed to stay at home. When I asked, Nurse simply clucked her tongue. But I found my own victory, hiding the hand warmer she gave me, slipping Mama's out of the trunk that holds her things, and placing the little Tara statue on a folded handkerchief where the coals should go. Why shouldn't I carry it with me? Surely that at least is my own affair.

Nurse shoos Wintersweet and Happiness and me ahead of her, as anxious as my cousin to enjoy the excitement and see the displays. This evening, she says, all Beijing will shine like the starry Silver River that pours across the sky. Or like the pearls on Wintersweet's new festival cap. Happiness nods, her round cheeks glowing even in the half-light.

"Do you like it, Lotus?" Wintersweet turns so I can admire the flashing kingfisher feathers woven into the black cap's stiff gauze. "Quite the grown-up lady, aren't I? For better or for worse." She whirls back around. "Never mind that. Soon you'll be grown up too, so we might as well be happy about it. Come on . . . my mother will be waiting."

I just nod and walk along with her, caught up in thinking how pretty Mama used to look in this cape I'm suddenly tall enough to wear. If the bamboo shoots embroidered near the hem had been real when she died, they'd be standing full grown now among the other silken stalks, leafy and frosted green, and empty inside.

Across the Front Courtyard two snowflake lanterns hang from a red pole tall enough to show them off to everyone who passes along our outer wall. The wind picks up; the lanterns twist and toss and go nowhere, their panes of mica glittering like the full moon beyond. As we start to walk toward them, passing the courtyard's little lotus pond, Wintersweet tells me Grandfather has declared we women are to stay in the Manchu City, and not to go into the Chinese part of town.

"Completely unreasonable," she whispers as her mother comes over to us, followed by Little Auntie Padma, First Uncle's concubine. Aunt Gao's two senior maids hurry after them, their chatter bright as their festival skirts and jackets.

But Aunt Gao overhears. "What's unreasonable, daughter?" Her voice slides clear and unyielding as the ice on the pond. The servants assembled over near the gate turn toward one another, suddenly busy with nothing much.

Wintersweet, as I expect, says what she thinks. And, as I expect, is upbraided for it: "Yes, we're Chinese, daughter. And yes, of course, Manchus, Chinese, Mongols, Muslims—all the people of the Great Qing are one family."

I glance toward round-faced Little Auntie Padma, who stands quietly with lowered eyes. No surprise that Aunt Gao has somehow forgotten to include Tibetans in the list. Despite her sharp northwestern tones, Padma speaks Chinese as easily as the rest of us. She grew up in Qing-hai, which some people say can't really be counted as Tibet—but my first aunt never lets her husband's concubine forget her family's foreign origins. Things got worse around the time Nurse told me Padma will have a baby before summer's end. I don't see why: the child will call Aunt Gao "Mother," and the family needs a son.

Aunt Gao fingers the pearls that hang from her earlobes. No need to seek out trouble among the Chinese of the Outer City, she tells us, not on Primal Night, when vulgar men are bound to be drinking heavily. Doesn't the law promote civil harmony by declaring that like must live with like? And even after all these years, how can the conquered Chinese help resenting the victorious Manchus and those who've fought underneath their banners? How can they help resenting *us*?

I know all that. But I nod anyway, and so does Wintersweet. Luckily, Third Aunt, dressed even tonight in drab widow's clothes, dashes in just then, all shy fluster and apologies, her maid, Partridge, trotting at her heels. So Wintersweet and I are spared the full lesson, at least.

Look at your new Manchu cap, Aunt Gao would say. Look at our great big unbound feet. Could the Chinese of the Outer City not know us for what we are?

The rest, of course, would hang unsaid: what we are is *not* Manchus, or even descendants of Chinese soldiers who chose to fight beside the Manchus to victory over a dying dynasty. Grandfather's grandfather's father, for all his bravery in battle, was no free warrior who threw his lot in with the conquerers. He had been captured. He was a slave.

And all of us—we Suns, the Gaos, Mama's family too—are still, despite our money and position, despite imperial favor, slaves. But now Wintersweet takes my hand, and we walk through the roofed double gate at the southeast corner of our compound, out into the world. It feels strange not to ride safe inside a closed cart or a sedan chair. Strange, and too much like last year's burial procession. Strange to be outside our home at all.

Wintersweet tugs away from her maid, and whispers to me with more restraint. "Sorry," she says. "And really, it's all because of me, isn't it? Now that I'm fifteen and my hair's pinned up, Grandfather's so strict. Chinese wives and girls in the Outer City go out more, I know it. And you've heard what Mother says about southern women's immodest ways! But," she tucks her chin and puffs out her cheeks, looks at me sternly, squints with an old man's eyes, "taking on those, *hrmpff-ah,* those loose modern habits would be most, *hrmpff-ah,* improper for—Aiiiii-ah!"

The rattle-clatter of firecrackers makes us both jump. And then start laughing, laughing. Fear and relief and amusement at our own silliness: I can hardly catch my breath. Two boys hoot and run away. I laugh. I gasp. Right there where our lane meets the avenue, not five feet from the police guards idling near the wooden street gate, tears leak onto my cheeks.

Nurse and Wintersweet and Happiness close in on me, pat my back, screen me from curious eyes. Padma sees what's going on and slips through the crowd to give me her handkerchief. Some of the junior maids gather round. If I don't stop, Aunt Gao or even Third Aunt will notice and everyone might have to go home before the evening's started.

I wouldn't mind, but poor Wintersweet! So I wipe my eyes with one hand, careful to keep the hand warmer tucked inside my other sleeve. I swallow. I know how to make crying stop.

"I'm fine, I'm fine," I murmur, though they probably can't hear me in the hubbub, can only see my forced smile and my upraised palm. Louder then:

"Oh, look! A toad lantern. And one shaped like a camel!" Happiness glances around. "There," I say, "near the cake vendor, just past the fortune-teller's umbrella."

"Fortune-teller?" Wintersweet wipes a last tear from my cheek, but her eyes flick toward the old man in the dirty fur-lined hat beneath his oiled-paper roof.

"Do you suppose—" Other lanterns, silver and golden, shaped like fish or scholars, hydrangeas or monkeys or moths, beckon us down the street. But Wintersweet is absorbed in reading the cloth sign hanging from the fortune-teller's table. "Happiness!" she says. "Quick, fetch Mother. I mean, ask her—Hurry, silly! Go."

She gives Happiness a tiny push and the chubby maid dashes forward through the swarm of people. It's easier to shape a smile this time, when I glimpse Aunt Gao and Third Aunt and the rest of the maids returning.

Aunt Gao reminds us that we've only begun to look about. "Perhaps later," she says, then makes a moue as someone spits a melon-seed hull nearby. "We'll walk toward the Imperial City, shall we, perhaps hear what's going on inside the villas and palaces there?" She motions to one of our gate boys to start pushing a way through the crowd. "Yes, later, daughter—I think it wise of you to want to know your fortune for *this* year."

Third Aunt smiles and covers her mouth. Partridge beside her titters. Wintersweet shoots me a look, then shrugs. Too much else for her to think about just now. A racket of horns and drums rises from behind a gray brick wall.

My own attention's taken up with navigating the crowds. Police with swords and handwhips keep watch from sentry stations; others brandish their long hooked poles as they patrol the avenues and lanes. They're out in full force. I should feel safer, but I've heard too many stories of what can happen to children on Primal Night. I might get separated, kidnapped, lost, or simply stepped on: This is the first time in months I've been outside. The burial procession drew onlookers, of course, even though it wasn't a fancy one. But people hardly jostled us when—

I must put the thought aside. And there's plenty of distraction tonight. Toy peddlers, ragged sages selling amulets, a monkey show man with flags and a hand gong and a curly-tailed dog on a leash. One pork-and-wine shop displays a glimmering candlelit ice statue of Old Master Longlife that Nurse can hardly tear herself away from. Soon we're admiring the boughs of paper plum blossoms at a night market booth. Wintersweet declares them cunning, but less beautiful than real flowers. Third Aunt peers nearsightedly and sighs that at least they'll last longer, whereupon Wintersweet tells Happiness to give the tired-looking woman behind the counter a few coins.

"Now, Third Aunt, Lotus, Mother—each of you pick the branch you like best." She hesitates. "Oh, Little Auntie Padma, too. Then we'll have an even number to put, to put wherever we decide to put them." But Wintersweet's tact fails. As the concubine selects a graceful spray, Aunt Gao refuses the one her daughter offers her, declaring them not to her taste.

Wintersweet only bows her head, but as her mother strikes up a conversation with Third Aunt and moves on, my cousin thrusts the pretty thing toward her maid. "Take it, Happiness," she says. "Why shouldn't you have one?"

The truth is, the branches soon become a nuisance, what with our hand warmers and capes and drooping sleeves. The junior maids and gate boys already have their hands filled with the poles of the tasseled lanterns that light our way, or other things—carry-boxes for purchases and handkerchiefs and umbrellas in case it starts to snow. Soon Nurse takes my branch, grumbling a bit, and Partridge holds Third Aunt's. Still, Happiness seems to enjoy watching the bits of paper flutter as she brandishes hers through the chilly air. And Padma continues to clasp her own small bough in silence; once I catch her lifting it against the glowing disk of the moon. She returns my cautious smile.

We visit two temples to see the picture-lantern exhibitions hung on their walls. I recall a year when I was very young, and Mama took me from Nurse and held me up herself and explained the holy stories that the lanterns showed. But the crowds are too thick here, and it's hard to glimpse more than a corner of any scene. Then what's the good, I think, of all that silk and fancy framing, all that careful painting?

My legs ache. People keep bumping into me, even when the gate boys remember their jobs and try to ward them off. The greasy smells from the food stalls cling to my hair; smoke scratches at my eyes. Each shout or bang of fireworks seems to nick a tiny piece of my skin. Even the hand warmer is a burden now. The chilly metal pulls heat from my hands, and I wish I hadn't brought it. Maybe I could give it to Nurse, tell her it's gone cold.

No. She'd notice the extra weight of the statue inside. I brought it out. I'll take it back. Besides, I meant to have a part of Mama with me.

That last thought sets me wondering where her spirit is. Maybe she passed through the underworld long ago. I'm sure my mama did nothing to be punished for, but I still hate to think of her there.

What is it like for her now? Does she long for what she can no longer touch? Perhaps she sees it all though my eyes, I think—if that's possible. If so, I ought to keep on looking, no matter how sleepy I am.

The watch drum booms across the crowded boulevard. I can hardly believe we're out so late. Aunt Gao picks up her pace, but we're headed away from home.

Before us, bearers with an elegant sedan chair shoulder through the mass of bodies. I'd rather be traveling that way, protected and warm and out of sight. No sense saying as much to Wintersweet, though. We've had that argument before.

I yawn. I've almost decided I *have* to ask Nurse to take me back when an odd thing happens. Aunt Gao has brought us to a halt at a busy intersection. She looks around, then sends her chief maid, Grace, and little Deucey to buy holiday rice dumplings for us to eat at home. When they finally return from the crowded stall, my first aunt lingers.

A squatting beggar monk claps his wooden blocks, announcing a tale to come: he's telling the story of the sutra-seeking monk who went to India with Monkey and his other disciples. That's not odd, but it's odd that Aunt Gao of all people leads us over to him, odder that she then doesn't really seem to listen after all. Instead, she keeps looking around at passersby.

Never mind, I think muzzily, shifting the hand warmer and rubbing my fist in my eye. I used to love this story, though it's been a year since I could pay much attention to any tale. "The mind monkey," Mama used to call him. He mostly goes by Sun Wu-kong; his family name is the same as ours—that always made me giggle—and Mama explained that "Wu-kong" means "Aware of the Emptiness." Once when we had a ballad singer in for a family party Mama confessed to me she liked that trickster's adventures far better than the romances Third Aunt favors, or the tales of girl heroes gone to war that Wintersweet always picks.

A mule cart preceded by shouting runners makes its way down the wide street. Aunt Gao's head snaps up. "Why, that must be the Jin family's Lady Ding," she says. "Wintersweet! Grace! Happiness! Harmony!"

Mother, daughter, and maids, accompanied by two of the more presentable gate boys, walk over to the mule cart. Their silks and satins shine in a hundred lanterns' light. Some kind of conversation's going on, greetings, polite introductions, but I pay more attention to the fantastic fight the red-robed monk's describing. Nurse puts an arm around my waist. I let her draw me close to her plump, warm side.

For a moment. The monk's voice goes high and sharp as he speaks for Monkey. Someone shoves in front of me. I can't see. I want to watch the monk's face stretch and squeeze and shift. It feels so good to be *interested* in something again, though I don't think about that for long as I slip forward through the ring of bodies.

There. The monk on his mat widens his eyes till they almost pop from his head. The crowd laughs. A skinny novice—also red robed; they must be from a Mongol or Tibetan temple—starts moving around with his begging bowl outstretched. Just as he comes to me, he stumbles. He falls forward. And then the oddest thing of all: I feel the novice's hand snake beneath the loose shield of my cape and up my sleeve; he grabs at the hand warmer and tugs.

"No!" I squawk, and pull back, hard. A few heads turn, and the old woman beside me starts to scold the novice, who ducks his scabby head and hurries on.

Why would he try to steal a shabby hand warmer, I wonder. Then I realize: it must have been the statue that he wanted. But why? And however did he know I had it there?

The monk chants his tale more loudly. Several people frown and shush the old woman. I've still got the hand warmer, and the Tara, but I'm frightened. I want Nurse.

Pushing out through the watchers is easier than pushing in. Most of them haven't noticed a thing; they're just anxious to see a little better themselves.

"I need to go home," I say to Nurse, who looks at me and nods and leads me to a quieter spot, and never asks me why.

It's only the next sleepy morning that Nurse explains what was going on last night with Lady Ding. "Common sense," she says, "for a mother to want to lay eyes on a prospective daughter-in-law, no matter how much she knows about her family standing and horoscope and such." Nurse stands behind me, fixing my hair for today's offerings to the ancestors' spirit tablets in the main hall, and I think she's talking to distract me. Or because she's Nurse, and so she talks. "So people—well-to-do folk, anyway—arrange these accidental meetings. And that's your poor cousin's problem."

"Because of her skin, you mean?"

"Exactly. Now you'd *expect* they'd be glad to get a girl as has survived the smallpox, since she's that much more likely to live to serve them in their old age, wouldn't you? But I'll warrant this Lady Ding will be thinking only of what her precious son will see when he first lifts the bridal veil." The comb tugs at a knot. "Well, there's time enough—she's still quite young, your cousin is. And at least her face protected her from being drafted as a palace maid, and with the dowry and connections this family can provide . . ."

She stops combing, and twitches my padded vest, to set it straight. "Not that a term of service in the Forbidden City is a *bad* thing, little missy, whatever outside people say. An honor and an opportunity, isn't it, even if some of the palace maids feel a little homesick now and then. Why, there's plenty of girls not . . . not registered under the Upper Banners the way you are, who'd give anything to be placed where they have the chance of catching a prince's eye."

"Are you done with my hair?" I ask. She starts fussing with the wooden comb again, but the talking doesn't stop.

"You must always remember His Majesty's own mother, Young Mistress, how she started low and came to be the most honored mother in all the world, and her father's position helping manage the princely household before His Late Majesty rose to the throne not so different from your father's—"

"I'll remember, Nurse. I could hardly ever forget, could I, I've heard it so many times." But she's only trying to make me feel better, though I hate it when she calls me "Young Mistress," as if I'm already grown. "Tell me . . . tell me why Wintersweet wasn't vaccinated the way I was?"

Nurse sighs heavily, and I hold my breath. No one ever talks about this, and I've never dared ask before. But now's a good time: Tetra and Quinta, the junior maids for our Upper Courtyard, can't overhear. They're over in Third Aunt's side building, across from ours, or maybe bringing hot water for Grandfather's morning washup next door in the big North Hall.

"Now that I can't say, missy. You wasn't born yet when Miss Wintersweet took sick and her poor little older brother met his fate, so I wasn't here. I just heard—"

She lowers her voice, though the breakfast things have already been taken back to the kitchen, and these days almost no one visits our building except Wintersweet and Happiness, and you can always hear them coming. "I know this. When you was just a tiny thing, your father said as how offerings to the Smallpox Goddess weren't enough—the palace folk rub bits of pox blossom scab in their babies' nostrils, and it protects them. His Majesty's grandfather started it, he said. But Missus—one of the other servants told me it was your late grandmother as had been against that idea, before, so this family had never done it. Your First Uncle was mostly off on business back when his own two babies should have been protected, and what could your Aunt Gao do against her mother-in-law?"

"So Wintersweet and her brother got smallpox after Third Uncle was killed so young in battle out in Kashgar, and then Grandmother died of coughing blood. Nurse, do you think Grandmother was being punished for—"

The comb scrapes my scalp, hard. "That's quite enough, Young Mistress! I was only answering your question, but I can see *that* was a mistake. Even if it's true, we need no unfilial, morbid talk from you." Her voice softens. "Your old nurse knows what's really bothering you. You'll feel better about everything after the one-year rites for your mother, I promise. Just three more days. When my Ma—but never mind."

She puts the comb down gently, seeing how ashamed I am by my outspokenness. I'm also shamed by this: I hadn't really thought before that Nurse must have had a mother once. She puts one warm, admonishing hand on my shoulder. "You want your father to come home from Nanjing to a nice young lady as knows how to behave, now don't you?"

Miserable, still facing away from her, I nod. Mama could have told me the whole story. She was here when the smallpox took my young boy-cousin away, but I always thought I'd ask her sometime later. Now all she knew is lost to me.

"Well, then, you must try a little harder, that's all. Remember, your cousin Wintersweet . . . she's got a ma here to protect her interests so it doesn't matter if she goes a bit far when she's excited, with her lively ways and all. Besides, right now we should feel sorry for her, shouldn't we, knowing she'll soon be leaving to go live out her life in some strange household. You're a good child, but the only one you feel sorry for is yourself." The hand on my shoulder squeezes gently. "You're forgetting that, sooner or later, everybody's mother dies."

My throat aches, so tight and close I think I might stop breathing. There's a cup of cold tea on my mother's dressing table, now mine. I gulp it down and the hurt of drinking chases the other hurt away.

"That's right, little missy. It's hard, I know, but we all learn to bear it." She gives my hair a final pat. "Now, you've got a while till you go pay your respects to your ancestors again, so—oh, your old nurse is turning into such a forgetful thing! Did you notice the package from my brother the lantern maker that arrived while we were out last night, or were you the sleepy melonhead you seemed?"

She makes me guess what's in it and—maybe she's right about how I'll be feeling better soon—I enjoy her teasing the way I used to. When I see what the present is, I forget about being almost grown up, and squeeze Nurse till she pretends to groan at my great strength.

A running horse lantern: as Nurse lights the candle under them, two galloping steeds pursued by two Mongol grooms start to revolve inside the pretty, fragile frame. After that, I forget as well that next winter it will be my turn to stand among the other bondservant girls for the annual selection of palace maids, forget Father's absence, forget just for a moment about being sad, and watch the paper figures turn and turn.

A TALE OF SILVER

Sixteen forty-four is as good a date as any to mark the start of the
Manchus' rule of China. But if their empire, *the Great Qing*, still lives,
it lives only in bright scenes laid out on silk and paper by visionary artists
or hungry hacks. In maps of the vanished. In sad ruins, seductive recon-
structions, conflicting histories.

This story of the Qing is one of them. This is where that scattered
rosary, that mandala-ring of pearly beads, came down to earth—in a new
form. And this is where the fragments must be gathered into one again.

This story, you might say, of a lotus coming into bloom: it has begun
in no particular year, early in the eighth decade of the eighteenth century,
as some reckon time. At the zenith, give or take a little, of the Qianlong
emperor's reign. The zenith, all in all, of the Qing dynasty.

An empire born of ferocious valor and unyielding discipline has grown
sleek with new food crops, booming commerce, babies, peace. Most peas-
ants prosper, relatively speaking. Art collections grow. Gentlemen—and
the more fortunate ladies—read poems, stories, plays. Outside the coastal
southeast, opium remains, as yet, more likely to be medicine than addic-
tion. The population has not quite outgrown the government's capacity to
oversee the functioning of the state, and official corruption has not gotten
entirely out of hand. The Grand Canal and the Yellow River levees will
remain in good condition for some while. The unwelcome greedy foreigners have, so far, been kept outside.

And in the capital city of Beijing, perhaps half a year before the death
of Lotus's mother, a smooth-faced artisan named Wu Ming hides in the
storeroom of a workshop devoted to making religious art. He can hear
Tantric Buddhist lamas in the nearby Yong-heh Palace Temple, chanting
by the light of smoky lamps. Casual footsteps sound. Two of the senior
metallurgists walk past the storeroom, talking of the project they'll begin
tomorrow morning. Wu Ming holds his breath.

He has planned carefully for what he'll do tonight. After four years' apprenticeship and six months as a junior sculptor, he knows the workshop's routines well. Soon all the work rooms will stand empty, as most of the unmarried men and boys retire to the dormitory off beyond the forge, and the others leave the compound, hurrying to reach their homes before the city's curfew falls.

He knows his motive, too: his father's dying. Despite the religious instruction that comes with his job, Wu Ming's not one to put much faith in Buddhist prayers. But the right medicine, he thinks, might save the man he's duty bound to save. Even at the price of his own flesh—young Wu grew up with tales of children who boiled chunks of meat cut from their bodies, that they might feed a starving parent broth.

Yet medicine costs money. Wu Ming's been paid mostly in room and board. And even the few taels of silver he's received in the half year since his promotion have gone to pay Wu family debts: they're bannerfolk, but in this time of peace, the emperor has less need of them. Especially Han Chinese like Wu Ming and his father, who are not bound to His Majesty the way Manchus, and his bondservants, are.

Squatting in the dusty storeroom, Wu Ming fights back a sneeze—and a flash of rage. My grandfathers, he thinks, fought bravely for the Manchu emperors. My father served for years in the Beijing Gendarmerie, until he grew too ill to serve. And now some whisper *turncoats*? Some dare call us Chinese bannermen faithless, betrayers of our own kind, and so potential traitors to the Qing?

He pictures, with the full force of the visual powers that helped him rise above the other apprentices, the two louts—two Chinese louts from the Outer City—who barely hid their sneers even as they suggested a sworn brotherhood that might lead to profit all around. Two louts perhaps descended from those who opened Beijing's gates to the Manchu army. Two dealers in religious art, eager to lay hands on the sacred objects Wu Ming touches every day.

Two arrogant, artless, greasy-fingered louts. Remembering, Wu Ming clamps his jaw shut, squeezes one fist until the muscles of his forearm quiver.

Nonetheless, a deal's been struck. Forty taels of silver in exchange for Wu Ming's help, including secret access to the workshop. The time's been chosen carefully: the night after a visit from the head lama of the Imperial

Office of Buddhist Paintings and Sculpture within the Forbidden City. This very night.

Someone else passes the storeroom door. A dragging step: the workshop gate guard, securing the building for the night. Wu Ming knows the old man well. He forces himself to open his clenched hands. Safe. He must believe he's safe, lest tension lead to fatal error. He feels his body shake.

His Holiness the head lama of the Imperial Office is primarily concerned with the artworks made for the imperial family in the studios of the Forbidden City's Hall of Central Uprightness. He leaves to the Yong-heh Palace Temple lamas the lesser business of this workshop that sees to the commercial trade. But Wu Ming knew what a flurry His Holiness's visit would cause here, and how on the evening after—this evening on which he hides and trembles—security might grow lax.

The slow footfalls fade away. The building's door bar thunks shut against the night, and only the one old guard remains on duty within the workshop grounds. What need for more? Who would be fool enough to steal sacred artworks from a workshop run by a temple favored by the emperor himself?

But to understand this poor fool Wu Ming, you need to see what he has seen in the light of earlier days. For one thing, his own name, which his mother wrote with difficulty, patiently, to teach him. He was a boy then, from a family not yet fallen on such hard times, a boy with hopes that education could win him a better life. A boy who knew his duty to his parents, and knew his gifts, and burned to enter his name, Wu Ming, Wu Ming, into the record book of history.

Here's another thing he's seen: not long ago, he spied a young girl's face and fell instantly in love. Just as happens in the amorous tales of the winsome big-drum singers his father likes so much.

Wu Ming doesn't know her name (her face flashed pale, pink tinged, a lotus bud). A girl from a banner family, evidently (she was leaving the Yong-heh Palace Temple as he passed by). Her clothing and her manner suggested a family of more taste than means, but of some standing nonetheless (menservants clustered round). The peek he caught (she'd come with her mother, two other women—aunts most likely—and a badly pock-marked older sister or a cousin, a gaggle of concubines or well-dressed maids) might not have stirred another man.

It stirred Wu Ming, with his discerning artist's eye.

A girl too young to marry (he saw her standing modest as a bride, then saw her glow with innocent passionate delight at something her mother said). The heart-wrenching lines of her face (he sensed a hint of an astounding self-possession that called to him, *possess*) shone softly, still cloaked by childhood, babyish. Her movements (the undeniably lovely mother drew the girl up beside her, into that cursed cart) beckoned, still unpracticed, even awkward—except in the eyes of a youth who'd already learned from a wine shop owner's wayward daughter what a subtle grace seduction offers up.

Wu Ming's family can't afford a marriage anyway. So he seizes the few sexual opportunities that come his way in an age that says quite distinctly one thing, but sometimes allows the daring or the driven—or the lower orders—the chance to do another. (He has known a lusty, lonely widow, a charming fellow apprentice, a well-to-do neighbor's careless maid.) He remembers still the face he saw, and vows to do whatever he must to take for himself the pleasures freely granted wealthy men.

He has seen too, what you perhaps have not. During his apprenticeship, Wu Ming studied under the Yong-heh lamas statues and tangka-paintings of Tantric Buddhist deities. Blue-skinned, immovable Achala, who grasps sword and noose; Mahakala, Great Black One, the Mongols' *Protector of the Tents*; ox-headed Yamantaka, slayer of Death itself: For an image to have sacred power, it must be precisely made. Now Wu Ming can sketch, and mold in wax, and cast in molten metal their individual attributes, their proper forms.

Many of the statues he has worked on sit serene, in meditation. But some wear ornaments of bone, or crowns of skulls, or garlands of severed heads—dripping blood, stripped of all flesh—draped round their waists and necks. Perhaps their fierceness fueled his own fierce sense of self-will, though that is not the best thing he might have learned from them.

Gazing at tangkas brought in from Tibet, Wu Ming has looked

unflinchingly at offering cups heaped with human entrails, at crushed bodies beneath the feet of fearsome guardians, at skull bowls and canopies of flayed human skin. At least, he tells himself he does not flinch.

Nor, he has resolved, will he flinch tonight. He's not devout, is in fact generally indifferent to things beyond this world, but to pass the time he sets his mind on the wrathful figure of Yamantaka. Protector, *adamantine terrifier,* Wisdom victorious over Death.

As the lame guard dozes in the gatehouse of the compound, Wu Ming's thoughts slip to another image of Yamantaka: the deity in union with his consort, an image he's not yet earned the right to see, not without more spiritual teaching, not without vows and an initiation. Then from that stolen vision, he turns again to the lesser unions in his own past. With enticing memories, he drugs away his fears.

At last the moment comes. Wu Ming returns to alertness as the city's Drum and Bell Towers sound the midnight watch. The neighborhood police stations repeat the count. The wooden rattles of the night patrol echo the number as they sweep the streets in their unvarying pattern, passing tallies lane to lane, reminding every citizen they are there.

The artisan eases from the storeroom. Even now, his two sworn brothers must be leaving their own hiding places in the alley just outside the workshop compound's outer wall.

His way is lighted by an unclouded gibbous moon. In a certain work room, a certain window opens onto the most shadowy corner of the compound, not far from the alley-side wall. Beneath the window, a useful table stands.

But before he lifts himself onto the table and out through the window into the yard, Wu Ming pauses. One set of thirty-seven small statues, recently completed, must not fall into those loutish hands. They wait, neatly boxed and awaiting consecration, where he left them after their final polishing. He slides the box beneath the table, in hopes it will pass unnoticed—until he can claim it, privately, for his own. A minor commission, among so many, but the first for which Wu Ming alone has overseen the casting.

When Mole and The Pebble—the only names Wu Ming knows these

art thieves by—have responded to the artisan's soft whistle, have dropped from a rope they leave dangling on the compound wall, they laugh. The Pebble bows an exaggerated, obsequious, quasi-gentleman's bow. Stocky Mole's teeth glint white above his dark clothing in the uncertain light. "Well met, Young Wu," they say. "Well met. Shall we proceed?"

"Show me my silver," Wu Ming says.

"Oho!" cries The Pebble in a stage whisper. "You fear treachery? From us?"

Mole hisses, "Lack of trust—and stupid dillydallying—brings failure. Where's the old man? Which window have you opened? Are you certain no one in the dormitory can hear us?" He thrusts a coarse-woven sack into the young man's hand. "Here's your bag! Carry your share of the load and then we'll talk of payment."

"Carry my share?" Wu Ming plants his feet, spread firm as unmoving Achala's, on the hard-packed earth. "But we part ways in the alley. You with the statues and the tangkas, I with forty taels. That's what we agreed."

The Pebble intervenes: yes, yes, so they did, it's only that they'll need his help—he's obviously quite strong, The Pebble says, the wiry type—in hoisting the booty up and over. "Look." He shakes his sleeve. In his broad dirty palm, a single tael of silver winks back at the moon.

Wu Ming reaches out. The first twenty taels will go to an herbalist. Then ten to the pawnshop near his home. But if his father mends, the last ten could help pay for gifts to a beautiful girl's family, and to a go-between . . .

The sting of the slap Mole administers shatters his calculations. "You'll get your reward *after*, pretty boy!" the squat man snarls. "Let's go."

Wu Ming's better at sculpting and metal casting than at the craft of establishing dominance. Narrow shoulders bent, red mouth sulky now, he leads the way to the sliding window he has left ajar.

The Pebble stays beside Wu Ming as they glide from room to room, rubbing his hands approvingly at the workshop's greatest prize: an offeratory model of Mount Meru circled by a golden sun and silver moon. He sighs, vexed, when he learns of the recent sale of a jeweled and gilded image of the wild, red-haired mother Penden Lhamo, who vanquishes egoism, and throws the dice that determine karmic fates. Neither he nor Wu Ming sees any irony in the loss.

In less than an hour of rummaging through rooms full of statues and clay molds and rolled-up tangka models, all three bags bulge. Mole awaits the others, leaning against the table by the window where they entered, tapping one cloth-shod foot. "About time," he says. "The old man just dragged himself around the building again. Anything in here we ought to pick up, sweetcheeks?"

Wu Ming shrugs. "I don't think we can carry much more."

"You don't think we'd want *this* then?" Mole leers as his foot nudges the wooden box he's dragged out from beneath the table, the one Wu Ming hid for himself.

Not worth the weight, Wu Ming hastily explains. A mandala set of statues that would have to be broken up before they sold it. "Too distinctive—that particular mandala's quite uncommon nowadays. The statues wouldn't bring much individually, or even if you kept the smaller groups together. No jewels, no gold, no silver. And they aren't consecrated yet."

Mole grins nastily. Wu Ming's armpits dampen. "Besides, how much can you two carry, once we're over the wall and we go our separate ways?"

"Lots of our retail trade isn't really consecrated," says Mole. "Except in the minds of those who buy the stuff. And we've got a—never you mind, pretty boy. We can handle the weight." Mole looks to The Pebble. "Must be something worth our while, or he wouldn't be so eager to hang onto it, eh?"

The Pebble nods. Wu Ming can't explain just why these statues mean so much to him. He did something in the making that he promised himself he'd tell no one, short of his appearance in the courtrooms of the afterlife a long long time from now. As a result, he can't bear—absolutely cannot *bear*—to see this particular set broken up.

Well, he thinks, the night's not over yet. The Pebble said they'd bribed a guard on the night patrol to help them get out of the area before dawn. Perhaps he'll just accompany the two thieves, instead of hiding in the alley as he'd planned. Perhaps he can talk them into giving him the statues as a kind of souvenir. Or he could let them keep a few taels . . .

"Come on." Mole or The Pebble? Wu Ming doesn't notice. His

heartbeat picks up as the three undertake the riskiest part of the whole affair: out the window, heavy burdened up the rope, over the wall, and down into the silent alleyway.

They make it. Get the silver now, thinks Wu Ming, and holds out his hand again.

"Oh. Right," says The Pebble, smiling brother-to-sworn-brother, and nods again, a message. "You want what you deserve. Of course."

The single tael of silver winks in his palm again. *One* tael? Wu Ming opens his mouth to protest. Opens his mouth to shriek, as Mole's knife cuts his windpipe and the great blood vessels of his neck. Opens his mouth and dies.

But you have not seen the last of him.

Now, if this were a tale doled out bit by bit in exchange for square-holed coins by a teahouse storyteller in Qing dynasty Beijing, you'd hear just at this moment (above your neighbors' chitchat and the caged birds' chirps and a clinking of thick cups) the attention-getting *clack* of a wooden block on a red-draped table, the snap shut of the storyteller's gesticulating fan: that's all, that's all for now!

A small wicker tray would pass before you. You'd toss in . . . well, surely not a tael of silver like the one for sake of which poor filial, vain Wu Ming met his breathless bloody death, but (surely?) a few copper cash.

And here's what the smiling pedagoguish storyteller (no posturing seductress like the big-drum singers Wu Ming's father dotes upon, but an impassioned lover nonetheless—of chimerical histories and castle-in-the-air romances), here's what that histrionical gabber, making use of one more time-silvered purloined formula, would say:

If you don't know what came of this audacious thievery, and of the foolish mortal artisan, please devote your attention to the installments that lie ahead.

A LOTUS BLOSSOMS: 2

On the eighteenth day of the first month, I wake before dawn, cold and empty and filled with a strange mixture of tension and relief: the three days of Lantern Festival offerings to the ancestors finally ended yesterday, the one-year ceremony for Mama won't be till tomorrow. But today, yes, I remember, there's a fortune-teller invited to come to us.

That's a better thing to think about. I draw in another breath of chilly air. What shall I ask her? Can she tell me when my father will come home?

Yet no matter what, he won't be here for Mama's anniversary offerings. I wish that I could miss them too. I know Aunt Gao will be glad to have them over with. Yesterday, I heard her say so.

If only my grandfather didn't insist that all his family continue to live together, no matter how awkward life in our household gets. I've heard a lot of my Aunt Gao's complaints: not just the expense of Mama's funeral, she likes to hint, or all the trouble fallen on *her* head, making arrangements and handling condolence calls and providing decent refreshment for the guests. It's the timing, she says, that really troubled her. Sad, of course, to lose a sister-in-law like that, but nonetheless . . .

Last year they had to paste white mourning paper on top of the red New Year's good-luck wishes beside our front gate while they were still fresh and new. Aunt Gao thinks that bad omen hurt the family's profits for the year—especially what First Uncle calls his *unofficial income*.

I heard a quarrel too, the day Mama died, though my aunt never brings that up. She and First Uncle wanted to post the death notice right on the wooden gate, on white paper, the way most Chinese people do. But Father and Grandfather insisted we stick to the ways of banner folk, and use a flagpole with a streamer instead.

It's always my uncle—or Aunt Gao, really—who points out that these days even Manchus wear Chinese clothing and follow Chinese customs. But they always get reminded that His Majesty despises bannermen who've lost the old ways and can't ride or shoot an arrow, that he chides banner families who fail to teach their children both languages. "We are who we are," Grandfather decrees to end those conversations. I realize now my father's never said exactly that.

What does it matter, really? I roll over onto my stomach. That always makes me feel safer somehow, even though nowadays it hurts the flesh around my nipples when I lie face down.

Mama agreed with Father—she was the one who taught Wintersweet and me to read Manchu versions of the old primers, as well as the Chinese instruction books for girls. Aunt Gao has no use for books at all. Yet if Mama had known a hundred languages, Mongolian and Tibetan and Sanskrit and the outlandish tongues of the empire's Muslims and the foreigners from Russia and Macao, it would be the same with her now.

Wind rattles the shutters, driving fine sand through every crack to settle on the furniture, my bedding, even on my face. The rhythmic clapping of the night patrolman's bamboo sticks drifts in from the street. The household itself remains wrapped in quiet, except for the guttural breathing coming from Nurse's couch. I yawn, and rub my aching eyes.

The sky outside must still be more dark than light. My hand brushes the cool metal of the Tara statue underneath a bolster, surprising as a buried memory returned: the statue, a moving hand not mine . . . Oh. The hand of the dirty novice monk, sliding into my satin sleeve. But I still can't imagine why. And how *would* he have known my secret? I drag the quilts over my head. Maybe the stuffy warmth of my own breath will put me back to sleep.

. . . .

$\mathcal{M}$other Jia wheezes, and pulls the hood of her cape up around her face. At a sharp glance from Aunt Gao, Grace feeds the fire beneath the wide, brick bed platform. The fortune-teller nods regally toward the maid's rustling skirts.

"Yesss," the old woman hisses, as if she were suddenly alone with Wintersweet here in Aunt Gao's inner room. "Yes." Her filmy eyes remain fixed on nothing as she runs her fingers over my cousin's scar-pitted face, stroking, squeezing, seeking out her fate from bones and features, size and placement and relationships. Jadewhite Rosary, her apprentice, watches every gesture, every measurement with her strange green-flecked eyes. Wintersweet winces as one yellowed fingernail flicks at a tiny upraised mole.

Biting her lips, Third Aunt leans forward from the backcushion in her warm nest between Aunt Gao and me on the bed platform. Little Auntie Padma keeps watching quietly from her chair near the door.

"First, madame . . ." The fortune-teller faces Aunt Gao precisely. "First, Mother Jia must remind you that her learning has been transmitted since the time of the Northern and Southern Dynasties. She follows the true teachings compiled in *The Spirit Mirror of Great Clarity* and *The Complete Guide to Numinous Observation*, not the idle speculations of the mob. Whatever predictions you've heard in the past, if they derive from vulgar rhymes and sayings, or cheap charts sold to any comer in the streets, must be ignored. For instance . . ."

She turns back to Wintersweet and strokes her eyebrow with a bony finger. "You've heard it said, no doubt, that large eyes and short brows, such as this young lady's, mean no brothers. Have you not? And is it true?"

Aunt Gao's face stiffens. "Not exactly," she says. "We shall be asking you—"

The physiognomist holds up a wrinkled hand. "Yes. The boy who perished. Mother Jia knows." Third Aunt gasps. "And you wish to ask about a future son, one perhaps being carried for you by the other, behind me, in the corner."

The silence now rings louder than any gasp, so pure I can hear the *pak* of a chair leg as Padma shifts her weight. "I shall advise you. And I can provide a most effective paper fetus-charm for the other, should you wish to acquire one. What Mother Jia sees, madame, ought to ease your mind."

The volume of her hoarse voice drops. "Among other things, you would do well to remember that the painful bearing of a family's children is often best left to younger women. But such things we shall speak of later, in private, if madame so desires."

Aunt Gao nods, remembers, agrees out loud, and hurriedly asks about Wintersweet.

The marred skin that secretly troubles the young lady so is nothing, says Mother Jia. Moreover, Wintersweet's well-formed ears reveal a lively intelligence. She need not worry overmuch about the meaning of the mole, only be very careful should she ever travel by water.

"The afflictions she must be wary of are the envy and resentment self-doubt brings," the old woman declares. My cousin blushed at the mention of her dark thoughts about her pock marks, thoughts I know she has shared only with Happiness and me. Now her face—for once—looks as if it were carved of wood. The fortune-teller goes on to predict an event that will bring joy to two households. A betrothal, soon. Wintersweet blushes more hotly than before.

"The young lady is by nature active, restless, almost boyish—the arrangement of the stars and planets on her face tells me so. And she enjoys good health, does she not? But here I must warn you—"

She gropes a bit, picks up Wintersweet's right hand, not to feel the bones, but to hold it in her own. "Young lady. For the next three years, you must be especially careful of your health. You will—it will be a difficult time for you, despite a certain happiness to come. You must, ah, but I won't say *must*. I only suggest that you may call on Mother Jia, at any time you feel the need.

"Take special pains in the early days to show your mother-in-law how dutiful you can be. She may not seem kind at first. I shall speak frankly with you on that point, but many a mother-in-law is strictest at the start, believing that her duty lies in seeming so. And—" She pats Wintersweet's hand, places it carefully back on my cousin's leg. "And supposing you traverse successfully the first years, then long life and honor and happiness and fine sons, at least three of them, I do believe, will be yours."

Long life. Tears well when I think once more how Mama was denied that, but I blink them back. The maids lined up at the sides of the room are all a-buzz. Third Aunt coughs, then offers her niece congratulations. Wintersweet laughs out loud, but not quite in her usual open way.

"Now, madame," says Mother Jia. "There is another here with a secret worry. I believe you said the heavy-hearted lady on your other side is your sister-in-law?"

"Ahh, no." Third Aunt's voice cracks like the string I broke the first time my father showed me how to play a few notes on his *chyn*. "That is—" and she returns to her usual shamefaced self, "that is, surely it's more proper for a useless widow to go last. If at all."

She raises her eyes, puts on a mask of pertness that would look unnatural even on Wintersweet. "Besides, we already know a widow's fate—a crab without legs, that's what I am! Our little Lotus is the one with something she wants to find out about, aren't you, Niece? Surely you're wondering when the *next* betrothal in the family will come?"

The maids giggle. So does Wintersweet. Everyone's looking at me now, even Mother Jia's apprentice—everyone except for Padma, who fixes her empty gaze on Third Aunt with an odd expression, as if she were turning something over in her mind. Jadewhite Rosary, standing beside the fortune-teller, nods as a ballad singer does when her listeners beg for more.

"As you wish, good lady," says Mother Jia to Third Aunt. She sounds pitying, almost sorrowful. Well, a young widow's lot *is* pitiable, even when her in-laws are proud to honor her pledge of lifelong fidelity, and support her as ungrudgingly as our family has. "So long as madame has no objections?"

Aunt Gao assents. She's waiting for that private conference now. I've barely time to put aside Mama's hand warmer—and the little statue of holy Tara I've hidden inside it again—before the fortune-teller steps over to my place at the front corner of the bed platform. She bids me stand, grasps my shoulders, pronounces my ruling element to be wood, for I've become tall for my age, and more slender than other girls. This means, she announces, that the karma of my past lives has molded my body in ways that indicate much human-heartedness.

"But *so* thin," Mother Jia murmurs when I sit back down and she begins to dig her fingers into my cheeks and jawline with surprising strength. "She'll soon grow to be more beautiful than you now suppose. Her bones tell me that much right away. And her destiny . . . not an ordinary one. Wait."

The others look impressed, but I soon decide that what lies behind her wisdom is not the teachings of old books: after I pull away, embarrassed, she calls me shy; after the back of her hand grazes my damp lashes, she speaks again of secret feelings, and of recent loss. Surely the fortune-teller and her apprentice could have learned a great deal about our family on visits to other households in our neighborhood. Or perhaps there's a reason Jadewhite Rosary seemed somehow familiar when she first walked in: perhaps I saw her gossiping with our servants once.

In a few minutes the tight muscles of my face relax under the slow, insistent massaging of the old woman's knotted hands. She calls me outwardly obedient, but explains that my face's Five Sacred Mountains hint at hidden pride, and deep emotions. I don't catch what Nurse mutters after that, but the maid beside her laughs.

Mother Jia ignores them, and when I ask about my father's return, she sighs, saying that's not the sort of thing revealed by the map of a person's face. "I have discerned your heart, young lady, and I calculate from the locations of the rivers, stars, and planets underneath my fingers now that, ah, before the year ends! And you so young! This year and the next will bring you great changes."

Now her hands run lightly, lightly, from the center of my forehead, across my temples, down to my chin. "Travel," she says. "The other young lady may be the one who would wish it, but travel you shall, some distance from our city, and sooner than you may think."

There's a good bit of discussion after that. Wintersweet jokingly proclaims she's miffed—*she* wants to be the one to see new places. Nurse breaks through the hubbub with a suggestion: Perhaps this means I ought to go along if Aunt Gao decides to make the fourth-month pilgrimage to Marvel Peak, as more and more people have begun to do?

The fortune-teller stares thoughtfully in the direction of Nurse's voice. "A pilgrimage of this family's ladies to offer incense to the Verdant Dawncloud Sovereign is certainly a likely possibility," says Mother Jia. "Indeed, you may find it beneficial to consult me, should you wish assistance in your preparations for asking blessings of Our Lady. And the girl will play her part there. But she will go farther from Beijing than just the Western Hills."

My stomach tightens. Does this mean I'll be chosen for service in the imperial palaces and will travel with the court? Or will I be married—but I'm too young!—to someone from a distant city? How awful to have to leave my family so soon!

"And now . . ." Mother Jia pats my hand, much as she patted

Wintersweet's, then steps back toward Third Aunt. Who pushes herself away from her backrest, slides forward on the bed platform with awkward haste and stands up, almost knocking the fortune-teller aside. "No!" she says, her voice shrill, and louder than I've ever heard it. "No, I've changed my mind. She—" My young aunt shakes her head. "I'm sorry. I don't feel well. Ask Partridge. This morning, no, I'm really not well at all. Please, Sister-in-law."

Third Aunt's about to throw herself down and kotow in supplication. Aunt Gao reaches out to stop her. "Of course," she says frostily. "If you'd like to be excused?"

We all—except the apprentice and Mother Jia—stare at Third Aunt, who stares down at the floor. Partridge hurries to take her mistress's arm and the two of them depart. Padma breaks the strained moment that follows, standing to ask softly if Aunt Gao would like the rest of us to withdraw.

It seems my uncle's concubine has judged correctly that her presence is not required for discussion of the child she is to bear; she slips out quickly. Wintersweet sweeps after her in the center of a knot of bantering maids. But as Nurse bustles me toward the door, the fortune-teller shoots out one bony hand to clutch my forearm.

"One moment!" she says. The wordless look of Jadewhite Rosary at her side tells me I must obey. "Young lady. You do not like what Mother Jia has told you, though I could have told you more. I *will* say you can count on your father returning in good health. Remember, winter travel on the Grand Canal can be slow. You will not, however, be altogether pleased by what he brings with him. But that is unimportant."

Aunt Gao is deep in conference with Grace. Nurse, who evidently took a great liking to Mother Jia after she recommended that I—and therefore Nurse, of course—go on a jaunt into the hills when the pilgrimage season comes, beams blandly. The others cluster out on the veranda, comparing opinions, oblivious. My breath runs fast and shallow. I stare into white eyes framed by the shadows of a heavy hood.

The grip of that powerful hand tightens around my arm. "This *is* important: what you need to remember, you do not know. Your destiny is indeed not ordinary. What you have to do . . . will not be easy. You must learn how to transmute passion, how to pass beyond fear and vacillation. You must learn how to see."

The blind fortune-teller drops my hand, so suddenly that it falls to my side like a lifeless thing. A thousand embroidery needles stitch my skin. I wrap my arms around myself and walk away.

Outside, Wintersweet is waiting, and invites me to come eat in her little side hall next door, where the north bedroom stands empty, waiting the birth of a brother. She and Happiness are full of talk about Mother Jia's predictions; so are the other maids, until Grace emerges and summons them to stand by in attendance in Aunt Gao's outer room. That means Nurse is the one who has to go from the West Courtyard to the kitchen in the front of the family's compound, and notify them where to deliver my lunch.

She's still grumpy when she returns, and says nothing of the fortune-teller's final words to me. Her one remark, as she and Happiness wait for my cousin and me to finish eating, is to comment darkly that Wintersweet's lucky about the placement of her mole.

"Lucky? Danger from water?" I ask. My father may be travelling by water at this very moment! Is it safe for him? I try to call up the details of his face, the exact location of the one mole I can remember.

"Lucky. There's people has moles as say *no sons*. Or worse."

"Nurse Gu, really! What could be worse?" Wintersweet's eyes sparkle as she lifts a mouthful of steaming noodles from her bowl.

"There's people, people we've all seen, mind you, bearing moles as tell the world their love of fornication. And—you girls must be old enough to hear this, judging from the grown-up way you order old women to scamper hither and yon as if they were junior maids—there's one in this household as bears an adulteress's mark. Leastways, if you believe what *I* always heard."

"Nurse Gu!" Wintersweet half laughs, half chokes as she talks and swallows all at once. "Who is it?"

"It's Old Lai's wife, isn't it?" whispers Happiness.

But Nurse will say no more. Wintersweet and Happiness return to selecting names for her future sons. I weary of the food and jokes and the talk of early marriage, and stare toward the dull light of the windows, wishing it were warm enough to eat outside. Small though it is, the West Courtyard with its little carp pond and arching crab apple tree always seems more pleasant than the Upper Courtyard, where a shout or a roar of laughter from Grand-father's North Hall can break the peace at any hour.

Wintersweet decides Mother Jia's forecast means that I won't have to go into service in the palaces, that Father will select some penniless but worthy scholar to take our family name as a married-in son-in-law. "So you'll have a smart husband, Lotus, and can stay here with the family until he wins top honors in the civil service exam and gets an important job in, in, Su-jou or Yang-jou or some other cultured city. But only for a couple years, until he's posted to the capital and then you can come back to us!"

Happiness hovers nearby, rosy faced, pouring tea and teasing us both. "Remember how they used to tell us that this night, the eighteenth of the first month, is when the mice get married? And made you hide your shoes, Miss Wintersweet, so one wouldn't be carried off as a mousie sedan chair? You used to throw such fits at *that* idea!"

I know who first told us that story. I can hardly stand all this, even though I also know one reason for the chatter is that my cousin wants to keep my mind off tomorrow's anniversary rites for Mama.

"And now it's you who'll soon be in a bridal chair," Happiness is saying, when I remember: Mama's hand warmer. The little statue. After Third Aunt's outburst, I left them in Aunt Gao's inner room.

How could I have forgotten? I nearly tip the low table as I jump off Wintersweet's bed platform and hurry out, Nurse fussing behind me as I run next door.

But they've vanished. No hand warmer, so of course, no statue. And Mother Jia and her snaky-eyed apprentice are gone as well; the junior maids left some time ago to escort them to the gate.

Grace and Harmony help me look around the room. My aunt soon turns to chiding me for suggesting that her new spiritual advisor might have stolen an old hand warmer. I can't bear to mention the little statue—none of them knows about it, and even if they believed me, they'd think me unforgivably dis-respectful. To put a holy statue, my mother's dying gift, inside a banged-up box for ash and coals! Only, I needed to have it with me.

I need it now.

"That thing? Really, Lotus." Aunt Gao waves dismissively. "That hand warmer was terribly corroded, and I believe I've seen a dent in it. I know who it belonged to, but it . . . Well. Your mother was a lovely lady, always careful not to squander the family's money. But to be honest, I remember it because it looked so shabby. Anyway, I'm certain it'll turn up. You *can't* think one of the West Courtyard's maids has taken it. My husband's concubine left empty handed, I assure you. Are you accusing your own courtyard's Tetra or Quinta? Or—not Partridge, surely?"

So now I must say I don't suspect any of the maids, for fear my aunt will have one of them beaten till she confesses. And in truth, I can't imagine Grace or Harmony or the others doing such a thing—not even the West Courtyard's little Deucey, or Trine, whom I know least well. Actually, my aunt is right: the hand warmer wasn't worth stealing, not for the coins it would bring. Besides, Mother Jia and her apprentice seemed to have other designs upon the family.

What can I do? I pretend to agree that I probably didn't really bring it along with me—Nurse shrugs when I look to her—and walk back to Wintersweet's room to pick at the food until it's all cold and I can leave.

During the first-year rites for Mama in the main hall, I keep thinking of the little Tara statue. Her mild face, the all-seeing eyes in the palms of her graceful hands, her full breasts draped with ropes of pearls: lost.

But each time, I push the picture from my mind and concentrate on the crowded family altar, its neat ranks of narrow wooden tablets bearing my ancestors' names, and the austere portrait of Grandfather's grandfather hanging above them, on the center of the north wall.

I must make Old Mister Jin, my grandfather's most scholarly friend and the ritual advisor for Mama's funeral, nod approvingly when he hears how well I've done this time. Not like a year ago, when I didn't join in the wailing and he scowled. It was his daughter-in-law Lady Ding who looked Wintersweet over, the night of the Lantern Festival. Best if the Jins think highly of the girls in our family.

Mama needed a son to cut off his queue and play the chief mourner's part. But I'm all she has. After she died, Father refused all suggestions that he adopt an heir, wryly asking which of his dissipated second cousin's two thick-witted sons would be more suitable, since there's no one else in the clan. "And no need to seek a boy outside," he said. "There's time enough."

So perhaps Wintersweet is right, perhaps he does intend to find me a husband willing to marry in, become one of the Suns, and carry on the family line. He'd take care of Mama's soul, and Father's when his time comes. And I'd be spared a life in some strangers' house.

But I must stop thinking, must do my part. I bow. I carry the hot rice and the five dishes to the table set before the spirit tablet that bears my mother's official posthumous name. I have no feelings at all.

Except this, one crack, one sliver in the wall I've built: I'm afraid I'll drop a chopstick, break the plate that holds the twisty buckwheat-millet pastries Mama always liked to eat. What if my failure a year ago means Mama's soul is trapped in hell? *Stop thinking, stop feeling, stop. Walk. Bow. Take refuge in careful form.*

I stare now at the high shadowy rafters of this double-roofed building, the tallest in our family compound. My father treated Mama well, whatever Nurse claims, insisting that—son or no son—she be honored in the family hall.

Afterward, the family eats and talks at tables set out before the main hall, in the surprising early-spring sunlight of the Front Courtyard. People open their fur-lined jackets in the unseasonable warmth, declaring themselves unable to have borne unbroken winter a moment longer, glad to be out in the fresh air and midday light, though the cold is bound to return. Ice still glazes the edge of the lotus pond, but the gardener has arranged pots of blooming narcissus around it. They touch the cool bright air with their green perfume.

I begin to feel better, and manage to force down enough food to keep Wintersweet from scolding me. At last it's over. Grandfather unbends, becoming almost merry, as people say one should do after first-year rites. But I'm relieved when my uncle jollies him out of playing the finger guessing game over cups of heated wine, quietly reminding him that his cronies may start arriving soon; Grandfather has invited them to an afternoon of mah-jongg in the guest hall opening onto this same courtyard.

Mama herself must surely be at rest now, an ancestor who will help the family even after the last living memory of her has gone. Surely she's comforted. And will be safely reborn. Thinking this, I join the other girls and women walking toward the back courtyards, glad to leave the front of the house before Grandfather's friends arrive.

Aunt Gao and Wintersweet and their maids turn into the passageway made when the West Courtyard was added to our compound; Third Aunt and Partridge scuttle off to Third Aunt's rooms, across the Upper Courtyard from my own. But I'm lingering outdoors, having stepped off my veranda to look at the tight leaf buds on the plum tree, when Harmony rushes up, and triumphantly puts something in my hands.

"Mah!" she says, eyes alight. "Here! I just now spotted it—such a peculiar place, I can't imagine—in the West Courtyard carp pond!"

Mama's hand warmer! Water still drains from it onto the paving stones. I thank Harmony, feel a smile tug at my mouth. But in the next instant the weight of the thing tells me what I needn't look inside to know. Empty. Whoever dropped it in the pond took the little Tara statue first.

Then I find a voice within me that can wail. Too late, too loudly for *this* day, my throat breaks open and I sob.

THE OUTER GATE

But where is the past, when it is gone from us? Somehow, you have entered into it, as if into a house of many rooms, a chain of corridors, a city of palaces and gardens. As if, perhaps, into a museum warehouse crowded with old statues, papery revolving lanterns, embroidered shoes, fragments saved from burned manuscripts and dubious biographies.

When you find them, pick them up. Remember or imagine those who walked these passageways, stepped through these entrances, desired or touched these things before.

Maybe the rooms are really quadrangles standing open to the heavens, their enclosure incomplete. Doors and gateways wait on every side. Behind some of them lies danger, behind some, a troubled happiness, or pleasures you yourself have never known. Each room connects with further shadowy rooms, each courtyard with another, deeper in. Which path among them will you choose to take?

One moon-shaped gate leads to a pond filled with pale rosy flowers. Their enormous saucer leaves rise above the still, green surface, hovering, a rippling maze of ruffled placidity, lapped one upon the next. Petal nuzzling petal, the large blossoms open, fleshy and ethereal at once.

Their roots reach into mud enriched by sunken moss and algae, the nutritious waste of long-dead fish, frog eggs decomposed, starry leaves gone scarlet, brown, then water-laden black. A detritus of words and syllables in a language you don't yet know.

The leaves' flat cups hold clear-silver pearls.

And look! A singer in a shallow-water boat. One hand stretches out from the floating skiff, tips those dewdrops into a bowl of porcelain glazed dark copper red. For tea.

I promise you a taste. If you walk farther in.

THE YEAR'S FIRST FULL MOON, AGAIN

Consider what else might be happening on the Lantern Festival night, the year after Lotus's mother dies. For example, off in Nanjing, *southern capital*, six hundred miles south—as the raven flies—from Beijing in the north.

Lovely Nanjing, embraced by the broad Yangzi's curve, and the inviting Finegold Hills: The city's name reminds the visitor that it ruled an empire more than once in history. A traveler arrived from our own time might walk an eighteenth-century boulevard and know that the city's fated to hold again in future centuries a few years' sway under more brief governments. And fated as well to be flooded anew by plunder and rape and death.

But not just yet. Tonight, the Manchu emperor controls the Pax Manjurica from a well-guarded palace in Beijing, while in this warm river-city's entertainment district, important men make merry. One of them is the visiting Specially Commissioned Imperial Household Assistant Department Director, Sun Taiyang, who soon must take his leave and return to the cold, dry home where his daughter waits. But, again, not yet.

Late on the fifteenth night of this year's first lunar month, all Nanjing celebrates. Even respectable women go out on the uproarious streets. In the entertainment quarter along the Qin-huai River, every winehouse glows with festival lanterns, burns bright with song and dance and unrestraint. In one of them, Taiyang joins his hosts and some of the captivating beauties whose fate and sustenance it is to display their talents, to stimulate men's conversations, to offer the refreshments of eros and the other arts.

A singer dressed in indigo and emerald begins another song. Tiny lanterns dangling from her hairpins shiver as she tilts her head.

Taiyang swallows a yawn, secretly stretches his shoulders up and back. It's getting late, and he's been in poor spirits awaiting the first anniversary of his wife's death. He once hoped to start the twenty-day journey home well before the new year came and the holiday season made travel too difficult. But persistence was called for, if he was to get a real sense of the situation here. Besides, the local officials know this Imperial Household official will report their doings directly to His Majesty; they've been anxious to keep him on through the weeks when gaiety must take precedence over investigations, anxious to blur his first impressions with a parade of rousing good times.

Well, and he must admit he's enjoyed the prolonged stay in the cultured southland, enjoyed being treated with so much respect. Any educated man can produce verse when called upon, of course, but here one can count on an official to know the difference between a good Chinese poem and a heap of clichéd doggerel. To say nothing of the elegant establishments like this place, outlawed in Beijing.

The next yawn catches Taiyang by surprise.

He's quick to shield his mouth. Still, the *musicienne* beside him— didn't someone call her Orchidheart?—tosses him a private half-smile and refills his cup with wine.

"Spring's first nights are long," she breathes beneath the singer's yearning southern melody. "Without intoxication, how dreary these tawdry entertainments must seem to a refined gentleman, even on Primal Night! Let me offer you another cup."

Nothing to do but drink it down, despite the bellyful he's had already. The place does deserve its reputation, and to insult the girls here would be to insult the man who arranged this gathering. Certainly the music this Orchidheart just drew forth from the strings of her paulownia-wood chyn suited Taiyang's melancholy mood, though his host seemed to find it a bit too elevated for this lively holiday.

Taiyang waves toward one of the engraved reflector lamps illuminating the performer, quotes a poem from bygone times. "Spring nights: bright and brief as a candle's flame," he says. The girl gestures to a little maid for fresh-warmed wine.

What a rude idiot he is, to allude to life's end at the new year's start! He knows what brought the line to mind, and thinks briefly of a happy Primal Night some years ago, thinks briefly of his wife. He coughs, and shakes his head.

But this pretty creature beside him will simply reckon him too gauche and muddle witted to avoid bringing bad fortune—or death itself—upon them with unlucky words. Better to begin the year speaking of spring and its fancies than the brevity of human lights and lives.

Quickly he quotes a more cheerful line, and quickly suggests they drink again. Her high-cheeked face retains its cool reserve, though she catches his eye for an instant as, together, they drain their cups. Surely someone has murmured in her hearing "imperial bondservant," the words he hates above all others, murmured them no doubt even while mentioning his respectable post within the Department of the Privy Purse, his access to the emperor's ear. Well, this courtesan shall know him for the educated, influential man he is. The emperor's man indeed. He has no need for shame.

"The Empress Dowager herself has lotus lamps not unlike that lot set out when she watches plays," he says. "Rather suitable for the holiday season, really, the colorful enameling, in spite of its gaudiness. And clever, the way the upturned leaf swivels to direct the beams on stage. The imperial palaces must be quite alive with actors' arias and moon-gongs and fireworks tonight." He shrugs, leans forward. "To be honest, I was rather sorry to be missing the Lantern Festival commotion in the capital, until Magistrate Hsiao invited me here."

Orchidheart lets her face hint that she's impressed, then before he can stop her, refills his cup. The house doesn't water down its wine, that much is certain. Thank Heaven it's not the fermented mare's milk favored by so many in the military!

The song ends, but no one suggests another drinking game. Officials and courtesans at small black-wood tables around the reception room joke and titter in twos and threes. A gust of shouting blows in from the street.

"We've a fair amount of commotion here too, haven't we?" says the musicienne, pursing her small red mouth.

"Too much for you, eh? And what would you rather pass this night by doing, then?" Taiyang picks up the rhythm of flirtation from his rising pulse beat. He knows a featured performer at an exclusive house like this one wouldn't make herself available on a first visit—but it is Primal Night, after all. Unhealthy for a man to sleep alone too long. Before dawn comes, many a couple will be celebrating the rising up of spring. One might at least play the game.

But her answer stops him cold. She looks at the lacquered wine tray, not at him, shifts it needlessly away as she tells him in her charming local accent that she'd rather play chess or *go* than most other things. "Almost anything, really," she adds, then blushes—actually blushes!—and confesses to dabbling in painting, when she has the time.

The girl has a mind then, as well as beauty. He might have known that from her music. But before he can inquire into her painting (does he remember young Hsiao waving toward a rather nice scroll of orchids in the anteroom?), an elbow catches Taiyang, sharp, in the ribs.

Dizziness seizes him even before he whirls around. Magistrate Hsiao is staring at him, pop eyed with chagrin, no, is scrambling from his seat to knock his own forehead against the floor, proclaiming himself a clumsy demon and begging Taiyang's forgiveness for his unforgivable affront.

The emperor's bondservant hears a rather artificial shriek of startled feminine laughter, but most of the party are too caught up in their own amusements to have noticed the incident. He stops young Hsiao's kotows, accepts perforce a mutual toast of friendship, makes some jest about how they must all play at being demons on Primal Night if they are to ward all demon work away from the new year's enterprises. And silently decides that Hsiao will do well to give him another little sum of silver as a parting gift—unless he doesn't care how he stands in Taiyang's report to His Majesty.

"He's a bit too tipsy, even for this occasion, eh?" Taiyang says sotto voce to his companion when things have settled down again. "But I suppose you see more than your share of that sort of thing."

It's actually the first time he's thought much about the life of a woman like this one. But the look of wary gratitude she gives him makes it clear he's hit home. Well, of course: she's confronted with such excess all year round. He supposes it can be difficult, really, for someone whose sensibilities remain unblunted.

She's a competent hostess, though, and smoothly turns the conversation away from whatever troubles she might have. "Odd," she tells him, "but I learned once that the ancients passed Primal Night quite differently, in prayer, as part of a ritual sacrifice."

But how does a courtesan know *The Records of the Grand Historian*? And a lost chapter at that!

Learned from a guest, of course. Taiyang shakes his head to drive off the mists gathering around the edges of his vision. Yet he can see the striking face of the musicienne so clearly, luminous as the fifteenth-night moon. Sometimes he used to call his wife Biyangga, "moonlike," when they spoke together in Manchu, because her Chinese name evoked old stories of the moon. Because he treasured her cool allure.

"A full moon," he says, a bit surprised to hear his voice articulate this private thought. His companion's high-arched eyebrows grow more and more distinct, as if a pale moth had landed on a lily flower lantern, as if he were bending closer to inspect its feathery antennae, as if he could caress each perfect curve with a finger's tip.

Orchidheart draws away, the corners of her lips lifting upward in— what? what? promise? mystery? scorn? "Ah," she says, in tones that mix something like admiration with faint reproof. "The moon. The gentleman must know the moon voyage story I heard recently?"

He's not too drunk to get the message. He leans back. He coughs again. And here, thank Heaven, is one of the maids with bowls of sticky-rice dumplings on a tray. Taiyang accepts one, pushes his cup aside, listens as Orchidheart begins to tell of a Tang-dynasty lutist and her wondrous trip by sky raft to the Moon Lady's crystalline palace. Stomach warmed, head clearing, he's just framing a compliment about the transcendent damsels of the divine realm he himself has been brought to this night when brisk hand claps demand his attention, and Magistrate Hsiao's voice rings out.

"Begging your pardon, Assistant Director Sun. Pardon, confreres and friends. Dear ladies, pardon me. This night of, of liberated feelings and brilliance amid the dark is quickly passing—and Miss Susu here, and the rest of these gifted beauties who practiced their music and, and such, so hard, have yet to view the lantern displays! Surely we should repay them for the pleasure they have given us—" His face freezes as one of his senior subordinates whispers something that elicits a smothered snort from the man beside him. "So. We'll, ah, we'll acknowledge their talents and their effort, and accompany them on a bit of an excursion."

That's that, of course. Nothing will do but that they all go out among the roistering crowds. Taiyang steps carefully toward the door. Someone has spilled a whole plate of slippery melon seeds, scattering them across the floor like a hot youth's—but enough of such thoughts; he must take care to stay near Orchidheart as she glides out, hips wavering deliciously, leaning on the arm of her little maid.

The hoi polloi have taken advantage of the occasion to swarm through the entertainment district, shoulder to shoulder, hip to hip, gawking at the courtesans and their well-to-do guests. Peddlers crowd close—no hint of respect in their manner this night—till Magistrate Hsiao's yamen-guards shove a few rowdies aside forcefully enough to make their point. The piquant strains of a moon-guitar waft from a winehouse across the lane, but the music's soon lost in the shouts and explosions and guffaws.

Still, it's all part of Primal Night, and Taiyang has to admit he finds something energizing in the carnival clamor. The year's newborn, the yang energy wells up, one ought to immerse oneself in the revelry and benefit from the rejuvenation of all things. As long as the yamen-guards clear a way though the hucksters and the vulgar mass.

He's stepping forward to say as much to Orchidheart—she's bright enough to appreciate the ironic side of his mixed feelings, and perhaps their interesting blend of vitality and fastidiousness as well—when she vanishes, like a kidnapped child or a heavenly jade maiden in a Lantern Festival tale. He blinks. A clash of brassy instruments draws his forehead tight.

Ah, there. She and the maid have paused with two of the other entertainers before a large gate hung with a cavalcade of bobbing faery-isle lanterns. All but Orchidheart are laughing, perhaps making fun of their rivals' display, faces flushed, plunging wholeheartedly into the tomfoolery. One of her companions motions carelessly toward the burnt-out lantern at one end; Orchidheart takes a half-step back.

Taiyang catches a glimpse of one tiny scarlet shoe beneath her skirts. *Oh.* Desire surges through the base of his jade stalk and back to the Cinnabar Field in his belly's pit. He has kept a full year's mourning—less but three days—for his wife. If he left this minute, he wouldn't reach Beijing until well into the second month anyway. A few more days will hardly matter.

Then, before Taiyang can catch his breath, a stocky, sun-burnt man in a scarred leather breastplate pushes through the herd of humanity in the street ahead. In one hand, a knife blade flares as it cuts through a beam of lantern light. He grasps Orchidheart by the elbow, urgent, and thrusts a small cloth-wrapped bundle—impossible to see more!—into her jacket's wide, loose sleeve. None of the other women notices. The nearby yamen-guard is turned away, glaring down at the ratty red-robed beggar monk who plucks at his arm.

The emperor's bondservant dashes forward. The warrior utters a few hoarse words in Mongolian: *safekeeping . . . unite them with the rest . . .* then one of those religious phrases. Taiyang knows he's heard it before, but he only has a smattering of—now look! It doesn't matter what the Mongol's saying; he's slipping off into a pack of carousing workmen. The package he gave Orchidheart has disappeared, and Taiyang's roar of frustrated valor drowns in the quicksand of a night when social order is set aside.

Yet a breezy fluke of air bears to him one last phrase, in the courtesan's dusky southern Chinese: *yes, yes, of course,* she's saying. But the warrior's gone, if he was ever really there.

The next morning, in Taiyang's headachy fragile sleep, those words— and Orchidheart's calm denial of the entire incident—entwine with the rare music that she played, and her invitation to return for another visit. "You should call me Inkscent," she said when he took his leave. "As do the few friends I really care about."

In his guest quarters at the hostelry, Taiyang fights his way up toward daylight from a well of tumultuous dreams, only to fall back into a chaos of danger and fruitless bravery. Again he sees, or remembers, or imagines, a burly man's weathered face that melts into a slim high-cheeked woman's. He coughs, his groin throbs, he mounts the black horse he left in Beijing, he takes aim at an invader in dirty rags. But the arrow in his crossbow melts away.

Just before he wakes, exhausted, for the last time, a giggling maid addresses him as "houseslave," and hands him a small object wrapped in silk. The cloth is the color of incense, which is the color of the skirt Orchidheart wore last night. The package is the one the Mongol forced upon her. When Taiyang opens it, he finds two small, red, flower-embroidered shoes.

UNOFFICIAL BIOGRAPHIES OF PAINTERS FROM THE WOMEN'S QUARTERS

CHAPTER 7, PAGES IA–B

attributed to Lian Jinlu [flourished after 1776]

Translator's Note:

Hailed by like-minded contemporaries as a champion of women's rights to education and artistic self-expression, the shadowy figure of Lian Jinlu will doubtless be viewed more skeptically by progressive poststructuralist critics as we enter the twenty-first century. Yet without this imperfect, fragmentary work, modern readers might know even less of female artists in Late Imperial China. Let us glean from Lian's unsubstantiated assertions what truths we can, and find in apocryphal anecdotes both imaginative understandings and the impetus for more research.

Auralie Nelsen-Jones

Tuo Muo-hsiang, whose name means "Inkscent," was also known as "Orchidheart." She was born into the Old Compound in Nanjing in the middle years of the Qianlong emperor's reign [1736–1796]. Although this pleasure quarter on the Qin-huai River—ravaged by war at the fall of the Ming, and suppressed by prohibitions in the Kangxi era [1661–1722]—had not yet restored the splendor of former times, in some houses the old traditions of womanly elegance survived.

In earliest childhood, Muo-hsiang loved to play with a calligrapher's brush. She was by nature perceptive and quick witted, yet refined and fond of quietness. Her slender body glided on petite and well-arched feet. Muo-hsiang's mother instructed her in the family heritage of music and calligraphy, as well as secret teachings of the Buddhist way.

By the time she reached womanhood and "broke the melon," Muo-hsiang had acquired a local reputation as a painter of orchids. Gallants and scholars who visited the establishment where she lived said she had about her the pure and upright air of that rare flower.

Although Muo-hsiang was much sought after for her musical ability, she disdained noisy gatherings on the colorful lantern boats along the river, refusing invitations when she was able to. Her rooms overlooked a quiet garden containing a dark clump of bamboo, with a wicker gate like that of a high-minded mountain recluse. At parties, she would pluck the strings of her chyn only after much urging, and having played a single lofty air, would push the instrument away.

Yet she had no way to remove herself from the register of female entertainers. And indeed, some say Muo-hsiang bore a deep resentment at those who came and went like butterflies among the flowers. Nonetheless, she hid it well, swallowing her bitterness as best she could.

Muo-hsiang's calligraphy resembled the lively "silver hooks" brushed by the Tang courtesan-poet Xue Tao. Her painting followed the vivacious style of Ma Shou-zhen, who lived in the Old Compound two hundred years before. Although she was a woman, her brushwork burst with ink-splashed energy; her line quality revealed her firm grace. One could sense the harmony of ink and paper in her daring compositions and lilting double-outline orchid leaves. Her paintings of chaste, enduring bamboo seemed ready to rise off the page.

As Muo-hsiang's fame grew, visitors to the district along the riverbank vied for introductions. Her sisters would entertain only the wealthy and generous, sending poor scholars away with no more than a bowl of rice gruel or a cup of tea. Yet Muo-hsiang was known to bestow a painted fan or an album leaf on the most impecunious of youths, if their spirits were in accord. Thus she could not acquire the means with which to buy her way free of the courtesan's life.

In time, a palace official came on imperial business to Nanjing. Muo-hsiang was among the entertainers asked to make music at a banquet in his honor.

Hanging back, she secretly observed his manner though pearl-sewn window blinds. The next day she put on the plain gown of a gentleman-student and paid a call, expressing her desire to study calligraphy with him.

The courtesan's dainty feet being deeply hidden in a pair of men's boots stuffed with crumpled binding cloths, the official was taken in by her disguise. "The young gentleman has a heavenly talent," he murmured when he saw Muo-hsiang write in the cursive style. "But, alas, I must soon leave the Southland and return to my home in Beijing."

"Then take me with you as your concubine!" replied the one in the student's gown, whisking off a manly cap to let down cloudy tresses of raven's wing, scented with honeywood.

"*Tsa!* What sort of person art thou?" asked the palace official. But when Muo-hsiang revealed her identity, he refused her, saying, "Beauty and skill you indeed possess, but what you lack is chastity."

At that, she seized the brush, and in an eye blink covered a sheet of paper with a clump of untainted orchids beside a noble stone. "It has been my fate since birth to associate with the profligates who linger in the lanes and byways of the Old Compound," she said. "And at times I could not but share my pillow with one of them. Yet I have always despised lewdness. Can the gentleman view my painting and not know my heart?"

SHOES

Place them before you for a moment, two pairs of women's shoes, come to you—somehow—out of the past. One pair is less than four inches long, one no more than seven. They can't be set aside, evaded, done away with.

Here, observe them: a few ounces of thread and fabric that tell a tale of lacerating aches and beauty's pride, of unrelieved itch and winter's bloodless cold. They rest now, weighed down by the daily lives of those who wore or stroked them, by the shameful fascination of the one thing some foreigners know about some Chinese women. Weighted, too, by a world of lip labrets and neck-extending rings, of ribs cut out to tighten a corset's cinch, of dangerous implants, and food-storage cells sucked from underneath the most esteemed of modern skins.

Let the smaller pair stand on your palm, arched and slender in the northern style. Floating clouds and tender peonies drift in hair-fine stitches made, it may be, by their wearer's own hand. Or were these shoes placed on an altar, presented to Guan-yin one auspicious day by a worried mother about to determine her well-loved daughter's fortune? The giver would have prayed for perfect form: not swollen or sharp pointed, but plump yet supple, curved and smooth.

These were "sleeping shoes." They peeped from underneath a quilt, they slyly—powerfully—brushed a husband's ankle, they yielded to his enraptured grasp. You examine them for tooth marks, stains, observe again the patience and endurance of the embroiderer's art. You imagine (if you want to know them fully for what they were) how their deep red artfully set off hidden jade-white skin.

And their effects upon the one who wore them? Praise. Respect. A chance of economic security. More defense against the blood-rush return of torment to numbed flesh than tight-wrapping cloths alone provide. The modest, seductive covering-up of unaesthetic, if exciting, crumpled skin.

One doctor won a bit of fame by placing shoes like these on the navels of old men with fevers, so they could draw out excess heat. Another described for a curious Royal Society the exotic deformations of a foot that might have worn this very pair of shoes, a foot found floating in a Chinese river, before it was detached and sent for dissection in his enlightened land.

A third civilized man of science analyzed the causes—the distorted forward curve of the lower vertebrae, perpetual tension in the lumbar musculature, a gradual alteration in the pelvis's actual size and shape—of a Chinese woman's distinctive gait. He concluded that the undulating, stimulating, sway was not inborn, not racial, after all. He might have said it was a successful adaptation to inescapable circumstances, a dignified bearing after childhood nights of bewildered tears and fire-knife pain.

Now place this pair aside. Turn your gaze (embarrassed? inquisitive?) to the other one. Though larger, they nonetheless will strike you as quite small, if you should judge by milk-fed Northern European standards. They too boast delightful images on crimson satin: a spray of long-life pine and a juicy peach. These shoes fit a Manchu woman, forbidden to take on the Chinese custom and bind her own, her girl-childrens', feet—or fit the daughter of a Chinese family bound to imperial servitude, and Manchu ways. Such shoes let her emulate the hobble Manchu men too had learned to prize; they rise on unstable tapered platforms that alter each pace as surely as do four-inch spike heels.

Enough of that. What use? Outrage, admiration, squeamishness will not make them go away. Finish the investigation. Pick up the first ones again.

Does any trace of the distinctive smell still linger? Some gold-lily shoes had fragrant soles of sandalwood. Some hid coy heel compartments to store perfumes. These sleeping shoes might have been filled by day with spicy sachets, stored away in a red and gold lacquer box.

With good reason. Just as new-bound feet were powdered with alum to purge the stench of pus and sloughing skin, so had each gold lily to be aired and washed, in private moments, against the intimate aromas of their yeasty moisture. Surely someone else in bygone times has pressed his nose to this silken cloth.

As he did, you do. But they are neither foul nor fragrant, are not even musty. Are odorless, lifeless, dry.

A LOTUS BLOSSOMS: 3

hortly after I've paid my morning respects to Grandfather, Wintersweet bursts into my room. "It's happened," she says, face flushed, and stands in the doorway, one hand pleating the edge of her other sleeve. "A jade necklace and . . . and things, I forget what all, just arrived from the Jin family. Wrapped in a red silk cloth."

"Cousin! You're getting married?" I push away the book of poems I was half trying to read, bumping the teapot on the low table set up on my bed platform, and gesture to her, *come sit beside me, do.*

"Ah, the Jins! Congratulations, Young Mistress," says Nurse, looking satisfied: her prediction has proved true.

Wintersweet seems not to hear her. "What else, silly Lotus? It turns out my parents have been talking with people, and having our horoscopes compared and all that ever since, oh, right after the start of the year. Grandfather proposed the match. No, no, I can't sit down. I'm too . . . excited."

Ducking underneath the door curtain, Happiness pops in. "I told her *weeks* ago there was talk." Her smile is even broader than usual. "But she wouldn't believe a word of it. I say she's lucky to have her future secured so young."

"Lucky?" Excited, yes, and jittery and rattle tongued, Wintersweet plops herself down. Then it comes tumbling out.

Lady Ding, daughter-in-law of Grandfather's friend Old Master Jin, *was* seeking a wife for her son at Lantern Festival time. Aunt Gao and First Uncle had already been to the Jins' substantial home on the pretext of holiday calls. First Uncle engaged the prospective groom in conversation there, and pronounced him "a splendid fellow." The Jins must have been waiting for a day unmarked by death—at least in our household—to formalize matters with the first betrothal presents. And now they have arrived, wrapped in the color of felicity.

"Anyway, he's one of us." A bondservant to the emperor, Wintersweet means, and from another family that has found its way by cleverness and study and loyal service, and well-placed daughters, to a certain social standing. Oh. They're related to the Jins whose daughter became an imperial concubine, and mother of three of His Majesty's sons! A family as influential as the most powerful of Aunt Gao's own relatives: a good match indeed.

I pour tea into my unused cup, press it on Wintersweet. She accepts it, but the flow of words doesn't stop.

"Papa says families like the Jins—they came from the Korean borderlands back before they started serving under the banners—keep up Manchu ways better than half the top bannerfolk these days! You know Grandfather would marry us both to Manchus if he could." She pauses to take one quick sip. "*Ake!* Too hot. He'd never let one of us go to a regular Chinese merchant family. If they'd even have big-footed us."

Poor Wintersweet. Does *she* sometimes secretly think of *me*, too much her mother's daughter? "I'm sure the Jins follow Confucian teachings too," I say as calmly as I can.

"I can't drink this." She plunks the cup back on the table. A few drops slosh out. "Oh, they're perfectly civilized, cousin. Papa says that he, my, you know, is a man of excellent taste. His family bought him a degree and he's waiting for a government job to open up. And of course they live here in the Manchu City, so I can easily come home to visit. He's the only son in his generation, which Mother says . . . which has its good side."

She smooths the lute-shaped lapel of her bright-pink sleeveless jacket, then continues. "So they really do have money. Maybe I *will* be the one to travel, Lotus, if he gets a post!"

I've never seen her this overwrought. Her large eyes grow larger, brighter. I put my hand on her rough cheek, as she did on mine, the first night of the Lantern Festival, to brush away my tears.

Wintersweet picks the cup up, twists it around. In a voice keen edged as Aunt Gao's, she orders Happiness to tell the rest.

"It's, well, the sons, miss. The ones old Mother Jia predicted? They're . . . already born. One to Young Master Jin's concubine. And the others to, to a lady who died almost two years ago. He's a widower, you see. But like I've told Miss Wintersweet already, that doesn't really matter. She's still going to be his formal wife. Not a concubine."

"His *second* wife! No wonder his family's willing to take an ugly pock-marked thing like me. He doesn't *need* to get married again. Someone in the family must be insisting—and how will *I* suit if a *proper* daughter-in-law's so important?"

Wintersweet sets the teacup down, stares into it as if it were a well. "You know we don't do all the Manchu rituals, whatever Grandfather tells his friends when they're drinking together. The Jins must be absolute sticklers for doing clan rites by the book! Some wife *I'll* be."

"Now, Young Mistress," Nurse can hold her tongue no longer. "Most people understand perfectly when a widower remarries. It's only some scholars as says—"

Wintersweet pushes my little brown-clay teapot back and forth across the table. "Their whole family will be watching me, comparing. How can those boys help but resent me? Everyone knows it's a mistake for a widower to take a successor wife! Either this Young Master Jin doesn't *care* about relationships within the household, or, or he's some kind of dreadful lecher, jumping at any excuse. And Lotus"—by now, her voice is faint and husky—"he's almost thirty, too old for me, I tried to tell them, but too young to *have* to take that concubine for having sons." My cousin doubles over and buries her face in her lap.

More tears. From both of us. Late last night, and as I started to read the poems, and now again: it seems that since I've started all I can do is cry. But Nurse asks sharply how I think I'm helping Wintersweet. I stop, and remind my poor cousin that the actual wedding may not take place for years.

That's no help at all: the date's not set, but Aunt Gao has made it clear that Mother Jia spoke truth. This year.

Which brings us dangerously close to the one thing no one says aloud.

Why are Wintersweet's parents so ready to accept this marriage offer? Granted, the match looks good at first, very good, given the Jins' connections. But she's young—there's plenty of time. Do they think no other suitable family will take a bride with a face as badly scarred as hers? Yet so many people have had smallpox . . .

Maybe it's the child Padma's carrying. Are they tired of worrying about a daughter who eventually must go, now there's the promise of a new son on the way? Or is it all the result of idle talk over too many cups of wine?

Then I think, they could wait and marry her to a good family in the Chinese part of town. After Grandfather dies. My hand jumps, and I knock the teapot off the table, making a huge wet mess of leaves and shattered clay.

$\mathcal{M}$y cousin and I spend the rest of the morning with Third Aunt in her side hall, in the north room we all call "the library," though no one forgets that before I was born it was Third Uncle's room. We drag ourselves through one of Bo Juyi's ballads under Third Aunt's blinking eyes, then move to the middle room for lunch. Eventually she lets us go and retreats to her own bedroom and the calligraphy practice that consumes her afternoons, as she brushes, over and over, the same dull words in the rigid clerkly style.

Later, I wake from yet another nap and sit in the sunny courtyard near some of Grandfather's potted chrysanthemums, trying to unsnarl the mess I've made of my embroidery. It tangles like my understanding of the elegy by Yuan Zhen that I was looking over in the morning. I tried to get my young aunt to help me with that, but she's not interested.

I pick at a knotted thread. Third Aunt prefers romantic lyrics over the older poetic forms; we're each to write a set of words to the pattern called "Partridge Skies." Maybe Wintersweet will come up with something about waiting for a lover's visit, but the phrases rising in my mind—the thread frays, I'll have to cut it—are more like those in the lament Pan Yue wrote for his wife hundreds of years before the days of Yuan and Bo. Or Mei Yaochen's sad elegy. I take up my little scissors. Why can't I write a poem like theirs?

The unusual warm spell that began on the day of Mama's one-year memorial service hasn't broken yet; I feel hot and itchy in my layers of padded clothes. At last I turn to Nurse. She's gossiping with one of the other older servants, Missus Jao, and only says the mess I've made is quite beyond her. "Why not go to Little Auntie Padma? She's good with her needle, I'll give her that."

"Good with her needle and good in First Young Master's eyes and probably good at the black arts too!" says Missus Jao, who has dragged my desk out into the sunshine and is supposed to be polishing it.

She puts down her cloth as if it were a judge's gavel. "A typical concubine, wouldn't you say? Puts on airs like she was better than us other servants, when her family took money for her contract the same as yours or mine, Missus Gu. And them no better than barbarians, way out there in Qing-hai! She acts the gentle thing, but mark my words, if that bump in her belly turns out a boy, there'll be no living with her."

"Well now, a boy cousin for my little missy here would be a blessing," says Nurse, shooting her friend a warning look. Does she think I'm still too young to notice? "But I do say I have to wonder about all her religious mumbo jumbo. Black arts, you think?"

Missus Jao slowly threads her cloth through the space within a cloud carving on one table leg. "I'm sure we both revere all the saints and sages and the buddhas and the bodhisattvas. But what those Tibetans and the Mongol hotheads call 'Buddhism.' *Unh!*" She pulls the rag in rhythm, in and out, and grunts again. "Of course the young lady knows I think all religions supported by our beloved imperial family are more than good enough for me. But they're special people, aren't they? Not like us Chinese. And that's my point."

The rag goes faster now, though there can't be a speck of dust left. "The question is, if this little auntie is the decent Chinese woman she claims to be, despite her dreadful accent, why's she so interested in foreign goddesses with naked . . . naked upper torsos? And you know what else—"

But Nurse interrupts to send me off to Padma by myself. I don't care. I'm glad enough to leave Missus Jao behind.

Little Auntie Padma has taken a chair out into the patch of sunlight in the tiny stone-paved yard west of her room. The room itself was only a small store-house until First Uncle returned from temporary duty in Qing-hai six months before Mama died, bringing his new concubine. Aunt Gao declared all other arrangements quite impossible. Then she suggested that as long as renovations on the storehouse were under way, a privy in the little yard beside it would be a convenience for all. But my uncle had a "hundred-sons" pomegranate shrub put there instead, and a narrow raised bed built for peonies.

This makes a funny sort of garden, with a bricked-in front gate filling most of its gray south wall; it was the entrance court for the people whose home became our West Courtyard back when our family bought them out and cut the vase-shaped doorway through the old dividing wall. But Padma prefers it to any other place: it's out of the way, at least compared to her room, which opens directly on the busy passageway to the rest of the family compound.

She mentions softly that there's a stool in her room I might want to bring out. After I'm settled, she makes short work of my tangled threads, and praises the one flower I've stitched that's smooth and even. I comment on the bamboo trellis that now shields her quiet outdoor corner from the rest of the West Courtyard. Padma's grateful, she says, that First Uncle agreed to have it built; a few paving stones have been removed beside it, so the gardener can put in a grapevine when warmer weather comes. We sit together, she working on a tiny jacket, I on my unsightly sash.

If Wintersweet wants to know something, I tell myself, she just asks. So when Padma sets down her needle for a moment and rubs her eyes and gives me a companionable look, I inquire about the strange green eight-armed female figure in the painting above the little altar I saw in her room.

"Does she make you feel frightened, Young Mistress?"

I mumble that she does, a little. The picture's worn, its paper creased. But the five skulls in the goddess's orange hair, her fiery halo and long necklace of severed human heads: I could make those out clearly enough.

"She *is* fierce. Yet her fierce kindness helps us. It's her power that can destroy what, what's walled up inside you. Or anyone."

I think of the tiger-skin skirt, the billowing folds of the short blouse pulled up and back to expose green breasts. "She's sitting on a lotus. Is she a buddha?"

"Some say bodhisattva. Some say mother of the buddhas. Some say goddess. We call what she's sitting on a moon disc. But under that's the lotus." Padma smiles. "Like our names."

"Our names?"

Padma tells me her name is popular for women where she grew up—she calls it "Amdo," not Qing-hai—and her parents liked it even though they mostly spoke Chinese at home. "Before we came here, your First Uncle said I couldn't go by my family name in the usual way. He thinks it's impossible to pronounce. I didn't care—we only have one for the government register, anyway. But "padma" in Chinese would be "*hehua*," or some other word for "lotus," like "*lian*"—

"Just like me!"

"Yes."

"And the, the goddess?"

"Green Tara is her name."

"Tara?" I try to sound natural, and fail.

"Like that statue."

I stare. She knows. But Mama told me the little statue was a secret.

"The statue your mother had was White Tara, Young Mistress, not Green. You could think of them as sisters."

"How do you—"

Padma tells me she let Mama have the statue, the day she first fell really ill. "Your mother was always kind to me, Young Mistress. You know she'd visit me too, sometimes, on a quiet afternoon like this one. We talked about that tangka—that painting of mine—more than once. She was my one friend here. Who doesn't need a little kindness, now and then?"

I've never seen Padma's broad smooth face twist with emotion as it does now, for just an instant. She's stopped work on the little jacket, but her needle begins to move again as she tells me the rest of the story: how she could bring only her few clothes and the tangka-painting on the long journey to Beijing. How First Uncle bought the statue for her after he caught her crying for home-sickness before the skimpy altar in her room. She doesn't say outright that the statue was a secret from Aunt Gao, but I can guess why Mama warned me to keep it hidden—to keep the family peace.

My mother had begun to believe deeply in the power and compassion of holy Tara, Padma says. But I know that. Mama talked to me about the goddess more than once in those last fevered days, though I couldn't make much sense out of her words. Padma had hoped the statue would help Mama overcome the illness.

Only it didn't. I think this, and then realize what Padma hasn't said: The statue Mama gave me was meant to be a loan to her and not a gift. Now I've lost it, or let it be stolen. Should I keep silent, pretend I didn't understand?

But I ought to tell the truth. After I do, Padma says nothing, only bends over her stitching. I watch the needle flash in the sun's long angled rays.

Finally, she speaks up. "It's done now. All year it made me feel better, to think White Tara was watching over you. The statue's not gilded, and it's so small, maybe whoever took it didn't think it worth melting down. People do peculiar things. We'll hope it was donated to some temple."

"Or maybe they needed it for themselves."

Her eyes flash toward me like the needle. "Maybe."

"Or maybe it will come—"

"—back to us." Her eyes look soft again. "I hope so, Young Mistress. Now I think you'd better go back to your own part of the house. It's getting cold."

I go. But the whole night, and after, I think how the sight of Green Tara, her awful garland of heads and her crown of skulls, shocked me into a kind of peacefulness, and how Padma—who is *lotus*—wears White Tara's sweet, mild face.

In the weeks that follow, Wintersweet's tied up with her mother every day, asking questions, listening to advice, learning how she keeps the household accounts—mostly in her head, since Aunt Gao can't read—and oversees the help. It's as if my cousin were a different person now: When I cautiously bring up her marriage, she just shrugs.

For practice, she's put in charge of all arrangements for this year's visit to the family graveyard on the Clearbright Festival. As we make the short trip out to the country, I look only at the first yellow-green haze on the willows, and try not to think too much of Mama, for fear I'll do the wrong thing. We sweep, set up willow branches, burn paper sacrifices, eat, and hurry back inside the Manchu City's ramparts. I do my part, but our family has never made much of this festival—as they say people did in olden times—so it's easy to notice only how well Wintersweet manages, and how much like a young matron she can act, for a few hours.

I visit Padma more than once, to listen to her stories, and sometimes help her with the sewing Aunt Gao's always telling her to do. I'm in her room one chilly afternoon halfway through the second month when the sound of shouts in the Front Courtyard drifts back to us. In a short while, Nurse comes in, clucking her tongue, to take me off to greet my father.

"Father! Nurse, should I put on nicer clothes?"

She looks me over. "You *should*, but he said to bring you in right away. He's paying his respects to the Old Master. In the North Hall."

For an instant I think of dashing to my room anyway, to snatch up the clean copy of the poem I finally finished. Third Aunt didn't say much about it, only pointed out two mistakes in the tonal pattern, but I think I've fixed them well enough. Wintersweet listened to me chant it, patted my hand, and called me a poor thing.

But Father's who I wrote it for, and Mama. Will he understand that I *know* how he must feel? Or will he think me presumptuous and unfilial?

Not Father. When I see him I remember how kind he is to me, when he has time to take notice, when he's not caught up in his duties in the Imperial Household. He stands stiffly, face creased, beside my grandfather's black-wood chair in the formal room of the North Hall. Grandfather's red-shot eyes gleam, but Father's are draped with shade.

Poor Father! The long journey down the Yangzi and along the Grand Canal must have exhausted him. But now I'm old enough to take care of him, at least when he isn't staying over in his quarters near the palaces.

As soon as I've made my kotows he pulls me up with both hands, pretending to groan from the effort. "So tall!" he says. "And so much like— suddenly so pretty too."

Grandfather cackles. I hang my head. Father coughs. A flick of movement draws my eyes to the shadows in one corner of the room. Where a silent woman stands.

"Lotus," Father says. "This is your new Little Auntie Tuo. Your grandfather tells me you're quite grown up enough to help her learn our family's ways. She will improve your playing of the chyn, and perhaps teach you a bit about painting as well. I expect you to work hard."

The woman keeps her head bowed. I turn to look at Father, but if my face reveals my shock, he ignores it. "She'll be staying in our side hall," he continues, "thanks to my father's kind permission." Through the blurring fringe of my lashes I can just make out Grandfather's smirk.

Father clears his throat. "Since I generally sleep in the Imperial City, I'll let her keep her things in my room. And you can stay on in, in your mother's old room."

My new little auntie. The polite words mean "mother's younger sister." My father has taken a concubine.

NIGHT MOORING ON THE YANGZI:
A LAMENT

Snow on the riverbank, washed away
    by rain at the start of spring.

Broad water, rich mud, faint first-month green,
    in this southland she never saw.

A cloud-blocked sun goes dim and sinks;
    on shore, the temple ruins fade.

At midnight the traveler, alone in his cabin,
    still peers through misty dark.

Small drops tap a sail made of reeds.

Dull flame trims an oil lamp's wick.

Its smoke forms a face with empty eyes,
    shapes words in a foreign script.

The smell of strange earth, the currents' soft rush
    mingle, ceaseless as grief.

Ravens mutter and stir in riverside trees:
    dawn and the rain still falls.

ANOTHER SOUL ADRIFT

Another story and another restless spirit, wind tossed on the dark spume beyond the edge of human life. Clad in new clothes of satin, dusted with the lime and ashes packed inside the coffin, it wanders, longing, through the gloom.

One of so many. They drift, they suffer, some are saved, and yet ten thousand thousands more are born to die and drift. And a hundred millions born to mourn them, till their own turn comes. Avalokiteshvara—as the bodhisattva Guan-yin is called in Sanskrit—Avalokiteshvara weeps.

He (for so Avalokiteshvara's most often pictured, and might as well be, after all) gazes tenderly at this new one now seeping through the borders of the visible, having died most recently in what you call *"eighteenth-century China."* It, she, poor roving ghost, first burned incense for Lady Guan-yin, Guan-yin of the Southern Sea, then for motherly, childless, White-Robed Guan-yin, giver of sons, though not to her. She next learned praise for the thousand-armed One called in Tibetan *Chenrezi.* And praise to holy Tara's name.

Her own name in the human realm was *Yueh-guei,* Lunar Kinnamomon, after the cinnamon-fragrant cassia tree that blossoms on the opal-dusty lunar plain. So you might say simply, Cassia.

Actually, you've already heard of her. Look closely: the thick hair she used to coif so neatly beneath a Manchu-style cap on holidays hangs down loose—as a mourner's hangs—around a face pallid and lovely as the mid-month moon. Lotus's dear "Mama." Taiyang's moonlike "Biyangga."

But why has she not found rest at her gravesite and in her spirit tablet? Why has some aspect of her being not made its way long months ago to the judgment rooms of hell?

It is not her daughter's failure in the mourning ritual that ties her to this fretful incompletion. Not the lack of a male descendant, nor her sister-in-law's stinginess with the postmortem rites. It's her daughter's yearning that has snared her—and it's her own hunger that keeps her trapped in this limitless place that is no place at all.

She has fixed her will upon the life that's ended. Desire claws at her like a five-clawed demon: she wants, wants only, to return. Confused as a ship that's lost its compass, hurled by wild seas of her own making, she whirls and wails. What good her husband's insistence that, live-born son or not, she deserved the comfort of full honors in his family's ancestral hall—what good, when she *will* have her way?

A new twist on the same old story. Avalokiteshvara feels the same new pity.

Once, in a moment such as this one, hot tears fell from the bodhisattva's eyes. From those two streams two lotuses rose and bloomed. Each blossom bore a female emanation, a goddess, if you will. Up from the left cheek sprang White Tara, giver of peace and plenty and long happy lives. Fierce Green Tara, compassionate action, was born from the right.

This is the truth that Padma taught to Cassia. A truth that, during her last months in the human realm, Cassia had begun to understand.

She, it, knows other truths, and only a dolt would quibble over logic. A soul's dark *po* sinks to the fecund earth, lingers at a carefully tended grave. Its *hun* parts rise, disperse like smoke, scatter like speeding light. And—some say—become the spirit of an ancestor accepting offerings of respect and food in the hall where its name tablet stands. Yet shades of the dead are also judged in hell, tormented or sent to take up long-term temporary residence and employment in the limbic towns on its ungentle plains, aided by paper houses, paper clothing, paper replicas of money, horses, maids, all burnt by dutiful progeny.

Grave po, ancestral hun, spirit in the underworld: These three are one. And each soul is reborn again, treading one of the Six Paths out of the tortuous underworld.

Yet a ghost unsatisfied does not go any of these various ways. It may appear in dreams, or deceive the living with illusory bodies, or roam as a dreadful beggar. As for salvation, escape from rebirth in the lotus pond of the Western Paradise, that is the deep belief—or destiny, or perhaps even the desire—of rather few. So she whom we may call Cassia, being one year dead, still roams, a disembodied personality at the shadowy perimeter of our world of light.

And, see? She has spied a glint of luminosity; she has somehow slipped toward it through the murky flux.

Cassia throws herself forward. The glittering arch she now discerns before her can be no other than the gateway to the heavenly headquarters! "Yang Purple Palace," a great sign proclaims in bold characters. She has stumbled upon the seat of the Jade Emperor, supreme lord of the divine bureaucracy that oversees all Under Heaven. Perhaps he will grant her what she craves: her old life in the flesh. Her home, her family, her things.

Or not. She pauses. An emperor—capricious, picky, autocratic—may not be the one to ask. Whom then?

Cassia knows that two youthful attendants stand on each side of his throne. Golden Lad and Jadewhite Girl have held their places there since well before the heavenly overlord's official recognition by a rather presumptuous earthly ruler of the Soong, more than six centuries prior to Cassia's birth.

She nods her head decisively. She'll beg them for their help. One who dares not approach an august monarch directly may profit from flattery or emoluments heaped upon his subordinants. Ask Sun Taiyang, proud holder of a key post in the Department of the Privy Purse.

"But wait," a pedant somewhere squeaks. "Wait. I've seen that boy-girl pair before. In Buddhist guise, on a Buddhist island mountain, not in this celestial Yang Purple Palace we'll classify under 'popular Taoism'." Wiser scholars nod, sigh patient sighs. A distant peal of thunder rolls across the sky.

Cassia pays no mind to all of that. She rushes on, past radiant cloud-banks: lavender, turquoise, lemon, topaz, flame, vermilion, ruby, shell, and rose.

Till someone blocks her way.

Her vaporous body somehow turns more solid as it bumps up against a chest and belly covered over by an official's embroidered robe, court rank three-B. Two grayed eyebrows rise in appreciation. A damp-lipped smile spreads across an oddly youthful face.

"Who are you?" Cassia asks. Then wipes the quaver from her voice: "I need to speak with . . . someone in the throne room. It's quite important."

"I," declares the official, "am Chief Secretary of the Joint Ministries of Baubles, Babble, and Extraneous Narratives. The question is, who are you?"

"I have business with the Dragon Dau—" (But what is she saying? Why does he make her so clumsy tongued, so nervous?) "—with Jadewhite Girl. Or Golden Lad. My name is not important. Will you let me pass?"

"Perhaps." The official appears to be considering options. Or perhaps the lady's clothing. She's lovely, he thinks, mettlesome, almost flaunting her unconquerability. Might she nonetheless be liable to deft persuasion? Backed by a genuine admiration? His curiosity slips like a single finger toward a tender imagined dampness. But, ah, didn't he put such entertainments well behind him, dynasties ago?

Cassia feels his gaze upon her. He can't possibly—she wouldn't—she has never used—except when her husband's stubborness—she's a lady! Yet such a thrilling novelty . . . (She notices her hand rising to brush back a strand of hair.) Ah, to be met with some masculine *something* other than fond complacent ownership, or polite aversion of the eyes . . . And what is it she wants to go back for, after . . .

"No!" Two chains of thought reach simultaneous finales, two voices cry out loud as one.

"Er, that is to say—"

"I wish, good sir—"

The pleasant baritone overrides the resonant contralto: "Madame, I already know just who you are. And what you would ask. We all knew, here at court, the moment you entered beneath the arch of gold. And just then—did you not hear the thunder?—His Majesty frowned."

"Oh."

Ah, such a pouty-ripe mouth. Can't he, with all his status and connections, do something for the charming little thing? A selfless tribute to her beauty and inner strength? "Truly, my dear, it's no good asking here now. But you might just try your luck with the Lord of Mount Tai. The Jade Emperor's principal aide, y'know. This sort of thing falls under his jurisdiction."

"The Lord of Mount Tai!" Cassia sets her mind on the peaks and ridges of the craggy massif rising above the Shandong plain, the rocky Eastern Guardian of states and empires long before the Qin, the Soong, the Tang, the Han, even before the Qing. She *will* go there. Now.

Tossing hasty thanks over one comely shoulder, she speeds away, past rose, cerise, magenta, apricot, sapphire, cobalt, amethyst, indigo, plum. If she hears the official's voice call out behind her, she pays it no heed.

Cassia knows how reverently men of power speak of Mount Tai's lord. Her own husband holds a special affection for the mountain, named as he is for its yang-side sunward slopes; a scroll that depicts its upthrust summit and misty grottos hangs in his room. Where sacrificial offerings have been made by rulers for twenty-three centuries, where even their own Qianlong emperor and his dowager mother have paid homage in grand procession—she must hurry, hurry.

"Stop."

No evading this voice. No avoiding the figure before her, beneath the glimmering arch. And no mistaking her: Jadewhite Girl, in a celestial courtier's garb. Cassia comes to a halt.

"Yes, ma'am? Miss? Ahh . . . your ladyship?" What above earth is the correct form of address?

"Before you go to Mount Tai . . ."

But can this heavenly maid be trusted? Why is she trying to slow Cassia down? Does she not have a snaky look about her green-flecked eyes? "Yes?"

Cassia's rudeness does not, it seems, go unnoticed. "Well. I'll just remind you that His Lordship has a daughter. You may go."

Yes, yes, of course, who doesn't know that? "Thank you, ma'am."

Which last words earn Cassia, as she speeds out and away, one more word to the wise: "Remember, you can always ask to be reborn! Or for sal-va-aa . . ."

The Jadewhite Girl's advice fades among the scudding mists beyond the Emperor's precincts, fades as Cassia flies, swift as an arrow shot from the crossbow of her own determination. Reborn, reborn! That's not what she wants.

She wants what she had, or what she remembers of it. Oh, and sons to continue her husband's line, and a good life for her own little girl, all that of course. But above everything, she wants to break free of this turbid purblind insubstantiality. To smell jasmine, and the packed dust of a roadway after rain. To eat *jiaozi* and *mudan efen* and sticky rice. To touch gauzy bed drapes and feel what that heavenly official made her feel. To hear a tea kettle simmering on the first cool day of fall. To see with clarity the lantern moon.

And dare we fault her, really? Rare the mortal who truly puts first the happiness of others. Rarer the one who recognizes the wellspring of unhappiness. And pleasant indeed, with luck, this pain-filled earthly life.

A LOTUS BLOSSOMS: 4

But why does he need a concubine? Of course I know the answer: to get a son. Wintersweet and I have talked it over many times these past few weeks; she keeps saying I wouldn't really want a husband desperate enough to give up his own family's name and marry in, and that Father's right about the risks in adopting some outside boy as heir.

"The little auntie's here to stay, cousin," she tells me. "You know what people say about listening to our fates. Heaven sends them, and what can we do?" I mustn't argue with Wintersweet. She's accepted her marriage—it would do her only harm to change her mind.

Still, Father needn't treat the woman like a wife. He needn't have summoned me into their room—no, his—to share their dinner this chilly evening. He needn't make such a fuss over the silly "plum blossom tray" she's had made, that covers five little serving plates with its stem-handled lid, and pushes them so intimately together. He calls it elegant, to arrange food in a flower design. I'd prefer it if we each ate from our own dishes, in the Manchu way.

I sit, because I have no choice, at the low table on their warm bed platform, wondering if they serve meals on trays like that in every southern winehouse. And Wintersweet says I should be glad this "Inkscent" is here because it means my father's less likely to take a new formal wife!

She's a finicky eater too, hinting he should tell Cook to order a better grade of vinegar all the way from Jin-jiang, and take pains not to mix flavors on the chopping board. She wants him to try rice flavored with dew gathered from wild roses when summer comes. I like imagining what they'll say about her in the kitchen if she succeeds.

"What do you think of the steamed yellow trout, Young Mistress?" she asks me with a look that feigns reserve. "When your father told me you'd be joining us, I sent word to use very little scallion and rely on ginger root to bring out the delicate flavor. I've noticed how sensitive your palate is."

I bend my lips upward and flick my ivory chopsticks out to the dish, stuffing a bite into my mouth so I won't have to reply in words. The fish is almost cold.

Father leans back and exhales deeply. "Ah, I remember that tasty Yang-jou fish you suggested when I hosted the dining-boat party there on our way north. I thought it as fine as the music you played!" He turns to me. "Lotus, learn to manage your kitchen well, and you'll make your husband a happy man."

"I'm sure Little Auntie Tuo can teach me many things about pleasing men."

Her face could be carved of ice, or bone. He narrows his eyes and makes a soft, thoughtful sound.

"Give me a bit more of that excellent sorghum wine, Inkscent. And tell me how my daughter's doing with her painting lessons."

As she tilts the wine pot, the southerner gracefully catches one flower-stitched sleeve with her other hand. "It's still too early to say much," she murmurs, eyes turned toward his cup. "But she has potential. A fine eye for what's wanted. It's clear she was raised to appreciate beauty."

She sets the wine pot down without a sound. "Her progress with the music is remarkable. She really has a superb touch on the chyn."

"Daughter." He swings the little cup in my direction, drains it. Above the warm maroon of his old riding jacket, his gaze is steady, his mouth set.

"Yes, Father?"

"Whether you marry young, or serve out ten years in the palaces first, or . . . stay on in some capacity, you'll do well to take with you all you can of connoisseurship. And the skills that please a connoisseur."

His eyes flick over to the concubine, then fix again on me. "You are a filial girl who values what your mother taught you. You have her feel for language, even poetry, in a properly feminine way. That pleases me. But your mother would not want you to keep forever to the knowledge—and *behavior*—of a child." He pauses, still unsmiling. "Do you understand me?"

"Yes, Father."

"Good. You'll soon be old enough to pin up your hair. I trust you'll apply yourself to your music and your stitchery and to your studies with Third Aunt. A wife who is cultivated as well as dutiful—and gracious to all around her—makes for a happy marriage." He picks up his chopsticks again. "I shall not forget I had that good fortune. On that point you may set your mind to rest."

"Yes, Father."

Little Auntie Tuo asks if she might pour a little sorghum wine for me, and when he agrees, takes a small jade cup, thin black-streaked verdant green, from its case.

I know what she's trying to do, and I set my heart against it, though I must accept the wine. But I resolve to work harder at my painting. Playing Father's chyn, even under her guidance, is hardly work—and she *is* helping me grow better.

Their talk soon turns to other Shandong drinks, and then to a millet liquor that Grandfather especially likes. My father rarely drinks more than a few small cups of anything—perhaps the reason is his own father's great fondness for any sort of wine.

"Ah, but Inkscent," he says, leaning back, "and you too, Lotus, I shall have to let you sample some fermented mare's milk the next night I can come home from my quarters. That will give you a taste of life in the lands north of the Long Wall! But I believe I'd best order in a kind less, ah, less fragrant than the sort my father favors. No, no more."

The little auntie replaces the wine pot in its bowl of warm water. "*Arjan*, we generally call it in this house," Father continues. Although our family speaks Chinese most of the time, we mix in Manchu words quite freely. But since my father's return from the south, this is almost the first syllable of Manchu that's crossed his lips.

"Arjan," repeats his concubine. "And all wines and such, in general, are . . . ?"

"*Arki.*"

Her high-cheeked face takes on an inward look. "Like *arahi*. Arki, arki."

"Arahi?" He jerks forward. "So you *do* speak Mongolian."

"It's Manchu I want to learn, now I serve this family."

"But you do know Mongol words."

"A few. One picks them up in . . . a busy city. Even in the south." My father's concubine toys with the slim vase of apricot blossoms on the table. I've almost stopped listening to her idle talk, musing instead on how she'd best first learn to speak Chinese northern style, as we do every day; the dialect she grew up with makes her unable to distinguish a *jing* from a *jin*. But I begin to pay attention now.

"We can repeat our old conversation again if the master wishes it," she says. "If in Nanjing I exaggerated my ignorance of the Mongol language—and I truly do not speak it, milord, only understand a bit—it was because the master seemed to have the impression . . . that something had happened that had not. But I must apologize for even slight exaggeration. Only a base person would be anything but completely open hearted with one who has shown her the overwhelming kindness—"

"Yes, yes."

"I am sincere, milord." She fixes her gaze on Father as if the world held nothing else worth seeing. "Listen. I will tell you of my lineage. Although at my mother's behest I have spoken of this to no outsider in the past. Not a few of my sisters in Nanjing bear the Mongol surnames Tuo and Dun . . ."

For the first time, I want to stay in the room. I sit motionless as the woman beguiles him with a story of Nanjing courtesans who claim descent through the entire Ming dynasty to captured noblewomen of the Mongol-ruled Yuan. Is it possible that generations of girls born fatherless in the winehouses could really have passed on Mongol teachings to their daughters, during all the difficulties of all those years?

"That is why I have asked your permission to go sometime to a temple cared for by Yellow Hat lamas, to burn incense there." Little Auntie Tuo sits with her hands folded carefully in her lap, eyes downward.

Is it possible? The Thunderbolt Way of the Tibetans is the same as the Mongols' secret teachings—and Padma also longs to visit the Yellow Hat lamas' Temple of the Five Pagodas or the Yong-heh Palace Temple, or one of the others. Perhaps this new concubine really did grow up with some trace of Mongol ways.

My father obviously believes her. Well, why not? And what difference does it make?

Then she adds in a sibilant undertone, "There are teachings my mother spoke of that I have not yet dared mention. The master knows that the official history of the Yuan dynasty describes how the Mongol emperor Huizong was patron to a Tibetan monk who taught him the secrets of paired practice. Which has . . . spiritual benefits, though it requires much preparation. If you wish, I could share with you the little that I—" Her glance flies quick as summer's distant heat lightning in my direction. "Perhaps later. If you wish."

Father reaches out to touch her cheek.

Soon I'm shuffled off to Nurse and her attentions and complaints. Soon after that I'm beneath my quilts, thinking about those last few minutes, how my father's room felt like the air in the courtyard when gray-purple clouds build up above the southern plain and the winds rise fast, before a cloudburst brings the sixth month's rains.

In the morning, my father leaves early to return to his duties in the Forbidden City. Both door-curtains are out sunning in the courtyard, so before he summoned me to the central room of our little building for a brief good-bye, I got a glimpse of him adjusting his cap in the little auntie's mirror. She stared at his back as if she were thinking deeply. But I'm sure she merely placed herself where he could catch her pose, over his shoulder, in the mirror's reversed image of the world.

In any case, today—the twentieth of the third month—has been set by the Ministry of Rites as this year's date for men to change to summer hats, so we girls and women will exchange our metal hairpins for cooler ornaments of jade. Nurse makes a great flurry of packing away the delicate bits of filigree that came to me from Mama, of unpacking other jewelry, of rummaging in the storage boxes to replace fur-lined clothes with lighter ones, and winter's padded door-curtains with airy bamboo blinds. The last time Nurse did this, Mama was barely two months dead.

I look away from the empty doorway. Luckily the weather turned overnight, and a light breeze warms the building. Nurse has opened the papered windows wide. Maybe the cold days have really gone at last.

In their end of our side hall, Inkscent and her new maid, Snow—a local girl about my age—seem to make short work of managing the belongings she brought with her from Nanjing. But how much finery will she extract from Father in the weeks and years to come? This hiring of Snow is no good sign.

Tetra and Quinta are assisting Grandfather's chambermaid, Prima, in the North Hall. As the junior maids for the Upper Courtyard, their first duty lies there. But soon a thin roar from Grandfather sends them out. I see Tetra scurry beneath the apricot tree across the courtyard to join Third Aunt and Partridge. Quinta ambles up to see what's needed in our hall.

A few moments later, the little auntie evidently decides to ingratiate herself with Aunt Gao by lending her a hand. But first she offers Nurse the assistance of Snow, saying the new maid would "benefit from Nurse Gu's experienced instruction, if you please." I watch through my bedroom window as the southerner takes herself off on lazy Quinta's arm. Wintersweet says this Inkscent is the first woman with gold-lily feet to live in our household since a concubine of Grandfather's who died before my birth.

This opportunity to quiz Snow with no one else but me around is one Nurse wouldn't miss, and soon the two of them are a-bustle in the middle room, though they chatter more quickly than they shake and fold or mend loosened seams.

"So how are you getting on with your new mistress now that it's been, what, three days?" Nurse asks. "It must be rather tiresome for you to catch her accent, being true Beijing born and bred yourself."

But Snow doesn't answer. Perhaps she's guarded because she knows I'm in the next room, leafing through the book of poems by Wang Wei that Father gave me yesterday.

Or perhaps she really's been taken in by her new mistress. She comes from a poor family in the Outer City, same as Nurse. Life must be better for her here. "Oh, I've gotten used to the way she talks," Snow finally says. "And such a pretty name she gave me, don't you think? At home I was just 'Puppy' or 'the Lins' fourth daughter,' but the mistress says she's named me for a lady painter who was famous for her landscape fans." I turn my head to peek through the doorway; the girl's face glows.

"A *lady* painter?"

"Well, a courtesan from Fujian who moved to Hang-jou. But the mistress told me her work was in the, the orthodox southern school of Mister Dong Qi-chang. And very pretty, it's said."

"The southern school, you say? Well, I suppose there's some southerners as aren't immoral. And I'm sure it's a very nice name for a nice girl like you— Lin Xue, Forest Snow, you might say. Clever. So she's good to you then?"

At times like this I miss Fidelity, the maid who came with Mama when she married into our family. *She* didn't have a showoffish name, and I remember Grandfather praising her virtue last spring before Aunt Gao found her a husband. Fidelity played games with me when I was little, but I haven't seen her since she paid her respects at New Year's. Nurse says she has a baby in her belly and a sickly mother-in-law, and is too busy for us now.

The sunlight glaring off the page before me makes my forehead tighten. But I mean to understand these poems before Father next comes home. Perhaps it's because he doesn't have a son that he takes interest in my studies. Anyway, I can make out something beautiful, and important, in the simple words.

Still, I want to close the book, maybe lie down and try to nap. But when I catch what Nurse is saying, I silently fold my arms on my desk and lay my head on them instead.

". . . four concubines over the years, the Old Master did, though they're all gone now. You can imagine how the late Old Mistress felt about that! They say she hounded one of them until . . ."

Her voice drops to a raspy whisper that floats in and out of hearing. ". . . should you have occasion to enter the Old Master's presence, if you know what I mean. Not that I'd say anything against him. But some in the household claim that after he's been out banqueting he can be a bit . . . you know."

"He—"

"Shhh." I keep my eyes closed and breathe evenly. Nurse continues, more softly still, "You'll want to watch yourself, that's all. But he's older now, and the only female he can stand to have around him since he actually packed his last concubine back to her family is Prima, his chambermaid as you've hardly laid eyes on yet. Not that you've missed much by *that*. She keeps Tetra and Quinta quite tied up with her fetching and carrying, lest he fly into a rage because she's stepped out for a moment. Makes it hard on the rest as works in this courtyard, when there's wash water wanted, or slops to take out, or messages and such. You'll see."

Nurse sighs. "But you've nothing to fear from my young charge's father, my dear. He's always been an upright sort. Growing up with all that jealousy and quarreling among his father's women must have done it. Mostly he seems to worry about how the imperial bondservants aren't favored by His Majesty as much as they were when the Old Master was a lad and His Majesty's blessed grandfather was on the throne. Or so the master used to say to his good wife.

"But—" I hear the sound of flapping cloth as Nurse begins to speak a bit more loudly, "what can we common folk do about what goes on inside the walls of the Forbidden City? How far above us is the sun? You've come to a good place, dearie, and if you have any little questions, you may come to old Nurse Gu. Ah, good morning, Miss Wintersweet! Isn't it a lovely day all of a sudden? I was just saying as much to young Snow here, wasn't I?"

My head snaps up. Wintersweet! I've hardly laid eyes on her these past few days, and I wonder what has freed her from the measuring and sewing that steal so much of her time now. We're due to meet with Third Aunt to review another chapter of Ban Zhao's *Admonitions for Women*, but not till later in the day. I'm sure Madame Ban deserves the respect she's had for all these centuries, but I don't see why my aunt wants us to go over it again.

"Cousin," I call. "How are you? Have you finished your essay on 'womanly words' for Third Aunt? Quick, come take a look at mine while I've still got time to fix it!"

Wintersweet bounces into my room, waving her arms as if she were fighting her way through clouds of dust. "*Aiii*, the only place you can smell more chase-moth herb is over in Mother's rooms!" She grimaces. "Yes, I came up with a little something. But it will be washed with more red ink than tears in the bitter sea. I'm claiming that when Madame Ban Zhao wrote of 'womanly words,' she was *supporting* the idea of women writing, and maybe even circulating their work outside their homes. Can you believe it?" She makes a comic grimace. "No doubt Third Aunt would prefer a nice little piece on one's duty to learn enough to teach one's children, or on holding one's tongue and not offending anyone."

"But—"

"You know, there are *throngs* of women from perfectly respectable families in the south who publish essays and poetry books and anthologies and plays.

And even some northerners, I hear. And think of the oldest poems there are. Doesn't *The Book of Odes* have folk songs that can only be woman's words? Isn't it one of the Six Classics?"

Her eyebrows fly up and down in mock surprise at the brilliance of her own argument. "*Mmm*, I'm worn out. I stayed up late to finish writing, and it's all just to tease Third Aunt out of her gloominess, anyway. I mean, what difference does it make? Do you think we could get some tea?"

"I'll ask Nurse. Or Snow could brew some for us, I expect. Remember how Mama taught us to recite from the *Odes* before we learned to read?"

My cousin walks over to stand by my chair and trace a faint tickle on the back of my neck. "I remember," she says quietly. Then her hand creeps toward my armpit and in a flash wriggling fingers attack me on both sides. I scream and gasp with laughter and beg for mercy, writhing wildly in my chair.

"Tea, tea, I must have tea! I am your respected elder cousin and you accused Zhu Shu-zhen of writing heartsick caterwauling—oh, I haven't forgotten what you said the other day—and you won't even offer me tea!"

"Stop! Oh, please!" I laugh till my cheeks turn wet. "Please. I'll give you tea."

"*And* declare that you would travel to the peak of the most rugged mountain under Heaven for your dear cousin's sake, and admit that Zhu Shu-zhen's saddest love lament is truer to most people's lives than . . ." She pauses to glance down at my book. ". . . than any of Wang Wei's poems! Even if she *was* a—do you declare it? Hurry. I want to get this over with. I came to tell you some enormous news."

"You are my dear cousin, and I would climb to the top of the Kunlun Range for you . . ." She stops the tickling and I take in a huge breath. "And, what was the rest?"

Wintersweet's fingers come toward my face like squirming crab claws. "You remember," she says, but in that instant I've slipped off my chair and out the door of my room to ask an astonished Snow to put a kettle of water on the little stove in Father's room.

And so Wintersweet's news: we will indeed make the pilgrimage to Marvel Peak to burn incense to the Verdant Dawncloud Sovereign and her companions in her palace shrine. Perhaps

Our Lady will cure Third Aunt's weakening eyes. Perhaps she'll grant the family sons.

We are to depart on the sixth day of the fourth month—Wintersweet, Happiness, Aunt Gao and Grace, Third Aunt and Partridge, Inkscent, little Snow, and Nurse and me. Cheerful Deucey will come too; she's smug at being chosen over Trine and the other junior maids. And it's been decided Padma must join us, to pray in person that the child she's carrying will be male.

For days the household is thick with the smells of cooking: peanuts boil in brine, sweet-potato cakes steam and then dry in the sun, vegetables are laid down to pickle, the tang of simmering black-bean paste drifts through the air. My father's concubine works her way into Aunt Gao's good graces, helping with lists and hemming indigo kerchiefs to hold our incense bundles. Snow is quite agog at the bustle and the great baskets of food and the prospect of travel three days' distance from Beijing. I can understand how she feels.

But who'll be our male escort? There will be far more men than women on the road, says Mother Jia, who drops by every few days. For us to travel with only menservants hardly suits our position in society—or the one we'd like to claim. Father can't leave his duties, and naturally no one suggests Grandfather make such a trip. Once he gets wind of the plan, though, he insists it be carried out. He wants an heir.

First Uncle is reluctant. He rubs his chin with one knuckle, says that a drawn-out investigation of the Eternally Auspicious Pawnshop ties him to the city just now. And so many are going already. The costs keep mounting, he points out—as if Wintersweet's dowry weren't strain enough.

But there's a good reason for every one of us to take part—except perhaps my cousin, since any sons she bears will be Jins, not Suns. Yet Wintersweet's wild to go, and First Uncle rarely denies his daughter anything. It's true a son of her own would secure her position in her new family. What's more, now a comfortable future's been arranged for her, Aunt Gao is reluctant to part from her only living child.

"I hear the First Young Master claims his duty lies in staying near his father, so as to keep an eye on the household staff with all the mistresses gone," Nurse whispers to her friend Missus Jao one afternoon. "As if you wasn't the one as really keeps in line those sluts and roughnecks in the Front Courtyard! But some say it's his wife's second maid he wants to keep his eye on, seeing as how she's being left behind to manage things. You watch that Harmony—she's just waiting to seize her chance with him, I guarantee it."

They're both annoyed because Big Jao, our chief steward, is going along to mind the arrangements and the other menservants, but Missus Jao is not. Yet the problem of a male relative to escort us remains. We've no suitable nephews or brothers-in-law among relatives outside the household: with Wintersweet betrothed, and me nearly grown, and a widow just turned thirty in the company, the candidates are few indeed.

But that becomes the clinching argument. The family needs sons. First Uncle will go along.

In the cool dim light of the fifth watch on the day of our departure, we rise, dress hastily, and stumble toward the front gate, where a line of donkeys—and the enclosed mule cart for Aunt Gao and Mother Jia and pregnant Padma—have been waiting since nightfall, when the police guards closed the street gates leading into our lane. "I still don't think it's right," Third Aunt mumbles to Partridge as we wait our turn to be assisted in mounting the animals, "for us to go out bare faced through the streets like this. Pilgrimage is just an excuse for vulgarity. For some women, I mean, and immodest behavior is forced by circumstances upon the rest of us. I wish we didn't have to go." Partridge clutches her arm more tightly, nods.

Wintersweet is almost dancing. She rushes back and forth across the flagstones of the Front Courtyard, in and out of the crowded vestibule off the gateway, as she did when she was a child. I stand behind Nurse, listening to the complaints and jests of the hired donkey grooms and baggage men out in the lane. My own eyes feel as puffy as Third Aunt's this morning. Early though it is, I woke up long ago, to lie staring into the darkness. Why didn't Mama ever make this journey? Why does Mother Jia insist that I take part?

The old fortune-teller has made arrangements for us to stop for breakfast and pay our respects at one of the older shrines to the Sovereign Lady, just outside the city wall, near Gaoliang Bridge. "There's reason aplenty why the Marvel Peak shrine has flourished so, though it *is* little more than a hundred years since a Master of the Taoist Way, and a wise Buddhist monk, and a devout layperson not unlike yourselves joined in founding it," she told us yesterday when we gathered in Aunt Gao's room for a final meeting. "Yet the efficacy of Our Lady at her other sites cannot be denied. Surely you've heard about the emperor's son of the last dynasty who was saved from smallpox after prayers at this smaller shrine?"

Did she deliberately bring on that twist of pain to shatter the composure of my first aunt's face? If so, and if the purpose was to bind Aunt Gao more tightly to her, I believe she was rewarded with success. Wintersweet, too, drew closer to the old woman in the hooded cape as she instructed us again: "Some say the Verdant Dawncloud Sovereign is the northern appearance of the Heavenly Empress of the Southern Sea, who of course is none other than Our Lady Guan-yin. And I will not deny it."

Even Third Aunt peered more intently from her corner then, as the fortune-teller's scratchy voice continued. "And surely in venerating the Sovereign, we may also gain the favor of the mighty Lord of Mount Tai, whom many hold to be Our Lady's father. Do not forget, it was on his Eastern Holy Mountain that this jade woman first revealed herself in the form of a statue found in the waters of a lofty spring-fed pool. More than seven centuries back it was that our Verdant Dawncloud Sovereign came to succor us."

Less than an hour ago, when Nurse finally stirred and I could step out on my veranda to glance toward the predawn sky, I saw how the gray clouds might be called "verdant," they looked so rich and lush in their green-tinged heaps. Now we move through empty streets, passing shadow-colored house walls, gates touched with dark emerald and red. Big Jao must have made a quiet financial arrangement with the officer in charge of the police guards for our neighborhood; although it's still more night than day, the wooden street gate at the head of our lane opens noiselessly before us.

We progress more swiftly than is possible at a later hour, so smoothly— and sleepily—it seems a wide eyed dream. My donkey trots amiably, and I find the riding pleasant, with its regular rock and sway. The gate boy who holds the halter plods steadily, head down.

I'm pleased, after all, that Wintersweet convinced Aunt Gao the seclusion of jouncing carts made little sense for most of us, since they'd have to be exchanged for donkeys anyway when the roads narrow as we approach the hills. "Some might call us pretentious, as well," my cousin told her mother, "to behave like ladies of the nobility when we travel for religious reasons." But I think it may have been the difference in cost that finally convinced my aunt.

Curfew's ended by the time we reach the twisting fortifications and imposing watchtower of the northernmost gate in the city's west wall. The central passageway's reserved for His Majesty, of course; I'm sure my father's seen it used when the emperor goes hunting in the Western Hills, or maybe when his household makes the short trip to the country palaces on the northern fringes of Beijing. But I have no desire to see those pretty gardens, let alone the foreign-looking fountains and marble villas: I know I'll only go there at the price of having left my family.

As we emerge from one of the side gates and turn west, the year's first rose vendor cries out on the road ahead of us, his baskets laden with furled buds of pink and mauve. Soon we stop at the shrine near the Gaoliang Bridge, to burn incense and make donations, and to eat. But Third Aunt slides from her donkey to stand stock still in the forecourt of the shrine.

"I, ah, believe I'll wait for you out here," she says, shoulders forward, the oval of her face tight set, eyelids pinched together to sharpen her view of the world. "After all"—her laugh tinkles suddenly—"we know that as far as having a child goes, this widow's fate is set. It's the Sovereign's companion, Our Lady Eyebright, whose help I need. I . . . understand *she*'s best beseeched atop Marvel Peak."

She laughs her new brittle laugh. "Anyway, that jouncing on the donkey has set my silly stomach churning. I'll just rest out here in the fresh air while you have your breakfast. Partridge can keep me company—Deucey, you'll run out with a steamed bun or two for her, won't you?"

Other visitors come and go around us. An old woman from the shrine's kitchen has stumped out to us, and appears to be on the brink of clutching Aunt Gao's sleeve and dragging her inside. Chief Steward Jao clears his throat.

"We've a long way to travel if we're to reach tonight's accommodations before dusk," says Mother Jia with a wave of her pilgrim staff. "I see no need to force anyone to pay her respects to Our Lady, if she finds the day or place unsuitable."

Oh, I think. An unsuitable day. Twice, Nurse counted up to be sure my monthly time would pass before we made the pilgrimage. When I asked why a goddess would take offense, she patted my hand and told me not to talk crazy talk.

Mother Jia's austere face turns kindly. Her thin-fleshed fingers grip my young aunt's forearm as they once gripped mine. "Mother Jia knows the goodness of your heart, dear madame," she says. "You may rely on me." Odd, I think, that no one else has noticed how easily the old woman gets around, or finds the thing she reaches for.

It's full daylight now. The predawn clouds have vanished into dry pale-blue air. Third Aunt blinks again.

The only place dirtier and more flea ridden than our temple lodgings the first night is the inn where we stop the next, in a shabby village in the shadow of Marvel Peak itself. By then, we've long since left Beijing's walls behind. How strange that felt, to turn my head and find them vanished! We've climbed west through the foothills, up and down and sharply up again. The mule cart was exchanged for three more don-keys—hired at twice the usual fee. In the morning we'll proceed up the last and steepest path on foot.

"How will Little Auntie Tuo get on?" my cousin breathes in my ear after we've finished the greasy, meatless so-called feast with dates and gritty congee. We've been sent off to a large bed platform in the women's side of the hostelry; Nurse was so tired she fell asleep the moment she stretched out at our feet. The other grown women still linger at the table: after dinner, Mother Jia gath-ered them around her with the promise of a tale of ghost possession not quite fit for young ears, yet edifying to married ladies in the end. Tomorrow, the eighth, is the best day in all the year to supplicate the Sovereign, so the com-pany's large and varied.

"Who cares?" I say, exhausted and still half hungry. I wish my Mama would appear like the ghostly mothers in stories who help their beloved chil-dren and punish wicked stepmothers or neglectful fathers. "We saw plenty of other gold-lily feet on the trail. Some of them must have walked the whole way from Beijing. Remember that man we saw this morning, stretching facedown on the ground every third step? What vow do you suppose he was carrying out?"

She purses her lips and shrugs. "Have you *seen* them yet?" she asks. "Without her shoes and binding cloths, I mean?"

"Wintersweet!"

A little girl with a cloth tied across her eyes rolls over on her pallet across the room. Nurse snores on. My cousin and I smile in the oil lamp's smoky light—the walls and ceiling here are pure black, I noticed when we first walked in. Better at least than out in the mat shed where our maids will sleep on rough board beds, while Big Jao and the rest of our men take turns standing guard.

"You know, my father told Mother the other day that Grandfather called the new little auntie the kind of wall-toppling beauty who can ruin a family," Wintersweet says quietly, slapping at something on her arm. "Papa thought it was because of her not speaking Manchu. The same old history book recitation again, he thought. But it turns out Grandfather meant because of her gold lilies. He was warning Papa to stay away from her." She shakes her head. "Papa told Mother that he almost broke his own teeth, keeping them locked together so he couldn't speak."

"His brother's concubine! What an awful idea!"

"Well, of course they'd been drinking when Grandfather said it. If you're shocked by that, I'd better not ask you my next question."

"What is it? About my father and the little auntie?"

"No."

"Good. What then?"

"About this bed platform, in this inn where new travelers pass night after night."

"Well?"

"Do you think that any—I mean, married couples must stay here when it isn't crowded." She pulls back her sleeve and inspects a spot on her arm. "How many people, do you suppose, have made this place where we're sitting a, a connubial bed?"

I shriek and hide my face in the quilt. I don't know what the blind girl thinks when we both collapse in mirth that soon becomes a breathless tickling session, ending only when we're both too sore sided to move. Nurse just snorts and goes back to sleep.

Actually, my father's concubine does admirably—it's the only word—on the last rough upward trail. Snow takes her arm every step of the way, and Mother Jia herself, who's surprisingly sure-footed, supports her on the other side. Perhaps it's this example that makes Aunt Gao solicitous of round-bellied Padma as our way twists past fearsome rock outcroppings and skirts the edges of sheer ravines. Looking down from the switchbacks, I can see others climbing after us, and sometimes I catch sight of more pilgrims where the trail crosses higher on the slope.

The weather's perfect, warm and clear, as the almanac predicted for this anniversary day of the Buddha's enlightenment. But we all need to stop often, despite the stone stairs built as a kind of offering in some of the steepest sections. Happiness's rosy face turns quite red with exertion. Nurse huffs and leans on the shiny-barked peachwood staff she bought yesterday. And when we come to a rest house set up for the two-week busy season by a charity club of bannerfolk, everyone in our party is grateful for the tea they press upon us with cries of "Welcome, Pious Ones!"

"There should be more of these rest houses," Wintersweet says as we leave the older women sitting on straw mats near the club's portrait of Our Lady, sipping and looking up toward the lotus flower shape of the peaks. "They do as much good for *us* in *this* life as for the donors in the next!" A new party arrives to bow before the flower-filled altar while devout society members sing and huge candles flare. The pilgrims all accept free millet porridge; some, like us, add food brought from home.

My cousin and I pass beneath a huge twisted pine tree as we amble arm in arm along a pretty side path to an overlook. She wants to light more sticks of incense at an altar the charity club has set up there. "Oh, Happiness!" She drops my arm, turns to her maid behind us. "Would you run back and get a couple tangerines from the red carry-basket for us to offer here?"

A little frown puckers Happiness's sweat-damp face. She must have a blister; she's been limping. How hard, to be a maid and have to do your mistress's bidding no matter what! To empty her chamber pot, to eat only after she finishes, to trudge on aching feet when she takes the notion to stroll. Of course Wintersweet knows the obligations of superiors toward those below them in society, and is thoughtful—when she thinks. Still. Then I remember: two or three years ago, Happiness's mother died. Happiness was given seven days off.

The words *I'll go get them* rush forward in my mouth. But just at that moment, Inkscent and Snow, carrying five tangerines, appear around the curve in the trail. I have no choice but to take one from the southerner's slim extended hand.

· · · · · · ·

The crowds at the peak are wild in their happy jostling. Bells and gongs and cymbals ring out, kettle drums rumble, horns blare, pilgrims chant or sing rice-planting songs. Near a stone memorial tablet, an old bannerman thumps a hand drum shaped like the moon. A group of acrobats has set up between bright pennants just outside the gate into the Sovereign's precincts, the Palace of Wondrous Responsiveness, and visitors who've already paid their respects inside gather around to watch them. Someone cheers.

They say more people make this pilgrimage every year. I wonder why troupes and troupes of performers haven't come to walk on stilts and strike bold poses, earning the favor of the goddess, and coins from travelers.

Within the shrine, bundles of incense sticks are piled so thickly they actually flame in the giant bronze burner. As my eyes adjust to the darkness and the smoke, I fix them on a wall plaque some thankful person's donated; "Pray, and you'll be answered," it proclaims. Men and boys, and a good many women and girls as well, cluster close, too packed together for me to see much else.

Nurse protects me as we step around a man kotowing furiously next to one of the carved pillars. The iron chain he's locked about his neck clanks heavily on the stone floor. A heap of baby figures, some of plaster, some of precious metals, rises at the left end of the altar, where Our Lady of Sons and Grandsons stands. There, Padma bows and prays just behind Aunt Gao. I see Partridge and Big Jao help Third Aunt slip forward to add to the pile of models of undamaged eyes before Our Lady Eyebright off to the right.

I never do catch more than the tiniest glimpse of the golden face of the Verdant Dawncloud Sovereign herself, though I jump up as Nurse gives me a boost, grunting at my weight. We toss our incense into the burner, pray quick prayers, and leave.

Our party is to reassemble near the stilt dancers. Metallic music adds to the clamor as their leader announces a performance of *The Romance of the Snake Girl and Sudhana the Devout Pilgrim Lad*. During the prologue, a painted-faced warrior brandishes his spear, rising a good four feet above the heads in front of me. But for an instant I lose sight of the winsome boy in the Snake Girl's garb; he drops down, then bobs up swiftly, stilts still tied to his feet. "Look at that!" someone up front cries out in Manchu. And in Chinese, another voice praises the young acrobat's perfect splits.

"Do you think the goddess will tell me how to have a happy marriage?" asks Wintersweet, coming up behind me at the edge of the ring of watchers. Her pocked face shines with earnestness, but in a flash it changes and she intones beneath the ruckus, "Please . . . your husband . . . and . . . he will . . . please you." She skips back as I reach out to give her lower lip a playful pinch.

Two sweaty bare-chested "mountain tigers" stop nearby to let a well-dressed old woman climb out of the swaying rattan chair in which they've carried her up to the peak. The sickish look on her face makes me glad Mother Jia advised us to express our devotion by making the climb on our own.

By now, most of our family party have arrived. Young Wang, the senior gate boy, informs us that First Uncle has already gone on to the Homeward Incense Pavilion to pay his respects to the Lord of Mount Tai. He's taken Little Auntie Padma with him, Young Wang says, so there's no need to look for her.

Grace hurries up, a butterfly made of red cloth tied to the front of her jacket, and I notice several of the others now wear souvenir emblems: tigers and flowers and lucky bats. Aunt Gao has bought a crimson sash inscribed "The mountain visited, incense offered, good fortune now borne home." "Where has my sister-in-law taken herself off to?" she asks, frowning as she looks around. Wintersweet says she saw Third Aunt and Partridge at the end of the row of thatched stalls hung with crimson lanterns, inspecting the colorful woven wheat-stalk fans and hats for sale.

Mother Jia raises her staff a foot or so, about to speak, when Partridge trots up. Alone.

"Has anyone—I've lost my mistress!" she almost wails. "It's so horribly crowded and noisy and . . ." Her plump face folds into itself.

"Never mind, my dear." The fortune-teller nods as if Partridge has just told her the answer to some difficult conundrum. "It *is* crowded and confusing, and this whole family knows you are a good girl and the most loyal of maids." She half shakes her head and continues with a lighter air, "Mother Jia believes she knows where the widow is. No one is to worry. Did I not hear that the family's First Young Master has gone on to the first stop on our homeward route?"

Aunt Gao draws in an exasperated breath; Partridge isn't the only one who's worn out by three days of hard travel and unfamiliar food. Wintersweet steps over to her mother's side. "Go, go," says Mother Jia, waving us onward with her staff. "I—we—will join you shortly, at the Homeward Incense Pavilion. I am sure you will want to give the Lord of the Eastern Peak his full due."

I fall in behind the others as they start to take the path around the goddess's palace and up the rise toward her father's shrine. I'm footsore too, and my calves ache and I don't really want to visit the Lord of Mount Tai at all. But I must, if only for Mama's sake. In case, just in case, she somehow hasn't yet safely passed through the infernal courts of judgment.

Five or six slow steps down the well-worn trail, someone clutches the hem of my jacket. Some awful beggar?

Mother Jia. "You must come with me," is all she says. The hood of her cape falls back, and I see her hair's still perfectly arranged, despite the difficult climb, piled up black as the hair of a woman half her age. "Shhh," she says when I open my mouth, and turns away, confident I'll follow.

I do. She steps smartly onto a narrow mossy path near a stand of fair-sized cypress trees, moving with the confidence of one blessed with perfect vision. Only after we've gone around a shoulder of the mountain, away from the music and excited voices, does the fortune-teller face me again and say, "Your young aunt needs you. Walk as quickly as you can."

She hurries on. The path grows fainter, crosses the hump of a side slope, ends on a wide flat ledge of rock. Where Third Aunt sits teetering, legs dangling above sheer air.

I freeze. My aunt's head whirls toward us. Mother Jia continues stepping forward, her staff tap-tapping on gray rock.

"The young lady believes she is all alone in this world," says the old woman. "But I have told her she may rely on me."

"Stay there!" shrills Third Aunt. "One more step and my death will be as certain as the falling of this stone." She picks up a stone from a small pile she's made beside herself and tosses it off the edge. I'm close enough to hear it thud on earth, clank twice. Then I hear no more.

Mother Jia stands still, her back toward me. "As you wish, my daughter. The choice to rely on me is yours alone. But now your dear niece will walk up and sit beside you." The tip of her staff wavers, gesturing me forward. I understand her, but my feet will not move. "The child is your student, and I know you care for her, more than she realizes. If you leap when *she* is coming toward you . . ." A half-breath's pause. The staff tip waves again. "What effect will it have on her? Sit there quietly, let her sit beside you as a comfort, and when you are ready, Mother Jia will listen to what you have to say."

"I have nothing to say, nothing to say to anyone." My aunt turns her face away, stares out over the gorge before her. But the words seem to have no meaning: all my attention now lies on setting down one foot, then the other, quietly, evenly, on the cracked rock of the ledge. As I pass the fortune-teller, her chin twitches toward the place I already know I must go and sit.

"Not too close," says Third Aunt, when I'm almost within arm's reach of her. "Sit then, Lotus, since you're here." She laughs the artificial laugh of these past few months. "Sit with me and enjoy the view of mountainsides from which clouds are born as if they were their own progenitors."

I sit, arms stiff, propping myself up. A half-glance down and giddiness surges through me. I won't look into those boulder-strewn depths again.

"They say," my aunt continues, gaze still fixed straight ahead, "that in Shandong, near the original palace of the Verdant Dawncloud Sovereign on Mount Tai, anyone who leaps from the Suicides' Terrace—with sufficient faith—will be saved by the goddess. That means—" She shoots a swift, angry look at the old woman. "That means, according to you, saved by the Compassionate Lady Guan-yin, does it not?"

The fortune-teller says mildly, "I have told you, you may rely on me."

"But what if someone *wants* to die? Wants to plunge to hell and suffer the cruelest tortures of the cruelest ox-head demons in the deepest pit? What if that is what the person *deserves*?"

Third Aunt? Impossible. Impossible too that I am here, feeling the ordinary heat of sun-warmed stone seep through my trousers and overskirt. Impossible that this meek woman, who pledged a lifetime's fidelity after word arrived of her husband's death on a frontier battlefield—

"*What* is going on here?" And a heartbeat after Nurse's voice cracks through my thoughts, I hear Partridge screaming, "Mistress! Mistress, no!"

Time, which snaked past slowly, slowly, after I saw Third Aunt sitting on the ledge, now hurtles forward. Mother Jia speaks low voiced, urgent words. Nurse ignores her, snatches me from the cliff's edge, falls back into a sitting position, and folds me against her soft breasts.

Partridge stumbles as she too runs across the rock, stumbles, sprawls, and howls. I catch sight of Third Aunt scrambling toward her maid and only friend, crawling, knees catching at her skirts. They kneel face to face and weep in one another's arms. Nurse weeps too, and pats my back, wiping the tears from my cheeks with her bare hands as I sob.

"That's enough now, little missy," Nurse says in a moment. "Your nurse has a handkerchief about her somewhere, and a good thing too. It's badly wanted, I must say."

I stand up to clean off my cheeks. Mother Jia has not moved. She's facing us with the same remote, absorbed expression I saw on the audience at the stilt dancers' show.

Third Aunt stands too, breathes deeply, smiles crookedly at Partridge still huddled near her feet.

"Mistress," the maid's voice quavers. "Did you tell them?"

Tell us what, I wonder. But what I hear instead is Nurse's voice, saying in her flat and soothing way, "About the child she's carrying, you mean? There's ways, if we act quickly—"

Again, time changes. Partridge gasps. Third Aunt hisses, "The father was a ghost, I tell you. The ghost of my husband, maybe. I had no choice."

Partridge says, "No, no, it wasn't. Why not tell them, mistress? *You* did nothing wrong."

Third Aunt stoops to pick up another of her stones, tosses it casually into the gorge, and casually steps after it, off the ledge of rock.

I throw my body forward, and throw my arms around her waist to stop her. But we both go down through the emptiness.

To land painfully on a narrow shelf of earth six feet below.

I sit up, remember to breathe, hear my poor aunt murmur, "It's none of your doing, Lotus. Be a good girl, as I've always taught you."

Then she rolls off the shelf and into the gulf of air.

No, she does not. Before she can move those last few inches, Nurse scrambles down to me, and her foot slips, and it is Nurse who rolls and falls, as swiftly and as fatally as any willing suicide, to the boulders far below.

After one look down, I turn away from the edge. I don't move again. How could I? I have become a stone.

Partridge arrives to help her mistress clamber in silence back up to the rock ledge. When I do not climb after them, Mother Jia reaches down with her staff.

"Take hold of this," she says. There is in her voice something—not authority, not command, something both cool and warm at once—that makes anything but obedience unthinkable. Though I don't much want to obey. Then, "Wait a moment," she says. And then, "Ah, now I understand."

I wait. I could just sit here on this shelf of mountain earth, facing the foot of the great rock ledge, and never move.

"Is there a cleft, an opening in the mountainside before you?" Mother Jia asks. There is. Perhaps I nod my head, as if the fortune-teller could see me. She tells me to reach inside.

What my hand grasps is metal-cold, and irregular, and heavy. It has the same heft as the Tara statue that disappeared from my keeping months ago. In the shadows where I'm sitting, I glance at it, not really interested. It isn't Tara, though it's a small image in the same style, the same color, a little taller perhaps. Its hands are held up at the level of the heart; each thumb and forefinger join to form a circle, one above the other.

To shift my gaze would require effort, so I continue to inspect it, observing the passionless face with no more interest than the bloody dirty scratches on my palm.

"Hide it beneath your skirt, in the waistband of your trousers," Mother Jia tells me. "Keep it safe. Tell no one. This is something you yourself must come to understand. Now grasp hold of my staff and climb up to me."

I do just as she says.

BEYOND THE CLOUDS AND UNDERNEATH THE EARTH

Hurtling away from the Jade Emperor's gleaming gate, as others have hurtled toward the edge of a drop-off above a rocky gorge, the ghost of Lotus's mother spins a thread within her mind: a thickening filament of silk, a woven cord, a rope. What does she know of Mount Tai and the subterranean courtroom to which that celestial bureaucrat the Chief Secretary suggested she take herself? How can she summon it into being; how can she find her way? How can she persuade the lord of the mountain to send her back to fleshly life?

Cassia remembers the scroll in Taiyang's room. Recalls sheer cliffs and spires higher than those near Beijing. Envisions gnarled oaks, red pines, a tunnel of cypresses. Casts these images like two cables out into the void.

Other visions rise: a waterfall emerging from a cave, the high-flown Ledge of Suicides above a sea of clouds, the poets' Sunrise Viewing Peak. These serve as boards and towers while Cassia builds her suspension bridge over, out of, nothingness.

And steps upon it, each step forward allowing her to thicken or extend the cables, to lay another girder. She can perceive the Red Gate shrine near the start of a pilgrim's final climb. Elaborate eaves emerge, deep blue-green against its faded garnet walls. A bent-backed graybeard sweeps the path below the steps. He glances in Cassia's direction, chuckles, taps his head to clear it.

She hurries on. Anxious local dignitaries and bored imperial guardsmen blink in and out of being at a spot where rituals of welcome for the Son of Heaven have been performed. Was that red-draped table set with flowers, candles, incense burner put up for a visit by the Kangxi emperor, she wonders, or for his grandson, who today rules nearly all the world?

Never mind. The rocks she's passing so closely at the moment are ancient Cambrian, as resistant as any rock can be. And solid, it now would seem. A geomancer of Cassia's time would speak of "earth's breath" within the hilltops and the winding ridges, would find their significance in their cosmological correlations and in pragmatic applications of the same. So would believe them real. A latter-day geologist, describing the crystalline structure of the rocks, would admit their substance to be no more than fluctuating "energy" in "sub-atomic" "space." Yet would believe them real.

Cassia reaches her goal: a nearby hillock called Haoli, Tombwort Village. Millennia ago, even before the ten elaborate hell courts took form beneath the earth of China, this place was known to be the primordial gateway to the shadowy underworld. Here, despite all shifts within the minds of men and women, the Lord of Mount Tai still holds sway.

"Oh, *dear*," the green-skinned deity is saying as the ghostly woman slips invisibly into his dim, chill judgment chambers, "here we *are* again. It's not the *wicked* who have no rest, it's those who have to *deal* with . . . well. To work, to work." He leans forward in his scarlet throne. "Who's *next*?"

Cassia's just about to reveal herself and make her plea when an unpleasant looking military type in a brass helmet dumps a tender-faced young man bound in chains on the floor before the monarch. "This one's been waiting quite a while, sir," he rumbles. "Bit of a tricky case, sir, but no one's come to, ah, make offerings on his behalf. Might as well clear him out of the way. Sir."

The Lord of Mount Tai taps the thick multicolored sole of his left shoe. "I believe I *will*," he says. "Never mind what little *gifts* have or have *not* been made. What does his *record* show?"

Not much good, it seems. Cassia's taken aback to hear what dreadful things the rather charming youth has done. The first crimes strike her as ordinary enough—indifference to the sufferings of people he saw daily; indifference to those he never laid eyes on, whose sufferings eased his days; a general indifference to suffering in general, except of course his own.

But the list goes on. A dollop of lust. A smidgen of greed, especially greed for others' admiration, though silver would do as second best. More envy than he'd ever admit, even in solitude. Occasional gluttony, mostly for intoxicants. Large doses of pride: He was given at times to pondering whether he was the voice through which society expressed its values, or the eye with which—yes—the universe beheld itself. Less sloth at least than wrath, the former being reserved for activities he believed beneath someone with his gifts, the latter arising chiefly when his work was stupidly or unfairly judged. Which he felt happened rather often.

Some kind of artist, then? Cassia observes the peculiar mixture of vulnerability and arrogance in the curl of his tender lower lip. She inspects the nimble fingers that again and again pull fruitlessly at his chains.

But wait. Let the helmeted bailiff answer her question, before curiosity drags Cassia too fully within the moment, spotlighting her into visibility in the murky room. "Did his apprenticeship as a lay metalsmith in a workshop associated with an imperially sponsored temple in Beijing, sir," the infernal officer is saying. "He had just finished making a set of Buddhist statues under the direction of several learned, ah, monks."

"Learned *monks*? Buddhists, eh?" A frown washes over the Lord of Mount Tai's broad face, then disappears as he waves a gracious— or judicious—hand. "Fine, fine. Monks. Ah! It's the *Qing* dynasty up there just now, isn't it? *Imperial* temple, you said? So they'd be *Tantric* Buddhists, I suppose?"

The bailiff braces, tucks his chin in smartly. "Yessir. Esoteric Buddhists, sir. Lamas, actually, most of them. Overseeing the quite prodigious production of paintings and images fashioned according to their particular . . . school of thought that present, ah, trends require. Sir."

The green hand waves an identically gracious—or judicious—wave. "Fine, fine. *Monks*. Go *on*."

"He'd risen to his position swiftly enough, having been selected from a minor Chinese banner family as a lad, moving from trainee to apprentice, and then to—"

Again the hand waves. Not, however, quite so graciously.

"Yessir. Well, the problem's this: Having reached a not unimpressive level of skill for an artisan so young—"

Cassia notices how the youth casts his gaze down modestly, then winces at the sound of "artisan."

"—he was assigned to a project worthy of a promising talent: a commission for a certain mandala consisting of thirty-six small bronze statues arranged around one of the cosmic buddha Vairochana. It seems a pilgrim to the Five Crest Mountains came across a badly faded painting of that particular grouping of buddhas and bodhisattvas . . . and guardians and so forth . . . in a temple there, and even though it's not a mandala especially favored by the Yellow Hat lamas nowadays, he vowed he'd donate a nice new three-dimensional replica as an act of merit, for his dear departed mother's sake. So, a week or two later, when this pilgrim got home to Beijing—Yessir."

The bailiff's chest swells as he breathes in deeply, hurries on. "In short, sir, this fellow here was allowed to model a few of the wax figures himself, and prepared the clay molds around all of them, as he was judged especially good at this, and helped pour the alloy into the molds, and so on."

"And?"

"Two sins, sir. First, he cunningly carved a tiny stamp with the characters for his own name. Warmed it, pressed it into each and every wax model, somewhere inside where it couldn't be seen. But of course that affected the molds, which affected the final form of the cooled metal, so that all thirty-seven images secretly bore his name out into the human world."

"His *name*? His name on a work of *religious* art?" The Lord of Mount Tai rolls his eyes.

"Yessir."

"*Hmmmf.* Gutsy. And *remarkably* dumb. Even allowing for his *species* and his line of work. *Two* sins, you said?"

The young man's well-modeled chin, which has been jutting forward in brave—if useless—defiance, drops to his chest.

"Yessir. Then he let the statues be stolen, sir. Along with more costly artifacts. Helped it happen, actually. And by way of thanks for his assistance, the thieves cut his throat."

"*Let* them be *stolen?*"

"My father was sick. He needed expensive medicine." The clear, intense timbre of the artist's voice carries only the tiniest hint of self-conscious modulation. "I had no choice but to—*Ai!* What's the point of poking me?"

The ox-headed demon next to him grunts, "Here's me point, laddie boy," but lowers his pikestaff when the Lord of Mount Tai shoots him an irritated look. Cassia recoils in fear.

As she draws herself more thinly back into the shadows, her eyes moisten, though whether for sake of the filial young man, or with longing for her own dead parents, or in memory of her daughter's clumsy attempts to nurse her on her deathbed, or in mourning for herself, she'd be hard pressed to say.

The bailiff's helmet gleams in the endless twilight of the courtroom as he reveals that the father had been scheduled all along to die just then, in the forty-fifth year of his life. A longer span than many are allotted, after all. "So the money this fellow would have gotten for helping the thieves slip into the workshop would have been wasted, actually, sir. Although it might have prevented the herbalist from selling off his youngest dau—but I digress."

"Indeed, you *do*."

"Yessir. Diphtheria took the girl the next month anyway, sir. Yessir. Sorry, sir. It's certain, ah, ecumenical aspects that have truly complicated the case, sir, as much as all these questions of motive and effects. That's why I've held it off, pending clarifications. Certain Buddhist . . . personages have been inquiring into the situation. Seems they're chiefly concerned about the mandala statues for some reason, sir. Want them reunited, sir, and delivered to their intended home in the Five Crest Mountains. Word came from Avalokiteshvara—"

"*Guan-yin's* in on this?" Great bulging eyes roll as exasperation washes over that green face. "*Well* now. We're all *in this* together, aren't we? Mustn't forget *that*." The Lord of Mount Tai chortles, though Cassia's not sure she sees the joke.

The divine magistrate then assumes the mask of august majesty, decrees that the young man's journey through the underworld shall be postponed until he's tidied up the mess. The statues are bound to have been sold off hither and yon: The one who made that possible will have to see they're brought together again.

"And I *believe*," he adds, "I can leave it to my Buddhist *colleagues* to decide whether the collected statues are to be consecrated in that temple at Five Crests anyway, or *what*. Given the *desecration*. Imagine! His own *name!*"

The artist bows his head.

"Very good, sir," replies the bailiff. "Now, apparently, Guan-yin decided it would not be inappropriate for her and her attendants to take some small part in the task. Given its complexity, on the human scale. In fact, she has already—"

"Well, that's not *my* problem, is it? Now. I've got a *great* many cases on the docket for today. *You*, son—what *is* this *name* you made so much of? *If* I may *inquire?*"

"Wu Ming, sire," the young man mumbles. And seems to brace himself, Cassia notices. Does he fear another pikestaff-poke?

"Wu Ming?" The Lord of Mount Tai roars with laughter. "Wu Ming? Your parents *named* you 'Anonymous'?"

"An accidental pun, sire. They forgot to take homophones into account. It's 'Wu,' the usual family name, sire, same as the ancient kingdom, not the 'wu' that means 'without.' And 'ming' like 'bright,' not 'ming' as in 'a name.' " The youth recites this rapid-fire, as if he has recited it many times before.

A second ox-headed demon guffaws, "But I heard Anonymous was a woman. *Har, har, har.*" Startled by the outburst, Cassia jumps. The demon's halberd gestures in Wu Ming's direction, then thunks end down on the courtroom floor—thunks so hard her breasts shimmy on her muscular chest. No one but Cassia pays her any mind.

"And that's the name you wanted to *advertise*? Well, well. Well." The deity shakes his large squarish head, flicks a tear of delight from his green cheek. "Well, young master Wu Ming." He raises his oblong gavel. "You are *condemned* to *return* to earth and see that *all* those statues of yours are *gathered up* and taken—"

"Oh, let me, let me!" With those words, Cassia dashes forward from her nebulous location. All eyes turn on her. And with the looking, she suddenly can be seen: the ghost of a woman of above-average height, her beauty ripened over her thirty-some years. Attractive despite the ashes smeared about her nicely tailored clothes.

She prostrates herself before the Lord of Mount Tai, begs him to allow her to return to her world. Quickly she begins to relate her urgent love of the life she had. When the deity's eyes glaze over, and the hand with the gavel twitches, she changes tack.

"I believe, Your Majesty, that I know already where one of the statues is. I—it would take rather a while to explain, but—" Cassia turns to Wu Ming. "They were smaller than the length of my hand, were they not?"

Wu Ming nods, though he looks a bit grudging.

"And one of them was Tara?"

Another nod.

The gavel bangs. "*Enough*. Humans may fill their *time* with questions, if they *wish* to. *I* have other interests. I've decided. You'll *both* go back."

Wu Ming casts a dubious eye at Cassia, whose lovely (and vaguely familiar) face radiates joy. The joy perhaps of a child about to eat all the sweet red-bean paste its stomach can hold, or a little more. The joy of a weak-willed nomad princeling who has just inherited his brother's wives. The joy of her father-in-law as he opens the first jar of the new season's unstrained wine.

"I prefer," the artist mutters, "to work alone. Nothing personal, ma'am." He's sure now that he saw her somewhere once. But his attention is devoted to the task at hand.

The two ox-headed demons step forward as one, weapons lowered, prepared to impress upon young Wu Ming the effectiveness of teamwork. The gavel bangs again. They halt.

"I'll send you *both*—work separately if you wish. Just get them to the proper temple in the Five Crest Mountains." The Lord of Mount Tai eyes the prisoner. "Wu Ming? Do you *accept* this task? Or shall I turn you over to my *assistants*?"

One more sullen nod.

"Madame?"

Cassia smiles her most winning smile.

"That's *that* then. You two may *go*."

Wu Ming's chains melt away. The male demon grasps his arm as the female clutches Cassia's. The two dazed humans are hustled toward the doorway that leads out of the hillock to the realm of living women and men.

"Ah, Wu Ming," the deity's voice calls out behind them, "You may *want* her assistance. You're both going to find it *trickier* than you *realize*, operating in the *human* world when you're *ghosts*."

Wu Ming shrugs, rather rudely. But Cassia stops short. "Ghost?" she cries. "But I want to live my old life again."

"Well, well," says the Lord of Mount Tai. *"That's* hardly possible, *is* it?"

"But why didn't you tell me I'd have to be a ghost?"

"Why didn't you ask? *Dismissed!*"

TALES OF THE STRANGE, FROM TERRACES OF JADE

NO. 14: THE STORY OF TSAO YUEH-GUEI

Introduction

T he compiler of the early–nineteenth-century collection in which this tale appears is known to us only by a penname, the Aging Lunatic of the Jade Terrace Studio. In publishing under this typical literary pseudonym, he (or, as "jade terrace" suggests, quite likely she) avoided disapproval for dabbling publicly in the vulgar pursuit of writing fictions. Anonymity also prevented repercussions from a government quick to censor, and sometimes to execute, a writer perceived as expressing seditious sentiments.

Internal evidence suggests "The Aging Lunatic" grew up in North China, possibly in one of the garrison communities where the Manchus and their military associates lived separately from the conquered populace. Although the characters in these stories appear to be Han Chinese, occasional details reveal the author's familiarity with the Manchu cultural sphere. One example is the curious name given to the old nurse in the story below: The Chinese "Meimei"—literally, Coal Eyebrows—would seem to be a transliteration of the Manchu term for a wet-nurse, *meme*.

If the author was indeed a bannerwoman, this might have increased the pressure toward anonymity. Despite the flourishing of literary women in the Yangzi delta region in the late Ming and the Qing, we have far fewer texts by women from the north, particularly those from the diverse groups lumped together as "the banners."[1] One new study hypothesizes that this may be the result of deliberate suppression of writings by women linked to the imperial clan. Restricting the circulation of such literary works would appear to have been grounded in the Qing debate on appropriate education for women, and in Manchu efforts to maintain a distinct cultural identity while winning the approval of conservative Chinese scholars.[2]

Like others of the period, these "Tales of the Strange" explore the boundaries and meaning of the transgressive, the disruptive, the anomalous, and the obsessive; their discourse claims the authority of historiography, even though they use a venerable genre (one that dated back over a thousand years, to the Tang dynasty) as a vehicle for self-expression overlaid with a thin gloss of conventional morality. The often sardonic comments offered by The Aging Lunatic at the end of each tale emphasize the importance of the interpretive act, and heighten readers' awareness of the interactive nature of each experience—each performance—of a text.

Elinora N. LaJeunesse
Ann Arbor, 1994

Yang Sun-tai, a native of Hsün-tian, was married to a woman of the Tsao family. The marriage turned out to be a happy one, but when their only child, a daughter, was about to enter adulthood, this Mistress Tsao suddenly fell ill and died.

Yang was a scholar of a progressive bent; though he did not follow Yuan Mei[3] in advocating spontaneous feeling and poetic freedom for educated women, he did hold with those who believe that a good education makes a good mother. "A

1. i.e., Manchus, many Mongol nations, Han Chinese from the Northeast whose ancestors had fought with the Manchus during the defeat of the Ming, bondservants of various ethnicities, and troopers and families from other minority populations—including Koreans, a few Russians, Evenki/Solon (Northern Tungus nomads), Dagur/Daghur (linguistically close cousins to other Mongols), and Xibo/Sibe (a Southern Tungus people originally from central Manchuria).
2. See Larsen, forthcoming. Despite conservative calls for "modesty," the historical record does include at least three eighteenth-century women poets associated with Manchu or Han Chinese banner units, as well as an imperial clanswoman-by-marriage (Gu Taiqing) and others in the nineteenth century.
3. (1716–1798): the preeminent poet of his age, and a strong supporter of literary women.

boy's earliest and deepest influences are the teachings he receives at his mother's knee," he would say. "This being so, should they not include the moral exemplars of poetry?"

But who was to educate his daughter? Lian-hua, as the girl was known, was already well versed in the basics of literacy as well as in the household arts. Although sometimes a bit stubborn, she was a good child, and showed signs of intelligence from an early age. Since there were no female relatives with a sufficient knowledge of literature, Yang was in a dilemma. His duties with the government kept him away from home; he could hardly teach her himself. After casting about for some time, he happened to mention the problem to an acquaintance newly come north to the capital from Hang-jou.

"Perhaps my wife's cousin could be of some assistance," the younger man said to Yang. "If I do not presume too greatly in suggesting it?" He went on to explain that this cousin[4] had appeared one day at his home in Hang-jou, recently widowed and begging to be taken in. Soon she acquired a local reputation as a poet and a "teacher of the inner chambers," of the sort who come and go among the women's quarters of various gentry households, hired to tutor other females in the art of poetry.[5]

"Although her parents-in-law shamelessly refused to support her after her husband died, and although her branch of the clan has fallen on hard times, nonetheless she is a woman of good family," the southerner said to Yang Sun-tai. "I dare not compare her to Madame Ban Zhao of the Han dynasty, but there are those who say she resembles Huang Yuanjie, who taught in Hang-jou over a hundred years ago. Huang's fame spread here to the capital, and her poems were passed around within the imperial palace itself."

"Indeed," said Yang, "having come to Beijing, your relative may be called a modern Wang Duanshu!"[6]

Soon all was decided. The female teacher would begin to teach Sun's daughter that very week. As the two men parted, Yang, begging pardon for his boldness, asked the tutor's name.

4. The original refers to her as a "younger sister of the same lineage," a vague term for junior distant relations.
5. The fullest study of such "teachers of the inner chambers" is Ko, 1994. For more on literary women in Late Imperial China, see especially Robertson, 1992.
6. (fl. 1660's) Painter, poet, essayist, literary critic, and editor of *An Appendix to the Classics: Poetry by Women of Note* and other anthologies, Wang—a southerner—was married to a native of Beijing. Daughter of a Ming loyalist, she evaded an invitation to serve as a tutor in the Manchu imperial palaces.

"My wife is a member of the Tsao clan. I believe her cousin signs her poems 'Yueh-guei.' "

Yang Sun-tai's eyes bulged in amazement: Tsao Yueh-guei was his late wife's very name! But he coughed to hide his emotions, reflecting that both names were actually rather common, and that history records many such coincidences. Later, when he first caught a glimpse of his daughter's tutor, he noted that she only somewhat resembled his northern-born wife: In speech and deportment, in the way she dressed her hair and the way she walked, the new teacher looked like nothing other than a woman of the southland.

Now, this Lian-hua, a most filial child, had long mourned her mother bitterly. In fact, Yang Sun-tai did not only want to prepare her to be a better wife and mother. He also hoped that study would ease the girl's heart, for her sorrow passed all limits and she fixed her every thought upon her grief; it seemed to deepen daily, and she was in danger of wasting away entirely. For this reason, he had already bidden his concubine, whose name was Orchidscent, teach Lian-hua how to paint.

Some weeks after the poetry lessons began, Yang returned home from the residence where his official post required him to live, and observed that his plan seemed to be working. Not only did his daughter take pleasure in her study of poetic prosody and allusions to the classics, but for the first time she showed interest in painting as well. The gloomy child he last saw had vanished, and in her place stood a slender, bright-eyed young beauty, who showed him the ambitious new painting she had been assigned to work on.

"See, Father?" said Lian-hua. "This one large wall scroll will resemble an album of seasonal tree and flower pictures. But rather than turning the pages one after another, people may view a plant for each of the twelve months in whatever order pleases them. They may move their gazes in a circle about the painting to see the flowers and greenery in the usual monthly arrangement, or may jump from end-of-summer lotuses to the early-blossoming plum and wintersweet,[7] then back to stalwart snow-dusted bamboo and over to late-spring peonies or this bowl of autumnal persimmons sitting by the desk."

The painting did portray a variety of plants, all arranged around the desk in an artist's studio. Some could be viewed through the door to a spring-filled court-

7. a fragrant shrub, *chimonanthus praecox*, the small bright yellow flowers of which appear long before its leaves.

yard, while a nearby window opened onto a wintry scene. Others were depicted in paintings—magnolia blossoms hanging on one wall of the studio and early-fall mallows on another. A small dish garden held a miniature red-leafed maple, and the girl showed him where she planned to add a potted chrysanthemum in bloom, after she had practiced more.

Though her brushwork was far from perfect, Yang discerned a fine sensibility in the girl's painting.

Exhorting his daughter to work hard, he remarked on the clever plan behind her work. "That was my poetry tutor's idea," exclaimed Lian-hua. "She says that turning the pages of an album forces one to follow strictly the plan of the album maker, while this painting is more like a poem."

"Ah," said Yang Sun-tai.

"She says that with this sort of design, one may hold the whole more easily in mind, selecting and juxtaposing various parts, and understanding them differently each time."

"Ah," said Yang Sun-tai again.

"Alas, I am still most clumsy at painting lotus leaves and blossoms," his daughter continued. "So I have merely sketched a hand scroll on the studio desk here, and will paint them on it later. My poetry tutor says I will find the ability when the time is right."

But when Yang next was able to return home, his daughter had changed utterly. The painting hung unfinished on the wall of her room, and she lay in bed, her body unnaturally warm, a hectic flush upon her cheeks. She had become dangerously thin, and barely recognized her father.

Yang's concubine—a gracious woman with no child of her own to look out for—told him she believed the girl's problem lay in her dreams. "Often at night," said Orchidscent, "I hear an eerie crooning in the girl's room. But if I go to see her, she appears to be fast asleep, with twin streams of tears, like chopsticks of clear jade, trailing down her face. The silly serving maids tell me they hear nothing except an occasional sob."

Indeed, the truth was this: Every night in her dreams, the girl greeted the figure of her old wet-nurse, who had also died recently. The nurse would hold Lian-hua in her arms, rocking her and singing and encouraging her to shed endless tears.

The girl told no one of these midnight visits, but so much crying had disturbed the balance of her vital forces, so that she was half awake by night and half asleep by day, leaving her too exhausted to eat or even speak. A doctor having been consulted, he prescribed a powerful tonic, but it could not overcome this insidious sapping of body and soul.

Yang Sun-tai could only stand above the bed and shake his head before returning to his duties. He left his daughter coughing listlessly, her eyes open but unseeing as she tossed and turned. Noting that the nearby painting now lacked only the lotus blossom, he wondered sadly if the girl would live to complete it.

Soon it was the fifteenth of the seventh month, the Festival of Ghosts. In Buddhist temples, paper dharma ships were burnt to help restless spirits cross over the sea of longing. Floating candles were set adrift on rivers and streams, glowing and diminishing in the twilight, as lost loved ones diminish and glow in memory. The smoke of mugwort incense[8] drifted through the courtyards of the Yangs' compound, and the shouts of common boys followed it in from the street. Holding fancy lotus lanterns made from multicolored paper, or simpler ones consisting of a real blossom or broad lotus leaf with a candle balanced on it, the urchins sang the familiar ditty:

> Lotus-leaf and -petal lanterns,
> Your candles nestle bright.
> Today, ignited, how you glow!
> Your light ends with the night.

The commotion pulled Lian-hua out of her stupor. Sitting bolt upright, she chanted the old rhyme once. But then she lay back, closed her eyes again, and sank into sleep. As twilight gathered, her poetry tutor paid a call, but seeing how it was with the girl, she quickly left.

Soon the apparition of her wet-nurse appeared to Lian-hua, but this time the woman did not encourage her to weep. Rather, she stood beside the bed, beckoning. "Come," she said. "You have recited your lesson. It is time for you to walk in the garden."

At that, Lian-hua felt her body—already made light by fever and starvation and too many tears—float up, as though she were riding a ribbon of mist. Before her, a door opened into a moonlit garden, where snowflakes sparkled on gray-

---

8. made from *haozi*, also known as tombwort, a member of the genus *artemisia*.

green bamboo and dewdrops glittered on apricot tree petals, where a ruby-red peony nodded in a puff of warm east breeze and a golden chrysanthemum stood upright in a chilly gust from the west.

"Coal Eyebrows!" she cried out. "What kind of place is this?" For she knew it could not be her own world, where apricot blossoms vanish long before fall's chrysanthemums bloom, and even that brave flower dies when winter decks all gardens with the snow that must someday melt away.

But the wet-nurse only tugged her sleeve and replied, "Do not ask such questions: This garden will exist so long as you will it to. Now hurry, the others await you." With that, she popped through a window next to the bamboo, and vanished. Lian-hua had no choice but to clamber after her.

She found herself in a spacious studio filled with the heavy scent of mugwort. Before her, an elaborately carved table held an inkstone, an inkstick, a brush, and an empty hand scroll. Pictures and potted plants decorated the room, but before she could examine them, ten laughing girls and women burst in through the moon-shaped doorway.

Now, some of the newcomers struck Lian-hua as oddly familiar, while others glanced at her with the look of an intimate friend, though she had never seen them before. And in truth, so quickly did they skip about the room, so merrily did they sway—first to the east and then to the west—that the girl could never quite look at one face for more than an instant. Moreover, thick veils of incense smoke swirled and hovered, now here, now there, making her dizzy every time she tried to focus her slippery gaze on any object or personage.

Each of the ten held a blossom or a branch, and each was garbed in silk robes of a matching color—sunny yellow for the girl who carried a spray of winter-sweet before her face, pink for the exotic-looking woman who grasped a many-petaled peony, light willow green for she who held a pale greenish orchid in her supple hand. Only the chrysanthemum bearer, clad in a robe of drab mauve, did not join in the gaiety, but kept herself turned away from the rest.

"Who are they?" she whispered to her wet-nurse beside her. And the wet-nurse whispered back, "They are flower spirits. They will exist so long as you choose to see them."

"So long as I—"

"Hush! The Queen of the Flowers is about to arrive."

At that, a stately woman dressed in the pure white of the first month's flow-ering plum—which is also the color of moonlight and mourning and the blank scroll on the desk beside which Lian-hua stood—stepped through the round doorway. The girl blinked at the sight of her, and hot tears welled spontaneously, blurring her vision.

Yet before she could quite identify the Flower Queen's moonlike face, a shadow swept across it. The Queen's robe shifted color, from pale plum-blossom white to the creamy yellow of old ivory. An intensely sweet cinnamon-like fragrance mingled with the mugwort, causing Lian-hua to cough furiously.[9]

Transformed, the flower spirit held up a mask made of dark leaves and dotted with tiny flowers the same hue as her robe. Then she covered her face with it. The spiny leaves looked slick, enduring. They bristled outward like an aura, hiding her tender cheeks and smiling lips, her soft tresses and smooth brow. Only the ardent black eyes shone through. The spirit said nothing, but she raised one arm and gestured to the girl with an air of incomprehensible need.

The girl turned to her nurse, feeling more frightened and bereft than ever. But the older woman did not cuddle her, did not sing, did not stroke Lian-hua's hair and encourage her to weep. "No more tears!" she said. "You have important work to do. Tell me, how many flower spirits have gathered here?"

Lian-hua saw the trick within the question; she did not know whether to say *eleven*, or to count the plum blossom-turned-cassia as two, and answer *twelve*. Several of the attendant flower spirits giggled gently. Something of the girl's old pride flashed within her: She would not answer incorrectly. And she would not cry. She bit her lips.

"Well then," said the nurse, "how many months in a single year?"

This question too defied a simple answer, for if Lian-hua answered *twelve*, Coal Eyebrows would remind her of those occasional years when the official calendar adds a thirteenth cycle of the moon, so that solar year and lunar may stay in harmony. Yet if the girl said *thirteen*, she would indicate one month too many for ordinary years.

Another giggle. Another flash of pride. "The flower spirits number"—she lifted her chin, dry eyed—"one fewer than the months in a year."

The spirit who hid her face behind the spray of wintersweet chuckled in a friendly way. The peony spirit smiled a pleased, mysterious, smile. And the

9. The *guei* trees of southern and western China—and of Chinese gardens as far north as climate will allow—are in fact various species of the genuses *cinnamomum* and *osmanthus*, some cultivated for their spicy bark, others for their fragrant blooms and evergreen leaves. Mythology and poetry long ago conflated them into a single kind of tree, often called "cassia" in English, and said to grow on the moon.

nurse nodded, lips pursed, as if relieved. "Right," she said, and added, "Can you figure out what's needed, then? If you do so, you will be given a thing *you* need."

Now all the flower spirits stood very still, as if much depended on what Lian-hua did next. She looked to them for help, but each one—reluctantly, it seemed—turned her face away. Coal Eyebrows assumed a stern expression, though a hint of loving urgency played about her mouth. The intense gaze of the cassia spirit remained fixed on the human girl.

Clearly what was needed was one more flower spirit for the remaining month. But Lian-hua knew herself to be a mortal creature. She could hardly become one of their company herself! Then she remembered the blank scroll on the table, and the ink and brush beside it. She knew what she must do.

But how? Lian-hua felt something crumple within her chest: Looking around, she realized the missing flower could only be a lotus, for no seasonal collection is complete without one. Yet she could not paint them well at all. If only she had a picture before her as a model, or even a real lotus bloom! If only she could leave this upsetting place and return to the time when her mother was alive!

Then the girl's gaze fell on the tranquil peony spirit. Lian-hua remembered seeing Buddhist paintings by artists of the cold western mountainlands, artists who lived where no lotus can grow.[10] The task before her was important for some reason, she told herself, and the past was gone. She would do her best.

In less time than it takes to eat a meal, the girl had prepared the ink and out-lined a single lotus blossom on the empty scroll. The flower spirits kept their dis-tance as she worked, and indeed Lian-hua became so absorbed that she forgot them—and the disturbing image of the harsh-masked queen. She set aside all thoughts of herself and her sorrows, feeling as she set down her brush only a quiet wish that it were possible to show her mother the painting, for it was rather better than Lian-hua had ever managed before.

Looking up, the girl found the room nearly empty: Coal Eyebrows and the cassia spirit alone remained.

"Where . . ." As Lian-hua began her question, the calmness that had wrapped itself around her as she painted shivered and cracked. Her throat tight-ened. She coughed. When she had finished coughing and opened her eyes again,

10. I am indebted to Ellen Johnston Laing for pointing out the peonylike representation of lotuses—which are of course necessary for correct iconography of many deities—in some Tibetan Buddhist paintings.

she saw all the flower spirits clustered here and there about the studio, just as before.

"I told you, they will exist here so long as you choose to see them," her wet-nurse said. "You must clarify your will. But if you have not come to understand that yet, you must learn it on your own. The Queen of the Flowers thanks you for your labors."

Coal Eyebrows paused and tilted her head toward the part of the cassia mask that covered the plum blossom spirit's tender mouth. "Ah," she added after a moment. "I am to tell you there will be another task for you to do. An important one. But meanwhile, you are to be given your reward."

At that, the wet-nurse held out a small package wrapped in silk. "This has some value as a merchant reckons value," she said. "But its true worth is far greater, for it may keep you from burning up in your own emotions. Guard it well. And remember that, just as the lotus you have brushed in black ink still lacks the tints of life, so you remain incomplete."

"I?"

"The you that you understand yourself to be." So saying, Coal Eyebrows thrust the heavy package into Lian-hua's hands. With that heaviness came the same peculiar lightness that had drawn the girl into this otherworldly place. The mugwort incense and the smell of cinnamon bark swirled inside her skull, so that she thought she saw the cassia mask drop away, she thought she saw the queen's robe go plum blossom white again, she thought she recognized that pure pale face at last—and yet she could not be sure.

Lian-hua's eyelids sank, her body rose once more as if upon a ribbon of mist, she fell into a swoon. Eventually, the touch of her summer coverlet on her skin told her she had returned to her own bed.

The household around her slept. But Lian-hua was used to waking too early, used to moving silently about her room by the faint dawn light. Rising, she walked over toward her uncompleted painting. It was no longer really incomplete, for she could just make out a lotus blossom—outlined in black ink though not colored in—on the scroll where she had planned to paint one, as soon as she felt up to it. Needless to say, although it resembled a peony, it was certainly a lotus.

It was the first morning in months that the girl had not awakened drained by tears. Stepping forward, she reached out a hand to touch the painting; she wanted to find out if the ink was wet.

As she stepped, her foot nudged something hidden in the shadows: a bundle wrapped in silk. Carrying it over to the window, Lian-hua removed the wrapper, and found a note in handwriting much like her mother's lithe calligraphy. "Keep this safe, and hidden from all human eyes," it commanded. "The fiery goddess may protect you from the danger into which your passions put you. As for the rest of them, they will come." At first that seemed to be the entire message, but then the puzzled girl turned the slip of paper over. "If you can learn how to see," it said.

Astounded, and still full of filial feeling but no longer weakened by melancholy, Lian-hua resolved to obey this command. The package, she discovered, held a large bamboo-and-paper lotus lantern, like those sold for the past night's festival. Inside the pretty thing, she found not a candle but a statue a little smaller than her hand: a graceful goddess, made of bronze. She hid it away in the chest that held her mother's belongings, and told no one of its existence.

Yang Sun-tai, on his next visit home, was greatly pleased by his daughter's recovery. Knowing she was but a beginner, and female besides, he said nothing of the uncompleted lotus, but simply praised her for her growing skill in painting. Tsao Yueh-guei, the poetry tutor, never returned to the Yang household, and when Sun-tai asked his southern acquaintance what had become of the younger man's wife's cousin, he was told that she had vanished—as unexpectedly as when she first arrived on the doorstep back in Hang-jou, claiming to be a relative in need. As for Coal Eyebrows, she appeared no more, and the girl slept easily at last.

The Aging Lunatic comments: In perusing this history of extraordinary events, one can see that the danger into which the girl put herself was nothing other than excessive indulgence in grief. The second Tsao Yueh-guei could only have been the ghost of the first, made restless by the daughter's inordinate longing. Having summoned her will and clarified her inner vision, Lian-hua received the holy statue, stopped her debilitating weeping, and neither ghost troubled her again.

Yet no flower on earth lives through the winter, and even the bamboo must someday die. Can we truly say then that human will is sufficient to bring into being all that we might wish?

SLEEPING AND WAKING

Who among us has never been reluctant to wake up? Since the deaths of her mother and her nurse, Lotus has returned from so many naps, so many troubled nights, heavy with the desire for sleep. And are you certain, gentle reader, that tomorrow morning you will not rise with sorrow, will not wish you could continue wandering the deep corridors of nonexistence, of blank relaxation and easy peace?

Think, too, of the artisan Wu Ming, how he found in sexual union more than the happy animal gratification of tickle, scratch, and rub. He learned the savor of a drug exceeding opium, learned how to lose for a few moments the dreadful cravings of his consciousness, learned he could set aside his acute needs and chronic fears, learned a false extinction's addictive bliss.

Who, on the other hand, has not wished (as fervidly as Cassia, it may be, or with Wu Ming's exquisite greed) to remain aware, alive? Each yearning comes to us in turn, in whatever order and proportion decreed by fortune or culture or karmic justice or what some call *the historical moment*—and our eyeblink niche within it.

And what delights you've found, once oblivion is left behind, in acts of perception! Such fine recompense for casting off unconsciousness, at least for one more hour, one more day!

Wake up then, if this be waking. Put together from the shards of speculations and idle chatter that surround you, the blossoming story of yourself. Assemble your vision of the cosmos, your own scattered mandala.

As you do, you make a thing of fearsome power, like the neck chain Green Tara wears. You create a garland of skulls.

A GARLAND OF SKULLS

Sun Taiyang coughs, and knows that someday death will win. Does he too carry the bodily disorder that pulled his mother, and his father's second concubine, years ago into the underworld?

He spits, and glances at his sputum. Good—no fleck of blood. This autumn afternoon's clear sunlight, the grassy smell of nearby dung, the comfortable balance of his body as he squats near a tall dark pine: All these assure him. He's meant to be alive, he'll live to sire an heir, he'll hold robust adorable grandsons on his knee.

Around him, the imperial hunting camp brings itself into being. Pack camels groan. Wagon wheels creak. Men labor to set up their temporary habitations. Taiyang removes his cap, slides one hand across the shaved front half of his scalp, touches the neat braid at the crown of his head. He pulls in a great gulp of air, and acknowledges the swell of his trim-muscled chest. He gives himself over to the falling heat of the day, the promise of the hunts to come, the rugged beauty of the northern game preserve, Mulan.

Behind him now lie fourteen days of travel. First, seven days' procession northeast from sultry Beijing, out past the Great Wall to the emperor's favorite summer residence: Thousands of troops accompanied His Majesty and half a hundred of his advisors, accompanied too His Majesty's beloved mother and a grand retinue of eunuchs, clerks, physicians, imperial consorts, artists, musicians, cooks, bondsmen, maids.

Then—once the great household settled into the palaces there, once Mongol *khans* and Muslim *begs* from Central Asia presented the best fruits of their homelands, received imperial beneficence and entertainments—then a smaller force set off again. Seven more days north into the wild dry mountains Lotus's father went, to camp within a palisade of living willows that marks as the emperor's huge hunting park what once was Mongol land.

Taiyang's duties remain behind him (he exhales gratefully, straightens his back, prolongs this peaceful moment beneath the tree) in the summer capital at Warmriver. He has not come to Mulan as an official in the Department of the Privy Purse. He is here as the great-great-grandson of a warrior, as bannerman—or, more precisely, as member of a bondservant company attached to the emperor's Plain Yellow Banner.

When His Majesty had just entered middle age and Taiyang was a youth studying in the best of the palace schools for bondservants' sons, he won imperial notice at a demonstration of mounted archery. His keen eye and good seat earned him a place among the guardsmen who accompanied the emperor's hunting trips. Later, Taiyang's intellect and diligence brought him better posts within the Imperial Household—and eventually the chance to serve as the emperor's eyes and ears in Nanjing. Now his success there last winter is being rewarded with another visit to Mulan.

Once more Taiyang will celebrate his body's vigor and the acuity of his vision, by pitting them against wild creatures' agility and speed. The Qianlong emperor's grandfather hunted for the same reasons, because he loved the test and risk of it, loved the open vistas outside the Great Wall, even though *his* father had assumed more sedentary Chinese ways. Qianlong's father preferred study, but Qianlong too rides the broad grasslands and untouched forests, takes pride in his prowess with horse and bow.

Still, the present emperor's great concern is this: Those about him must not lose the martial skills that brought their ancestors into power over millions who knew only how to farm or trade or toy with bookishness. True, the hunt's a pleasure. But it also means discipline, marksmanship, practice for battle. It provides animal flesh for ritual sacrifice in the old Manchu way. Provides the means to bond khan and beg to emperor in blood-sealed camaraderie, to remind subjects and tributaries from outside China that the Manchus have not forgotten their origins. In Beijing, the Qing empire's Son of Heaven performs an age-old Han Chinese rite when he plows the earth as the Yellow Emperor once did. But here at Mulan, he and nobles who care not a whit for agriculture lay siege to mighty stags.

Taiyang watches a knot of horses eating, a man who swings two heavy buckets from his shoulder pole, whip-thin hunting dogs being led out for exercise. Smoke sifts upward from the first small cooking fires. Off to his right, gray-blue tents and round white yurts rise in clumps that straggle toward the creek where the drovers and the other laborers stay. To his left, more such nomad shelters spring up in orderly ranks around the imperial-yellow curtains shielding the larger tents and yurts of the emperor and those closest to him.

Guards stand at attention outside the first ring of tents separating the emperor's camp from the support units where Taiyang has come to stretch his legs. He knows that, within the imperial precincts, nobles and generals watch high-booted wrestlers, met to amuse His Majesty. But for the moment Taiyang is content not to rank among the honored audience. He clears his throat and spits again.

This place between, thinks Taiyang, is my place: no longer a soldier in anything but registration, too important to have to do with the laborers here, not yet risen to the rank my talents deserve. Not a freeman, yet. But even a bondservant may hope for more than service as a commissioner sent out by the emperor to watch over his interests in trade and manufacture. Where would the customs bureau be without us? Do some of us not run local governments as magistrates and prefects? Have others not held office in the Department of Medicine, or among the empire's top scholars in the Hanlin Academy, or even in the Grand Secretariat itself? And what of the provincial governors Wu and Chen and Lu in His Majesty's grandfather's reign?

Such men may be few, but they have lived. Let my Lotus make a fortunate career within the palaces, let her bear a son to the right man and we'll see what offices—and what respect—will come my way. Or let my concubine give me a healthy boy, and he will study his way to a position that brings honor to our ancestors.

Taiyang flicks his eyes toward the damp (but bloodless) spot where he spat in the dust. He stands up. He strides away.

A few days later, just after dawn, a miles-long line of mounted soldiers crests the hills that form one side of a U-shaped valley, one of some seventy within the game preserve. Their squads advance with a discipline that seems effortless. Red pennants whipping, they press on, at first an arrow's flight apart, then converging as they pass over brambles, ledges, treacherous gullies.

Taiyang rides among these beaters, as he did when he was young.

They drive before them deer, game birds, perhaps with luck a wolf or lynx or one rare tiger. Drums sound. They move in closer. The weight of his quiver pulls Taiyang's shoulder down and back. He sucks in the cool dry air, catches a brief whiff of salt. His own or his mount's, he wonders. Delicious. Who would ever wish not to be alive?

Shouts rip the air. A few guns fire upward, adding to the commotion. Stag and doe alike flee downhill, along faint trails and dry waterways leading toward the valley's mouth. Others run from a second line of beaters, now visible on the opposite slope. The sparse wood grows thick with animals. Do they take delight, Taiyang wonders, in the stretch of their flesh even as they leap and dodge, thinking to evade the danger at their heels?

Mahaga, shout the leaders in Mongolian, and wave their hats atop long poles to give the sign: The circle is complete. The guardsmen move in closer. A horn sounds. The men to either side of Taiyang halt, as half the force drops back, forming an outer circle that will shoot any fugitive animals who break past the human barrier.

Taiyang's pulse rises. He can see, within the grassy clearing before them, the emperor emerging from his watchtower to mount his horse and lead a dozen eager nobles—and, for security, several hand-picked musketeers—into the center of the ring. The panicked deer leap in all directions. Round-eyed hares, black grouse with tail feathers curved like lyres, nut-brown chukar partridges scatter. Each one is distinctly beautiful.

Should any animal try to burst free near Taiyang, he is to drive it back with shouts or gestures or the hollow clapping of his stirrups against the leather that shields his horse's sides. A glance toward one hilltop shows him the screened shelter where a few imperial ladies watch in privacy. He can hear the yaps of the hunting dogs straining to be set loose.

Straight backed and spare in his early sixties, His Majesty draws his heavy longbow. A young buck stumbles. Bright blood spurts. A favored courtier leans forward on his mount to hand the emperor a second arrow. No one else shoots. The Son of Heaven nocks the arrow, draws, releases. The buck falls. Then another. His marksmanship is superb.

Eventually, the emperor indicates that the princes and the honored guests beside him may join in with sword or bow and arrow. By day's end, the bodies will pile high, their numbers inexhaustible, or so it seems.

Enough to feast the aristocracy and favor the troops with meat from the Son of Heaven's table. Enough for a garland of skulls.

In the next days this process is repeated in other valleys. Sometimes the emperor goes instead on what's called the little hunt: Backed by a small half-ring of soldiers, flanked by falconers with "clearwhites" and "grayheads" and other hunting hawks, he leads a more casual pursuit of pheasants, badgers, hare, and deer. Archery competitions, and races and more wrestling, fill the few daylight hours in camp.

Once, part of the force breaks the usual nighttime discipline of silence, setting out long before sunrise. At first light, His Majesty and seven hunters dressed in deerskin leave Taiyang and the others at the foot of a hill. They vanish up the slope.

Taiyang watches the full moon sink, wondering if the emperor will notice him again, will remember that he invited his special commissioner to Nanjing to take part in this year's Mulan hunt. Is Taiyang to play no greater role than any capable trooper might?

Then a high eerie whistle shrills from the hillcrest, driving all speculation from Taiyang's mind. He envisions the deer lure of gilded sandalwood, long and curved. It shrills again, as if with untellable longing. He can almost see the man in the deer's-head mask who calls a great buck before the emperor, calls him to his death as a doe calls out for a mate, as a Manchu shaman calls when summoning a god.

On one of the last days before the return to the estate at Warmriver, Taiyang's moment comes. He is commanded to join the small group accompanying the emperor to a mountain cove two hours' swift ride from base camp. The bannermen stationed at the small post here at Mulan know it to be the home range of a great wild boar. The ride is rough; Taiyang finds it satisfying.

The guides cry out. The boar appears. Routed out of bed by the dogs, harried easily into shortsighted rage, it charges the trespassers, determined, powerful, fast. Taiyang and the other riders dodge, then turn and pursue. A horse whinnies. Dogs and footmen risk their lives. Those who ride endanger themselves as well: A mount spooked by the stink of boar, and ill controlled, could toss any one of them to his death.

The dogs corner their prey against a high outcropping of stone. They circle, and snap their teeth. A tan hound feints forward. He's caught by a curved tusk and pushed aside, raked across one hindquarter and flank.

A Mongol prince, now imperial son-in-law, rides close behind His Majesty's sleek roan favorite, as footmen beat back the dogs. The emperor shoots an arrow through the animal's coarse-furred belly. The boar breaks away. He seems not to notice the wound, except that he whirls and lowers his head, ready to charge again.

The emperor dismounts, takes up a pike. His long face remains composed. Taiyang presses a hand on his mount's wet withers. His mind seizes on the old story of how, when His Majesty was about Lotus's age, he sat calmly on his pony as a huge bear attacked, until the beast had been dispatched.

Now the boar charges. The emperor steps toward him, driving the weapon into the animal's narrow chest, using the practiced power of his arms and back, and the force of his adversary's forward motion, to make the kill. The pike goes deep. Blood flies. The boar squeals. Its legs pump as if to outrun mortality by scrambling up a stony slope of air.

Manchu and Mongol warriors cheer, joined by Taiyang and a few other favored sons of China. Even the Muslim beg from an oasis city conquered less than twenty years ago grunts with approval. Troopers prepare the motionless boar for the return to camp, the wounded dog is tied behind a saddle, the party turns toward home.

On the way back, the emperor's Mongol son-in-law shoots two "flying dragons," hazel grouse with speckled breasts and red streaks near their eyes. More hares start up, and fall, impaled by arrow shafts. Taiyang adds a brown-eared pheasant to the day's bag; its long plumes will be awarded some valorous general, to be displayed, soft and full as a horse's tail, upon his military cap.

So, thinks this imperial bondservant as they pass the first camp sentry, I have ridden again in company with the Son of Heaven. How many in the empire, whatever their rank, can make that claim?

He will think that once more, years from now, as he lies on his bed at home, thin and weary, his forehead damp, dying peacefully of tuberculosis. He will envision His Majesty reviewing the imperial guard, eyelids heavy, eyes hawk bright beneath a sable tasseled helmet of lacquered leather marked with pearls and a golden mantra charm, cheeks papery with age but still taut as his will, riding in formal armor that bears embroidered five-clawed dragons and a mirror on the chest. In that moment, Taiyang will feel a respect and awe as profound as any love for kin or lover. *I have ridden in company with the Son of Heaven. How many can make that claim?*

The Son of Heaven, Taiyang knows, is also Khan of Khans, acknowledged by the nomads, farmers, townsfolk, traders from the cold lands north and east of Korea and the Amur River, to distant Bukhara and north Afghanistan—to say nothing of Burma and Annam, of Tibetan territories annexed and the empire's complex, militarily enforced relations with the Lhasa government: The empire straddles the Great Wall, and the other barriers—the deserts, jungles, mountains—around the Chinese heartland. Just, thinks Taiyang when the hunting party reaches the heart of the Mulan base camp, as in sleeping tonight I will straddle the border between nothingness and life. Just as I am in my fortune and my abilities something that partakes of both Manchu and Chinese. And am seen as fully neither one.

Orders are shouted. Those who've stayed behind brace at attention, or dismount in the presence of His Majesty, or prostrate themselves, according to their place in life. The wounded hound, unconscious now, is carried away to have a poultice applied to the bloody gouge in his haunch. Eventually, Taiyang is dismissed—with an unforgettable word of praise— and leads his horse over to be groomed.

The emperor's bondservant walks toward the creek, its water so clean you can drink it unboiled—a foolish risk south of the Wall. Even His Majesty's hunting dogs bear names in two tongues, he muses. No wonder I'm a man of two languages, and two minds.

The swift hound Tsang-shui chiou, "Darkwater Two-horned Dragon," is called in Manchu *Solomtu*, "Antlers." Lean white Shuang-hua yao, "Frost-flower Raptor," is *Silmetu*, "Sparrowhawk." The Chinese names are more poetic, but what these dogs do is the work and play of harsher lands: The Manchu names are easier to yell. And they're the ones the dogs responded to as they closed in on the boar.

Smothered laughter, the frayed edge of a witless jest, pulls Taiyang from his reverie. The skinny groom who just took his horse's bridle seemed respectful. But what has the other groom muttered as Taiyang turned and walked away? Something like "Mean spirited as all those slaves" and "wouldn't give a fart away for free."

A great heat fills Taiyang's chest. He, whom the Son of Heaven has just now praised! He could have made them both his indentured servants, before they entered imperial service, and never noticed the price. Even now he could see that they are beaten with heavy bamboo poles until they bleed.

Supposing that he heard correctly. Supposing he cared to acknowledge it, and make a scene, and so draw attention to the charge.

Taiyang coughs and walks away, tugging one of his horse-hoof sleeves back to its proper place. As if those lumpish grooms know what skill or self-control or learning or refinement are, in Manchu or Chinese!

And my daughter? Taiyang thinks of Lotus as he passes a man bent under a load of firewood. What might she make of a life where she is—not an ignoble *slave*, the Manchu word *booi* means merely "person of the house"—a life where she is a bondservant who could, with luck and cleverness, become the mother of a prince? Then none will dare whisper the smallest slur, and perhaps the histories will be a bit imprecise about our origins. Not that I myself would wish them to. Ah, she will bless my father's insistence that we maintain both Manchu and Chinese in our house.

Yet times have changed. This doubleness of speech and writing, this ease with two ways of living made Taiyang's great-grandfather's fortune in an age when few knew both worlds well. The emperor then wrote Chinese as a well-learned foreigner does; now, his grandson issues querulous edicts demanding that Manchu language and customs not be forgotten— edicts written in flawless Chinese, translated for the archives by one of ever fewer Manchus competent in their ancestors' tongue.

But won't His Majesty or one of his sons, thinks Taiyang, be all the more interested in a beauty educated in both languages, in the daughter of a Han Chinese who's proven himself at mounted archery in the Manchu style? The emperor's man breathes deeply, turns back toward his dinner. Already he can taste the salty sweetness of roast meat.

Where does the circle formed by a garland—or a rosary—begin? Count backward now through time, bead by bead, or skull by skull, or day by day.

Before Taiyang leaves the palaces at Warmriver in the eighth month, to join the autumn excursion to the Mulan hunting camp, before grape vendors in Beijing fill the lanes with cries that mark the hot season's diminishing, before Wintersweet steps wet eyed into a red sedan chair and is carried to her new life in the Jin household, before the end of the seventh month when fighting crickets in carved clay jars sing, before the disappearance of Lotus's new poetry tutor some ten days earlier during the Festival of Ghosts, before ice peddlers first clink brass cups to advertise cool ephemeral chunks off great blocks buried under straw and earth half a year ago, before the summer rains, when Lotus sits indifferent in her room and does not join her cousin in cutting out a paper girl with a paper broom to sweep clear weather in, before Padma gives birth to a lovely disappointing daughter, before melons of spotted green and ivory and honey gold fill the markets at the fifth month's end, before the pomegranates bloom, voluptuous and delicate, before the ancient holiday on the fifth of the fifth, with its amulets and offerings of dumplings made of sticky rice: Before all these things, in the fourth month, rose-petal cakes and new ripe cherries and the young shoots of asparagus-rushes delight pilgrims recently returned from Marvel Peak. Orioles call. Mulberry trees spread their downy leaves. A young widow in the house of the Suns stares at the dark tabletop in front of her.

Third Aunt has been alive for thirty years, and faithful to her husband's memory for almost fifteen of them. She is long widowed, but her belly is newly round and she is newly beautiful. Her small breasts have filled. Her sallow skin has taken on a soft flush. Above her high forehead, her hair shines, thicker and glossier than it has ever been. She has only days till someone reads the signs. It is as certain as the ripening of mulberries, as the orioles' annual departure at the fourth month's end.

Her maid, Partridge, has known from the first, but Partridge would never tell. Nurse Gu is dead, her cozy nagging sensible voice irrevocably stilled. Mother Jia kept a stern abstracted silence during the family's return from the ill-fated pilgrimage. Nor has she visited the Suns in the ten days since. And apparently Lotus did not catch the telltale frantic words exchanged at cliff's edge—at any rate, Lotus says nothing much to anyone these days.

But even a widow with few duties beyond the informal education of two girls distracted by depression or impending marriage cannot linger in her apartments forever. Soon—perhaps on the first of next month, at the family's gathering for the regular offerings to the ancestors in the Main Hall—sharp eyes will fall upon Third Aunt's growing roundness. What will she do then?

The child of a ghost casts no shadow; a widow bearing her late husband such a child cannot be blamed, and cases of this have been recorded. But this child's father is no ghost. When it is born—and neither Third Aunt nor Partridge knows anything of how less sheltered women may try to prevent a birth—its shadow will lie long and heavy across the family's honor. Across Third Aunt's.

For some months now, she has managed to hide away from herself her knowledge of the inevitable. But when the child is born, and this young widow is no longer protected from punishment by her pregnancy, she will be punished in the prescribed degree: with strangulation. Worse, she'll lose the obscurity she's cherished all these years, her one defense against the world's demands. She'll gain not peace, but infamy, and the comfortless disposal of her remains at the public crematory.

What is she to do? "To starve to death is nothing, to lose one's chastity is serious indeed," the saying goes. Yet Third Aunt knows she can't sustain the will to starve herself. And look, she thinks, what happened at Marvel Peak. Given a second chance, I could not bear the thought of feeling my bones smash against those rocks. Nor can I choose to sink under cold water in the well, or to hang from a rafter gasping in futile panic, as my own sash about my neck chokes off all air.

Third Aunt places one hand on her belly. She hears the gardener outside planting morning glories beneath the trellis screening the Upper Courtyard from male visitors admitted to the front part of the compound.

She wonders idly if the vines will bloom white or blue. Then Partridge slips in to tell her that a toy peddler has come to the gate; does the mistress want to buy some trinkets for her nieces, as she said the other day? Third Aunt waves her chubby maid away.

To lose one's chastity is serious indeed. And to be raped without resisting to (or better yet, beyond) the point of death, is to be unchaste: This is more than proverb, this is law. The woman who fails to scream without stopping, the woman who gives up her struggles, no matter what pain the struggling brings, that woman acquiesces. Third Aunt was not maimed or murdered, she did not kill herself rather than submit, so she assented. She is an adulteress.

I did not cry out, she thinks. I only lay there, unable to believe I was awake, too dumbfounded—too slow and stupid and irresolute—to do anything at all. Yet what could I have done? And to name him now, to bring down punishment upon him, would only send my own name deeper into this pit of shame. Third Aunt pulls one soft-stemmed peony from the vase at her elbow, ignores the water dripping on the polished rosewood, begins to pluck the crimson petals, one by one.

Partridge still hopes that a fire of anger within her mistress will bring on a miscarriage. But proper women don't harbor such emotions: What looks like anger (see how Third Aunt snatches one deep red petal, how she tears it, how she rolls the tender shreds between her fingers, drops them moist to the cool gray floor) must be dejection, or sorrow, or guilt.

Growing up, Third Aunt also learned that a woman of quality remains faithful to her deceased husband, and is rewarded, at a lifetime's end, with public honor and a place in history. The government promotes Confucian scholars' ideas of womanly virtue by giving the families of chaste widows silk and silver, and wine and mutton for sacrifice to their souls. A useful system: Otherwise, a childless bereaved young woman faced with long decades on the margins of a household that must support her with no return—beyond her constant service to her parents-in-law—might choose to end her life. His Majesty's father proclaimed that such a woman's duty lies in living on.

Third Aunt rips another petal. A suicide can be denied the first step toward peace that comes with entry into the underworld, can be doomed to malicious and tormented wandering as a restless ghost. The thought held her in place, paralyzed, after Nurse Gu slipped and screamed. It holds her every time she hears that scream again.

"Mistress?" Partridge tiptoes once more into the library. "Look. Miss Wintersweet has sent you a present." She carries a cream-yellow chrysanthemum made of silk. "The toy man had a basket of artificial flowers too, so the young mistress gave Miss Lotus a pink camellia for her hair. And she thought you might like this." The maid ignores the mess beside the vase, as she's learned to ignore the deepening shadows under Third Aunt's eyes. "She bought some nice jasmine for one of her new caps."

"That's nice." Third Aunt rolls the stripped peony stem across the table with her palm. She seems utterly absorbed in the sight, or feel, of it. Every flower dies, she thinks, and which of them can determine the hour or manner of its going?

"A lovely trousseau Miss Wintersweet's going to have." Partridge has learned that her mistress still welcomes such normal chatter. Only the truth must not be spoken of.

Third Aunt's head jerks up. She begins to brush the petals briskly off the rosewood. "There's more to marriage than new clothes!" she snaps. The maid swallows her surprise and mumbles an agreement, but before she can think what to say next, the porcelain vase crashes to the floor.

Partridge starts to clear away the mess. Third Aunt walks over to the open window. She stares at the apricot tree outside. The petals have long fallen from its flowers, leaving only tattered sepals and ugly swelling knobs of green among its young leaves. She turns a large fragment of the vase over and over in her hands, talking of how she is too weak, too unfortunate, to do anything well. "You see, Partridge?" she says. "I can't even smash a vase properly."

"Accidents—" the maid begins, when a drunken shout from the courtyard hushes them both.

Third Aunt jumps back from the window. Old Master Sun has returned from a peony-viewing party at a monastery among the fields in the Chinese section of Beijing. He's calling out to his chambermaid that he has added an appreciative poem of his own to the scroll-full of others attached to a famous painting there.

Third Aunt stoops down beside the table, scrapes the knifelike piece of porcelain up one elaborately carved leg. She hums a song—"Orioles among the Willow Trees"—about the end of spring. She draws the edge of the shard a second time along the gouge she made, paring away a thin strip of the gleaming wood.

Partridge's eyes grow wide. What can she say to distract her mistress? "That one!" she blurts. "A pity he prefers the wine cup to the pipe! They may say that the fashion for smoking opium straight shows we're heading into sinful times—but at least it keeps people quiet. Better for certain parties to fall asleep on their couches than to carry on yelling and disrupting and, and such like!"

Third Aunt ought to scold her maid for such disrespect toward the master of the household. She ought to have her beaten and dismissed. Instead, she looks up, rubs her eyes, smiles broadly, begins to wonder aloud what sort of trinket she might come up with after all to cheer Lotus, and thank Wintersweet. "We haven't had a lesson since, in weeks," she says. Her voice bristles with unnatural gaiety. "And something must be done about that poor child." She sends Partridge to fetch a box from the bedroom at the other end of the hall.

The two of them look over the childhood mementos the maid carries in. Third Aunt seems more her former gentle self—neither brittle nor immobilized with fear and shame—as she settles on a packet of toys from Su-jou's Tiger Hill, the last gift her dear father gave her before he died. Wintersweet shall have the little man whose arms and legs wave so merrily when he's turned upright and sand runs through his torso from his head. To Lotus will go the set of tiny acrobats filled with quicksilver; they tumble wildly across the tabletop, perhaps of their own volition, perhaps propelled by the simple fact of what they are.

"And Partridge, when the time comes, I want you to have my fur-lined vest and—"

Before this conversation can continue, Old Master Sun calls out for the gardener to report to him, posthaste. It's Third Aunt who breaks the silence afterward. Her old flustering, her more recent shrillness, the gloom of the past weeks—all these have dropped away, as if the undignified, petulant voice had been a knife slicing cleanly through a stem. Only one possible act of self-will is left to her, after a lifetime spent extinguishing self-will.

Third Aunt hands the maid her husband's carved jade thumb ring. "Partridge, there's something only you can do for me," she begins.

So, on this pleasant day late in the fourth month, Partridge leaves the household on a secret errand. Sniffling quietly, she returns from pawnshop and apothecary, ignoring the hostas unfurling this year's broad leaves beside the stone steps to the veranda as she pauses at the sight of her mistress framed by an open window.

Look at this pregnant widow now, as she sits unmoving at the writing table in the library—once her husband's room—adjacent to the tiny garden in the northeast corner of the Suns' compound. Some say a mole above the starting point of a woman's left eyebrow means she'll marry more than once. Third Aunt's brow is clear. A mole beneath the right eye, over halfway out, is believed to indicate a taste for adultery. She has no mole beneath her right eye.

One small brown spot underneath the outer corner of the left—in the opinion of some—gives the truth away: It marks her as a woman with an unseemly love of sex. Her late mother-in-law might have disregarded such vulgar superstition when she chose a bride for her youngest son, preferring more advanced prognostications. Third Aunt herself might never have heard of this particular omen, for the fortune-tellers' schools and teachings vary. But others in the household made note.

Made note, and eventually one old man, sodden with drink and a vague sense of wrongs done against him in a changing world, irked by the wastefulness of supporting this withered (yet attractive) branch—irked too by the forbiddenness of his desire—crept out of his apartments, through that private garden, and into the side hall where Third Aunt slept.

Remember: A virtuous woman would not have allowed herself to be shocked into silence, would have cast off a lifetime's teachings on dutiful submission, would have summoned the physical strength a lady's not supposed to have. A virtuous woman would have brought unthinkable disgrace upon the most important person in the family and so upon them all. A virtuous woman would have fought him off, would have killed herself—somehow—before he could commit the act, would certainly have cried out.

And did Partridge sin? Surely she ought to have ignored, for the first time in her life, the wishes of the master, when he stumbled over her sleeping form on his way out and ordered silence. I could do nothing, she thinks as she wipes her eyes and makes the preparations, as she sets a tea cup on the table where her mistress sits. Let today's sad business atone for the nothing I did.

A strong smell burns through the air, rising from the red-black liquid in the cup. Third Aunt contemplates how she will simply fall into sleep, the heavy untroubled sleep of too much opium, and how Partridge has promised to offer spirit-money for her soul's repose. So easy. Why did she not think of this before?

Simple memorial rites will be hurried through, just enough to ward off harm to the family from a suicide's nasty soul, just enough to keep the curiosity of servants and neighbors at bay. A childless widow married in from an unimportant family needs little fuss. *A swift decline, doubtless brought on by the shock of witnessing that bizarre accident of poor Nurse Gu's,* Aunt Gao will murmur to the few callers. *We'll be applying for official recognition of chaste widowhood, of course, but you know how long the paperwork can take.* She'll soon marry Partridge off, to a loyal retired manservant in a country town.

Third Aunt's hand shakes. A few blood-dark drops fall like petals on her ice-blue dress. Then her small jaw tightens as it seldom has. She will go *now.* At a time of her own choosing, her reputation undefiled. She lifts the cup.

One more death, among so many. Old Master Sun will quietly order prayers said on Third Aunt's behalf at the very temple where his own richly lacquered coffin is stored, visible evidence of wealth and foresight, and the family's propriety.

All summer—count forward through the months again—as people mark the season with salt eggs and sour-plum lemonade, as Lotus grieves for mother and nurse and aunt, weeping herself into a sickly stupor despite all her cousin and her father and his concubine can think of to distract her, as Padma's girl-child's born and the household begins a month of taboos occasioned by the powerful yin-blood of birth, as the imperial elephants are given their annual bath in the city moat, as Taiyang departs for the imperial mountain estate at Warmriver, as the soldiers' horse god and then the war god, Lord Guan, are worshiped on their festival days, as bug peddlers carry baskets filled with amusing beetles and whirring dragonflies tethered to reeds and decorative live butterflies held by their legs in split sticks, as Lotus mysteriously returns to health in the middle of the seventh month, as Wintersweet puts her hair up in a married woman's style, as the first fluke of cool air comes one evening to the sun-pressed city: All summer and on into the autumn, Lotus's grandfather mourns his daughter-in-law.

Not openly. Not reasonably. *Had she been virtuous, she would have resisted,* the old man tells himself, again and yet again, as if counting off prayers on a sandalwood rosary. But night after night, deep in his cups, he thinks of her as one tragically lost, the way his prized chrysanthemums are, every winter, claimed by cold.

He pulls at his mustache, bids Prima heat another jar of wine and fetch his chamber pot. He stares out at the moonlit courtyard, toward the plum tree and the apricot his wife ordered planted years ago—or into the shadows of the tiny corner garden between his hall and the one where his youngest son, and his youngest daughter-in-law, used to live. It is as if her skull hung on a chain draped round his neck. He broods and drinks and cannot achieve forgetfulness.

There is still that other road to the obliteration of the self. Ambitious young Wu Ming hopes to satisfy his taste for it, as he attempts the difficult task assigned him by the Lord of Mount Tai. But so far he can only worry: Just how is he to find the scattered statues, when he can't even gain full entry into the human realm?

Observe what happens one evening late in the sultry seventh month, three months after Third Aunt's death. Ever since his painful interview in the subterranean courtroom, Wu Ming has hovered about the margins of human space and time, looking for the gateway that will allow him to slip back in.

The reason for this long delay is simple: The Lord of Mount Tai's ox-headed demons expected a token of appreciation before they'd give the two disembodied spirits that final ectoplasmic shove across the boundary between their murky domain and our brighter one. *Cash on the spot or you'll be stuck*, they said in unison. *Neither here nor there*, har, har! Lacking funds to pay the squeeze, Wu Ming and Lotus's mother were dumped at the portal of the underworld, able to see what the living do, but not to be seen, or act. Infuriating, to watch human folly yet remain unable to take part!

Then Cassia managed a temporary return: She simply waited till simultaneous surges of her daughter's longing and her own compelling need drew her into dream, and the semblance of materiality. But no living soul mourns Wu Ming with such intensity, and—luckily for us—a greed for frivolous delights does not suffice to allow ghosts back into our realm. So Wu Ming's been limited to hazy exploration of what happened to some of the mandala statues, with no way to take action, no way to avoid the painful punishments the Lord of Mount Tai is quite capable of heaping upon his rather handsome head. Until tonight.

Wu Ming knows the exact look of a necklace of skulls. He might have concentrated on other attributes of the images he studied during his apprenticeship—the luminosity of a flame aura, the dispassionate steadiness of ego-smashing arms and legs, the tranquility of small figures in monk's garb accompanying a mesmerizing protector. He did not.

He looked upon those death's-head chains and devoted himself, when chance allowed, to stealing peeks at secret deities united with their consorts in *yabyum*—the father-mother pose, where male enters female and female takes in male. For Wu Ming, the Yamantaka to be envisioned was the one who—even as he brandishes his death-defeating sword—joins his swooning wide-eyed consort in the blissful merging of wisdom and compassion.

But Wu Ming did not properly understand what yabyum meant. He also neither longed for, nor much feared, his death; he merely wished to live forever, making better and better artifacts, tasting again and again the gladness that the body gives, spewing his name out over and over for posterity. He was a young man, and death seemed to have little to do with him—until he helped in the theft of a mandala of statues, and was swiftly killed. To his considerable regret.

Just now, he has traced Cassia to Lotus's room. The girl still grieves, but ever since the Ghost Festival, she has returned to normal sadness, normal moments of near contentment, normal activity. Her music and her painting prosper under the guidance of her father's concubine. She continues to read poetry. She helps her cousin with the final preparations for the wedding just days away. She believes her Aunt Gao's vague explanation of her third aunt's death.

And tonight after dark, alone in her bed with no one closer by than Inkscent's maid, Snow, snoring lightly next to Quinta in the outer room, Lotus remembers her secret game.

It's an amusement she invented when she was quite a little girl. Nurse disapproved, and so did Mama, so Lotus played it only on the sly. In the dolors of the past year and a half, the game slid from her thoughts completely. But in the sultry midnight a restlessness quite unlike the dreary insomnia of the recent past suggests to her that she might try riding her wild horse once more.

Wu Ming responds. As Lotus saddles a bolster with a folded coverlet, as she straddles this Mongol pony and silently begins to rock across the grasslands atop her bed, as she squeezes her thighs and tilts her pelvis and presses down at the exact unforgotten spot, Wu Ming responds.

He feels her breathing speed up and go shallow. He regards the small points her nipples make as they rise against her silky sleeping tunic. He has spent so much time in recent months dangling disembodied in her vicinity that he can almost (almost!) touch with his own hand (his hand again, his aching hand!) the tingling swelling flesh pressed to that illusory saddle as she rides.

And then, at last, he knows her for who she is: the girl he saw once at the Yong-heh Palace Temple, the secretly passionate child with the face of a lotus bud. The nameless girl he desired—he fell in love with—just as in the storytellers' fables: at first sight.

Lotus shivers wildly when the pony bucks and leaps. Soon, she's sprawled atop the covers, sound asleep, while Wu Ming lingers invisible in the shadows. How he would pant, if he had lungs. If he had flesh, how it would throb. How greatly (his eye that is no eye turns to the cream-gold skin at the girl's nape as she sighs and, still sleeping, brushes her dampened hair away), how greatly he desires that throbbing.

The bond between them's not yet strong enough to draw him into her world. But now Wu Ming knows how he can begin to carry out the task he has to do—and how he might have again what he misses most about his human life besides. One more skull dangles from the chain.

After her marriage, Wintersweet too sets foot upon that road to forgetfulness. When she comes home—as young brides do—for a visit in the middle of the eighth month, she finds a chance to sit alone with her cousin, and speak of it.

It is the afternoon of the sixteenth, the day after the Midautumn Festival. Last night, a perfect harvest moon ignited the dry air. In the court-yards of the Suns, the Jins, in all the family courtyards of Beijing, women set up altars bearing round mooncakes, candles, incense burners, melons cut in lotus-petal shapes. Beside each altar stood a painting of the Moon Lady—depicted these days with a strong resemblance to Guan-yin—or perhaps one of the jadewhite moonhare, who after centuries still pounds in his mortar the elusive medicine of immortality.

Wintersweet has already talked about all this. She's told her mother and Lotus and the concubines and maids gathered this afternoon in the West Courtyard for a second party in her honor how for this festival, at least, the customs of the Jins are the same as those here at home. There, too, last night's altar faced east, waiting for the full moon's rising, laden with scarlet cockscomb flowers, with grapes and pomegranates, with green stalks of tasty soybeans for the moonhare and a spray of yellow blooms from a cassia tree.

True, the Jins' family-sized mooncake was filled with nuts and honey, rather than the date paste or haw jelly Wintersweet prefers. True, Happiness nearly disgraced herself by weeping for homesickness, as she sat in attendance with the other maids of the Jin household. True, last night each of the Suns thought sadly of how so many they have loved—Wintersweet among them now—could no longer eat a slice of their family-circle cake.

But smaller cakes in many flavors, and fruit and wine, have made a festive second party. Tonight, only a slight diminishing will mar the roundness of the moon; by then, however, Wintersweet will have returned to her husband, for they must not spend a single night apart in this first month of their married life.

"I wish you didn't have to leave so quickly, cousin," says Lotus as the two of them, accompanied only by Happiness, go to Lotus's room to look at her recent paintings. "It's ridiculous for us to celebrate the full moon in the afternoon! Do you think Lady Ding will let you visit for a whole week when the first month's up?"

"Don't let's talk about my mother-in-law." For an instant Wintersweet's bright eyes dim. "Show me what you've been doing. Then I've got something to show you."

When she's admired Lotus's delicate ink-flowers, Wintersweet sends Happiness out to the veranda to keep watch, and pulls her cousin down to sit beside her on the bed platform. "You're sure Grandfather's not coming home soon?" she asks, slipping a hand inside her peach-colored jacket.

Lotus blushes. "I heard Prima telling Snow he was off to visit some boy-actresses. He's bound to be gone for hours."

A shrug from Wintersweet, as if to say, *harmless enough.* "Then look." She pulls out a little wooden mirror case, opens it like a book. "See your pretty face?"

An unfamiliar note in her voice makes Lotus look instead into her cousin's eyes. But at Wintersweet's insistence, she glances into the silver-backed rectangle of glass inside the sandalwood case: nothing new.

Wintersweet closes the case, turns it over, surprises Lotus by sliding out the panel behind the little mirror. This reveals a shallow compartment hiding a painting on another piece of glass. "Look again," she says.

Lotus sees what Wintersweet saw on her wedding night, when Young Master Jin, with a tolerant smile, gave the mirror case to his nervous bride. A tiny woman in a loose red robe looks up in coquettish surprise from the mirror in her hand. A tiny man leans forward through her bedroom door. He reaches playfully toward her mirror, gazes into her eyes.

"He got it on a trip to Yang-jou. I told you things are different in the south." Lotus understands who *he* is, finds the hidden picture clever—if somehow unsettling—but feels she's not getting the point.

"It's—well, you'd never be able to buy something like this here in the capital. But he says that in spite of all His Majesty's decrees about morality, such things are actually finding their way into the palaces again."

"Again?" asks Lotus, thoroughly confused.

"Like in the last dynasty, he says. That people say was so, you know, degenerate. And there's a book we're going to read together, a novel—oh, Lotus, I'm trying to tell you about something. But I don't—remember when we were little and you went with us to visit Mother's family and that big dog climbed on top of their Blackie and Mother snatched us away but Nurse Gu said later they were only making puppies?"

Lotus remembers. She nods.

"Well—" Now it's Wintersweet who blushes. "I know it's rude to talk about, but *I* say, Blackie must have liked it, at least a little. I mean, what she and the other dog—oh, just look."

Now she shows Lotus that the hidden picture slides, just as the back panel did, out of the wooden frame of the case. Another, more secret, picture lies beneath. Seconds pass before Lotus can make sense of the red and turquoise and iron gray and pink and white. The same woman now looks out to meet Lotus's gaze quite steadily with her own. She kneels astride the same man, who smiles a different sort of smile as he leans back on a couch and lifts her skirts. A candle burns. He is naked, actually naked, except for his shoes. His long queue remains wrapped atop his head. The woman too wears tiny shoes, red ones, on her gold-lily feet. Lotus can see his erect penis. She can see the few strands of black hair about each lover's genitals, every detail precisely laid in paint beneath the glass.

"Miss Wintersweet?" Happiness calls in from the veranda. "Deucey and Trine are here to fetch us back to the West Courtyard." The other two maids call out that the First Mistress wants to know what's keeping them so long.

Wintersweet assures them they'll be right out. Quickly, she turns the first picture over, gives Lotus a glimpse of a third one shining through the other side of the double sheet of glass: the same couple, the man stretched out facedown in satisfied sleep, a quilt tossed across his shoulders for warmth. The woman, now wearing only her ordinary little belly-apron to protect her modesty, leans over him with a tender anxiousness, as if about to rouse him with the touch of her nipples on his back.

Lotus feels her throat close. She wants to snatch the pictures out of her cousin's hand, throw them against the room's far wall.

"We're just putting Miss Lotus's paintings away," calls Wintersweet. "You can stay there."

As she reassembles the mirror case and tucks it into the pocket inside her jacket, she whispers, "You see? I know it looks disgusting, but we don't—I mean, at night you don't have to show yourself like that. And I refuse to do the really—well, you can see from the picture that the woman likes it." Wintersweet's muted grin brings forth the beauty beneath the deep pockmarks on her face. "It helps her forget about scoldings and insults and the strangers she has to live with. Wait and see, cousin. Wait and see." She takes Lotus by the hand, pulls her out toward the maids.

Later, leaning on the rail of the veranda to look up at a nearly perfect moon, Lotus thinks about the glassy paintings, and about the wanting that rose within her as she looked at them. Yet she doesn't know what it is she wanted, exactly, or why it came to her to smash the fragile images, or even the reason Wintersweet's last words made her feel so sad.

Nearby, watching her, Inkscent wonders about this oddly solitary girl, who refused any substitute after her nurse died, and makes do now with only aimless Quinta, to the annoyance of the Upper Courtyard's other maids. Madame Gao is quick enough to save a bit of money when she can, the southerner says to herself. I'm lucky the girl's father is more generous than her aunt.

Inkscent sighs and looks toward the moon herself. Months now since Taiyang left Beijing for the summer capital: She knows the longing that Lotus feels. But better that they both go back into their building. Snow and Quinta too. The old master's home and Inkscent doesn't want him to send word bidding her play a romantic melody upon her chyn, or summoning his granddaughter to keep him company.

Unthinkable that he'd do more, but Inkscent could see the cause of Third Aunt's death; she figured out what happened from all that no one said. Lucky that the old man is so reclusive in his ways. Still, since chains of circumstance have thrown them all improperly together in this courtyard, she'll keep herself and the girl away from him.

The concubine's stomach tightens. *She* feels the anger Third Aunt wouldn't, heavy as a crown of skulls upon her head, and nothing to be done about it. Restless and weary, she sends the girls to bed, draws out her polished instrument after all, and plucks the melody, "Ah, Orchid Flourishing Alone"—till her mood eases and she too lies down.

Lotus listens, wakeful, decides to ask her father's concubine to teach her that famous old song. When the music ends, she considers playing the pony game again. But no.

Instead she slides one hand beneath her tunic and her rumpled trousers, slides it past the scant silk of new hairs, into the warm crevice between her legs. Wu Ming, come to look at her again, lets loose an inaudible gasp: one more watcher, among so many.

Toward the end of the ninth month, Taiyang will take his place in the imperial procession back to Beijing. He'll come home, and he and Inkscent will give one another a taste of the scant forgetfulness that is Wintersweet's only opiate. Not long after, the rosary of Lotus's life will count forward into new knowledge she cannot imagine yet.

But first, at the start of that same month, First Uncle will bid farewell to his wife and his concubine as he leaves Beijing to oversee the confiscation of a hapless official's country estate. Aunt Gao, to tell the truth, will miss his lovemaking more than Padma will.

A few days later, the old master's chrysanthemums will begin to bloom: a Tawny Lion, a River-light, a Drunken Poet, a Gold Buddha's Throne. On the ninth of the ninth, the city will celebrate the holiday of Double Yang, the last efflorescence of the bright force before winter brings in the rule of the dark yin.

It's another occasion for reunions: Wintersweet will come home again, to eat pickled crabs and yellow-duckling pears, to drink wine and write poems as people have done for almost two millennia. It won't be much of a holiday for this dwindled family, though the cousins will be glad to see each other—especially Wintersweet, for by then the better part of her husband's attentions will have returned to his concubine.

Both girls' poetic efforts will be judged passable by their grandfather.

Lotus, especially, will be praised for capturing the spirit of Old Master Sun's favorite poet Tao Qian, long-ago aficionado of chrysanthemums and wine.

After the womenfolk have gone off to bed, the old man will stay up with patient Prima, sleepless again, leafing through an old book about the arcane correspondences of seasons, directions, colors, the elements. Then he'll cast philosophy aside, and sit in the lamplight, thinking of all those who have died. Of his youngest daughter-in-law.

The next morning, he'll scrawl a poem of his own. He will drink and mourn and, mourning, will count off one more on a chain of skulls.

LATE FALL:
GAZING AT CHRYSANTHEMUMS,
REMEMBERING OLD BOOKS

1.

They bloom dull gold and bronze by my east fence,
Sending winter's scent aloft on northerly winds.

The yin comes round again in the seasons' stir.
I only want this one clear day to last.

A single frost-tipped flower in my cup:
Tao Qian's poems linger. Tao is gone.

Who has walked this earth and not departed?
Easier to pour wine from a broken jar!

2.

The air today is washed fall's piercing blue—
Let my melody suit these flowers, and such skies!

I twist the pegs and tune to a minor key;
White weather rises, metallic, in the west.

Color, direction, music, elements, mind:
Grasp cosmic order, and live in harmony.

Last night's sleepless book explained this well,
But what sounds ease the heart when petals freeze?

3.

Leave treatises and poems, leave ink and brush,
Leave fall's last flowers. Leave the city's walls.

What I knew, of gardens, or old texts,
Lies dead with my ambitions, my lost past.

Ride out past quick-sprung poplars, white-barked pines,
Past farmers' shacks—and past more sallow blooms.

Yet no road quits self-pity, outruns sorrow.
Better to stay, and taste what's in the cup.

A LOTUS BLOSSOMS: 5

The rich spice of Tibetan incense drifts from my father's room. Inside, his concubine copies out by lamplight the sutra she wants to donate to one of the Yellow Hats' temples. I stare from the veranda, past the low roof of what were Third Aunt's rooms, toward a rising moon turned amber by the tenth month's early dusk.

Cold burns my hands, my face and feet. But I won't go in. When I am dead, when everyone I know is dead, and everyone who remembers us as well, the moon will still go through its unchanging transformations in the sky. There's comfort in the thought, but not much.

Stop. I have sworn off such thinking. The moon's full: three months exactly since my dream about the garden of the flower spirits at Ghost Festival time. Three months since the Queen of the Flowers let me know I had an important task to do—but did not, could not, tell me what. And three months tomorrow morning since I looked inside the paper lotus lantern my mysterious poetry tutor left me as a parting gift.

I've been keeping the statue of the buddha goddess I found there hidden away, as my tutor's farewell note commanded. Easy not to speak of it to

Wintersweet in the flurry of last-minute wedding preparations or on her visits home. She's taken up by her new life and can't talk of anything but the customs of the Jin household, the schemes of her husband's concubine, the boys who call her "Mother" now. If she spoke more of what happens in her marriage bed, I know I would listen. But I will not ask.

"Young Mistress?" A reedy voice behind me, Snow. "Your Little Auntie Tuo says if you're not going to sleep or practice your music, would you care to join her for a game of chess?"

No, I would not care to, I almost say. I'm glad to study painting and the chyn with my father's concubine, but I don't see any reason to act like she's really part of our family. It's uncomfortable enough that I must give her the respect owed a teacher, when Father bought her contract like that of any servant. When he could sell her off next month, next year, if she fails to give him a son.

But I doubt he will. I look down at the little maid shivering beneath her layers of clothes. "Snow?" I say. "Am I taller than I was when you came to us last spring?"

The two tufts of hair atop her head bob as she nods. "Oh yes, Young Mistress. Taller, and your face has changed. Not just from the way your little auntie has taught you to wear makeup. You used to be a girl like me—not like *me*, of course, but—now your eyebrows and the shape of your face . . . well, you've become quite . . ." She reaches toward me in the moonlight, hesitates. "Sorry, Young Mistress. I'm not to speak so freely. It's what they call, inelegant." She clasps her hands before her and looks down.

So I'm not the only one receiving lessons from the former courtesan. It occurs to me that Inkscent's life in Nanjing must have been altogether different: surrounded by admirers of her music, by apprentices anxious to learn from her.

Still, I wish this lesson in reticence hadn't taken root. After Wintersweet married, Snow and I began to talk sometimes; who else did I have, with Nurse and Third Aunt and even Partridge gone, and the other maids so dull, and Little Auntie Padma quite taken up by her baby daughter and her improved relations with Aunt Gao? Not that it matters. I may be leaving the family soon myself, leaving everyone I know behind.

"Never mind, Snow," I say. "Let's go inside."

She lifts the door-curtain as I enter; it's warm in my father's room, where

Quinta is putting away the writing things. The little auntie nods quietly, then invites me to sit on the bed platform. A sulky haze creeps into Quinta's eyes when she and Snow are sent to the kitchen to fetch us roasted chestnuts, but her face brightens when they are promised some. Once she's in the Front Courtyard, she'll be happy to stay there gossiping with the other servants while she waits for Cook to stir and toss the chestnuts in his wok.

Remnants of incense linger in the room. Heat rises through the bricks of the bed platform, soaking into me. We divide the round wooden chess pieces in silence, mine marked in black and Little Auntie Tuo's in red, sixteen on either side of the river dividing my territory from hers. My general taps down on the paper playing board atop the table between us, protected on either side by officer, battle-elephant, horse, and chariot.

"I'll have Snow make fresh tea when they return, shall I?" says the concubine. "Your father brought some first-grade Dragonwell when he came home for the ancestral offerings on the first."

I nod, and begin to set my soldiers and my cannons out in front of the other pieces.

"You'll have a real feast when you go to Old Lady Jin's birthday celebration tomorrow. And seeing your cousin—I know you'll like that." Her smooth voice still carries accents of the south, but I have no trouble understanding her now.

I nod again. I don't mean to be rude; I simply don't know what to say. It's not like when we're talking about painting, or she's offering calm corrections to my playing on the chyn. Besides, she should know that everyday conversation never comes easily to me. When Aunt Gao's sister or other ladies come to call, no one minds that I sit quietly listening to my elders, though surely they preferred Wintersweet's amusing chatter when she was here.

"Would you like to accompany me to the temple if your father lets me present my sutra copy in person, Lotus?"

Teacher or not, she oughtn't speak to me so familiarly. I'm no longer a child; I'm a young mistress of this family. I don't see why Father didn't move her over into Third Aunt's empty apartment, instead of keeping her on here. I don't need company, whatever people say.

Yet what can I do besides put up with her? *Patience,* Mama used to tell me, though it's hard to be patient when people are stupid or improper or wrong. "As you wish," I say, and nudge one of my cannons needlessly into place.

Little Auntie Tuo says nothing, only moves a chariot two squares forward.

I send a battle-elephant up two squares and over one. The lamp's light flickers, sets our shadows swaying on the wall. "You know, Young Mistress," says my father's concubine. "You have a great deal to learn in a short time."

My head jerks up before I can stop it. She holds my gaze with her own. "Not about chess or music or painting," she says, "though you would do well to work seriously at each of those. Not about making your face and hair more beautiful—you took to that quickly enough." One corner of her mouth curves upward. "But you'll be eaten alive in the palaces—*if* you're chosen—unless you learn how to manage all your feelings." She moves one of her soldiers toward the river's edge. "And how to make people want what you want them to."

My face grows hot. Speech is utterly impossible.

"This family needs you to succeed," my father's concubine continues. "And you could. If not in the Forbidden City, at least in an advantageous marriage. You have it in you to make some man forget everything but his desire for you—and make the women around you compete to win your friendship or your favor. But you have no idea . . ."

That must be what the Queen of the Flowers meant about my important task. To help my family. If I can become the right man's consort . . .

The understanding loosens my tongue, and I apologize. "I don't," I say, "don't even understand my, what I . . ." For an instant my body forgets that I have given over weeping.

My will remembers, though, and I see Inkscent see me conquer myself. A look of cool approval crosses that lovely face.

"It's like chess," she says, and a flush of rose amber comes to her cheeks. "What happens between men and women. A pleasant game that need hurt no one. But only one can win. Sometimes of course—" She purses her lips and tilts her chin toward my grandfather's North Hall. "Sometimes there is nothing one can do." She sweeps away half the pieces on her side of the board, ruining the game, leaving her general vulnerable to my attack.

"But sometimes," she continues, "you can achieve exactly what you want." Against all rules, her slim hand makes a foray into my territory, flicks just one piece into my lap. "Checkmate in three moves," she says. "Would you like to play it out?"

I open my mouth, then shut it. I've never heard, never heard *about*, any woman who spoke like this. Yet I've seen her dutiful tenderness toward my father, seen how she works to make the household more harmonious.

The window rattles and the lamplight shifts again. Of course. Only a stupid woman works against the interests of the family she enters. Mama was a Tsao, not a Sun, but she served Grandfather and Grandmother well, she tried to give the family a son, she kept the servants happy and hard working. Aunt Gao may do what she can for her sister, but she does more for us.

Leaning forward, I stare at that moonlike face. There's nothing cruel or grasping about it, only a self-possession that—yes—would make me struggle against anyone to win her regard. "Tell me," I say. "Teach me what I need to know."

Winter rain on the phoenix tree," sings the little actor, her voice high and clear as the bamboo flute accompanying her, "strange winds out of the south."

One of the two Jin girls beside me—Wintersweet's unmarried sisters-in-law—whispers to the other, who steals a glance at me and whispers something back. It's hard to believe they're both at least five years older than I am. The fourth at our table, a young cousin of theirs from the Fu clan, sighs and leans forward, toward the stage.

"In a shaded courtyard, piled snow melts," the lonely beauty sings, "into gutters deep with tears."

In fact, the courtyard where the stage has been set up remains sunny and cold and dry. Few of the women crowded cosily into Old Lady Jin's reception room to watch seem much interested in loneliness or sorrow. At the head of the room, Aunt Gao and the other senior guests seated close to the old lady laugh at something she's just said. Wintersweet stands behind Lady Ding, in case her mother-in-law or Old Lady Jin herself should want for something. The other young wife in the group waits upon her own mother-in-law, the married daughter of Old Lady Jin, come home from the Fus with her little girl and this harried-looking daughter-in-law, to celebrate the matriarch's seventieth birthday.

For several days, Wintersweet has told me, ladies of good family paid calls to congratulate Old Lady Jin, and a throng of well-wishers—including men of great influence—came to offer their respects yesterday, on the actual anniversary of the old lady's birth. When Aunt Gao made her formal visit, she was invited to return today for the women's family party: The Jins seem as intent as she on building the relationship forged when Wintersweet married the old lady's grandson.

Is that why Aunt Gao was asked to bring me along as well? Am I being inspected as a possible wife for some Jin nephew, a Fu cousin, the son of a relative of the Dings? But Old Lady Jin seems more interested in the flattering conversation of the older guests. When we arrived, she examined my new rose-pink jacket, my honey-colored brocade robe, my pale green underskirt, pronounced me "utterly fetching," and sent me to sit with the other girls near the wide doorway of the room.

". . . but perhaps *dangerously* beautiful," I heard someone murmuring behind me as I went. Or—what nonsense—thought I heard.

A relief, then, to be so easily excused, a relief that no one seems to notice how the tight sleeves of my robe hardly cover the new length of my bare wrists. It's colder here, but we can see out into the courtyard easily—and it's warmer than the veranda, where the Jins' female servants watch the performance alongside Quinta and the other visiting maids.

Now a handsome youth in scholar's clothes steps gracefully onstage in high black boots. The wistful singer has fallen asleep at her desk. Her eyes remain closed as the intruder begins an aria with a laugh like the call of an astonished bird. He sees no danger in her loveliness.

A fleet of serving women arrives with steaming dishes. I catch sight of more food being carried over to the side hall where the Jin concubines and nurses and the little boys are. There's a new stiffness to Wintersweet's movements as she oversees the serving of Old Lady Jin and the senior ladies. Yet anyone who didn't notice the knotted set of her shoulders would think my cousin a natural at the part of a large family's youngest wife.

Soon, the other three unmarried girls turn their attention from the play to the greasy duck and the smoked pheasant with pickled cabbage. I pick up a slice of steamed sweetbean curlup, and hope no one will think me rude. The performances began several hours ago, but I'd still rather keep my eyes on the stage.

The beardless scholar waves and twists his fan as he jokes with the demure young woman before him. The music twines and rises higher. The invisible landscape they construct with fan flutter and teasing question and shy rebuke grows solid. Watching a silk sleeve unfurl when the beauty gestures, I can see it make the man beside her wonder what lies beneath that self-control.

The orchestra seated along the edge of the stage seems indifferent to the flirtation. Yet I know the little musicians have spent hours of practice putting themselves flawlessly in its service. Or is it they, and their flutes and wooden clapper and drum and lutes, who hold the power here? Is it the music that leads the characters deeper into their emotions, as it leads me?

At the urging of the Jin girls, Euphonia and Constance, I drink a bowl of soup with some kind of fancy mushroom they make a great fuss about. The sort of delicacy that my father's concubine would savor, I think, though she would never utter a word about its cost. When everyone is finished, as baskets of treats are being sent out to the servants on the veranda, I catch myself wishing Little Auntie Tuo could hear some of the southern music that persists—breathy and sinuous and captivating—despite the hubbub in the reception room.

"*Ai ya!*" puffs Wintersweet, plopping down on an empty seat. "Grandmother Jin's in a merry mood! With Mother Ding excused from daughter-in-law duties, I've nearly run my feet off tending to the two of them *and* the guests. Some things you just can't trust the servants to do properly."

Her mother has said those words a hundred times. I squeeze Wintersweet's hand as she turns to little Cousin Fu. "Of course, your brother's wife has been in the same state, I imagine—but who had time to ask her?"

Her husband's cousin pushes her mouth into a tiny knot, as if to say, what else should a young married woman do, save please all those around her? She's nearly my age, I realize; her eyes look vacant as those of Padma's baby girl.

Aunt Gao stands to drain her wine cup amid a burst of laughter—Old Lady Jin has imposed some kind of playful penalty. "Typical," breathes Wintersweet in my ear, "that we young ones aren't invited to have more than a cup or two. These Jins may indulge themselves by calling in a troupe of players at every excuse, but let the juniors have a little extra fun? A dreadful affront of propriety that would be!"

My aunt looks flushed and uncomfortable as she drops back to her seat. Her face clears quickly: Wintersweet's stepsons rush into the room and up to the head table, followed by their nurses.

The two older boys—neither more than five or six—pay their respects quite charmingly, dropping to one knee, right arm extended Manchu style. They could be twins from the look of them, for all that they were born to different mothers. "Thank you, Great-grandmother," they chorus, "for the feast." The third lisps his thanks from his nurse's arms. The guests all coo and nod as Old Lady Jin beams.

I raise an eyebrow, and Wintersweet whispers to me again. "Oh yes, they're good boys really. Especially when I've told the nurses what to have them do—oh, watch Mother now!"

Aunt Gao has waved the youngest's nursemaid over, and seizing Little Treasure, plunks him on her lap. She praises him loudly, pointing out his resemblances to this relative or that, offering him a fried pastry and chuckling as it crumbles onto her dress. Onstage, a new scene begins with a stirring martial air. The older boys turn toward the courtyard, and Little Treasure wriggles. My aunt squeezes him affectionately. He squawks.

All the ladies laugh, some to cover the awkwardness, some genuinely amused. Aunt Gao's face grows redder as she lets the boy slide from her lap, and he stumps like a fat-legged turnip in split baby trousers to take his nurse's hand.

A noble young bandit dressed in black leaps onstage and brandishes a glittering sword. Old Lady Jin cries out, "Let them go back where they can sit comfortably and watch! If Madame Gao will excuse my little ruffian?"

More laughter. My aunt bows in her seat, lips pulled into a wide smile. The bandit dives across the boards to battle a corrupt constable. The boys and their entourage hurry toward the doorway. The old lady focuses her attention on the stage and the other ladies do the same. Except my aunt: I think I see her eyes grow moist as they follow Little Treasure in his open-crotched pants, his penis bobbing between his legs. He passes her, passes me, toddles out the door.

In a flurry of feints and blocks and midair gyrations, the constable is defeated. The entire audience, from serving women to Old Lady Jin, bursts out in admiring cries. I hear one of the older boys call "well done!" from the side hall. I've been waiting for a chance to talk with Wintersweet, but I can't stop watching the lithe black-clad body as the noble rebel vows to continue the fight against injustice until all wrongs within the four seas have been made right. Is this distraction where the danger of beauty lies?

Euphonia reminds us that the next scene will be *Longing for the Worldly*, the story of a lovesick novice nun. "So romantic!" she sighs, and her Cousin Fu beside her sighs a half-breath later. Only an eyebrow twitch from Constance questions the wisdom of preferring a bridal chamber to a convent cell. But she holds her peace.

A tiny girl-actor waving a white horsehair fly-whisk begins her plaintive solo, accompanied by a single flute: "Long long ago, pious Maudgalyayana, ah!, tried to save his mother from the depths of hell." A long wooden rosary sways before the blue-and-white patchwork of her sleeveless jacket. Her half-dance of pose and gesture reminds me of the easy precision of my little auntie's finger as she flicked my chess piece off the board last night. I resolve to move more mindfully when we leave.

Wintersweet tugs at my sleeve, which makes me cross: She needn't think I have to be protected every time someone mentions mothers. I whirl to tell her so, forgetting entirely how anxious I have been for this reunion with my cousin.

A small gong sounds, saving me from hasty words. "How pitiful," the young nun is saying, "to have my hair shaved off. How pitiful to pass the night with no companion, save one lone altar lamp!"

My cousin too is drawn into the story; she nods, agreeing with the nun. But is that true? Isn't the girl better off without the prettiness she's cut away?

Before I can say anything to Wintersweet, cries of delight arise from the senior ladies. On Old Lady Jin's orders, two maids are returning from the stage area, leading the beardless scholar, face still made up in pink and white, and the appealing gymnast who played the black-clad noble bandit. Unlike the little nun and the others who play female parts, these two actors have unbound feet. The scholar-actor moves lightly, but even here in the reception room, there's an odd boldness to the girl gymnast's gait.

Of course they're girls. I kept forgetting as I watched the plays, but everyone made much of that—a troupe not of men who've trained since childhood, but of girls no older than thirteen. "However do they manage to act and sing and play so skillfully?" I hear my Aunt Gao exclaim. And Lady Ding asks how a ten-year-old can understand so well the longing of a lonely wife.

I think it possible. But however did a girl of twelve or so come to harbor the martial spirit of a young man unjustly outlawed and gone to live by his wits in the marshlands? I ask as much of Wintersweet, who shrugs, replying that it's not a matter of what they feel but what they do. "Something in a past life sent them to be actors," she says, "some on gold-lily feet and some in soft-soled boots. The point is that they do it well, and bring honor to their troupe."

Before we can pursue the conversation, Old Lady Jin calls Wintersweet up to the head of the room. It seems these two boyish girls have caught the old lady's fancy; Wintersweet is to squeeze them in at our table, and see that they eat their fill. Then, when this last play has ended and the servants have emptied the baskets of coins on stage, she and the Jin girls are to take the two performers on a tour of the family's garden.

"Oh, yes," Old Lady Jin adds as Wintersweet smiles and Lady Ding swallows a brief frown. "Of course you'll want to take the girls' Cousin Fu and your pretty Cousin Sun along. We won't bore Madame Gao and our other relatives with it again. But the young ones might as well stretch their legs and have a quick look round."

The older ladies begin a lively drinking game. Euphonia and Cousin Fu begin to quiz the actors: Where are they from and how long have they belonged to the troupe and what do they do when they aren't called in to some private household? Dazzler, the long-eared young scholar with the painted face, reveals that they've been asked to perform for the emperor's ladies in the Forbidden City. Wintersweet joins in the congratulations, and even Constance looks impressed.

I try not to be. Dazzler's singing voice has a remarkable range, from a deep resonance to fine falsetto, and I know no one with the limber strength of the other performer—Blackdragon, her name is. But Aunt Gao always says that actors and popular musicians come from the lowest sorts of families and hardly lead proper lives: Why, this girl Blackdragon strides about as if she still carried a sword.

The conversation wanders on as the two actors eat with surprising daintiness. One of their "sisters" strums background music on her lute. *With your ear,* Little Auntie Tuo said recently, *you could learn to play passably on the lute or the Tartar fiddle in a few months—but the nuances of the chyn take years to master.*

Suddenly Blackdragon catches my eye. "Does the refined Miss Sun ever stoop to reading novels?" she asks in her peculiar, not-quite-placeable accent. "Or does she prefer only the higher, more proper sorts of literature?"

I blush, afraid I've actually said my thoughts out loud.

But the black-clad actor's voice turns kindly: "I fear we're boring you, Miss. Your cousin was just mentioning your love of poetry."

"Oh, Lotus!" Wintersweet breaks in gaily. "Were you off in ethereal realms again?" Nothing for it but to join in the laughter. My cousin isn't one to help my new resolve to emulate my little auntie's fascinating reserve.

Nor is she one to leave me suffering for long. "I quite like novels," Wintersweet announces. "Why do you ask?"

While I toy with my empty tea cup, Blackdragon—who evidently can read quite ably—explains she's heard talk of manuscript sections from a long, unfinished novel circulating though the booksellers' stalls at temple market fairs. She says the Jin family's garden made her think of it; this *Reannotated Story of the Stone* is set largely in the great garden of a wealthy family right here in Beijing.

"Goodness!" Euphonia's eyes narrow. "I hope no, no literary *thief* is peddling some crude pack of lies stolen from our Southland Garden!"

"Surely not." Blackdragon smiles a private smile. "Who would mistake your distinguished household for the silly stick puppets of a made-up fable? But I thought it an odd coincidence, to hear one day about such a flight of fancy, and the very next to have an opportunity to see the real thing."

Constance looks bored, and Euphonia faintly disapproving. According to Wintersweet, neither of her sisters-in-law can read a word, or see much need for the skill.

Wintersweet calls for fresh tea. "Perhaps—it sounds like the sort of thing my husband might care for, to pass a dull afternoon. I'll have to mention it to him."

It's hard to come by, Blackdragon tells her, and the most you can get at any one time is a section of ten or so chapters copied out from some third-hand manuscript. "So you, ah, Young Master Jin would have to make his way through fragments out of order. And they've gotten a bit garbled with all that recopying, I was told." She smiles again. "Rather like getting lost among the pathways and miniature hills and waters of a fine garden, I suppose! But how else does one make one's way through this confusing world?"

Rather like a waste of time says Euphonia's face. "Surely we'd do better to rely upon the buddhas and the bodhisattvas and the other gods, as our mama does?" puts in Constance. Cousin Fu just blinks.

"Ah!" Dazzler accepts a cup of tea from an eagerly listening maid. "Surely,

indeed. Besides, these grounds of the Jins' are an entire Southland in miniature, aren't they? Far better than the fragments of some book! Why, Blackdragon, you yourself have told us that this *Reannotated Story* thing is
incomplete. And think of all the parts of the world, or even just the characters'
lives, that any such tale omits."

"Some parts of life are better left out!" I don't think my sally deserves the
ripple of laughter it receives. But at least it gets us off the subject of the novel
and moving toward the garden. I can see my cousin longs to lay hands on as
many chapters as she can; it comes to me that reading it might ease her
through this new life of hers. Besides, plays can be just as sensational and
vulgar as a storyteller's make-believe. Yet didn't Blackdragon just now teach us
something about courage, and Dazzler about tenderness?

A cluster of maids joins us as we take leave of the elders and walk through
the gate into Southland Park. Funny, I think, that for all their talk of pre-
serving the Manchu *old way*, even the Jins can't resist the lure of China's
loveliest scenes.

How could they? There must be grander gardens in Beijing—to say
nothing of the South—but even in the tenth month, I feel I've wandered into a
faery realm of fresh-looking evergreens and interlaced bare branches and fantastic gnarled stones. Each hillock is a mountain, and every turn in a path
takes us to new vistas.

Yet I'm still smarting from Blackdragon's sarcasm, and the way she struts
about in her black silk trousers. "You'll have to forgive me," I say quietly when
I find myself beside her. "But I don't think any storyteller could invent views as
grand as these."

"Quite right, Miss." She's not smiling now, and she doesn't mention the
frost-ruined leaves cluttering the lotus pond before us. "Better if we listened to
Miss Constance, or my brother Dazzler."

Brother? But who knows the ways of theater folk? So much she says is
unlike the speech of anyone I've ever met.

Then Blackdragon takes my hand, just for an instant. The touch is like a
diamond-flash of lightning. She inclines her head as a grand lady might, and
drifts away when the group moves on, leaving me to stand stock-still, gazing
after her.

At first, it's Wintersweet who reels off the names of the pavilions and summer houses and rare trees. But Euphonia soon takes over, to the accompaniment of occasional murmured corrections from her sister. As we cross a footbridge over a winding pond, my cousin falls behind to walk with me.

"You see what they're like," she whispers. "Father Jin's concubines' daughters, both of them are, remember. Not bad—not like Mother Ding, always calling me a long-tongued know-nothing, no matter how I try to hold my peace or learn how things are done here—but a little . . . well. At least I've got my dowry. Amazing what a small present, or a bit of silver contributed toward a family party, can do!"

She laughs naturally for the first time today. "Mother and Papa and Grandfather were right, to go a little into debt to set me up securely in a well-connected family. Everyone in this neighborhood remembers the procession with my dowry chests. And my husband's grandparents are pleased at how I'm learning their family's ways. Even Mother Ding admitted the other day she's glad to be relieved of some of the household management, so if I can just—ah, quick!"

Wintersweet tugs my sleeve. The others have all stepped into a little white-walled building done in Su-jou style, to admire the paintings on the rafters. "This way," she hisses, and disappears down a side path curving round a thick clump of purplish-black bamboo.

"My secret refuge," my cousin says quite seriously, then grins more sharply than she used to. "At least when I can get away, and my mother-in-law isn't here herself." The windows of the tiny structure before us are papered on the outside, Manchu style. We step inside.

I can see almost nothing—dull glints of silver, a bit of turquoise, or perhaps enamel, two small glimmering flames. The air is heavy with stale smoke of aloeswood and the spoiled, milklike smell of the burning lamps. My eyes adjust. We're standing before an altar.

Ranged upon its three steps stands a profusion of ornate objects: a brass vase that holds a brilliant peacock feather, a conical reliquary, the smoking lamps and an incense burner and other bronze or gilt or silvery forms, all deep in shade.

One line of vague shapes might be the Eight Buddhist Treasures; I can't be sure. There's too much to take in. Bowls with offerings of nuts and fruit and rice. A brocade-wrapped sutra box. Flowers. A shell-shaped dish of yogurt.

Long white silk scarves that seem to shine out from within. A hand drum made from a cup of . . . ivory? Bone? My gaze flies upward, relieved by the sight of familiar pale-pink lotus flowers painted on the wall above.

"Look quickly!" Wintersweet's low, urgent voice breaks my trance, telling me there's more she wants to show me, and that we've got to hurry back before the others find us here. "There, above the altar. The bodhisattva Manjushri! Though he's really a buddha, I know that now, when he's in his own Pure Land. I heard Mother Ding's teacher-lama say so."

In the Jins' big ancestral hall, my cousin reminds me, they make sacrifice to Manchu gods: Omosimama for luck and babies, Mulihan, Banaji, the horse divinity and the Painted God. Her voice fills with a fervor I'd rather think of as piety than self-pity: "Here at least is a holy being that I came here knowing how to pray to."

This more than anything tells me how homesick the Jin family's rituals make Wintersweet: Naturally, we Suns respect each of the Three Religions, but we've never done all that much in the way of Buddhist devotions, especially since Mama died. Still, the look on my cousin's shadowy, scarred face shows how important this little chapel has become to her. As my eyes grow more used to the gloom, I begin to make out what's painted on the cloth hanging in the niche of the altar-screen.

Pale gold skin, a flame-tipped sword, a volume that must be the Perfect Wisdom Sutra: This Manjushri has the beauty of a princely youth. He sits in full lotus above the petals of his throne. His graceful naked torso, his floating shawl, the oddly pleasing blue-greens and reddish orange of the elaborate background and his richly patterned clothes remind me of Padma's picture of Green Tara. In fact, I realize, one of the host of small holy beings surrounding him must be the goddess. And that's White Tara in the other corner, then . . .

"I think the temple there, behind him, must be in the Five Crest Mountains," says Wintersweet. "My mother-in-law actually went there on pilgrimage, some years back. If only you and I—"

A footstep sounds. *"Ai ya!"* she shrills. Her sudden grip on my arm feels like the bony fingers of Mother Jia, long months ago.

But it's no more than two bamboo stalks creaking against one another in a breath of wind.

The dusky chapel's atmosphere soon smothers our edgy laughter.

Wintersweet's grip eases. She begins to pull me into the tiny space behind the altar screen.

And stops halfway. "Don't think—this isn't like those mirror paintings I showed you once. Those are just . . ." She gulps in air. "They're like the primers we used to read. Really, it's all right for me, us, to come to Lady Ding's chapel. But if she finds out I've seen *this*, before her lama has given me the right . . . let alone showing it to someone else . . ." Another breath. "I don't understand it. Except that it's really Manjushri. In another form."

It hangs on the far side of the altar screen, illuminated only by a tiny papered window. *It* is another tangka-painting, ablaze with a ring of swirling flames against a ground of milky green and midnight blue. *It* portrays within that burning aura a disturbing deity. Neither of us can loose even a faint whisper; I feel my own throat close, hear Wintersweet exhale and try to speak.

Deep blue skin. Legs spread wide in a lunging, upright stance. The raging, skull-crowned, horned head of a bull-buffalo. Flanked by other faces on that same head, glaring, snarling. Many powerful arms fan out from the torso, each hand gripping—what?—a trident, a small dharma wheel, a thunderbolt-chopper, dagger, ax, an iron hook. My eyes dart at random. A noose, a cranium bowl, another rope—no, intestines. Jewels perhaps. Perhaps a scepter. A drum, a mirror, an elephant's hide.

The dharma wheel: That, surely, is what I ought to fix my eyes on. The Wheel of the Buddhist Law: He's not a demon, then, despite his demonic looks. But there's more to see.

Not one deity, but two. At last my mind acknowledges that the swath of lighter blue against the torso of this fierce being is, can only be, his consort.

They embrace, so tightly that I thought their flesh was one. One of her legs stands planted flush with his upon a mass of tiny writhing bodies. The other wraps around his other thigh. Her head's thrown back. Her teeth gleam with undeniable delight. She too wears a skull diadem, a garland of severed heads.

The small sack of his sex dangles just below the cleft between her buttocks. Another hanging chain of skulls curves tenderly beneath this intimate joining.

Littler figures, most many armed, most paired in the same union, float and burn around them. I begin to burn and float.

"I described it to Padma." Wintersweet's tentative croak calls me back from far away. "She says he is Yamantaka. The slayer of Death, she says. And the other one's name means Diamond Zombie. But that's all she would tell me."

And then, another footstep. Softer than bamboo's creak.

An unfamiliar, eerily familiar voice calls out gently. For the past few moments I'd forgotten there was such a thing as gentleness. "Lotus? Wintersweet? It's only me."

"Blackdragon?" my brave cousin responds.

"That name will do as well as any." The boyish gymnast chuckles. "Never mind. Come here."

I breathe easier in the main part of the little chapel, where the actor's face looms above her black clothes in the dim air. "Don't worry," she says as we gape at her in heart-thumping silence. "Dazzler is keeping the others busy with a fine display. But even my brother can only carry on so long."

Blackdragon takes my hand, as she did earlier. "Lotus," she says, "there's something else here you need to see, and to remember. Look at the altar again."

With a wave as masterly as a practiced sword thrust, as enticing as a stage flirtation, Blackdragon draws my attention to the set of figures I took to be the Eight Buddhist Treasures. They're not.

Stepping closer, I can tell that these metal images aren't the usual parasol, paired fish, eternal knot and other good-luck offerings. No: eight . . . goddesses, I decide, made like the paintings in a Tibetan-looking style. Yet it's not the tangkas they remind me of, but something else.

I can't think what. It seems like hours since we walked into the garden, weeks since I left home this morning for the Jins'. Or has it been just hours since Nurse slipped off that narrow shelf of mountain earth, and saw the face of the one this Death-slayer slays?

"The Goddesses of the Offerings: Vajradhupa, Vajragiti, Vajranritya . . ." Blackdragon points to one and then another as she reels off their names. "Oh, but you don't know Sanskrit."

How, after these overwhelming sights, can I feel this wire-fine blaze of pride? But I do. "I, we know *vajra*, of course," I snap. "*Diamond* or *thunderbolt*, take your pick."

Young as she is, the actor looks at me with a mother's amused affection. "Of course you do. And I expect you'll learn the rest, but meanwhile, if you'll forgive my showing off, I'll translate: 'Vajra Incense,' 'Vajra Song,' 'Vajra Lamp' . . ."

The names glow within me as she indicates each little statue. I suppose it's because I've been so long in semidarkness that I can see them clearly now. Wintersweet too stares as if she'd never noticed their drifting scarves, their fluid bodies and enchanting faces. Eight perfect statues, cast in metal, each one smaller than my hand.

"You'll want to see them again someday, Lotus," the actor says. A dispassionate pressure heightens her unusual accent. "Remember where they are."

"They'll be right here, I'm sure. My mother-in-law's not likely to let them go." Wintersweet's irrepressible humor wins her one of Blackdragon's gracious nods.

"Should your mother-in-law keep you sometimes from this best of refuges," she says as my cousin's face goes somber, "you might make yourself another. From that little studio over by the lotus pond, it may be. Or from paper, brush, and ink."

She turns to me. "Remember this too, little Lotus: I'll see you again. Perhaps within the walls of another garden. Now we'd better go back to the others."

We file out quickly and slip up to the ring of watchers transfixed by the swaggering routine Dazzler's putting on. His arms sweep wide and, as Blackdragon joins him, they move like a pair of tigers boxing off a shadow host from the underworld.

What garden was she speaking of just now, and why will I be there?

I won't forget a single thing about this day, I think. And suddenly I remember what the eight goddess statues resemble: The figure of fiery Pandaravashini that my poetry tutor gave to me.

THE MEMOIRS OF EUGENHO DA ROANOCA

BEING AN AUTHENTIC ACCOUNT
OF TWENTY-FIVE YEARS IN MACAO,
CANTON, ILHA FORMOSA, DEJIMA
(OR, NAGASAKI), AND ALONG THE
CHINA COAST, AND OF THE MANNERS
AND USAGES OF THE PERSONS THERE,
PUBLISHED IN OBEDIENCE
TO THE PUBLIC VOICE

Selected and Translated from the Portuguese by Joaõ-Luis Larasaõ, Lately of This City

London:
Printed by Elliott, Eliot, & Elliot, Booksellers, Pall Mall
MDCCLXXXVIII

Chapter XIX

As a result of those unfortunate misunderstandings previously related, I, Eugenho da Roanoca, having been unjustly sent to languish in gaol in Macao until my timely pardon by His Excellency the Governor, did there make the acquaintance of one known as Father Umberto, formerly a Jesuit, who as he lay afflicted in our common cell gave testimony to me, and me alone, of his experiences at the Man-joo court of China. He did press me to convey to all the world some part at least of his stories, and I shall endeavour to acquit myself of that duty, for by what motive should one labor with ink and pen if not to carry forward the memory of those whom one has known, and to tell the Truth?

Renegade and apostate tho he was judged to be, I believe this Father Umberto (and even now I cannot deny him the priestly title he cherished, despite his unhappy History and the crimes of which he stood accused) to have been an honourable man, and an unparalleled teller of tales. Notwithstanding the ill health to which the trials of his flight from Pekin and the deadly climate of the Summer in South China had driven him, his mind and tongue did function admirably. Yet perhaps I shall not prove the only person to greet with initial doubts some part of that which he recounted; so curious does it seem.

He was resident in Pekin for many years, until word reached the Jesuitical Mission there on the Fifth day of August, *Anno Domini* 1774, of the dissolution of their Order by decree of Pope Clement XIV; and had been moreover a painter serving in the court of the Chinese Emperor himself. Fr. Umberto was consequently acquainted with many particulars of the Man-joo court; and spoke their speech with that same ease with which he could converse in Italian, Portuguese, or less elegant tongues. He said he did prefer the Man-joo language, it having an apprehensible grammar not unlike that of Latin; yet he had thro daily necessity become fluent as well in the Northern vernacular of China.

It was to one series of events, which took place only the Winter before the news of his Order's dissolution, or mayhap a year or two earlier (for in time if in nothing else, the richly burdened memory of the ailing Fr. Umberto did sometimes swerve), that he in his narratives repeatedly returned. The Reader may suspect this Ecclesiastic of an unchaste, and dangerous, interest in the Lady of whom he spoke; but he swore otherwise.

It being a quiet period just before the celebrations of the Lunar New Year, which is the chiefest feast day of China, the Imperial Household and all attendant upon it were in residence in the Ze-Kin-Tcheng (which signifies, the Prohibited Walled Borough Which Is Like Unto the Pole Star), a grand aggregation of palaces and audience halls, of atria and treasuries and offices of superintendence, forming as it were the very Centre of Pekin.

Each year, in the Spring and early Summer, the Emperor and his Ladies repair to their residential parks in the environs of the Capital; and from Summer well into the Autumn, he removes himself and a goodly portion of his Court from Pekin's cruel heat, proceeding Northward to the mountains of Eastern Tartary. The requirements of Law and Custom do, however, prevail upon the Imperial Household to pass the harsh Winter in the Ze-Kin-Tcheng: in the ornified captivity of lamp-lit stone-paved passageways between high walls; and apartments luxurious but viewless, where the healthy amusements of the countryside are gainsaid those to whom no delicacy or fine raiment (excepting only should it be the privileged mark of a more august Rank) is denied.

That Winter, as usual, Fr. Umberto laboured daily at his painting in the draughty Imperial Studios within the outer, or Southern, section of the Ze-Kin-Tcheng. He and other priestly Artists, along with various Astronomers, Mathematicians, Clockmakers and Architects belonging to the Jesuit or other Catholick Orders, have long been the only Europeans, save a small number of Russians, who may reside within the Man-joo Empire proper. The influence of the Missionaries at Court having been for many decades in decline, Fr. Umberto was pleased when he was summoned by a factotum of the Imperial Household Staff and given a special commission from the Emperor.

This man's family name was Suen, or Soon, and he was not one of the two thousand Eunuchs in service in the household; but was rather one of his Imperial Majesty's own hereditary servants, a powerful caste. Fr. Umberto had always found this Suen an intelligent and cultured, if sometimes proud or dreamful, man (which last Fr. Umberto supposed to result from the Consumption he suspected to be lurking within the lungs of the good Suen), tho he had politely declined all invitations to discuss the teachings of Holy Writ, preferring to fix his attentions upon his standing in this world.

"Sir," said Suen. "I must desire you to adopt your most circumspect manner and prepare to exercise your utmost skill." He explained that his Imperial Majesty (whom the Chinese in their own tongue do call *Wann Suey Yeeh*, or Master of Ten Thousand Years, which is to signify their wishes for his longevity) had commanded the Italian to paint for him a portrait of a certain Concubine of the Second Rank.

Now, Fr. Umberto, no matter how feverish or wracked by ague, forbore to describe this Concubine; except to say she was a favourite among all the twenty or more Queens espoused to the Emperor, and daughter to a great clan of a Turanian oasis town (which is to say, a kingdom of certain Eastern Toorks) in the far West of Tartary, lately conquered by the Man-joo. When I inquired of my sickly companion if she was not therefore what we style a Musulman, who submits to the teachings of the prophet Mahomet, he conceded it. When I inquired of him, could she be called a beauty, he asked if I supposed Eve seemed fair to our apple-eating father Adam, when she stood before him unclothed and holding the Fruit of that forbidden tree, whose mortal taste brought all our woe.

Perhaps because of her Religion, or perhaps because of jealousy on the part of the Man-joo and Chinese Queens in the seraglio, this Turanian Concubine did not dwell alongside the others within the Ze-Kin-Tcheng. She passed her Winters instead in a nearby belvedere among the noble abodes and governmental bureaux of the so-called Imperial City, a fortified six-gated district surrounding the moat and ramparts of the Ze-Kin-Tcheng, and nested in turn at the core of Pekin's lightsome Man-joo City; which is itself walled away from the habitations of the subject populace.

Fr. Umberto later learned that the Concubine's Winter residence, the Precious Moon Tower, stood overlooking the Southern wall of the Imperial City. So infatuated was the Emperor that, to prevent in her the indisposition some call home-sickness, he had ordered the settlement, just outside that wall, of a number of his Musulman subjects, complete with a Mosque and a bazaar resembling those of her native land, that the Lady might have the comfort of familiar sights and sounds nearby. Indeed, someone within the Mission told my companion that his deceased compatriot, Fr. Giuseppe Castiglione, had some years previously executed for this Concubine's sake a series of oil paintings depicting scenes of the beauty's home.

At any rate, his Imperial Majesty had decreed that no man, save Himself and his Eunuchs, was to enter this Precious Moon Tower. Consequently, despite Fr. Umberto's priestly celibacy, the portrait must needs be painted elsewhere.

On that first day, and for many afterward, the factotum Suen ushered Fr. Umberto Northward thro the most private section of the Ze-Kin-Tcheng, thro internal portals and twisting passages between claret-coloured walls topped with tiles glazed in golden ochre, leading him almost to the limits of its confines, and thence thro the gate in the Southwestern corner of the Imperial Garden. The Turanian Concubine was borne thither in her palanquin by a different route, entering the Ze-Kin-Tcheng, and directly thereupon the Garden, thro doubled gates to the North; and was brought to where the Artist waited, his paints kept warm beside a great bronze charcoal braziere in the bitter Pekin cold, within a two-storied building called the Yang-Sing-Jai, or Lodge for Nourishing the Disposition, where the course of Fr. Umberto's passions was to be most profoundly altered.

This Yang-Sing-Jai was not the grandest building within the Garden; but it was more substantial than the Summer-houses within those precincts, allowing for sufficient light as well as warmth and a privacy unavailable in the busy Imperial Studios, where it was unthinkable that such a highly placed Lady should show her face. And since the Lodge stood adjacent to the wall of that Northwestern quarter of the Ze-Kin-Tcheng where the Empress Dowager and many of the Queens did dwell, Fr. Umberto thought perhaps it had been selected for that reason; as tho the nearness of the seraglio lent a protective shield, even tho its denizens were spared by secrecy the agony of knowing his Imperial Majesty so favoured their Turanian rival as to order this special portrait.

The Concubine seemed indifferent to all such matters, maintaining a delicate decorum that never smacked of haughtiness. Suen whispered once to Fr. Umberto that the temper of this Lady could flare passing fierce, rumour having it that she had been so strong of will as to refuse the favour of the Emperor repeatedly during her first years in Pekin, before she began to rise in Rank among his Queens; yet as the days and weeks passed, the Artist observed no indication of such a trait, only an absence of the fawning and simpering which he held to be the chief weaknesses of Womankind. (I, Eugenho, hold no such brief against the distaff side; but saw little hope of reasoning my ailing companion into an approbation of that Sex for whom his subsequent ill-managed passion had led to our vile and malodorous cell.)

While Fr. Umberto worked, the Turanian Concubine's two Eunuch-guards idled on the portico. Her maids and ladies-in-waiting would amuse themselves with their needlework, or in conversation, occasionally commenting on the unusual effects of Fr. Umberto's oil paints upon the portrait; for his Imperial Majesty had decreed that this depiction of his beloved be rendered in exotic and delectable European dress, and in the painterly manner peculiar to such foreigners, rather than in the translucent Chinese tempera colours with which the Court artists were usually required to work.

Freed to paint in the style of his youthful training, Fr. Umberto eschewed the flat look of the usual Chinese full-faced portrait, showing rather the Lady's lovely head turned slightly to one side, its sleek curvature finely modeled by that judicious touch of shadows to which the Reader's eye is doubtless well accustomed. Yet her attendants perceived the shading as mere laughable smudges upon their mistress's face; as for the Turanian Concubine, even when the Artist repeatedly invited her, she made no comment whatsoever.

One day, it being sunny and windless and warmer than usual for the season, three maids were granted leave to walk about the Garden and examine the condition of the ice atop its twin lotos ponds. Fr. Umberto laboured mightily that day, for the factotum Suen had begun to press him with word of Imperial inquiries as to his progress; and I do now suspect my friend of lingering overlong upon the fanciful landscape of the portrait's background (tho I know not whether it repre-

sented Italy, or Turanian lands, or the sylvan groves of Arcady) in order to post-
pone the day of separation.

The three maids, bobbing hastily on the high soles of their oddish Man-joo
shoes, burst thro an archway of grotesque water-riven limestone before the Yang-
Sing-Jai, calling to their mistress that some other maid unknown to them was
being severely beaten by a deranged Eunuch labourer in a deserted courtyard
adjacent to the Garden. The Turanian Concubine's compassion (or her curiosity)
being immediately ignited, she dispatched her own guardian Eunuchs to fetch the
two forthwith.

The toothless menial in his Man-joo cap and dirty padded robe knelt sullenly
in the well-lighted chamber Fr. Umberto had taken as his studio within the Lodge,
where the guards had thrown him down before their mistress. He refused all
questions, only humming some popular theatrical melody. As for the girl, the dis-
array of her coiffure and clothing suggested that she had indeed suffered as fierce
a beating as the gaunt old man might manage; yet she swallowed her tears and
when bade speak, prostrated herself before the Concubine, then quickly and
intelligently told her tale.

At first, my cellmate told me, he took her for a maiden of perhaps fifteen
years, come into the palace as a lady-in-waiting from some noble Man-joo clan;
but he soon deduced from her plain blue gown and simple plait of hair that,
despite her slender height and the elusive air of worldly sorrow beneath her fresh-
faced beauty, she was indeed only a serving-maid, and younger than she
seemed. All eyes, even those of the two Eunuch-guards, fixed upon her as she
spoke. Only the old man crouched alone, staring at the floor, mumbling and humming from time to time.

The girl Lien-Wha, whose name might be rendered Nenuphar, or Flower of
the Lotos, had but recently entered into the service of his Imperial Majesty's
revered Mother. This aged Empress Dowager, according to the girl, had just the
day before attended theatricals performed by the Imperial Castrati-actors on a
small stage in the grounds of the Tchung-Wha-Gung (or, Palace of Doubled
Glory), just West of the Garden. It was thro a side-gate leading directly from the
Northwest corner of Garden to this same palace that the girl's cries of pain and
fear had reached the ears of the Concubine's own maids.

But how had the unreasoning Eunuch come to unleash his rage upon the
girl? The Empress Dowager having discovered the loss of a favorite handkerchief,

Nenuphar explained, she and another new maid were dispatched to see if they might not find it in the Tchung-Wha-Gung. After some time, the girls spotted the bit of broidered silk in the corner of an empty courtyard, snatched it up, and gaily prepared to return past the Six Western Palaces of the seraglio to their mistress's own dwelling-place. The old Eunuch leapt upon them utterly without cause, said Nenuphar, seizing and striking her, while the other maid fled.

"You lie!" Rising up from his crouch with a shriek, the Dotard leapt again upon the maid, encircling her neck with long thin fingers, and crying out incoherent vilifications: that she had desecrated the stage with female filth; and had slipped away from her young companion and stolen some tiny pagan Idol from a little shrine within the Tchung-Wha-Gung.

Nenuphar gasped. The old man's fingers tightened. The Concubine's lounging guards were slow to act; but she was not. Casting aside her usual languor, she too leapt up, pulling a small dagger from her sleeve as she ran toward the struggling pair. The guards and other attendants (and Fr. Umberto, aghast) stood as if they had been transformed to statuary, more shocked by their mistress's actions than by any other thing.

She cut a deep gash into the Eunuch's wrist. Blood poured out. With a great sigh, the madman released his grip, sank to the floor, and took up his demented crooning once again, while the guards, at last, rushed toward him.

Great confusion followed. Several among the Concubine's attendants wept or swooned, tho Nenuphar forbore to do so, merely standing motionless, her arms wrapped tightly across the breast of her blood-spotted gown. Fr. Umberto found himself so affected, so riven by charity and pity and admiration, that he reached forth and rested a trembling hand, for what was at once the first and last of times, upon the smaller hand of the Turanian Concubine, fearing, as he told me, that she might otherwise succumb to hystericks; but she calmly laid his hand aside.

Meanwhile, before her laggard guards had fairly bound up the raving would-be murderer, a further pair of Eunuch-guards could be heard clattering through the side-gate from the Tchung-Wha-Gung into the garden, led by Nenuphar's companion. It was but a matter of a few shouts and fewer moments before they found their way to Fr. Umberto's former studio.

I say "former" because these events brought an end to the portrait-sittings, the Artist being later obliged to finish up his work from memory, in which the image of the Lady remained perfectly unobscured. Of course he realized that the Eunuch's allegations upon the innocent maid were groundless. In order to maintain the wall of secrecy around the painting of the portrait, thus sparing the sensibilities of the other Queens, all present were enjoined an absolute silence.

My ill-fated cellmate did tell this tale, as I have said, more times than any of his others, desiring me to inform the world of the valour of the Turanian Concubine, and told it consistently in all particulars; except the last time, which was the last time he did recount to me any tale whatsoever, when he confided two more minutiae concerning his final moments in the Garden. Many a story grows in the telling of it, I do admit; but I herewith bear witness that Fr. Umberto's nobility of spirit confirmed that what follows can only have been the Truth.

The first: As the Concubine, her attendants, and her personal guards prepared to make their way to the North gate of the precincts, outside which her palanquin and bearers and more guards waited, the maid Nenuphar, resembling nothing so much as one awakening from a deep dream, hurled herself face down before the Concubine, knocking her forehead against the floor, in order to express her deep gratitude in the Chinese manner. The Lady, gently condescending to stretch forth that same small hand and raise up the servant girl, did murmur, so softly that my feverish friend declared that altho he had pondered the moment for years, he could not be altogether certain he had heard it, "If indeed you have taken something you so value, guard it fiercely, guard it well." Then she herself, in her only sign of discomposure, did also blink as if returning from a dream, and did turn immediately away.

No, did not immediately turn, for Fr. Umberto forthwith retracted that statement, and sobbingly declared to me the second new particular of the scene: that the lovely Turanian thereupon raised her face from the maid's, and cast to him a look heavy with scorn, as if to say, *I am not that for which you have taken me!* It was then, he confessed, that the Principles upon which he had built his life were shaken, leading to a new way of seeing—and, alas, to the unhappy events of the years that carried him from Pekin to our cell in Macao. He confessed this, and rolled to face the dank stones of the wall, stones that in time following for me did echo with his name. O Excellent Umberto! The fever took him shortly afterward.

AT THE PRECIOUS-MOON TOWER, RESIDENCE OF THE MUSLIM CONCUBINE FROM OUR NEW WESTERN TERRITORIES

By Aisin Gioro Hongli (1711–1799)
[reigned as the Qianlong emperor]

North of this tower of story on story:
   the Imperial City's three lakes.

South of the wall that walls in these walls:
   a mosque and a Turkic bazaar.

A settlement ordered, Muslims moved in—
   within sight of this uppermost floor.

A distant bride summoned to pass her days here—
   within sound of the mullah's prayer call.

From her room, one can see in a mirror of glass
   that replica town of the West.

Or admire on the walls, in paintings in oils,
   her desert, her scent-trees, her home.

What need for daggers, for a heart falcon-keen?
  Better musk, and soft skin bathed in milk!

A nation is conquered, a woman is wed;
  the harem, the empire, the same.

A Note on the Poem: More than forty thousand poems are attributed to China's Qianlong emperor, many of them doubtless "corrected" (if not actually written) by his subordinates. The authorship of this example remains an open question. Although the aviatrix and memoirist Hedda Svensdatter claimed in 1933 to have found it among a bundle of old papers purchased in Beijing from an impoverished Manchu bannerman, the noted scholar Mi Huajian cites glaring linguistic evidence indicating that it is a crude forgery, probably by Svensdatter herself.

—Janus Allrise O'Neene

ARTIFICIAL VISTAS

How many counterfeit panoramas, how many mirages and facsimiles you have seen! It seems the Qianlong emperor really did order the construction of an Islamic quarter (or something like one: barracks for Muslim bannermen, with a tower that might have been a mosque) within eye- and earshot of a building once called Precious Moon.

But be careful. Those paintings in the ersatz poem you've read (the aromatic sand date trees, the thirsty hills) are actually reported to have hung inside a different villa. You can't trust every poet's fabrication, or all that glib da Roanoca represents as true.

The figures just portrayed, for instance. The Giuseppe Castiglione whom da Roanoca mentions seems a fair enough reproduction of the bona fide Italian Jesuit (born in 1688; died, alas, in 1766) who served three emperors, and was transformed in dress and name to the Chinese courtier Liang Shi'ning. Engravings still exist of structures he helped design for the imperial retreat a few miles north of Beijing's walls: faux baroque fountains, Sino-Portuguese belvederes, Italianate chateaux out of some Euro-*Arabian Nights*, Chinese-roofed versions of Versailles.

But da Roanoca's storytelling Father Umberto? A sadly flawed simulacrum, at best. And the Muslim lady from the arid basin west of China—so vaguely known and named by Europeans of her day—that some today call Xinjiang and some, East Turkestan? Well. Her story's been recounted many times.

If Father Umberto saw her as another Eve responsible for his illicit longings, perhaps she held for the Qianlong emperor the thrill of conquest consummated: his empire's *xin jiang*, "new territories," redolent of difference and laid before him in exotic dress. To her turncoat brothers and uncle, who'd cast their lots in with the Qing forces during the 1750s' desert war, her entry into the emperor's harem must have been another emblem (like their fine new Beijing mansions, their fancy imperial ranks) of their ennoblement.

Soon, wild stories sprang up: the Muslim's titillating bathing habits, her unnatural natural fragrance, her shocking dagger turned against the emperor in vengeance for a (nonexistent) slain Altishahri husband. All depict a woman—and a people—alien and untrustworthy. And desirable: Name it Altishahr or Turkestan or Xinjiang Province (or even, as that questionable da Roanoca did, the home of nebulous "Turanians," of *certain Eastern Toorks*) it's a lot of land.

Rebellious Han Chinese circulated tales of how the Manchu ruler's mother (the very Empress Dowager in whose employ you've discovered our own sweetly blooming Lotus) coolly ordered strangulation for the perfumed consort Hsiang Fei, thus bringing her besotted son's obsession to an end. Then westward-looking playwrights or revolutionary theater troupes made Hsiang Fei walk and talk like a strong-minded New Woman or a happy minority-nationality comrade-ette.

For some descendants of her people, she has become the heroine Iparhan, resistance fighter against eighteenth-century Chinese overlords—who look a lot like modern communist bureaucrats. And there's no denying it: Western writers in this century have sketched for us a *Fragrant Concubine* with all the qualities of their Orients, sensual, irrational, possessed (it would seem) of a need to be possessed. But what would Inkscent—or Third Aunt—make of their self-gratifying fantasies?

Seeking traces of the woman outlined in all these looking glasses, a reflective scholar now in Arizona visits her several gravesites, translates court records, deconstructs the legends. In an academic journal, he reproduces paintings alleged to show this Uyghur, or Muslim, or Khoja-clan, or *Rong*, ("fine countenanced," "forbearing") concubine, or consort, queen, or secondary wife. He even notes one dubious portrait that's painted on— a mirror.

Lotus, too, will speculate upon the woman's knife-blade courage, her murmured words. She will ask herself again, again, just what they signify. And one day, when she most needs it, she'll construct an answer for herself.

Gaze, then, at all these likenesses. What story have *we* made of her, I and my collaborators? Is she flesh and blood and vital forces, or ink on paper? A woman or a canvas? One who looks and acts, or merely silvered glass on which some eye perceives its own framed image, in reverse?

. . . .

Or Lotus: Where shall we place her, among the winding lanes and mise-en-scène walled courtyards of this history we're contriving? At the moment, perhaps, she has yet to enter the service of the Empress Dowager. Perhaps she and the other bondservant daughters liable for this year's draft of palace maids have just now gone in through the great rear gate of the Forbidden City for the first time, sleepy, wide eyed, and nervous, all at once. Do you see in the early morning light of that same Imperial Garden, how they line up in tens beneath the eunuchs' appraising eyes?

Tall and slender, Lotus stands out among the candidates, a light-boned crane amid a flock of neckless chickens. Because she was excused from the selection during her official period of mourning for her mother, she's a full year older than the other awed and anxious girls.

Nothing for it but to hold my head high, Lotus thinks, though she keeps her eyes properly downcast. The chief eunuch purses his full lips and points: She's chosen. Ten years inside palace walls. She stops breathing for a moment and stares ahead at last, through the garden's leafless trees to the small Temple of Four Gods. *But I feel glad, really,* she tells herself. *This is what Nurse and Mama wanted for me. What my family wants.*

So, blankly observing the casual grandeur of the emerald and carnelian and lapis painted on the temple's beams, Lotus tints another pretty scene for the picture book of her own life. She tries hard to imagine how she might bring the tale to the end her father so desires.

Easy to paint what we see. Hard to see what we paint. Another example? In mid–eighteenth-century Europe, chinoiserie is all the rage. In a park near Father Umberto's hometown, a small pagoda breaks the stale neoclassical balance. Da Roanoca's bourgeois sister hangs fanciful Chinese paper on her modish walls. In the same moment that a red-veiled bride you know as Wintersweet steps, Manchu style, over a nomad saddle and a small fire in the Jins' front courtyard, a pair of gorgeous Asian pheasants come to roost on an English mantel. Their heads are cocked as if they heard the hoofbeats of Sun Taiyang's horse—so lifelike are these bright enameled porcelains made for the export trade.

But so much is scrambled in translation. A Cantonese painting on glass gleams on a wall in Gloucestershire or Jersey, framed by Thomas Chippendale in Sino-rococo: A lady in a Qing aristocrat's headdress appears to wear a corset beneath her high-collared robe. A French tapestry offers up a fabulous fleshy despot lounging cross-legged on his sumptuous hallucinatory throne—a far cry from the spare keen-eyed archer Taiyang admires.

And early in the Seven Years War, in the fine engravings of one Wm. Chambers, a sharp-goateed Buddhist bonze evokes a muscular Hanoverian Mephistopheles. Chambers's buxom country women, his provocative lady of quality—arm akimbo, bodice tight—radiate an anatomical roundness that the Qianlong emperor, and Cassia, would have scorned. Even his "Chinefe Nun" has a shocking boldness about her eyes, as if she were free-and-easy countess in the kingdom of George Augustus, at a midnight masquerade.

Intellectuals throughout what's called the Age of Reason inscribe their own stylized designs on China. Leibnitz, Voltaire, Quesnay, Montesquieu, learn from the Jesuits' reports of philosopher-kings. The ideal they transplant, or reinvent, strikes sparks in the pyrotechnic mind of a red-haired colonist called Tom Jefferson: the United States owes the Central Kingdom for more than sizzling skyrockets on Independence Day.

So few beggars, the travelers report, compared to what we have at home! Such love of books! An economy so well developed as to win the admiration of Adam Smith! Those other, terribly convenient, images of Oriental decadence and mass poverty belong to overpopulated later times, when administrative breakdown—and a ruinous balance of trade (all that silver heading east in exchange for tea and silk and prettified *objets!*)—will make it clearer to the West how badly China needs help. Or at least a bit of intervention.

When that day comes, the Qing view of smelly, ignorant, *ignor-able* outlanders will have to be remade. Meanwhile, during this height of

Manchu power and self-confidence, there's a minor curiosity about the trappings of the pushy barbarians. A vogue for Chinese porcelain copies of Limoges enamels and Venetian glass sweeps Qianlong's court.

Some hybrid geegaws made for European export linger in the homeland where they can't quite be at home. Eggshell-fine bowls show monstrous sandy-haired women got up as shepherdesses, with lumpish men in knee breeches and tricorn hats. (Aunt Gao sees one, and sighs that such an appalling female could have a loyal mate.) Folding fans display the foreign flags and Greek-columned buildings along the Canton waterfront. (Lady Ding stares at hers, thinks of her long-absent husband, who must deal with the unruly European traders some twelve hundred miles off to the south.)

The power of the exotic is a strong thing, is it not? Just look at that immodest neckline, those beaky noses and blatant legs, the freakishly discolored hair! Marvel at that little dollhouse of a temple, the funny pigtailed chap groveling facedown—as surely no civilized man would lower himself to do!—before an impossibly ornate throne. How bizarre! How charming! What fun to gawp and wonder if true human feeling can exist within!

Of course some bits of Europe are welcomed, though they're altered. Even now, as Lotus learns the byways and cul-de-sacs and inner gateways of the women's palaces, two of Beijing's four Roman Catholic churches offer huge murals in tricksy trompe l'oeil: Rooms and corridors and piazzas tempt the viewer to walk into a world within a wall. This new way of painting will catch the Manchu ruling family's fancy. Eventually unreal scenes equally realistic, from the well-loved *Story of the Stone*, will adorn chambers inside the Forbidden City. A few more steps and there you'd be, in a pseudo-Nanjing garden grander than the Jins'.

Hard to paint what we really see. Yet surely there's something more than just the wish to conquer behind all these urges to make palpable a reverie of the faraway. Can Lotus learn nothing from her dreamscapes? And after all, have you and I not chosen to gaze upon such scenes?

But something's happening in another section of Beijing's Manchu City, northwest of the great palace complex, where those registered to the Plain Yellow Banner—and the emperor's

Plain Yellow Banner bondservants—make their homes. No touch of trivial barbarous Europe here, no interest in the costly Muslim territories, only an uneasy balancing of Manchu and Han. And fantastic landscapes of another sort.

Twigs of a courtyard apricot tree and an early-budding plum bow down, iced by a freak of weather: Their thin glaze fell, rare winter rain, through the freezing air. The sky stretches dull as courtyard paving stones. Yet a few rays leak through, transforming familiar branches to filigrees of light. There in his North Hall sits Old Master Sun, caught in his depression. Doubtless he does not feel as much guilt as we think he should. Perhaps he feels more than he knows.

"Prima!" he shouts, and the maid hurries over, to see if he wants more wine, or his chamber pot, or clarifying tea.

No, he has another diversion in mind. (What good to brood on old friends dead, on chances for authority and respect now slipped away, on one son killed in battle out in Xinjiang and the others heirless, on a useless careless widow and his hazy loss of self-control, on the impotence that descends on him so often since that fit of lust?) He bids the maid bring to his study the dish garden he's been preparing as a gift for Old Master Jin. Prima scurries off; she carries the treasure in.

Four winters ago he selected the antique bowl, bought a gnarled stone. He sifted dried mud, soaked it with liquid dung. Dried and soaked and sifted again, and packed the scanty dirt into crevices among the stone's soaring peaks. When spring came, the old man planted a seedling pine below a miniature grotto, near the base of the tiny mountain in the bowl. He scored the bark and bent the branches, holding them down with fibrous strings. Since then, he's kept it carefully underwatered and half-starved.

Now he prunes the dormant tree once more, snipping off twiglets, needles, one by one. On the backs of his hands, the veins stand out, but his touch is sure: The tree has the look of flourishing endurance in old age. He bids Prima—simple, uncomplaining Prima—bring him a certain box.

Inside lies a tiny hut crafted from slivers of wood and thatched with slender grass. Old Master Sun dabs its base with a bit of mortar, affixes it to the false mountain. He recalls a story he read years ago, about an alchemist who escaped all mundane woes the day he shrank and strolled into a diminutive cave in a container garden such as this.

A thread of music enters the room: His second son's concubine must have returned from the West Courtyard, where she spends so much time. He snips another twig. Now that Lotus has gone into service in the palace, when Taiyang's away, there's only the maids and the haughty concubine here with Old Master Sun in the Upper Courtyard. Hardly the usual thing, he must admit, at least on the face of it.

Not that he wants her, certainly not. Even if she weren't his son's, this concubine harbors too much resentment for the old man's taste. Her courteous frostiness can't fool *him*. He wonders why Taiyang does not prefer an untroublesome woman like Prima in his bed.

The melody swells, turns back on itself. Odd how the family has taken its present stunted shape over the years. A shape not like the rhythmic patterns and recurring themes of the southern woman's music. Not like the planned asymmetry of the small pine.

Old Master Sun glances out to the icy lonely courtyard, that once threatened to fill to bursting, before they bought the West Courtyard for his first son, before his wife and his favorite concubine—and his brave third son, and his toddling grandson—died.

He calls for wine to be heated, gazes at the dish garden, wonders if today his spirit will at last be freed to slip inside the small world he has made. And never wonders if the Prima whom he sees, the one he's fashioned for himself, is the Prima Prima knows.

A silk string snaps. Inkscent puts her chyn aside, invites Snow and Quinta to come sit on the heated bed platform. The little maids demur at taking the liberty, but soon concede that they do feel the day's unusually damp chill. They perch on a corner of the woolen rug that covers the brick ledge, agree when Inkscent remarks that the trees in the courtyard resemble perfect sculptures of spun ice.

Snow asks when the master is next expected to come home. Inkscent shrugs. The truth is, she wants very much—to her surprise—to see

Taiyang again. She wishes she did not; he already rules too much of her life.

And yet, *why not care for him?* she thinks. *It's not like in Nanjing.* There, she would have been a fool (as her mother was, as are so many in the winehouses) to give up her self-control. To allow herself to love the way her Ma did, pining after a Mongol officer transferred years before to another garrison.

Still, safer to bear, and love, a son. Best till then to think of other matters. Inkscent gives the two girls a few cash and sends them off to the Front Courtyard to find a gate boy to go out and buy her a replacement string for her chyn. "Tell him you'll wait there till he returns," she says. "That will hurry him along."

This gives Inkscent that rarity, a few moments all alone. She opens the trunk she brought with her up the Grand Canal, looking for a package wrapped in silk. Until now, Inkscent has kept it in reserve, like some hidden thought, undisplayed but present. As her Ma might have wished.

A shrouded memory: She can be no more than six, for Mummy Jang has brought her in from her foster home in the country for a visit. Ma pets her, promises that next year her little girl can come to stay for good in Nanjing's pleasure quarter and begin her apprenticeship. Then Ma for some reason starts to weep. She makes her rambling claim of their descent from captured noblewomen of the Mongol dynasty, reveals her memories of Inkscent's father—that same departed banner officer—and urges the little girl to keep to the Mongols' version of the Buddhist way. *There's secrets, daughter. I swear I'll teach you what I can, even without a lama's blessing. They may sustain you when love deserts you, when looks and talent drain away.*

There was time, before Ma's final illness, for Inkscent to learn a few traditions of their lineage—or the lineage her mother had constructed for them. Among them, the importance, for her next rebirth, of piling up religious merit by charity and gifts to temples, by chanting mantras, by pilgrimage. By offerings before a deity.

Yet she hasn't done much of those things. Inkscent lays hands on the angular silken package, asks herself with an angry inward laugh just how she could have, taken up as she has been with making her way to a decent life? Her talents won a name for her in the pleasure quarters; they kept her from despair and aimlessness. But developing them has taken so much time! And more time taken since she came to Beijing, to win Taiyang truly over—and Madame Gao.

Inkscent wonders if she can find a lama, now that she's settled in, who might be willing to teach her more. Perhaps a priest from the Mahakala Shrine, where they chant the liturgy in the Mongol tongue. If Taiyang will allow it.

Yet perhaps it's still too soon to ask him, he might be annoyed, she'd better bide her—but why must she always—oh, enough, enough!

Inkscent unwraps the five small statues that were thrust at her by that other unknown Mongol warrior during the Lantern Festival that now seems so long ago. Yes: the transcendent buddha Akshobhya and four bodhisattvas to surround him. Imperturbable Akshobhya, whose right hand reaches down to touch the earth, whose left hand holds a vajra scepter, a diamond thunderbolt.

She arranges the faintly smiling figures on her writing desk. Akshobhya formed the center of the faded mandala painting her mother hung above the altar in her room. *See?* Ma would say. *His right hand shows us what we know without a lot of talk, like the ground beneath our feet. The other holds the power of—what truly is. Someday you'll learn.*

And once she whispered, *Daughter, Akshobhya transmutes hate and anger into the clear reflection of his mirror wisdom. Remember that.*

Frowning, Inkscent shakes her head, lights incense. The smoke of sandalwood twines and stretches, describing vaporous feelings not to be put in words. She wonders why that mysterious warrior chose her to give the statues to, and just what his muttered urgings meant. She thinks of her mother. She does not think, no does not, think of Taiyang.

Reader, are these statues but another projection of human longing for what humans lack? Are they empty artifice, these graceful bodhi-sattvas, this tranquil buddha who looks outward through half-lidded eyes, and does not meet a human gaze? These molded lumps of metal that bear, impressed profanely within their hollow centers, the laughable name Wu Ming?

No time to speculate. A footstep falls on the veranda's creaky board. Inkscent whirls. Whatever the Mongol warrior's purposes, her secret's precious to her for no greater reason than: it is her secret. And for no lesser one. She backs up against the desk to block the figures from the intruder's view. Unlikely that Snow and Quinta would be back so soon. Taiyang? Can he have found time to come home?

"Come in," she calls. Her voice is perfectly controlled.

Prima. Only Prima. Who naturally thinks nothing of a whiff of incense, and would not in any case presume to ask. Her slight wry smile (the one Old Master Sun has never seen) plays around her mouth as she passes on the old gentleman's request: Would Little Auntie Tuo play a while longer on her chyn? The master's deep in melancholy this gray day, and reposeful music might ease the pain that troubles his lower back and hips, might stimulate and regulate his inner energies.

"Something moderate, the Old Master says. Restrained." Prima doesn't add his other fretful phrases, how, frustrated that once more he'd failed to slip from this world into the cave paradise inside his fantasy mountain, he drained his cup again and lectured the air about long-ago Physician Heh. Who taught that a man always near the women's chambers will suffer afflictions as cruel as those of one who swallows the venom of snakes, toads, scorpions. And taught that decorous, regulated music was the means used by sages to subdue untoward passions. *Nothing seductive, tell her,* the Old Master mumbled. *Nothing depraved. Now go!*

Even so, heat rises behind Inkscent's composed, high-cheekboned face. Of course she knows the old man listens. But he's never directly asked, not like this, with no sons or guests about.

Although young Lotus left for the Forbidden City still oblivious, Inkscent understands—as surely as if Third Aunt had told her—what must have happened about this time last year. The sodden, dolorous old man might as well have plunged a knife into his daughter-in-law (his daughter-in-law!), might as well have slit her swelling belly and her throat.

What can Inkscent do about it? Out of sight of Prima, she drives the fingernails of one hand deep into the flesh at the palm's base.

The dolorous, sodden old man. She'll simply say she doesn't have a string to replace the one that broke. Or say she's been taken ill. The unnameable smells of sandalwood weave beneath her nostrils. She feigns a cough.

And coughing, Inkscent catches the suggestion deep in Prima's eyes. Silent, patient, raging Prima. So.

So: not out of forgiveness, but for Prima. And perhaps for the safer place outward obedience can earn her in this household, Inkscent will play. She inclines her head.

She'll play for vengeance too. Inkscent knows what Prima does, how artful gliding notes can resonate with the mind's internal vistas. How, if she strains the coarseness from her anger, her music can paint an invisible landscape that would drive a stronger man than the Old Master to lay his head on a tabletop, and sob. Who can say what effects such anguish might have on the old man's health?

Let go of that imagined melody. Look into another corner of this panorama. It's all true, what adroit Umberto and prevaricating da Roanoca set before us, about the layout of the Imperial Garden, the Forbidden City's maze of palaces and passageways, the rest of Beijing's domains inside domains like nested, fretworked ivory boxes. At least, it's true as far as can be determined from eye-blurring study of old accounts and tourist guidebooks, of maps hand drawn or xerographed or made from woodblocks, of scholarly monographs and their puzzle-knot citations, of handsome coffee-table photo essays from Hong Kong or the Palace Museum in Beijing or its doppelgänger in Taipei.

It's not far from the Suns' faltering household to the anxious one of the Jins, where Wintersweet now lives. This morning, as the cold rain fell and froze, she stiffly played the young wife's part in the Manchu-style sacrifice of a pig in the Manchu-style worship hall of this Korean-Chinese, determinedly Manchu-style family.

Following the Qing conquest, a Ming dynasty building at the heart of the Forbidden City was remodeled to look like a wing of the Manchu ruler's old palace back in Mukden, their capital in the far northeast. Its Chinese windows were redone, its Chinese symmetry broken, its entrance moved off to one side. Great cookstoves and cauldrons for Manchu ritual feasts of offertory meat were installed opposite the new door. Years later, Old Master Jin had a similar, smaller, copy of that Mukden sacrificial hall built within his family's compound.

Wintersweet has long since learned her role: *manjurambi*, in the Manchu language, to act and speak and write like a Manchu. Yet she's noticed her mother-in-law enjoys the Chinese abbess she's at this very moment welcoming to her rooms, as much as visits from her outland lama—and more, it seems, than she cares for the long ceremonies of the drum-beating Manchu shaman favored by Old Lady Jin.

What's more, Wintersweet's figured out that both ladies colluded with her pleasure-loving husband in winning the old man over to the construction of the family's stylish, and very Chinese, Southland Garden. Where just now Wintersweet walks in silence with Young Master Jin's concubine, Redgirl, to admire the prospect of the ice.

Wintersweet pauses to touch a frosted branch and contemplate the power of names. This morning, Lady Ding scolded her roundly, creating an ugly Wintersweet with no more than the Manchu *mase*, "pock-marked one." And Wintersweet's husband, when he visits her bedroom, has taken to calling her—in Chinese—"Little Miss Prim Piety."

Yet she can't imagine what it is, beyond what they have already shared, he wants. Surely no nice woman would do the shameless things depicted in that banned book he gave her yesterday, with a half-smile and a wordless jerk of his chin.

Things done by daylight, and stark naked. Things out of line with everything Wintersweet was taught about a good wife's ways. All quite embarrassing, like her husband's hints that she should beg for mercy at the sight of his hugeness, and later cry out regardless of who might overhear. Like his teasing insistence that her own parents do such things.

Her fingers cling to the cold branch. Redgirl, who has been teetering with unwonted energy a few feet behind Wintersweet along the covered promenade, catches up. "See, Young Madame?" she chirps as she points toward the cold webwork of an ice-covered thorny quince. "How all the world is changed today? Those pricking thorns are captured."

Oddly imaginative words from Redgirl. Wintersweet wonders for an instant if there is more to the vacuous, greedy concubine than she has noticed.

Then Redgirl titters. "But think how they will drip now that the sun's returning!" Her sly glance sends Wintersweet's gaze to the toes of her high-platformed shoes.

I wasn't always like this, thinks Wintersweet. *I used to enjoy a joke—at least if it wasn't crude.*

She forces herself to turn her head up as if admiring the ice work of the bush, and the frozen waterway beyond. Yes, she's changed: The last time she saw Lotus, when she went home for farewells on the eve of the palace maids' selection, it was she and not her young cousin who wept. Saying good-bye to Lotus was like saying good-bye to her own childhood self, and even to the dizzied confiding bride of her marriage's first month.

"Your pardon, ladies!" But what is her husband's page, Tobacco, doing here in the garden, carrying a charcoal-basket? "Excuse me! I was sent to—by the Young Master. Pardon me." He ducks his head and hurries past them down the promenade.

Tobacco disappears into the tunnel through the mount of pitted Lake Tai limestone at the garden's center; it seems he's headed toward the Old Master's study, the Lodge of the Immortals' Isles. But no, that's unlikely— Wintersweet knows her husband's grandfather will be gone all day. Perhaps the abbess has left quickly for once, and for some reason Tobacco was the one ordered to warm the little chapel for Lady Ding and her two daughters? Most improbable, but where else in Southland Garden does anybody go in wintertime?

"Let's follow him, Young Madame!" Redgirl's eyes gleam as they do when her son outshines his two half-brothers. "He must be up to something. Let's find out what!"

Her plain wool cloak falls partway open as she strides past Wintersweet, ruder than ever, falls open to show she's garbed like a man in knee-high deerskin boots and a tunic jacket over a short riding robe. With her fur scarf muffling her neck and chin, she looks like—almost like—a groom come south from the grasslands of the steppes. At the mouth of the tunnel, she turns her head back. She flings a daring grin.

Until now, Wintersweet has preferred simply to remain above the concubine's vulgarities, despite her mother's counsels that a good beating is what's needed. Certainly there's risk in making a companion of the rival she resents, but Euphonia and Constance have proven little solace for Wintersweet's loneliness, and a lingering winter malady has left Happiness sickly, snuffling, poor company.

So enough of playing the proper junior lady of the household! She need not be so fearsome. Wintersweet picks up her skirts and hurries after, emerging from the far side of the limestone mount in time to see Redgirl pause, framed in a bottle gourd–shaped gate beneath a sign that declares the courtyard and the lodge within to be the Immortals' Isles. Again she turns her head back for a look. Again she grins a boyish grin.

Wintersweet walks carefully across slick stepping stones and through the gourd-shaped gate. Redgirl has vanished.

Now what? No lady would barge uninvited into her grandfather-in-law's study, even when he's gone. The brief thrill of the chase—of playing any game after these long months of criticism and anxiety and jealousy—damps down within her.

Silly of her to pretend to be a child again. If only she could *not care*, as Redgirl does! Well, at least she can have a quick look around; she's never seen this courtyard before.

A water gate allowing the ingeniously engineered stream into the garden must lie beyond the small whitewashed building before her. The waterway curves through the forecourt before passing under its front wall and off to the rest of this false Southland. Wintersweet rests one hand on a rough pillar rising well above her head—more grotesque expensive Lake Tai stone.

Ice shatters. Redgirl? A bird? A frozen late persimmon just now fallen from that deserted tree? No sign of—

Blind: She's blind. Can hardly breathe though the thick cloth swaddling her head. Can hear the muffled mannish laugh of whoever's caught her from behind.

A real man, not dressed-up Redgirl. His body tall and pressing now into her. She feels him swell and harden against her buttocks. One arm tightens around her; the other hand slips inside her cape, reaches for a breast.

Too remote a place for anyone to—but where are Redgirl and Tobacco? She'll scream. Scream as she never has, as she threatened to last week when her husband wanted her to take off every stitch of clothing in broad daylight and let him summon Redgirl and compare their nakedness.

But two more hands push themselves across her mouth, scrabble to hold their place as the man behind her picks her up and carries her into the silence of the lodge.

Which is warm, so warm it must have heaps of charcoal burning inside several braziers. This can't be the work of criminals who've managed to clamber over the compound's high outer wall. The hands fall from her mouth but now Wintersweet is too stunned to scream, or even speak.

Then two things happen in the same moment. She hears Redgirl's giggle. And hears the voice of the man who captured her—her husband's voice!—ordering someone (Tobacco, it has to be Tobacco) to go stand guard outside the gate.

Reader, stop and look. Within yourself: What tableaux do you find for what comes next? Is Wintersweet stripped, are her wrists bound with a sash, does Young Master Jin allow his concubine to inspect his wife at leisure, then bid the other woman to disrobe? Does Redgirl stand by—or turn away, or leave, her mission done—as the man plays out a vile game of rape and humiliation upon the body of his wife?

Or is Wintersweet apologized to, gentled, tantalized with silken words and satin fingertips until a lifetime of inhibitions falls away? In this room apart from all she's ever known, does she begin to learn the pure abandon that will heighten her own pleasure and her husband's joy?

The forbidden erotica left us by her puritanical age might help fill in this blank in the spectacle. Some seem cruel, some dull or pathetically one sided. Some are funny. Some were banned simply for preferring the sensuous to the procreative. Some were framed by warnings of the dangers (physical, familial, spiritual) of sexual excess. All would show you bits of Wintersweet's world, scenes you might otherwise have missed.

Consider: A man seduces the new wife he calls a prude—though she says she's merely proper—with a sequence of frank pictures. (Look. First this, then this and, see? Now this.) He slides his tongue into her finally unprotesting mouth, tells her all he wants to do that they have not yet done, restrains himself as he hasn't in times past, touches her till the couch beneath her's dampened, parts her legs and moves within her slowly, slowly. At last, she lifts her hips in rhythm, finds at last the spot that gives her (in the words of Li Yu) *a strange new sensation, not pain*

*or itch or tickle, almost too much too endure, yet unendurable that it
should end.*

Soon afterward, this young married woman discovers the further
shuddering thrills of acknowledging propriety through its clandestine vio-
lation, by her own—and not her husband's—will.

Or, a woman of experience knows she can heighten her wanting, and
hence her satisfaction, by listening while a novice cries out with ecstasy at
the efforts of their mutual lover. She begins by bringing up conversations
and pastimes (aren't they fascinating, she says, the illustrations on these
playing cards? No two of them the same!) that will lead the novice to a
new state of resistless eagerness. Sets her at ease and teases and guides
her on.

Then the novice learns the rewards of forgetting all she's been taught
of feminine reticence. She lets her moans ring in the lover's ears and her
own. Unabashed, she rises to new heights.

Or again, a shy wife comes to understand why she might choose for
her own enjoyment to play a song of breath and lips and tongue upon the
jadewhite flute.

And then someone jokes about an oral examination of his beloved, or
sings of human rapture literally divine, or delights in a double-play of
words from calligraphy or some other art. For what else loosens the mind,
and thighs, like the yoking together of two different things by wit?

After which, a man teaches a woman deeper pleasure by pleasuring
her intently. Then stops short. *Little oily mouth,* he whispers in her ear
as he lets her learn for herself the savor purchased by frustration, and
the power and pride of making him unable not to return to her. And
both learn the gratification of something more than the countless (but
endlessly counted) thrusts and obsessive penile size of less imaginative tales.

Over and over—in miraculously unburned book and narrowly surviving print, where windows beckon and screens or garden rocks con-
ceal—you, gentle reader, would spy artificial vistas that celebrate the
tingle of the imagination. They engage us both (right now, reader! now!)
in the naughty, sometimes irresistible, treat of looking on.

But let us stroll no farther down the garden path of the erotic fancy.

We'll put away those carved woodblock aphrodisiacs and erection rings of words, leave the airy castles of cross-dressing, staged encounters, invented reveries. We'll even ignore young Tobacco when he peeps at a long sinuous golden dragon easing down above his master's pulsing genitals.

And we won't forget—we really mustn't—the burgeoning Hell-Fire Clubs, the breathless libidinous memoirs and trendy bawdy limericks abounding in the London of da Roanoca's day. Too many sex-laden Western Orients have been trumped up out of Asia to allow us to do otherwise. But if the weight of that history presses on us, the rush of other histories presses us on.

So we'll turn resolutely to another manufactured landscape, away from desire and its sticky consequences, as Sun Taiyang has done. He rubs his chin and coughs to drive away a moon-pale image of his lost wife. Coughs to drive away the longing he's just now engendered with his mind's one eye. Coughs once more and casts a measuring gaze toward another dreamlike artifact on this wintry day.

Wait. Before we try to see what Taiyang sees, we must acknowledge what else happens in the moment of that cough.

First this: The ghost of Cassia, held in a bondage more torturous than any Wintersweet or Young Master Jin or Redgirl will ever know—at least while they're still alive—has caught a glimpse of the construction site that Taiyang was observing. Drawn to the Forbidden City by the force of his amorous memories, she saw what he saw. And when he coughed, was brushed dizzily away.

Then this: Wintersweet, before she leaves the lodge (damp eyed and dazed by newfound ecstasies? sunk in the swift return of ingrained shame? outraged, or amazed, that she was raised to loathe what now she finds so good? relaxed, loose limbed and slippery lipped, her vision rinsed by the calming elevation of her pulse?), Wintersweet catches sight of five small metal statues on an altar in the central room.

She notices them, of course, because they resemble so exactly, in size and style and color, the eight goddesses of the offering in Lady Ding's garden chapel, the ones the actress Blackdragon took such pains to show to Lotus. Remarkable, thinks Wintersweet, and steps out of the Immortals' Isles.

And, see? Now this: What Wintersweet does *not* notice is the approach of racing sperm to receptive ovum in her sweat-drenched cooling belly, the readiness of her blood-thick uterus, two sets of haploid chromosomes entwining in irrevocable embrace. One cell complete. Then two cells, four. Then eight. Soon, embryo, then fetus. Someday, child: Her body has begun to assemble a replica of herself and of her mate, a creation that will transform her life's terrain.

But at this moment, she merely sighs (weary? regretfully? content?), leans on Redgirl's arm, gives herself over to the visible, dripping, scenery.

As Sun Taiyang must, and does. With the impure vision of everyday reality, he stares again at the strip of foundation stones laid in stairstep "cosmic mountain" style, where the bright-hued tiles of a glorious Nine-Dragon Screen are to be installed. He shrugs, turns round, dodges a workman burdened with a load of more white stones. *Over eight hundred thousand taels of silver,* he thinks, looking northward into the great gateway of the complex the dragons will guard, *for all this building and planting and refurbishing. And not to be finished this year, or the next.*

But he does not doubt the importance of the task, whatever its toll on the Privy Purse. In just over two more decades, His Majesty will have reigned as long as his glorious grandfather did: one full cycle of the Heavenly Stems and Earthly Branches, sixty years. He's declared his intention to step down then, rather than presume to surpass that unsurpassable precedent; this long red-walled rectangle in the northeast corner of the longer broader rectangle of the Forbidden City is to be his retirement home.

And hang the expense, of course. Just as the Qianlong emperor emulates the model of his greatest ancestors, so this Palace of Peace and Longevity—with its majestic offices and throne room to the south, its comfortable northern bedchambers, studies, chapels, and enticing garden—will replicate the august front half of the Forbidden City and the more intimate quarters to the rear.

At least that's the plan, and sixty thousand artisans labor to make it so. In fact, though the emperor will survive more than three years past his abdication, he'll never give up preeminence, will never relinquish the cozy central residence of the reigning monarch, will only visit this mere likeness of the zone of power. But Taiyang won't live to know that, anyway.

A damp, finger-numbing day: The emperor's bondservant coughs again. Again he sees that moonlike vision of his wife. *Almost as if she were insisting on returning to my memory,* he thinks as he winces at the frost blade in his chest. *Almost as if she were present, somehow, not nearly two years gone.* For a moment he considers buying some kind of holy object (*a pair of altar lamps? a little statue? a painted mandala?*) to donate on her behalf to, ah, perhaps to the Yellow Hats, since her interests seemed to be tending toward their sort of Buddhism in the last months of her life.

No, better not to. Taiyang appreciates a womanly sensitivity toward religion, but he learned well in his schoolboy days the respectful reservations of Master Kong: With so much in human life and society that requires attention to the here and now, so much lack of virtue in the realm of the everyday, why speak of ghosts and spirits? Certainly, the proper rites must be performed, if only for the living's sake. But how false—however dear—Taiyang considers them to be, his enticing visions of the dead. Again, he brushes away the semblance of Cassia's face.

It's the future he must look toward. Today Taiyang's working on a plan to replace the funds this project's draining from the Privy Purse—if he can pull it off. His motives look like passionate loyalty, or a greed for influence and money, or necessary striving in a ruthless world, depending on the angle of your view.

In any case, his physical view is clear cut, framed by the entrance of the new retirement palace, the Gate of Imperial Supremacy: the foundations for a second grand gate across a stone-paved plaza, and beyond that, the site where a double-roofed edifice will hold a throne. But Taiyang enters only the first gate, then walks north outside the wall containing the formal buildings and their courtyards.

He pauses to inspect the sky. Good. Dry winds are moving in. He can feel his chest expand.

A few more paces take him to the Gate of Ample Blessings, the portal of the long garden area west of the four residential halls. Yesterday Old

Shyr, one of the top eunuchs in personal attendance on His Majesty, murmured that he would wait inside the garden at this hour. *A fine spot for a private chat,* he added. Taiyang breathes in till he aches, steps through the studded double door.

Now he walks around the screening rocks, on a charming pathway crazy paved with multicolored slabs quite unlike the usual identical marble oblongs. But where's Old Shyr? Has he changed his mind? Has Taiyang been betrayed?

The eunuch's not in the open-sided building at the far end of this first informal courtyard, where five woodcarvers squat beneath the catalpa tree out front. Not on the still roofless gallery to Taiyang's right, and surely not on the half-finished terrace atop the stone hill up ahead, with its cypress saplings and newly planted pines. Four more idyllic courtyards lie beyond: Taiyang has reviewed the requisition lists. The plans for the garden area show more than twenty buildings completed or restored or under way— why did the cagey eunuch mumble only, *I'll wait someplace we'll have reason to talk at length, and ignite no curiosity as to why?*

The Imperial Household official peers about like a careful money manager on a surprise inspection tour. The woodcarvers bend low over panels of fragrant nanmu cedar brought all the way from Yunnan province. The laborers installing a marble balustrade up on the terrace shout lustily as they hoist and shove. And the raspy voice of Old Shyr calls a soft ironic welcome from the little pavilion to Taiyang's left, where someday cups of wine will meander along a rivulet that curves and recurves like a symmetrical labyrinth.

Sun Taiyang clasps his hands before him and bows with careful graciousness. Old Shyr clasps his own hands and, more deeply, bows. The bent figure in his fur-trimmed overgown begins to show the bondservant how clever engineering will float winecups to where the drinkers sit, composing poems.

But why must these two be secretive? Why perform this charade of gesturing toward water vat and trench and well, while they speak of other things?

More than a century earlier, an emperor changed the political landscape. Aware of the disastrous influence of palace eunuchs upon the imperial family of the defeated Ming, he created the Imperial Household

Department and staffed it with his personal bondservants. Eunuchs, all agreed, were necessary to a smooth-running palace life, but men like Taiyang ought to oversee them, and balance their inevitable access to power.

After that emperor's decree, *death by slicing* was the punishment for any Qing eunuch found *guilty of interfering with government affairs*, of combining his daily access to the ears of princeling or consort or monarch with *friendship with Manchu and Han officials*, with *accepting bribes*, with *reporting on things that are not his duty or suggesting whether an official is good or bad.*

And Taiyang wants to persuade Old Shyr to do just that. Unlike a eunuch, he may move freely outside the Forbidden City, can gather information about which bondservant customs officer or imperial manufactory supervisor does what. Old Shyr can pass on that information with His Majesty's morning tea. Taiyang's plan will bring profit to them both: For one thing, power. For another, silver skimmed off when a new Bureau of Secret Accounts is quietly established for, call them *donations*, from corrupt bondservant officials whose names will wend from Taiyang to Old Shyr to the emperor.

Only the most outrageously greedy of those in His Majesty's service shall have this private opportunity to atone for incompetence and graft. And the frugal, spendthrift emperor won't object to fattening his Privy Purse.

What's more, Taiyang tells himself, this scheme may help keep the most rapacious of his fellow bondservants in line—to the benefit of the reputation of them all.

So Sun Taiyang bends closer to his stoop-shouldered companion's black velvet cap. It's a household official's duty to support the emperor's financial needs, given so many palaces, temples, gardens yet to build, given such grand-scale imperial tours and pilgrimages and birthday celebrations and charities to fund. Certainly it's a good man's responsibility to sustain his family by rising higher in his world—and a maltreated eunuch's necessity to store up for his old age. Taiyang takes the crucial step: He clears his throat.

. . . .

While those two in the garden of the Palace of Peace and Longevity build their half-unspoken understanding, a front has pushed in Beijing's usual crisp winter air. On the far side of the Forbidden City, Lotus feels a gash of longing for her mother, and wonders what has touched it off. She shivers as she fetches for her new mistress the Empress Dowager a broad leaf from a bodhi tree, meticulously painted with Guan-yin of the Southern Sea and her attendant Pilgrim Lad.

And in the same breath of time, in the northeast corner of the emperor's retirement palace, a boy appears. Literally: appears. If you saw him, you might rub your eyes and convince yourself he'd clambered stealthily over the adjacent outer wall of the whole palace complex. He did not.

He's dressed like a novice of the Yellow Hat school. He pops into being in a quiet spot between two half-built chapels where cloisonné stupas and gilded miniatures of famous teacher-priests and breathtaking Tantric Buddhist murals (here on the ground floor, fiery guardian gods; there, in a more secluded upper room, deities and consorts joined in yab-yum) will survive even the spiteful looting of 1900, and the avarice of subsequent years.

By now, the last clouds over Beijing have broken up and gone. Screwing up his eyes in the clear light, the boy carries a small basket on his arm as he leaves those mute shadows and makes his way past gangs of weary workers and lean construction bosses. Nothing out of the ordinary, in the Forbidden City, about a boy-eunuch on an errand. Nothing out of the ordinary, in the Forbidden City, about a lama or a novice who's a eunuch: That's how the various requirements of palace custom and religion are met.

Soon he arrives at the Gate of Ample Blessings, and steps, as Sun Taiyang did, along that gaudy crazy-paved path. "Sirs!" he calls out modestly, coming up behind the two figures now leaning down as though to admire the bamboo carved into the low stone fence around the winding wine cup rivulet.

Taiyang is startled, stung, as if by the incoming Mongolian wind. He lifts his head one heartbeat too hastily. Old Shyr, a more experienced conspirator, waits, eyes the lad so obviously his junior, grunts.

If either of them paid more attention to the icons venerated by so many in the palace and the empire, if either one had seen that painting on the bodhi leaf Lotus just now fetched (hooded Lady Guan-yin seated before a shady bamboo grove, a white parrot holding a rosary in its beak, and, *oh!* a slightly squint-eyed boy with longish earlobes, standing prayerfully atop a lotus blossom), he might look differently upon this intruder who blinks and bows before them. Whose ears have an uncommonly soft, elongated look.

"Well?" Old Shyr's tone is slick as the last trace of ice in the shade of the bamboo-carved fence.

"Your pardon, sirs. I was told to bring you these." The boy reaches into his basket, presents each with a brocade bag. And in the instant that their eyes flick to the vermilion silk placed into their hands, he unappears.

Only Taiyang notices this final peculiarity. Old Shyr is busy maintaining an air of mild bored irritation as he opens the small bag stitched with the characters of his name and title. Ah, exquisite! A snuff bottle of lapis lazuli carved with a prospect of cliffs and evergreens and a long-legged crane. The stopper knob is coral, the dipping spoon, ivory. A handsome gift indeed.

But . . . a gift from whom? Who chose this roundabout taunting way to say, *I know you two are here, together?* The old eunuch's head jerks up. "Who sent—"

No one there, of course, to answer. No one nearby except a smooth-tongued proud intelligent Imperial Household bondservant gone absolutely speechless.

Taiyang finally remembers to exhale. He loosens the drawstring on the bag embroidered with his name and rank. His gift's considerably larger, heavier, than Old Shyr's palm-sized bottle of fashionable rose jasmine–scented snuff.

Reader, you know what sort of thing it is. More bronze goddesses perhaps, or the guardian deities of the four directions, or another buddha with encircling bodhisattvas—that is to say, more imitations forged by Wu Ming's human hands. And another stone laid into a mosaic pathway of narrative tease and factitious step-by-step fulfillment. Of artificial scenes.

But remember, these statues (five, it turns out—Taiyang examines them one by one) have yet to make their way from the astounded father to the daughter secluded in the palace women's quarters, whom he may no longer see. They still must find their place in a scattered microcosm, in a regathered mandala of thirty-seven images.

Well, then, since Taiyang remains stunned, a little frightened, unable to utter a word, Lotus herself must lead us farther down the garden path. She'll show us the next in this series of effigies, paintings, tapestries, murals, pasticci, vistas.

In the meantime, kindly reader, do overlook all this metaphorical abandon, these cheap or playful come-ons of juxtaposed like-yet-not-alikes. Perhaps you wished only to read a girl's straightforward story of her career in an eighteenth-century palace. Here it—finally—comes.

Oh, but wait. You must beware: It *is*, finally, a story. Finally, Lotus is no more to be trusted than the wily da Roanoca. She's not double-dealing da Roanoca's simpler alternate, not mendacious da Roanoca's guileless better half. She's da Roanoca's artful slippery twin.

A LOTUS BLOSSOMS: 6

Why won't you believe me?" I know that what I've said is true, or might as well be. Yet now I wish I'd held my tongue.

Ten days ago, the Empress Dowager's residence within the Forbidden City was new and frightening to me, though I hid my feelings and tried to look as serene as my father's concubine, or Padma. But today I allowed another long dull morning in the Palace of Compassion and Tranquility to lead me into foolish talk.

I'm on duty with two other maids in the chilly waiting room by the front gate of Her Dowager Majesty's palace, on duty with nothing much to do. Putting my embroidery down, I rub one finger along the edge of a blackwood tabletop. What I told them *could* be true.

Greenplum beside me smirks and glances knowingly into little Yura's wide-open eyes. "Oh certainly," she says to me, "I'd believe you could ride the fastest, wildest pony that ever was . . ." Since the Empress Dowager, her attendant ladies, and most of her other maids are at devotions in the Buddha Hall behind the palace's main building, Greenplum's free to let her voice take on its natural sharpness. ". . . *if* I didn't know you'd spent your whole life here in

Beijing, like me. But remember, Yura's from a Mongol family . . . and she grew up at Warmriver. Out there beyond the Long Wall, they learn the old Mongol and Manchu ways. And riding those horses is no easy thing, is it Yura?"

Yura looks down at the red silk peony she's making. "I've never ridden anything but a donkey," she mumbles. "And that was only when—"

But Greenplum interrupts. I turn my gaze to the curled leaf growing at my needletip. From beneath my lashes, I see her narrow lips move in her narrow face. But perhaps if I concentrate, I can catch the chanting of the eunuch-lamas in Her Dowager Majesty's chapel, instead of Greenplum's words.

Anyway, I know she'll say whatever she thinks might convince us family lineage makes us who we are. Never mind customs or languages or ways of worship, or where your family has lived or anything you've done—or been told or imagined. Never mind that emperors, and mere banner-company captains, move clans easily among the three different sorts of banners, Manchu and Mongol and Han Chinese, changing their registries with a few words that outweigh ancestry. Never mind that a waking dream can carry a Han girl from Beijing off to gallop through a grassy valley in a khanate on the steppes.

Never mind, in fact, that Greenplum—the very name she uses is Chinese—speaks Manchu only haltingly. She likes to point out that nowadays His Majesty is having the genealogies cleaned up. And that, bondservants though we all are, she is a Manchu, and Yura and I are not.

Does that matter, really? My family has served the heads of the Aisin Gioro clan since my grandfather's great-grandfather was captured as a boy, before they fought their way in through the Shanhai Pass and then through all China. He must have seen, on the summer day when the gates of Beijing were opened to the Manchu forces, that Heaven truly favored them over the Ming. Well, I would choose a firm gold pear over one splotched brown, and winey sour at the core.

I can hear my grandfather telling the story. First far-seeing Nurgaci, who brought the rival clans of the northeast together, then his bold son Abahai, then the young Shunzhi emperor, the first Aisin Gioro to reign over China; they recognized my ancestors' bravery and loyalty, and their usefulness. And Han or Manchu, how could we not be faithful to the man who's meant to rule the world?

Now Greenplum talks, and I sew in silence by the window, the droning of the lamas too far away to hear. I doubt her father's half the bowman mine is. Has *he* ever ridden beside His Majesty in the imperial hunting grounds?

This struggle between us began the wintry morning after I was chosen to enter the palaces. Waking from that first restless night in a room filled with sniffling newcomers and disdainful older maids, I was unsettled by all the strangers and the Forbidden City's complicated rules. So when Greenplum, oldest in the room, finished making the new girls repeat our names and banner registrations, and began to ask who was really Manchu and who was not, I lost my control.

My face grows hot with the memory. I bend closer to the handkerchief I'm working on. A dozen girls were listening, and two eunuchs, who smirked as they doled out our morning bread. *The peach tree and the plum don't speak,* Third Aunt used to say to Wintersweet and me, *yet people beat paths to see them bloom.* Mama knew her mind, but she never quarreled with her elders. How could I have put myself and my opinions forward in that way?

Still, I was right. Bannerfolk are bannerfolk, I said. Every city has its garrison—we live there, the local people live outside, and the laws keep places for men of both kinds in His Majesty's government. Doesn't the whole country prosper? I asked. The border tribes are pacified, and tiny uprisings in the hinterlands mean nothing—the Great Qing has brought about a happy peace.

Greenplum could only shrug and turn away. She's my senior by eight years; if not from respect, then out of common sense I should have held my tongue and watched how she pleases the Empress Dowager and her attendant ladies, how she stays on the eunuchs' good side. But that morning I knew one thing only: If I yielded to Greenplum—as Third Aunt would have—she'd pick at me till I broke and cried.

A day later she did just that to poor homesick Yura. As she led us new girls to the wardrobe room, Greenplum went on and on about plague-ridden Mongols, and how we must beware of catching smallpox from the Tümet and Ordos and Khorchin soldiers if we travel with the court.

"Oh, but excuse me, ah, Yura, isn't it?" she said as we left the room, carrying the heavy robes Her Dowager Majesty would choose among that day. "I wouldn't say that about Chahars like your family—why you've fought beside us Manchus since long before we entered the Pass, and anyway, descendants of Chinggis Kahn have been marrying into our imperial clan for, forever. I only mean the uncivilized, untrustworthy ones." Her voice was honeyed; her smile flashed sharp. "Like those dirty Oirats from out west. They really are agents of the smallpox goddess, you know."

Certainly a Chahar's not an Oirat—and Yura's family must have served the imperial line for generations. But after a full day of such remarks, she stopped eating altogether.

The next morning Yura looked to me like a very little girl, hunched over, dully piling up torn bits of cold steamed bread in the gray light. I know the heavy tightness that can fill an empty stomach, though the eunuchs give us no more than they must. I went and sat beside her.

"Would you like to hear a poem?" I asked. She said nothing, but looked up, shy and surprised. Except for my one outburst, I'd had little to say to anyone.

My father taught the poem to me, I told her. It describes the Old North Gate in the Long Wall, a stop on the Warmriver road. Yura had passed through the place herself on her way to Beijing from her home in the summer capital, so of course she wanted me to recite the poem. And of course Greenplum and several others listened in. I chanted the last line slowly, clearly: "Within the Wall, beyond the Wall—one empire, and one family."

Greenplum sniffed. She hardly could have spoken out against what everyone knows is true. We are one empire, and were meant to be. Treasonous—and ridiculous—to say otherwise. Yet we all saw her wrinkle her nose and lift her chin. "One family?" she drawled, as if breaking out of a half-doze of boredom. "Well, it fits the meter, doesn't it? Has your father written other poems?" *One family, perhaps,* her expression said. *But every family has its elders and its juniors, its main branch and its lesser ones.*

I have no quarrel with the way things are. But I will quarrel with stupidity, and with someone who twists a truth into something ugly as a hateful lie. So I just said, "A few," and stood up, adding that I thought it time to see if Lady Brightcloud needed anything; she's the first among Her Dowager Majesty's highborn attendants, so we all do what we can to earn her favor. Greenplum smiled a thin smile.

But on my way out the door, I turned back and added, "Oh! Did I make it sound like that poem's by my father? How stupid of me." I even slapped my face, the way the girls here do. "I'm sure he would be honored to know you thought so. He heard a Grand Council minister call it his favorite of all the thousands His Majesty has written . . ."

Little Yura gasped before she could think to stifle the sound. No one said a word. How ill-bred, to criticize a poem by the Son of Heaven—what *could* anybody say? From the corner of my eye, I saw Greenplum turn red, and swallow hard. The others looked at me with the beginnings of wary respect.

It turns out I was lucky to have made a friend of Yura. A few days later I gave in to a dreamlike urge to take—no, to rescue from a dusty shrine in the Palace of Doubled Glory the little figure of a round-breasted goddess resembling the lost Tara that Mama gave me. And Yura defended me against the crazy old eunuch's accusations with full belief in my innocence. If my thick winter clothing saved me from serious bruising when he hit me, her obvious sincerity saved me from far worse . . . as long as no one finds the lovely thing I stole.

Today, however, I was only talking about what's possible, because I let Greenplum lure me into speaking. I won't slip again. She can like me or not, as she pleases, but I want no enemy working against my future here in the Forbidden City. So I nod as she talks, and thread a new color into my needle, and when she pauses, I offer to make fresh tea.

While it steeps, I wrap my hands around the indigo-glazed teapot, thinking how it *is* possible that I could ride a racing half-tamed horse. I've done so, in the way that matters. And now I have the courage to do so in the way Greenplum means, on a horse of bones and flesh.

I pour out three steaming cups of tea, capably as a grown woman pleasing an honored guest, gracefully as Mama used to. Once, I wouldn't have believed I might do by daylight the bold things I do in dreams. I was too weak to bear what life brings, and wept easily, like Yura. Before that, I loved the world with a child's love, unaware, and laughed with Wintersweet. Then I grew sad and soft as poor Third Aunt. But I finally buried my sadness in music and painting and preparing myself for life here, for my family's sake. And I learned to save my softness, the way Nurse did, for those few moments when someone like Yura needs kindness more than common sense.

I sip from my cup, and burn my tongue, and grimace to make Greenplum and Yura laugh. An easy game to play: One face crinkles inward, pleased, one opens out and shines.

Easy—when, then, did I stop playing? Have I changed as much as Wintersweet? The last time I saw my cousin she'd grown too anxious about her position in her new household; her lively ways had disappeared. By then, I knew why: Tender skin can feel a hundred burns, a thousand tiny slices in a single day. If you allow it to.

And what if the Mongol pony I used to ride within my bedcurtains is not exactly like the ponies guardsmen, soldiers, hunters, ride? When a teapot is shaped into a porcelain peach, with a curved branch for its handle and a well-placed leaf for a lid, no one tries to take a bite of it. Yet hasn't baked clay taken on the spirit of the fruit?

In my family's house this blue peach would be valued; here, where every dish and cup's a treasure, it has fallen out of favor, and is left to the maids. Yet it has outlasted any peach that grew on a living tree. I sip once more, feel the warm tea bathe my mouth and throat. At any rate, I can trust what I envision. That pony is my own. It won't desert me as a real horse, unhobbled, might.

Still, in the future I'll hold my tongue. I won't tell anyone about the strange pleasure of my childish pillow-riding. Anyway, for the next ten years, I must sleep quietly among the other maids, wherever our duty to Her Dowager Majesty takes us. Unless my luck is very good.

Besides, I never heard of any other girl who feels the breathless hunger that filled me when I shut my eyes and rode. Or the tremors and the sleepiness that came afterward. I doubt people would believe me if I did try to tell.

Not luck, but will: That's what determines the future of a palace maid. Or will and cleverness, despite whatever luck and karma bring. Remember, the late emperor's mother was a bondservant girl like you. When I begin to get lost in the unfamiliarity of my new life, the eunuchs' harshness, or the slow length of the short winter days, I remind myself of what Little Auntie Tuo said the night before I left for the Forbidden City.

I think this over again today, in the antechamber to Her Dowager Majesty's inner apartment. Yura dozes in the corner, near two maids who've been in service several years now, a complacent, heavy-featured girl named Goldflower and her friend Clarity. Often, there's work aplenty, but we've little to do just now save wait in case we're needed. Sewing the hair flowers and scarves and fancy shoes the eunuchs sell for us on the outside is forbidden when we're here—as if earning a bit of pocket money would slow us down when the Empress Dowager needs a message taken or something fetched.

Clarity has been combing and arranging Goldflower's hair for nearly an hour. She strokes and praises its thick darkness as they talk in an undertone. Goldflower allows her to try one fanciful style after another, though she never takes a turn at combing Clarity's.

They offered to quiz Yura and me on yesterday's lesson in palace regulations. I didn't like the forced arch of Goldflower's eyebrow, and said no. Memorizing comes naturally to me, after years of practice under Mama and Third Aunt. Yura just shook her head. She was already half asleep; last night, she sat nightshift with two ladies-in-waiting and another maid outside Her Dowager Majesty's bedroom. But when the eunuch who's always whispering with Greenplum put Yura on duty again today, she never said a word of protest.

Clarity's perfumed comb clatters to the floor. She jumps away from her friend. Yura blinks awake. But the stout senior eunuch who marches into the antechamber pays no mind. He hurries to the next room, where Her Majesty, Lady Brightcloud, and several other ladies sit. He must bear important news.

After he's admitted, Goldflower and Clarity giggle with relief and hide the evidence of their distraction from duty, weaving Clarity's hair into a maid's thick single braid, slipping the comb into a sleeve. Yura straightens her compact body. I think again of how we make our own luck. The eunuch might have been Chief Bao. Two nights ago I saw him personally beat a maid for little more than playing with a girlfriend's hair.

Perhaps he did so because of the dreary tension hanging over the palace these past few days. Yesterday the emperor left for the Temple of Heaven in the south part of Beijing; he was to stay in the Hall of Abstinence and make the winter solstice sacrifice before this morning's sunrise. Of course we maids had nothing to do with so important an event, but I've felt the unspoken nervousness since he began his three days of purification. All the palaces must have felt it: Even Her Dowager Majesty observed the prohibitions on meat and wine and strong-flavored food.

No commoner may watch the emperor's procession to the Temple of Heaven, but Greenplum seemed to know all about the musicians and the regiments of young noblemen, the expensive trappings of the imperial elephants, the officials' special robes. What she didn't know, what no one can, is whether everything went flawlessly this year, whether the kneelings and prostrations, the offering of the pigs and bullocks and sheep, were performed precisely as the ancient ways require. They must be: Heaven's favor, and earthly order, depend on success in the rituals.

The eunuch cuts his eyes toward us as he leaves, but we all four stand at the ready, and he goes on without a word. Soon Lady Brightcloud walks into the antechamber, smiling. "Ah, Little Miss Sun!" she says, "You're here," then nods to the other three.

Despite Greenplum's obvious efforts, Her Dowager Majesty's favorite has taken a liking to me. It started when she discovered how smoothly I read and even wrote both Manchu and Chinese: Although the lady-in-waiting is the daughter of a top Manchu banner officer, she speaks that language no better than Greenplum does. But she loves poetry, and twice now, when other matters occupied Her Dowager Majesty, the lady has summoned me to read quietly aloud to her.

How wise my parents were, when they prepared me for my life here! *Let me repay them,* I thought the first time Lady Brightcloud bade me lift a thin paper volume from its case and chant out its words. *Let me bring our family honor!*

Now Lady Brightcloud tells us what the eunuch said: that the imperial procession along the central avenue of the Chinese City, the rites, the prayers, the offering of the animals, went off without misstep or bad omen. Earth and Heaven move in accord; next year will go well. Her silent relief is like the change in Grandfather's moods at winter's end, when the yang light grows.

Her Dowager Majesty's in high spirits now, the lady-in-waiting says, and ready for an outing. Tomorrow, as we begin the weeks of greatest cold, the emperor will undertake a more festive duty: reviewing some of the empire's most skillful banner soldiers while they skate, shoot arrows, and compete with one another on the thick ice of the Great Liquid Pools, just outside the Forbidden City. His mother has decided to watch.

Lady Brightcloud takes a half-step toward me, moving smoothly on her high-platformed shoes. She tells me I'm to come along and help serve Her Dowager Majesty, adding that for this occasion I should wear something prettier—and warmer—than my plain blue maid's gown. "Manchu clothes, not

Han. But no need," she pauses and glances at the two older maids, "to take special pains with your hair."

So she could see what was going on out here in the antechamber. Or heard Clarity and Goldflower discussing styles, or the clatter of the comb. No one says a word.

Lady Brightcloud's voice continues evenly. "Imagine! Well past eighty and still willing to brave the cold. No wonder we all admire Her Dowager Majesty so." This isn't just a holiday outing, she says. I remember Father's descriptions from his days in the palace guard—nonetheless, I nod as I'm reminded how important it is that the bannermen maintain their readiness in these blessed peaceful times.

Goldflower's eyebrows knit. She doesn't like it that the lady-in-waiting addresses herself to me alone.

"Her Majesty the First Consort will be there as well," Lady Brightcloud adds. "Of course she'll have her own ladies and maids and eunuchs in attendance, but our mistress has decided her kitchen will provide a feast for all."

Yura's shoulder brushes my arm. *The emperor's First Consort!* her touch says, and I know that now she wants to go. Never mind that His Majesty hasn't promoted this daughter of the Wei-jia clan to empress; when his last empress died, he declared he'd never take another. With no living empress, the First Consort is second only to the Empress Dowager. And there can be but one First Consort at a time: She'll never have to share her station with another.

I must admit, Yura's not the only one who wants to see her. We know the First Consort leads the emperor's other ladies in his affections as well as in the rank he's raised her to—she's the mother of his two youngest daughters, and his last four sons. Father says the two boys still living both have a good chance at being named heir to the throne.

Yura says she has no desire to prolong her time in imperial service, but we always watch the First Consort carefully when she comes to pay her respects to the emperor's mother. We've discussed her more than once with other maids. Some call her weak chinned and weak spirited; I think her pretty, though she's well into her forties. And she's a lady of culture, with a connoisseur's love of paintings and fine calligraphy.

We watch her for another reason too. No maid in the Forbidden City can forget the First Consort is from a bondservant clan. Father told me that because of her, her family's registration changed. They are bondservants no more.

Lady Brightcloud's gaze falls on Yura's round, pleading face. Irresistible. A slight smile—perhaps at her own power to bestow happiness—and a few light words: Tomorrow my friend will also go along.

Once the lady-in-waiting has left to speak with the head eunuch in Her Dowager Majesty's kitchen, Goldflower's quick to tell us what a miserable time she had, the year *she* attended at one of the skating reviews. "The only place colder than the pavilion where you two will be scurrying about would be next to His Majesty's sledge, right out in the middle of the ice." She nods as if approving her own statement, and smooths the hair above her low forehead. "Of course, it's only men out there. But don't expect a good show. It's hard to see much from the shore, even when you aren't running your feet off."

Who cares what Goldflower says? I'll be leaving the countless gates and knotted passageways of the Forbidden City, at least for a few hours. I'll see a grand display of soldiers skimming free as dragonflies on the frozen lake. And then it comes to me: Perhaps I'll see my father somehow, on the way. Maybe I could even . . . Yes—he could take that dangerous stolen statue home, and end the foolish risk I've thoughtlessly created for myself.

I set the thought aside. Yura's frowning, her pleasure in the prospect spoiled as Goldflower describes the hurly-burly of keeping bored ladies happy at a banquet in the bitter cold.

But it's not hard to turn the older maid onto a different track. Who else might be there, I ask, trying to look as admiring of her knowledge as Yura often does. "Not the Dowager First Consort Geng, surely?"

Goldflower shakes her head, and Clarity snickers to show how little I know about what's what.

This second surviving lady of the late emperor's is a few years older even than the Empress Dowager, Goldflower points out. She rarely leaves her Palace of Tranquil Old Age off on the far side of the widows' quarters. Except when she pays her respects to Her Dowager Majesty: Our mistress out-ranked the older lady even before His Late Majesty died and the present emperor raised his mother to the highest rank of all.

In the end, Goldflower reveals how clearly she remembers an event she claims was a miserable blur of frigid dusty winds and crossness and overwork. "Both of His Majesty's two youngest sons are likely to be freezing with you in the pavilion again this year. The Fifteenth Prince may be the only person who won't mind the weather. In fact . . ." She whispers now: "he won't pay much attention to anything except the archery displays. His little brother will cling to his mother, then dash about and beg to be allowed out on the ice. Just as one might expect of him."

None of the imperial ladies at the three lowest ranks will be there; Goldflower's certain of that. As for the emperor's second-rank consorts, she continues, the Barin Mongol lady who bears the title of *The Distinguished* is not much in favor just now. "She's not bad looking for a Khalkha, but . . ." Goldflower purses her lips before continuing, as if I'd never heard. "She's never had a child, you know."

Clarity opens her mouth, but Goldflower nods her head decisively, and hurries on. "And we all know His Majesty spends little time these days with the daughter of the Lus, even if he did promote her to Felicitious Second-Ranked Consort a year or two ago." I know she too is childless, though word is she's a motherly sort and has won some of the cautious boyish affection of His Majesty's fifteenth son away from the First Consort.

But before Goldflower can continue her catalog, running through the consorts at the third rank and the fourth, Clarity breaks in. "You two must tell us if the Fourth-ranked Consort from the Uang family is there," she whispers softly, careful now. "The one titled *The Sincere*." Her face goes sly. "She's hot tempered, Lotus, and hard on her maids, they say. So you'd best not put on your airs." She looks quickly toward the next room. "But I also hear she's becoming a new favorite of His Majesty's."

Clarity leans close, and doles out her news, declaring that The Sincere Fourth-Ranked Consort is bound to be promoted if she bears a child. Goldflower tries to look like she's heard it all, but Clarity's as triumphant as if she herself had won the favor of an emperor. This leads to yet another low-voiced discussion of how the Dowager Empress became the handmaid of a future emperor when she was about my age, and talk of the late First Consorts Gao and Jin.

Yura looks troubled as she turns to Goldflower. "I know those two did well in life, considering they were once bondservant girls. But their promotions to First Consort came after they were dead! What good was that to them?"

Good for their families, I think. That branch of the Gaos was freed decades ago, and Father's sure the same will happen someday to the Jin lady's closest relatives: Her father's career still flourishes, and who knows what the future holds for her princely sons?

Clarity squeezes Yura's hand and grins. "Better than a posthumous *demo-tion!*" she hisses. She flashes two fingers in silent reference to His Majesty's second empress. The whole empire mourned when the first Manchu lady to be raised to empress died—but her successor somehow angered him so greatly that she received only a First Consort's honors at her death.

Empress or imperial consort, low-ranked concubine or palace maid, it's all the same to me, says Yura's face. But the shock on Goldflower's looks like it has more to do with jealousy—Clarity only now lets go of Yura's hand—than with this bold allusion to a scandal nearly ten years old.

I've heard enough. My mind turns briefly to the skating review, then to the way the courtyards looked the other day, when early morning light reflected off that rare glaze of ice. Far thinner than a lake, I think, yet as beautiful as any-thing I may hope to see tomorrow. And vanished now.

The others talk on. No one, I notice, mentions the Muslim Fourth-ranked Consort from the New Territories. Not surprising, really, since she lives out in the Imperial City, and keeps to herself as much as she can. They don't even know she came into the Forbidden City to have her portrait painted by that hairy foreigner.

Yet I still remember everything the Muslim woman said and did the day it came to me that the goddess statue did not belong in that neglected shrine. The lady in no way resembles the First Consort, and she's hardly from a loyal family that keeps to Manchu ways. What is it about her, then, that has won the favor of His Majesty? What can I learn from my memory of her?

Yura and I walk together among the maids behind the Empress Dowager's huge palanquin as it's borne toward the West Glorious Gate of the Forbidden City. And toward my father. Breathe in, I tell myself. You have to breathe.

My friend too looks sharp around us when we pass the offices of the Imperial Household Bureau near the gate, though she still knows nothing of the bronze goddess I am carrying. But we see no one who comes close to my descriptions of my handsome father; I let my head drop, and feel the weight of my hidden burden, and refuse to regret that mysterious urge to take it for my own.

Out the gate and across the Forbidden City's moat, into the Imperial City parkland around the Great Liquid Pools: a clear, nearly windless day. Except for being hustled with the other new maids to lessons in deportment at the temple school outside the rear gate, this is the first time I've left the high red walls. My heart lifts. Still, it's cold enough to keep both me and Yura head-down as we make our way to the Gold Tortoise and Jade Rainbow Bridge, the elaborate span of marble dividing the central and northern sections of the lake.

Flags wave along the shore and atop three large archways set up on the ice. Well over a thousand skaters, half in scarlet jackets, half in gold, talk or glide or limber up for the races, the ice-wrestling and ice-football to come. Yura's delighted by the sight, though in truth I prefer the colorless droop of the bare willow trees on the sloping bank.

As the ladies take their places in the prettiest of the lakeside buildings, the eunuchs fan the charcoal fires, prepare plates of appetizers, and order us maids about. I hand Lady Brightcloud a fox-fur lap robe for Her Majesty, and realize it used all my luck just to get here: How silly to think I might get a glimpse of Father, much less pass him a stolen statue with a whispered suppli-cation to take it home for me! Unfilial to put him to such risk. Stupid to sup-pose I'd have the chance.

Back in the kitchen behind the pavilion where the ladies have settled in, I crumple the note I wrote Father and toss it on the blazing coals. A few cash and a smile for one of the friendlier eunuchs will get my letters to his office. As for the statue, I can return it to its hiding place behind the sliding panel in my jewelry box. But that can't last forever: What if someone finds it, recalls seeing it in that dusty shrine? Perhaps I ought to drop it down a well. If I ever knew why I took it, I can't remember now. It looks like so many others I—

"Girl!"

I whirl, and recognize the young man—boy, really, he's little older than I, and no taller—by his clothing: the Fifteenth Prince. He waves away the eunuch who bustles up to him, and grants me a practiced smile. "Give me some bread, or whatever's hot and plain," he says, demanding and tentative at once, as if he were any well-mannered but hungry youth in his grandmother's kitchen, and I were any serving maid.

He's not. And I'm not. I refuse to be: I didn't need Little Auntie Tuo's advice to know that much. So I keep my spine straight as hers, even when I drop my eyes and take the plate the head cook himself has thrust in my hands. Is this odd, indecorous meeting to be my great chance? Somehow Mama found a safe place in my father's heart, a place not guaranteed to every wife. Somehow, his concubine—but how?

Surely not by staring gape-mouthed, as Yura's staring now. And not, I think, with the simpers of the maids clustered close beside her.

"You're new." The prince is still addressing me. He asks my family's name, and what they call me. I feel the absolute attention of every person in the kitchen upon the two of us.

This husky boy could be the next emperor. I could—

Someone looses a high-pitched giggle. The prince's eyes flash over to her face. "Another young beauty!" he exclaims, as if human beauty were a new thing to him. "I had no idea my grandmother's garden held so many flowers in the wintertime."

The guardsman beside him laughs heartily. The kitchen eunuchs soon join in. "Well said, Your Highness," the guardsman says. "A winter-blooming lotus, the tall one is!"

I ought to peek at the prince from beneath my eyelashes. I ought to purse my lips as if both pleased and displeased by his impetuosity, or maybe let their corners lift in a hint of pleasure held back. But something in me—not modesty, and not simply embarrassment—refuses to let me move.

The prince asks the other maid her name, seizes the steamed roll from my plate, and strides away, leaving the women's world to join his father on the ice. My gaze fixes on his shoulders, strong looking as those of any of the full-grown guards falling into place in the prince's wake. The shoulders of an expert bowman. Like my father's, I think.

Then he turns around. Meets my eyes. Stares at the girl he's caught daring to stare back at him, and turns away.

The buzz of talk that follows—did his father summon him? did his mother send him out? did he himself choose to stop here first for simple food rather than banquet delicacies?—is broken a few moments later by the appearance of one of Her Dowager Majesty's attendant eunuchs, come to see what's holding up the service of the venison, the chicken stewed with mushrooms, and the rest.

A great relief: I'm tired of fending off silly questions and sillier jokes. Soon we maids are dismissed for the moment, as the eunuchs and ladies-in-waiting attend to the senior ladies and the noisy little Seventeenth Prince, with hot food and warm wine.

We huddle at one end of the veranda. Yura and the other girls return to their talk of the Fifteenth Prince, who now stands on the ice beside his father's yellow boat-shaped sledge. Absorbed in informing one another of the prince's reputation for patience and obedience, his skill with bow and gun and reins, they leave me in peace; I look beyond the crowd around His Majesty, to the long line of skaters that curves and coils like a swimming dragon.

A hundred soldiers in winter uniforms spread their arms as they twist and turn in single file, though I suspect their posture serves mostly to point out to us the difficulty of what they do with such assurance. Some bear flags in the colors of the eight banner units—yellow and white and red and blue, half plain and half with broad elaborate borders. Others shoot at targets dangling over-head, as they pass one man behind the next, precisely spaced, through the three archways on the ice.

Beyond the chatter of the girls around me, I catch the announcement of a eunuch messenger that after this company presents the "Great Scorpion" for-mation, another group will form a human pyramid. But it's the burst of laughter from the nearby ladies that silences the other maids.

Lady Brightcloud's voice rings loudly in the sudden hush. "Little Miss Sun!" she calls. I hurry to her side.

The Fifteenth Prince, she tells me, has kindly sent word asking his grand-mother to favor her new maids with a tidbit from her own table—and men-tioned me by name. I stand unmoving, dumb. "You'll want to thank Her Dowager Majesty before you receive her bounty," the lady-in-waiting says. I fall to my knees, grateful to hide my blazing face as I touch my forehead to the pavilion floor.

But when I stand, one sight blurs out Lady Brightcloud's thoughtful coun-tenance and the amused or waspish looks of the other ladies-in-waiting. It's not the inward, distant cast of Her Dowager Majesty's wrinkled squarish face; I've seen that often enough. It's certainly not the frosty whiteness of the sugar-koumiss candies, each shaped into a plum blossom, in the fancy box Lady Brightcloud lifts from the Dowager Empress's table and places directly into the hands I can only just keep from shaking. It's the measuring—and skeptical—

expression of the prince's mother, the fading, lovely, tight-mouthed First Consort, as she looks at me.

That night, I dream a powerful dream. Yura and I race on horseback across the stone-strewn lower slope of a huge brown mountainside. I pull ahead, breathing hard, urging my mount as I lean forward, as I squeeze my thighs against its heated flanks. The sound of hoof-beats behind me drops away.

And then returns. *Faster,* I think, and *harder.* It's no longer Yura I ride with, I know that, but I'm not afraid, only anxious to win the game. I look back over my shoulder and laugh, though I can't make out my pursuer's face. Someone whoops. The wide sky and the valley swell around us. We race on, unrestrained.

I approach a pile of stones that supports a pole tied with fluttering strips of cloth. Words—prayers?—wave in the head wind. But before I can make out the script, I've passed the whole thing by.

My pony stops short before a round white tent. A yurt, of course. Suddenly, I'm inside.

It's dusky, despite the light that streams in through the wood-framed doorway and the circular opening at the peak of the roof. Dusky, but not with the chill shadows of the Forbidden City's lanes: The inside of the yurt spreads out warm with patterned rugs and gaily decorated chests, with a crowded altar beneath a dazzling newly painted tangka, with a neatly cluttered cupboard, rumpled bedding, a tidy heap of clothes. The coals of the dung fire in the tent's center glow, though no one's tending them.

The altar, I realize. *I'm supposed to look at the altar.* I glimpse a supple-bodied woman cast in bronze, and start to move closer. But then it vanishes into the cosy jumble of the owners' lives.

Instead, I reach down and feel the bedding. It too is colorful, and warm.

A shadow falls across the light. *The Fifteenth Prince,* I think. *That's who rode the other horse!*

No. The boy, the man, who walks toward me now is taller, slimmer, a little older. His gaze rests steady, no hint of anxiety at the corners of his eyes. This time I don't refuse it. In fact, I don't think at all about what I should or shouldn't do. I stare back. He pinches my cheek lightly, playfully. He begins to say my name.

"Lotus." Again: "Lotus. Lotus!"

A square room crowded with sleeping bodies. A single guttering candle. A shining, worried face looms near mine. I see the delicate brown mole—sign of great change in a single lifetime—upon its chin: Yura, leaning toward me from her spot on the bed we share.

"Lotus," she says again, her whisper hoarse. "You were, you were dreaming." She grins. "You kicked me awake, you know, with your thrashing. But I don't think the other girls would appreciate—"

Someone half snores in her sleep. Yura grins again. She reaches into the shadows, opens a carefully folded handkerchief, shows me two perfect plum blossoms. Not plum blossoms. Sugar-koumiss candies.

"I saved one for each of us," she says, and crunches down on the tip of one white petal. "They taste of the northland, don't you think? The koumiss, I suppose. I'll pretend I'm back home, eating snow."

Then she stops grinning.

Home, I think. Yura puts her arms around me as I bite my lip. I feel our bodies start to shake with noiseless sobs.

Days later, I must push the memory of that dream, and of that waking, aside again as I stare out into the bare branched phoenix trees and gingkos, the somber cypresses of the Garden of Compassion and Tranquility—all overlaid with windblown winter dust. Her Dowager Majesty has left the rush and fuss of preparations for the New Year's season, to make a day-long retreat. And I am in disgrace. My stomach squeezes into a knot of shame.

I brought it on myself, in the central worship hall of this garden enclosure the emperor's mother loves even more than the chapel in her palace or the Flower Glory Hall, where she meets the other senior ladies to receive the lamas' blessings and watch them drive evil spirits off. On her lama's instructions, Her Dowager Majesty has come to ward off a danger to her health forseen by an oracle. Here of all places, today of all days, I ought to have maintained my control.

We maids have fasted since noon yesterday. The Empress Dowager wanted us to take part in this small pilgrimage; she wanted out attentions fixed, our spirits pure. We followed Her Dowager Majesty and her ladies-in-waiting, bowing down full length at each stop on the circuit of the stately buildings framing the north end of the garden: the Hall of Auspicious Clouds, the Hall of Compassionate Shelter, the Hall of Precious Images with its magnificent bronze pantheon.

She lighted altar lamps and recited mantra chants. By the time we finished the circuit for the third time, my head spun with the buddhas, guardians, goddesses, bodhisattvas that floated on murals or filled niches, that sat cross-legged above altars or covered the outsides of shrines. We paused for a moment before the wide-eaved central hall. I breathed in, and in that instant saw how the garden and its ring of worship halls formed a kind of mandala, a palace for these deities: so many faces, benevolent, ferocious, wrapped in contemplation. So many arms, signing grace or bearing emblems of unimaginable force.

I wanted to make the round again, to look at every detail of each holy one, their brilliant pigments shining beneath canopies in ill-lit inner rooms. Each seemed to know what Padma told me once: *This world that causes you such unhappiness is a buddha field, a pure land, a paradise for practicing the dharma law—if you can see it so.*

I never can. But just then it flickered through my mind that if this garden is like a mandala, then perhaps the same could be said of the Forbidden City's rows and rings of palaces, its web of corridors that branch and turn. Light-headedness rushed over me. I blinked and steadied myself by looking down at the pavement's checkerboard of mosaic river pebbles and smooth stone squares.

We followed the Empress Dowager into the central worship hall. The eunuch lamas repeated their sacred words. My arms ached from all the prostrations, but perhaps today, I thought, I would learn to see what Padma sees.

There, the incense hung more heavily, one day's smoke layered over the smokes of months and years before. Beyond rafters painted with flaming jewels and gilt dragons, beyond the candlesticks and vases, the embroidered cutwork hangings and ornate emblems of the Eight Buddhist Treasures, stood an altar I was finally unable—or unwilling—to see after all.

I don't know why. Perhaps hunger stole my energies, perhaps the stale air or the crowd before me: half a dozen ladies-in-waiting, twice as many maids, the rows of lamas with Her Dowager Majesty's teacher at their head. Perhaps tiredness—I woke this morning weary.

I squinted at the endless gilded-metal knot standing on its pedestal at one side of the altar. To the left, I could just make out lines of Sanskrit glittering on the wall above orderly ranks of small image plaques. My head throbbed. I began to count: on each narrow shelf, fifteen flame-shaped plaques—identical lustrous images of a holy being whose name I did not know. Was it Amitayus, buddha of boundless life? Yet someday even Her Dowager Majesty—

Don't think that. On the side walls, more shelves, more deities with their auras. How many? More chanting of the sutras, more golden flames, more smoke.

More prostrations: Blindly following Yura and Clarity beside me, I bent down over a wide polished board, pushed my hands along it till I lay stretched out full length, facedown, and bent my arms to clasp my hands above my head. Then I stood up quickly, dropped and flattened and raised my hands in salutation once again. Stood up, swayed toward a flurry of trembling aura flames. Dropped and felt the giddy air rush out as I stood up again.

My stomach slipped. I couldn't have eaten if I'd wanted to. Ten days ago, we broke another fast with Twelfthmonth Eighthday porridge, in honor of the day the Buddha Shakyamuni achieved enlightenment. Now I was remembering how the familiar saltless taste of soupy rice and sticky millet and red beans had reminded me of Mama making the porridge with her own slim hands. Every year, she gave me red jujubes to form a lion atop each serving in the special bowls. Every year, Nurse joined her in praising my clumsy skill.

The prostrations stopped. We maids stood silent. I knew I had to think of something besides the Twelfthmonth Eighthdays of my childhood, besides the cheery gatherings and solemn sacrifices approaching as the year turns and carries me still farther from the time when my mother was alive. Something besides the gaudy Lantern Festival, and then the anniversary, that await me when the New Year's season ends.

More sutras swirled into my ears. I couldn't see what the lamas and Her Dowager Majesty were doing. But I wasn't meant to. I only had to keep myself from crying. I only had to think of other things.

We began again: stand, drop, flatten, stand. The rhythm, like a pony's hoofbeats. The breathless dizziness. My dream, the young man taller than the

Fifteenth Prince, pressing closer, warmth in a world of cold. I want him to come back, but I don't know what he wants of me.

And then that young man reached toward me, through rows of shifting gilded aura flames. His hand was as finely molded as the hands of the stolen goddess hidden in my jewelry box. It touched me, just as in my dreams.

Lady Brightcloud said I shrieked before I fainted. I only remember that he pulled me toward him, as if through a gauzy cutwork drapery, or an unending weave of knotted silken cord.

The next moment I looked up at Yura and a circle of other faces, like a wheel of guardian goddesses set a-spin. Each watcher showed her own blend of concern or shock or fear or secretive amusement. Only Yura's large eyes hinted that she might have caught sight of what I saw—if not the insistent, almost girlishly beautiful youth, at least a glimpse of the living golden flames.

Now I sit alone, banished to one of the deserted side halls at the south end of the garden. Lady Brightcloud herself, and Goldflower, pulled me hastily out of the worship hall. Seeing I was all right, the lady-in-waiting pressed her lips together, ordered Goldflower to see me to a safe resting place, and hurried back to join the Empress Dowager in her devotions.

Goldflower half led, half supported me down the long walk through the trees south of the worship halls, past curving roofs and a courtyard gate, past the rectangular pond straddled by a small pavilion. She let me sit on the step to a well-house near the rockery at the bottom of the garden, while she herself drew up water for me to drink.

In all this time, neither of us said a word. The water might have been sweet dew. I sipped it slowly, afraid of what could happen if I gulped, then thanked Goldflower for her kindness.

"I'm hungry too," she muttered. "And it isn't you or me we're asking bless-ings for."

Dangerous words. The well-rope creaked. If I'd brought that stolen statue along, I could get rid of it.

Goldflower's full mouth twisted. Less than ten years, she blurted, since they put up most of the garden's buildings—at a cost of nearly sixty thousand taels of silver. Enough to keep each of the thousands of maids and eunuchs in the Forbidden City well fed for years.

I shrugged. She nodded. "You'd best wait in the side hall there," she said, the usual matter-of-fact tone returning to her voice. "It's empty now, but it looks as if one of the lamas has been inside since the dust storm ended yesterday. Perhaps he's left you a few coals in the brazier. I'll make sure you're not forgotten when we finally leave." She gave me a wry smile, and walked away.

So now I stare from the side hall's veranda out into bare branches and somber evergreens. Or at the marble railing around the pond, at its pavilion's latticed windows, tightly closed today. Or across the garden to another side hall. Or back to the trees again.

When I've had enough of fresh cold air, I discover Goldflower's sharp eyes caught the truth: Earlier today, someone made a fire in a brazier in the center of the long single room. The embers warm my hands; I shudder once, violently, throwing off the chill.

My stomach eases. My headache's gone. The charcoal burns more evenly than the dung fire in the yurt I dreamed about. It glows too weakly to form a veil of flames.

That last thought sets me moving, pacing the length and width of the side hall, tracing its shape as earlier our procession traced the squared-off ring of image halls, up and over and down and over again.

In a corner, I come across a gray-bronze censer, mottled green with age, standing alone on a simple table. Whoever lighted the fire in the brazier must have left this incense smoking too. The last vapors unwind in a papered window's light.

The censer looks like a mountain on a lotus stem, or an island floating above the shallow sea in its base. There's a name for this special shape. But what?

Broadmountain. Mama taught me that. *A broadmountain censer, a relic of the Han dynasty.* She must have—yes, I remember her showing one to me, when I was no more than four or five. Where is it now? Did the family have to sell it in a bad year? Had Father brought it home on loan from an antiques dealer, pretending he might buy it so she could enjoy it for a while?

She valued its fine crafting, its perfectly cast details: I remember that. And she took my small hand in hers and waved it through the smoke, and when I tried to catch a handful she laughed the sweetest possible laugh.

The tiny figures covering the upper half of the censer now before me blur and waver. Whatever else happened the day Mama taught me its name, that day is lost now. Lost entirely, if I hadn't grasped this fragment out of memory. Lost forever, when I forget again.

THE CENSER

Vou too now stare at a smoking censer: tarnished, beautiful, cast two millennia ago in broadmountain form. It rises from a shallow basin, like a bronze goblet—or a lotus bud above a pond—on a stem wound round by water dragons, gold inlaid.

Smoke slides, fragrant as remembrance, from the openwork of the conical lid. Between those airy crevices, incised deer and tigers wander wild metallic peaks that lift one above another to the central summit. Woodcutters and hunting hounds, one-horned spirit beasts and birds with swirling wings roam among its sheer cliffs and secret caves. This mountain island is a realm alive with powers mortals may confront, but never tame.

For you, it is the realm of the lost, the only, past. Those fine-line figures beneath the dull patina were caught up by the artist in one instant out of time. And so were caught forever *in* it.

Do you mourn them? Do you envy? The censer was made to comfort its owner with a vision of transcendence: Crafted two millennia ago, in the imperial workshops of the Han dynasty, it was presented to a prince's wife by her sister, who'd just been named empress. A few years or decades later, the censer—and its owner—were entombed.

And then? Long repose within the earth, while a body made from dust returned to its element. Grave robbers. Clandestine sales. Generations of appreciative connoisseurs, acquisitive collectors, greedy heirs.

Once, the censer came by chance to a stoop-shouldered scholar from the Soong capital of Lin-an, but he soon died far away, in the malarial swamplands of the south. At the time of the Mongol conquest, it was reburied for safekeeping, in a household courtyard; its next owner dug it up from beneath a still-warm heap of ash. During the Ming, a long-armed storyteller glimpsed its green-gray crags, briefly sunstruck on a shelf in an antiques dealer's shop. Two hundred years later, a musician in Nanjing caught the scent of their smoke clouds as she played her chyn. Her song of longing for one departed twined with those tenuous vapors; perhaps her other losses, her buried griefs, wove among them too.

This mountain of spirits rising from the world ocean might eventually have made its way to some museum, to stand glass boxed, climate controlled, on the arid plains of the American Midwest. Instead, it has come to you. Hold it for a moment, feel its weight cupped in the moistureless skin of your two hands. Let your gaze follow the hilltops' upward forms. This small terrain, this cosmos poured in hot to a lost wax mold, reaches from the liquid abyss at its base toward the elusive realms of immortality.

Place the thing now carefully back upon the table. How long since someone else burnt incense beneath that tapering lid?

Pungent clouds stream forth like warm fog rising up from hillsides after rain, like mists from long cascades. They are the life waters of the highlands, made aerial, trailing skyward. May they ease the roving souls who have known the sight or heft of this craggy long-lived thing. May they ease the souls all who breathe in and remember and who mourn.

AN UNOFFICIAL HISTORY OF THE LADIES AND THE SERVING GIRLS IN THE MANCHU PALACES

Preface to the English Edition

As a lad in Old Peking before the fall of the Manchu dynasty, I would listen for hours as my grandfather told me stories he had heard in his youth, especially tales of the grandest and cruelest of the Manchu emperors, whose reign began precisely two hundred years ago, in 1736.

How remarkable I find it, that I had history itself from the living mouth of one who had it from the mouths of witnesses, or at any rate from persons at no more than one or two removes from actuality! The old gentleman held a special feeling for those hapless young females pressed into imperial service; it is their legacy I feel I must transmit as best I can, supplementing it with my own casual researches into the written record.

My grandfather spoke in the argot of the true Peking-ese, spiced with its tongue-curling *r*s and distinctive idioms—including, it must be admitted, a few words judiciously selected from the degenerate Manchu tongue. To the shaven-headed chappie I was then, his reminiscences surpassed the "victory songs" of the Manchu street entertainers with their eight-sided drums, and even the historical romances or fairy tales expounded from the raised platform in the smoky tea shop where idle Bannermen often sat but a threadbare-elbow's width away from me, my grandfather, and his chums.

Many of the events described below took place within Peking's "Forbidden

City." I beg the reader to bear in mind that in those times the opulent edifices and marble-paved peristyles yielded an impression quite unlike that of the pillaged, weedy derelicts of these latter days.

Other notable incidents occurred in the sumptuous Old Summer Palace (the Yuan-ming Yuan) just outside the city, as it was not burnt and looted by the Anglo-French forces until October 1860. Some episodes, of course, came to pass in the nearby Yi-ho Yuan, as we now call the summer palace favored, in the final decades of the dying regime, by the infamous dowager who ruled from behind a screen behind the throne.

Still others are set (most entrancingly of all to the young dreamer I was) upon the stage, as it were, of the remote summer capital Jehol, or "Warm River." The Manchu rulers traveled thither almost annually from the establishment, in 1703, of what was soon dubbed "The Mountain Estate for Escaping Hot Weather," until the death there of the Hsien Feng emperor in 1861, the year of my own birth.

Now I am grown old, and the Manchus have been overthrown by patriotic native Chinese. Peking, the "Northern Capital" that was, is known these days as Pei-p'ing, "Northern Peace," and other alien invaders threaten our homeland: the Japanese puppet masters in the Northeast's so-called nation of "Manchukuo"—which recently swallowed up Jehol. Defense against any future incursions into China must perforce be guided by the government of our Republic from this ancient southern capital where I now make my home.

I shall not comment on the present state of my valiant yet battle-weary nation, for who can say what may transpire tomorrow, or next year? Rather, I shall merely express the hope that European and New-World readers will join me in a fond look back at the beauties and the blemishes of another China, long ago. Although my foreign friends are bound to find oddities and even shocks herein, I trust they will remember that every nation has its sorrows, and its puzzle knots.

> "The Old Codger of the Lotus Pond"
> Nanking, December 11, 1936
> *beneath the lamp*

According to regulations published in the time of the Ch'ien-lung emperor (who officially reigned 1736–1796, but after abdication maintained power until his death early in 1799), the Empress Dowager's annual household allotment included 20 taels (Chinese ounces) of gold, 2,000 of silver, and over a hundred bolts of various cloths, along with special threads and furs.

One day's food ration for her palace begins, "50 *chin* (Chinese pounds) of dressed meat, one pig, one sheep . . ." and runs to 32 items in all. This is to say nothing of the lavish supply of charcoal, candles, and the like, nor of her official share of such regional offerings as delicious Hami melons, litchee fruits, prized fish from the Northeast, and top-grade Dragonwell tea.

By way of comparison, a palace maid annually received anywhere from 6 taels of silver, to none at all. Their rations of cloth and foodstuffs were similarly small.

Although the regulations limited the Empress Dowager to 12 maids (with 10 allowed to the Empress when there was one, 8 apiece to the First Imperial Consort and the consorts of the second rank, 6 to those of the third, et cetera), there were actually many more.

When the Banner girls of various ranks lined up for the selections of maids, ladies-in-waiting, or concubines to the imperial house, they were said to resemble strings of pearls.

Grandfather and I used to wonder how many deliberately failed the serving-girls' entry tests of embroidery and housekeeping skills. As they bid farewell to the families they might never visit again, what must they have felt?

Once in the second lunar month, when the Imperial Household had settled into the extravagant palazzos of the Yuan-ming Yuan in the suburbs, two maids attached to the emperor's mother took advantage of a rare free hour to play alone upon a swing in a garden modeled after Suchow's finest.

One flower-faced girl stood on the swing that hung from its scarlet frame beside some budding willow trees. Her young friend, a Mongol lass, pushed her 'til she soared beyond the railing of the terrace which held the garden.

We may imagine how their blossom-pink cheeks glowed with pleasure and exertion, how the multicolored streamers of their springtime dresses trailed and fluttered in the breeze.

A son of the emperor happened to pass below the garden terrace. Looking up, he caught sight of a flying maiden come from fairy land, and swore to take her for his own.

The smoking of opium in any form was forbidden within the Manchu palaces. But more than one frustrated lady or despairing eunuch turned to it "on the sly."

I apologize for pointing out to my foreign friends that one reason the Western traders, and governments, of the last two centuries insisted they be allowed to import this pernicious drug to China was to fill the empty holds of ships arriving in our ports to purchase silks—and to balance out the great eastward flow of Western silver bullion in exchange for Chinese tea. One of my American friends (who herself takes no beverage stronger than boiled water) has remarked that the first "dope fiends" involved in this sad transaction were, therefore, not among the Chinese!

Yet many of my countrymen also lined their pockets with profits from this miserable trade. What purpose in quarreling over the division of regret and blame when there is enough and plenty for all?

The problem of opium within the very Forbidden City appears to have begun before 1800: My grandfather had the following pathetic story from his elder uncle.

A maid in the Palace of Compassion and Tranquility named Ch'ing-mei, or "Green Plum," had formed a romantic attachment with a eunuch. (I hasten to inform my readers that the poor unmanned creatures whom poverty or ambition had led into palace service were inspected most thoroughly! Nevertheless, such liaisons, however fruitless or risible they may seem to the modern mind, were quite "the thing" within that closed-in miniature metropolis.)

The eunuch's taste for a soporific smoke led to quarrels between the sweethearts. After one such altercation, perhaps to prove the depth of his feeling, or his rage that Ch'ing-mei had hidden his long-stemmed pipe, he slashed his wrist with a knife. Though the wound was not unduly serious, in accord with the palace regulations forbidding the desecration of the imperial home by any attempt at self-inflicted death, he was executed.

Wracked with anguish and guilt, Ch'ing-mei hanged herself from a storeroom rafter. Again the regulations dictated the punishment: Her entire family were sent off to a remote desert region to eke out their lives as military slaves.

Selected ladies of the emperor awaited his nightly pleasure in resting rooms behind his living quarters within the Forbidden City, the Hall of Mental Cultivation. A eunuch presented a trayful of cards at suppertime, each inscribed with a lady's name, that the emperor might make his choice. Gossip reports that the eunuchs would call in through the bedroom window if the emperor dallied beyond the allotted time!

In the various summer palaces, such matters were handled in a less constrained fashion, which perhaps helps explain their popularity as the seats of court.

At Jehol, for example, the ladies' quarters adjacent to the emperor's own Main Palace were renovated and enlarged by order of the Ch'ien-lung emperor in the fourteenth year of his reign (1749); after this, his ladies no longer dwelt in the "bookchambers" next to his bedroom in the Main Palace's Hall of Mists and Waves. Instead, a little-known side door—which could only be opened from within—allowed whichever lady the emperor fancied to be brought from the nearby zenana to the Hall of Mists and Waves.

I do not know if they were really stripped, as people said, by the attendant eunuchs and carried into the imperial bedroom wrapped only in a quilt.

Although the Manchus claimed to uphold a strict morality between the sexes, the truth is that before the end of the eighteenth century, corruption had already begun to weaken the denizens of the court. In those days, a certain retired palace official had a son who succeeded him in the imperial service. Though the son was obedient and respectful, he privately disdained his father's taste for unhealthy habits, and for illegal books and "curios" devoted to the *ars amatoria*.

One day the father presented the son with a picture album of "clandestine amusements," ordering him to use his connections among the eunuchs to introduce the illicit paintings into the residence of a susceptible prince. Later, when the son examined the album, he discovered that the face of the young woman lewdly cavorting in scene after scene strongly resembled the innocent countenance of his only daughter!

I was a newly married stripling when Grandfather related this, and he unfortunately had entered his dotage. So I cannot confirm how he learned of it, or indeed whether it is true. Yet I myself have read an account of a not-dissimilar album featuring the visage of an emperor.

Official records indicate that the Ch'ien-lung emperor had twenty-nine empresses, consorts, and concubines in all. Yet no fewer than forty-one women were buried in his dark palatial crypt in the Eastern Imperial Tombs.

Grandfather once overheard his mother discussing with a friend an event at one of the "travel palaces" where the Imperial Household stopped during the seven-day journey to the Jehol estate. As usual, the military attendants and lesser palace functionaries made camp outside the small courtyard around the rather simple building. Personal servants took their places in tents within the courtyard wall. The emperor and ladies of rank slept inside the lodge.

But somehow in the "hurly-burly," a servant girl became separated from the other women. Being a person of extraordinary disposition—at once proud and melancholic—she seized the chance to wander while the summer twilight lingered among the picturesque pinewoods beyond the camp, for it was her first journey thither with the court.

Even my Western readers will remark the girl's unusual degree of independence, not to say foolhardiness. Yet I daresay she felt protected by her connection to the imperial family, and of course by all those soldiers milling about within the range of a single scream.

Then, in a shady glen, she encountered the one sort of man who could dare attempt to make something of the situation: a young imperial clansman of the highest rank. He too had wandered off, weary of the clamor and bustle of the imperial passage, and in the deepening shadows he approached her courteously.

The husband of my great-grandmother's friend, a faithful attendant of this young man, had secretly followed his master, desiring that the imperial youth come to no harm. He saw the meeting in the glade, saw that the girl was a veritable "Helen of Troy" or "Aphrodite," but discretion urged him to fall back and wait some distance away, so he never knew exactly what transpired.

The next day, this same attendant was bidden to take a small religious artifact of some sort, and quietly bribe a eunuch to deliver it to a particular tall and noble-spirited servant girl in the employ of an imperial lady. One supposes it was intended as a gift to woo her heart.

As the Manchus did not automatically make the first-born son his father's heir, the future Chia-ch'ing emperor was secretly selected successor to the throne late in 1773, when he was in his early teens. Later, the imperial genealogies recorded him as the Fifth Prince, the actual fifth son of the emperor having died at a young age, although he was in fact the fifteenth boy-child born to the emperor. Such a "retroactive promotion" of a monarch was not without precedent.

His father's selection of this hunt-loving Fifteenth Prince over the best of his half-brothers seems to have been a choice of the Manchu martial virtues over the literary and artistic talents of the Fourth, Sixth, and Eleventh Princes. But it may also have been the result of persuasions exercised by the mother of the new heir, the First Imperial Consort from the Wei clan.

The Chia-ch'ing emperor's affection for his first empress (born to the bondservant Hetala clan and mother of his heir, the Tao-kuang emperor) is well known. Several of his lower-ranking ladies also came from the loyal bondservant class. People whispered, moreover, that his first real love had been a bondservant girl.

My grandfather took quite an interest in the history of the First Imperial Consort who had given birth to the Chia-ch'ing emperor, during whose reign he himself was born. Although her clan name was given out to be "Wei-jia" (a Chinese rendering of a Manchu name, "Weyigiya" or some such, I believe), she was born to a Chinese family with the perfectly regular Chinese name of "Wei."

This First Imperial Consort was only in her late forties when she died in 1775.

She was posthumously promoted to empress when her son's rank as crown prince was made public in 1795.

The official story came to be that the family of this favorite of the Ch'ien-lung emperor had long served the dynasty as members of one of the "Chinese-martial" Banners, and were promoted to a Manchu Banner (and given their "Manchu" clan name) after their daughter's rise within the harem. But in fact they were known to have been bondservants to the Imperial Household.

Such was the need of the Ch'ien-lung and the Chia-ch'ing emperors, father and son, to declare their "Manchu-ness"!

One year in midspring, at the time imperial offerings were to be made at the Altar of the Goddess of Silkworms (sometimes styled the "Silkweb Empress," wife of the legendary Yellow Emperor) an interesting thing happened. Since there was no empress living, it fell to this same First Imperial Consort Wei-jia, or Wei, to perform the rite, this being considered the "distaff" equivalent of the annual Primal Plowing by the emperor at the Altar of Agriculture.

A few days before the ritual, the First Consort and her suite left her palazzo in the suburban Yuan-ming Yuan, returning to the capital by boat through the Yi-ho Yuan's Lake K'un-ming and the Ch'ang-ho Canal, to the northwest corner of the city walls. Other ladies of rank followed, hurrying to arrive in time to welcome the Empress Dowager, who with her attendants made her grand entry last of all.

The day before the silkworm rites, the First Consort was required to go to the Hall of Union in the Forbidden City, there to examine the baskets and hooks for picking the mulberry leaves fed to the silkworms after hatching. This year, the elderly Empress Dowager decided to observe her—she must have been a fearsome mother-in-law indeed!

Naturally, First Consort Wei could say nothing directly about the old harridan breathing down her neck. Her ire fell rather upon one of the maids in the dowager's retinue. "That girl again!" she whispered loudly to a confidante. "That haughty girl! Do you see how rudely she stares at me?"

Needless to say, word of this swiftly reached the senior lady, who only nodded her head at this criticism of one of her own. The next day, First Consort Wei went to a stone terrace in the mulberry grove just outside the Forbidden City, performed her kow-tows at the altar there, made libation, and completed her worship of the Silkworm Goddess, careful to commit no error that might bring upon her criticism from the dowager.

When the silkworms hatched, all the consorts, princesses, and other ladies went again to the pleasance of the mulberry grove for the feeding ritual. Court musicians played the ceremonial music as first the emperor's top lady, and then the princesses and others of high rank plucked the mulberry leaves, giving them over to be examined for "bad spots" upon another sacred terrace of stone. The Empress Dowager sat on a special stage to admire the vernal scene. Servants took over the real work of tending to the voracious worms, and the imperial ladies toasted one another and began a banquet to restore themselves from their "labors."

The atmosphere grew a bit less formal, and the Empress Dowager announced a new entertainment. From behind a screen of downy green mulberry trees rose the first dulcet notes of a simple springtime song played upon a Chinese zither. Though it was not the performance of a highly trained master, the melody conveyed with gossamer sensitivity the agreeable pastoral mood of the time and place.

"Your new musician is a person of outstanding feeling!" exclaimed the First Imperial Consort. Even those ladies who did not share her reputation for fine taste agreed.

At that, the Empress Dowager summoned the musician forth. It was the very maid First Consort Wei had criticized.

As for all this taking of bondservant daughters into the imperial harem, my Western readers would do well to remember that in the old Manchu (and Mongolian) traditions, *all* followers of the ruling Khan, even the upper orders, stood to him in a relation of servitude.

This is quite unlike the Confucian ministers of the native dynasties of China, who might fulfill their moral duty to withdraw from the court of an immoral emperor. The highest Manchu nobleman existed purely on the bounty, and the booty, provided by his master—and referred to himself in their language as "aha," or "slave."

· · · · · ·

Within the gloomy section of the Forbidden City to which the harem inmates of a deceased emperor were relegated, in the Palace of Tranquil Old Age, a theater stood until the year 1799. Once a company of girl-actors was invited to perform there for the aged ladies of the late Yung-cheng emperor, father of Ch'ien-lung. One of their stars, who always played the acrobatic parts of young outlaws or supernatural beings, bore the name of Chiang Hei-lung. The reader may guess what her name signified when I explain that she dressed by preference in ebony, and moved with a dragon's sinuous grace.

This Chiang Hei-lung quite won the hearts of one and all, until time came for the company to make its farewells. The gimlet eye of the Empress Dowager apparently caught sight of a bundle the performer had secreted beneath her folded cape.

A sturdy eunuch took the bundle and opened it, revealing five small Buddhistic statues, property of the chief lady of that palace. With a wild cry, Chiang Hei-lung broke free of the guards restraining her, snatching back the bronze images and their wrapping-cloth.

To the astonishment of all, the actress then sprang right over the high compound wall, like a warrior woman out of a Chinese "penny dreadful." Thence she must have cleared, as if with supernatural ability, the nearby outer wall of the Forbidden City, and its adjacent moat, for she and the statues were never seen or heard of again.

The Ch'ien-lung emperor's youngest daughter, the Tenth Princess, was born to "the Sincere" Consort of the Uang family in 1775. The Uang consort was promoted to the Third Rank about the time the child was conceived. A few years after the birth of the Princess, her mother was temporarily demoted one grade for beating a maidservant to death.

The little girl loved to dress up in boy's clothing, and to ride with her father in the imperial hunting parks. She could shoot well with a heavy bow. After her marriage early in 1790 to the son of the hated and powerful Manchu Ho-shen, she managed her husband's household most excellently.

The emperor supposedly told the girl, "Were you a boy, I would surely make you my heir."

. . . .

Regarding the secret Manchu rites per-
formed by the imperial clan at New Year's, my grandfather of course knew
nothing. Even the top Chinese officials were "excused" from attending such
events. But he did hear of a curious incident in their Manchu-style ritual hall
within the Forbidden City on the twenty-fourth night of one year's last month.

A Manchu "spirit pole" stood before this hall, on which bones and flesh from
the sacrifices were hung. The ancient religion required at certain times the performance of magical masques reenacting the epic bear and tiger hunts of Nurhachi
(1559–1626), the soi-disant emperor "by Heaven's mandate" ["T'ien-ming," or
"abkai fulingga" in Manchu], though he never ruled in China proper. Costumed in
animal pelts and masks, and wearing tall hats adorned with feathers, two lines of
Manchu braves would fall or flee before the arrows of a warrior gotten up as a fan-
tastically garbed Nurhachi. In other such sacraments, whinnying martial cele-
brants capered about upon hobbyhorses, all in honor of the Eight Banner Corps
and the emperor.

On this particular night, the Ch'ien-lung emperor had joined his first lady to
make burnt sacrifice. Religious functionaries stood about to watch as he sat on
the k'ang (the heated brick sleeping-and-lounging platform ubiquitous throughout
North China and peripheral lands). He beat the ceremonial clappers and sang a
song to "invite the spirits" while the lady harmonized, in the manner decreed by
their archaic religious beliefs.

Before time came to "bid farewell to the spirits," the aging emperor suddenly
spoke out, as a spirit medium or witch doctor of their traditions might, in an
unknown soprano voice! "Tell my daughter," it said with great determination, "that
she must bring again together the dispersed mandala." Evidently this referred to
one of the circular god-palaces or representations of the kosmos so important in
the religions of the Hindoos and Thibetans, as well those Manchus who adopted
the Buddhism of the "Secret Teachings" schools.

Later, the emperor remembered nothing of this. And though the words had
been clear enough, their full meaning remained a mystery.

Over the centuries, China has had its
goodly share of poets among the fair sex. This is even true of the Manchus and

their followers in the "Chinese-martial" Banners. I have only recently come across this fragment:

> *Dawn vapors trail . . .*
> *the cleft of River Wu-lieh's fertile vale.*
> *Firm spires stark . . .*
> *guard the Ghost-Gate of the royal park!*

These lines are attributed to a female of uncertain rank within the palaces (a beautiful native Chinese, according to the secret history in which they are recorded), and describe the Mountain Estate for Escaping Hot Weather. The traditional Chinese "Master of Wind and Water" warns his clients that baleful influences are most likely to enter their homes from the northeast, which direction he styles "The Gateway of Ghosts"; the Manchu rulers embraced this belief when they spent huge sums constructing guardian Buddhistic temples north and east of their pleasant walled estate at Jehol.

(Warm thanks to my friend and English tutor Jane Lawson—who hesitates to style herself a "poetess"—for her assistance in rendering this couplet in a modern style.)

One more poem, of sorts: The story goes that one sultry day in the reign of the Ch'ien-lung emperor, when some of the imperial ladies were boating on the chain of artificial lakes just north of the major palaces in The Mountain Estate for Escaping Hot Weather, a Mongol bondservant girl among their suite fell into a fit. They had been drifting through the landscape that so charmingly replicated the delights of China's Yangtse delta lands, admiring the arched bridges, green islands, Southern-style kiosks, and the rounded hills beyond, when she turned ghastly pale.

"What place is this?" she demanded of someone next to her, although she herself was a native of the nearby town. "Is this not Mongol land, outside the Great Wall?"

The birdlike banter of the maids and ladies ceased. The eunuch boatmen stared. A companion told her, "We've just left Lake As-you-like-it. We're on Clarifying Lake. See? There's the Gold Mountain, built to be His Majesty's own Mount Meru—and Pounder Rock erect on the ridge across the river!"

At that, the girl's eyes rolled upward in their sockets and she moaned as if possessed by a demon, or a ghost: an act which may have spared her a charge of treason from her Manchu overlords!

Now, my grandfather knew that the pagoda and the temple hall on this ersatz Gold Mountain had been precisely modeled after those on the famous Gold Mountain in the city of Chen-chiang, on the Yangtse River. (Rather a neat way for the Manchus to gloat over their conquests, I later came to think.) So he always said he understood why the poor girl chanted out, before she swooned,

> "Gold Mountain in the North, or in the South?
> Gold Mountain made by human arts, or cosmic Mount Meru?
> A rock? A hammer? Something else?
> A valley or a woman? Are they one or are they two?"

Editor's note: The above is my 1995 transcription of an unpublished manuscript recently found in a steamer trunk belonging to my grandmother, Jane Lewis Lawson (1910–1994). She taught at the Presbyterian mission school in Nanking (Nanjing) until she fled the Japanese invasion in 1937, barely escaping its dreadful aftermath.

Jennie Lawson

BIRTHDAYS PRESENT, AND TO COME

Beautiful as a flower, her lovely feet unbound and bare, the bodhi-sattva Guan-yin sits upon a diamond boulder-sized. Thick woods rise quiet and cool behind her, dark-brilliant as a peacock's neck. Nearby, a brilliant-dark cascade plashes over mossy stones. In one hand she holds a long-necked bottle of pure water and in the other, a greening willow branch.

This might be any day, of course, but it might as well be the nine-teenth of the second lunar month, when Guan-yin's birthday is celebrated in the human realm. It might as well be just a few months after the girl Lotus enters service as a palace maid, the spring before she travels with the court to the Warmriver estate—though it could be any other year.

The Dragon Daughter and Pilgrim Lad appear (appear!) and take their places at the bodhisattva's sides. The two attendants offer Guan-yin birthday congratulations. Then, entering the reminiscent mood such days can bring, they talk over their forays into the world of the Dragon Daughter's story, in pursuit of stolen statues, of a mandala strewn about like a broken chain of pearls.

They journeyed to last year's Lantern Festival, playing red-robed storytelling beggar monk and snaky-fingered novice, to impress upon the human girl the importance of the Tara statue her mother gave her. They whisked to Nanjing that same night, and Pilgrim Lad took on a Mongol warrior's form, all to catch up a cultivated courtesan in the story's web.

Alas, neither mortal fully got the point. The courtesan, her heart dis-tracted by a lingering grain of ice, can't see why an image of the buddha Akshobhya, transmuter of human anger, would have come to her. And this Lotus still needed to be taught a lesson: She left the Tara statue unat-tended, and so doesn't even know now where it is!

Still, there's only so much he and his companion ought to do, Pilgrim Lad points out, and not for the first time. Otherwise, the game—the Dragon Daughter's story, the regathering of the scattered mandala,

Lotus's unfolding into life—the serious, playful, possibly enlightening game loses all its worth.

So stiff-necked Pilgrim Lad has begun to balk. As the boyish girl-actor Dazzler, he helped acrobatic Blackdragon reveal to Lotus eight bronze altar goddesses in a garden chapel. And of course he held his tongue, back when Guan-yin herself, as the fortune-teller Mother Jia, led a pilgrimage to Marvel Peak—and allowed the humans to do the foolish things that humans do. Each action had its cause in earlier actions and emotions, and how else can they learn? But the day the Dragon Daughter proposed forays into the imperial palaces, he started to refuse.

"I'll be a eunuch-lama for an hour," he said then, nodding his shaven head, "and deliver the blessed Ratnasambhava and his bodhisattvas to the girl's pride-driven father. A good deed, to be sure, considering his needs. Let *them* work out the next step, though. Or not. After all, she knew enough to take that little figure of clear-seeing Lochana from the unused palace shrine—and to keep it when the old cleaning eunuch caught her, didn't she?"

Here, the Dragon Daughter smiled a secret smile, but Pilgrim Lad, oblivious, lectured on. "She's beginning to show signs of exchanging self-pity and the heart's delusions for vision and perseverance." He pulled a pious face. "It's our duty to give her a chance to learn for herself."

So they agreed they'd simply leave one set of statues where Wintersweet saw them after that memorable ice storm, in Old Master Jin's Lodge of the Immortals' Isles, and outside Lotus's ken. Later, the storyteller didn't bother mentioning to her companion a certain little wall-jumping escapade—even though she doesn't know how best to get into Lotus's hands the small bronze Amitabha and attendants she took from the Dowager Consort's palace.

Yet it's crucial, too, the Dragon Daughter muses now, that the girl's attention should be drawn to that very buddha, who helps transform the tenderest, most seductive, human passions—contemplative Amitabha, whose manifestations include no lesser figure than their own Guan-yin!

The storyteller's eyes flash green. She decides that if she should whisper into the mind of a certain desire-stricken prince that a little statue of a goddess—Mamaki, say, who loves all equally—might make a suitable gift to that maid of his grandmama's he's hoping for a chance to frolic with . . . well, Pilgrim Lad needn't be informed. Not every part of a story has to be spelled out.

Certainly not. The tiniest rustle, as of one bamboo leaf against another, impinges on the Dragon Daughter's thoughts. She turns her head, and blushes beneath Guan-yin's kindly dispassionate smile.

A warm breeze comes up like a blessing from the Southern Sea. Surely this much is true—call it delusion, call it karma, call it free will and human perversity, call it the zigs and zags of narrative complications or tangled chains of psychological cause and effect: Neither storyteller nor incarnate being travels an easy straight-line road.

Yet Guan-yin's blessings may arise like that balmy southerly breeze. The Dragon Daughter clears her throat. "About the mother of the human girl," she says. "When she was alive, she always made devotions on this day. And now the Lord of Mount Tai has stuck her in a dreadful ghostly state, not living, rarely able to communicate with those who are, and certainly not able to ease on to what comes next. Couldn't she be allowed—"

"The Lord of Mount Tai did that?" Pilgrim Lad's voice cracks with indignation. "Her silly daughter's clinging—and her own silly attachment to human life, you mean!"

But merciful Guan-yin ignores this lapse. She nods consent.

The nineteenth day of the second lunar month: Across the grounds of the imperial residences outside Beijing at Yuan-ming-yuan, spring brushes the scene with fresh green and earliest pink. Pools and lakes and curved canals link and loop, lying tangled over rolling acres like strands of silvery beads.

All at once, the ghost of Cassia finds herself there, free to see and smell and hear again. Snared as she is in the web of her own, her daughter's longing, something in her aches. Happiness at this moment, and yearning for the future, and the sadness of recollection: all at once.

The day's unusual warmth promises greater heat to come. The Qian-long emperor sits by a pine tree, resting after hours of reading and consultations, admiring the scroll held up before him, contemplating the inner meaning of the Buddhist elephant bathing it depicts. But the love of illusion is not so easily washed away: He feels a great pride of possession as he prepares to stamp the painting with his large red chop.

Some way off, beneath an Italianate colonnade, eunuchs fret over preparations for receiving a minor outland delegation. In studios named "Days of Transformation Long Drawn Out" and "The Library of Delight," painters labor (some nervous, some annoyed, some smug) to please the emperor they've just followed in their annual move out from the Forbidden City. Others—joined by clockmakers, enamel artists, carvers of ivory, bamboo, gnarled roots, and jade—quarrel and joke and envy in a four-courtyard complex over in the section known as "The Cave-Heaven's Depths."

Cassia passes all these by. She flits here and there, drawn first by one burst of feeling, then another, driven always by her desire to have again what each of the emotion-laden figures strewn across this marvelous landscape has.

On the shore of a sun-sparked lake, the Fifteenth Prince and his younger brother have assembled with assorted nephews and boy-cousins for archery practice under the vigilant single eye of an aged Mongol officer. Mount a-gallop, long queue flying, the secret heir to the throne hits the target squarely in its center, and exults. Elsewhere, in the Garden of Long-Lasting Spring, the emperor's Muslim consort approaches two mirror-image curving outdoor staircases. *Let the other women make their infidel devotions!* she thinks. *I will find my solace in prayer to Allah the Sustainer.* Cassia hurries on.

She picks up the trace of another mood. Her daughter! Passing the scarlet frame of a garden swing, Lotus and Yura giggle, remembering the last time they managed to slip away from the others. Today, Yura feigned a stomachache. (Easily done: She hates her life in the Empress Dowager's service, feels it in her belly every day.) Greenplum ordered Lotus to stay behind and care for her while the others went off to enjoy this foretaste of pleasant weather; they're attending the Empress Dowager in the garden of the marble labyrinth near Seacalm Palace and its zodiacal fountain clock.

Lotus makes a joke. The girls laugh harder, giddy, a little edgy, actually. They were nearly caught as they slipped past the eunuch-guards with their mumbled glib excuses. Cassia feels the fear of punishment mingled with their relishing of freedom, and of their cleverness. Her daughter's not the child she used to be.

A fat bee bumbles by, heading for early flowers marked with ultraviolet colors humans cannot see. The trees are hazed by splitting buds, and Cassia observes how the entire parkland's draped with soft green garlands, like the scented garlands on an altar, the foam garlands on the streams that course through Guan-yin's island-mountain home.

Dashing round a corner at the warning sound of high-pitched eunuch voices, Yura stubs her toe. Even the everyday cotton shoes issued to the junior maids aren't made for running. "Never mind!" she whispers, sharp, to Lotus. "I'm fine, I'm fine. Come on!"

Hovering invisible beside them, Cassia comes to understand that the two are half pretending they're headed for the great aviary where peacocks, parrots, hornbills, pheasants, egrets, nightjars, warblers, flashing kingfishers, all are sheltered in a building with a mazy cagelike wrought-iron door. But they know they don't know how to find it, or how far away it is.

And she, ectoplasmic Cassia, has no idea how she can reach her fleshly daughter, how she can get the girl to bring together the mandala as the Lord of Mount Tai ordered.

The bee, or its sister, passes by again. Last year, by concentrating on the impending Ghost Festival, when the shade world and the bright one meet, Cassia was able—briefly, briefly!—to cross over, to play the parts of a widowed poetry tutor, and a regal flower-spirit in a garbled dream. But communication is so limited! Cassia keeps running into the insensible wall, the depthless imperceptible abyss, that blocks her actions in the human realm.

What a failure, the night she begged a Manchu spirit to let her speak through the Manchu emperor as if through a shaman's mouth! What frustration that the youth Wu Ming has gone off half cocked, full cocked, somewhere on his own. What dizziness, to sweep here and there on the winds of passions, and never know what place, what time, she'll come to next.

It's as though she were wandering slick-sided marble puzzle-paths, were the blindfolded child in a game of "Guess the Fruits" on a winding Beijing lane, were caught in a bit of fanciful tomfoolery with rules no one will explain. Cassia can feel a special receptivity in her daughter's friend—but she can't, she *can't*, get through.

Nothing for it but to make do. As Lotus and Yura do: they're tiptoeing toward a pond where two wing-clipped Mandarin ducks lead a line of nestlings on their first swim. Tawny and downy and quacking tiny perfect quacks, the babies take to the pollen-swirled pool like—

Like bees to nectar. Someone's danced a message-dance within a hidden hive: Two more purposeful workers hustle by.

Who cares about being spotted by the eunuchs? How could disaster fall on such an agreeable day? In silent accord, the friends edge closer, closer to the darling fluff-tousled ducklings, hearts set, eyes fixed, ready to leap and grab.

Lotus signals with her chin. They tense, breathe in, prepare to spring.

And Yura sneezes. Duck and drake fly up, awkward, quacking loudly, *gua-gua! danger! danger! gua, gua, gua!* The babies flutter after. The family flaps and hops and tumbles to the safety of the marsh below the outlet of the pond.

A few cross words, a curt reminder that sneezes can't be stopped: Two girls sit unspeaking on a large stone by the shore. The breeze cools. The sunlight dulls. Cassia watches Lotus lean forward, plunge one hand into the water, shudder at the tarrying wintry cold.

"Sorry," Lotus says, because she knows she ought to. "Of course you couldn't help it." Yura mutters her own apology.

Nonetheless, their silence stretches out. Then the sky goes bright again. Lotus, leaning once more forward, begins to examine the face she sees within the pond.

I look like Mama, she thinks. *So much like Mama! I never used to believe I did, whatever people said.* The face (her own? her mother's?) bites its lips.

Here's Cassia's chance to bridge the gap! To speak through the watery glare of the tremulous mirage, to tell her daughter: Don't grieve, or not too much, keep looking for the holy statues, you should ask your cousin and your father and, and his concubine—

A flash of jealousy blinds Cassia. A thunderpeal of anger deafens her. But no, she will not—there's no reason Taiyang shouldn't—the important thing is getting through to Lotus. Summoning all her determination, she smooths this storm of temperament.

Now Lotus is tossed on a tempest of her own, as if she's inhaled the yellow wind that sweeps in from the Gobi. To evade the sorrow stirred within her by the specter, she swallows, and turns toward Yura. She will confess. "There's something I have to tell you, about the day that old eunuch accused me of stealing from the shrine in the Palace of Doubled Glory, and we wound up in the Imperial Garden with His Majesty's Muslim lady . . ."

Some word, some fragment—*statues*—must have slipped between the realms from mother's thoughts to daughter's. Cassia watches, listens amazed as Lotus blurts that she really did take the holy figure, that she's hidden it behind a secret panel in her wooden jewelry box, that she suddenly feels Yura ought to know the truth, that maybe Yura can help her find others . . .

"It was so strange. But I think there're more." She hurries on, oblivious of the clouds gathering on the visage of her friend. "It reminded me of a Tara that my mama gave me, or maybe a statue I found on that terrible pilgrimage to Marvel Peak I told you all about, and then my poetry tutor—"

"Told me *all* about?" snaps Yura. "Don't say *all* about. You never mentioned finding a holy image. Sounds like just another of your lies!"

The hot flush of anger—sharp as the stinging of a thousand bees—washes over Lotus. The venomous, painful swarm of feelings that has engulfed poor Yura (her friend lies to her! her only friend! can *any*thing be trusted, in worldly life?) now clusters on the fragile skin of Cassia's little girl. Their poison pumps, pricking, nettling, goading as they fill Lotus's mouth and nostrils, as they cover her eyes and ears.

Eventually, the two friends will manage apologies, will sneak back to the maids' room before the others return to Her Dowager Majesty's residence, before the dust storm hits. But all that will take every bit of Lotus's attention. Cassia knows there's no hope she'll get through to the human realm today. Where, then? How, then? When, oh when?

· · · · · · ·

Late in the third month: A group of women and their servants join the crowds departing Beijing's Manchu City for the Temple of the Eastern Peak a few minutes' walk outside the wall. The name of the temple marks it as a counterpart of far-off sacred Mount Tai itself. For two weeks each year, the Beijing sanctum stands open to the public; heaps of paper flowers and paper money are offered along with prayers and incense to a multitude of gods. Officially honored as chief among them is the god of the Eastern Peak, first magistrate in the netherworld, the stern Lord of Mount Tai.

Who are they, who come to pay respects during the celebration of the birthday of the mountain's lord? Cassia knows most of them, and quickly flicking—sent once more by Guan-yin's mercy—into their midst, finds out about the rest.

Cassia's niece Wintersweet chats gaily with her mother. Then, suddenly slump shouldered and uncertain, she urges her donkey forward to the side of her mother-in-law's cart. Lady Ding's two unmarried daughters, Euphonia and Constance, ride nearby, whispering busily of their plans to buy and set free caged sparrows (or maybe magpies, why not, they can afford it!) for the benefit of their souls.

Familiar maids—Madame Gao's Harmony and Grace, Wintersweet's Happiness (who looks different now, wan, eyes dulled and shadowed)—walk with others Cassia doesn't know, surrounded by older serving women and menservants from the Sun house, and the Jins'.

But who's this exquisite beauty managing somehow to stand alone among the crush of others? Clearly not a maid: too well dressed, too self-assured. And not a bannerwoman: Cassia gets a glimpse of tiny gold-lily feet. There's something . . . For an instant, Cassia imagines she might have had a sister who was stolen away at birth.

Of course. No! Yes. Face serene as the full moon, features delicate yet definite as the new moon's curve. *But not,* thinks Cassia, *a bit like me!*: She recognizes her husband's concubine. How could she have forgotten the woman she couldn't avoid when she returned to her own home as an outsider, as hired poetry tutor to her own child?

And yet, how can she bear to recognize the high-cheeked countenance she's seen looming in her husband's thoughts?

Well, Cassia won't be like her sister-in-law, who evidently forced

Padma to stay at home. There's a place for a concubine in a well-ordered household. Taiyang needs to preserve his health. The family needs a son. And the woman did treat Lotus well. Cassia's been told all her life how feminine resentment, feminine bitterness, excessive feminine desire, can disrupt a lineage, drive it into ruin. That may not be the entire story, she thinks, but as far as it goes, it's true.

Those feelings can disrupt the woman's body too: She overhears Euphonia and Constance discussing their father's married sister. "It's her jealousy that brought it on, you know," says Euphonia. "Since Uncle Fu has only the one son, he can't be blamed for taking a concubine. Especially after Aunt, you know, miscarried. She has no excuse to carry on the way she's done."

Constance nods. "I hope I'm never like that," she says. "They say jealousy's a vinegar so strong, it's poison! So Aunt just keeps seeping blood? Down there? How awful! Perhaps we ought to release a pair of magpies for her sake."

"Or sparrows, anyway," Euphonia is saying, when they see their mother's mule cart stop near the temple gate.

Cassia knows what will happen next. She can almost heft a worshiper's feather duster in her hand, as she did when she too would help sweep a year's worth of cobwebs from some of the seventy-two side shrines in the courtyard where the great hall stands. She can see without looking the rows of inkstones and writing bushes in front of the Literature God. And she can actually feel the cool smooth metal of the Healing Mule, the year she rubbed his ear to cure a throbbing in her own.

Why, Cassia remembers her first visit after Lotus was born. How much grander the shrine complex had become that spring; how the buildings and porches had grown! His Majesty had sponsored repairs and enlargements throughout, just as eighty years earlier his grandfather set up stones inscribed with a temple history that even then stretched back some three centuries and a half. After Cassia married Taiyang, she came nearly every year to place a tablet before the God of Official Promotion, and a little plaster baby before Our Lady of Sons and Grandsons.

That's it! Of course! Cassia twitches with comprehension, and a ripple in the sun-warmed air makes a laborer reverently lighting a pile of paper scraps stop to rub his eyes.

Our Lady is the party's real goal. Oh, they'll struggle through the crowds that fill the temple's main courtyard. They'll pay homage at shrines that offer wealth and timely marriage and long life—each cubicle the seat of a divine department head in the celestial bureaucracy. They might stop at a few of the less popular bureaus too, paying their respects to various deities in charge of handicrafts, or sheep or cattle or assorted birds, or the Yellow River or rain, or freedom from plagues and boils. They'll bow in front of the great hall dedicated to the god of the Eastern Peak, where everyone makes reverence, and some ask questions, and some have questions answered, assuming they can understand what they are told.

But eventually, the party Cassia's trailing will surely go on to the next courtyard and pay homage to Our Lady. Last year's ill-fated pilgrimage to Marvel Peak in the Western Hills failed to yield a boy-child for the house of the Suns. Perhaps this year, offerings at a local temple will.

And surely Wintersweet (oh! Cassia notices at last her niece's swollen face, her swollen belly and breasts) wants nothing so much as she wants to bear a grandson for Lady Ding.

The young wife's stomach clenches. If only she can do what her husband's first wife—*and his vulgar concubine*—have done. Overhearing this one thought, Cassia catches a sudden blast of nervousness and longing.

Will Wintersweet be granted what she needs to free her from this snarl of envy and self-doubt? Cassia can envision the building in the northern courtyard of this temple: not three goddesses as atop Marvel Peak, but nine, in three groups of three; deities emerge in response to human fervor, just as temples grow in response to human gifts, and human lacks. There's a Smallpox Goddess among them (*poor Wintersweet!*), and Our Lady Eyebright (*poor Third Aunt!*), and goddesses who ease childbirth's danger and its pain. But two will receive the most of this group's devotions: Our Lady of Sons and Grandsons—and the chief among them, the Verdant Dawncloud Sovereign herself.

The Verdant Dawncloud Sovereign! The ghost-woman's heart yaws and pitches. It was Cassia's own mother who told her about the Lord of Mount Tai's daughter, about the Lady's compassion, and how she gives life—unlike her father, implacable judge of the dead.

Perhaps the Sovereign will help Cassia return to her old circumstances! Why didn't she think of this long ago? A half-memory surfaces (was it that Jadewhite Girl, among the vivid clouds near the celestial Yang Purple Palace?), a half- or merely quarter-memory of some mention of the goddess . . .

But what's this? Before Cassia can make her way to the two-story building dedicated to the Sovereign and her associates, a vaporous slap of anger and resentment and humiliation slashes across her face.

Two slaps: one from Wintersweet (Cassia sees it happen, right here in public, a dreadful loss of dignity) and one answering, in the fleshless form of a single reproachful look from Happiness, against the sensitive pock-scarred skin of her beloved mistress. But no one else (save the maid and Wintersweet) can sense the second blow; its existence lies outside the realm of flesh and sight and sound.

For some in the crowd of temple visitors, the scene blends comedy with elbow-nudging satisfaction. *Get that, will you? A grand household's lah-dee-dah young lady, ha, ha, brawling like Missus Fishmonger with a little scullion in the market street!* For others, it's a mere inconvenience. *Quarrel if you like, dearie, but step aside. Don't conduct your trivial business between me and the altar of the god.*

Madame Gao hangs her head in rare shame. *Now what will Lady Ding think of my headstrong daughter, and how I brought her up? I told her father a thousand times he shouldn't spoil her.* Constance stares, puzzled, shocked, embarrassed. *Goodness! Granted, Happiness has turned sullen lately, but this is hardly the place to correct her. My sister-in-law's been so moody. I'm sure I'll never let a pregnancy make me act like this.*

Cassia feels it all. She wishes she could weep.

And for others in the party—Lady Ding and Euphonia and the Jin family's sharper maids—it's the last clue confirming what they have suspected for some time. Whatever little thing Happiness just now did, or mis-did, or failed to do, her real transgression's obvious: She didn't fend off the Young Master. Somewhere, sometime, she's let Wintersweet's husband open her skirts.

All right, then. The girl's no better than she should be. But the Young Master—here the thoughts of the various observers diverge slightly for a moment—*the Young Master's so high spirited,* or *he's so persistent,* or *at least he's got the sense to keep his little peccadillos within the household.* And re-converge: *Lucky the woman whose husband has a taste for home cooking. Didn't she herself bring the maid into our midst? There's advantage for a clever wife in this sort of situation. And no reason to shame us all with a public scene.*

Oh, Wintersweet! Oh, Happiness! If she had lungs, Cassia would shriek with outrage and pity. No, no—the wind shifts—she would stroke each poor stinging reddened cheek with fingertips feather tender, if she had hands.

Instead, she's buffeted away from the two blood-tinged faces, away from all the tongue cluckers, the snickerers and prigs. Away from the jostling, away from the grasping, away from the very stuff of the life she covets so.

And into the presence of the Verdant Dawncloud Sovereign. Cassia's pulse—or what feels like her pulse—rushes as if she were climbing six thousand steep stone stairs. Clouds swirl and melt around her. The hubbub of the worshipers is replaced by a distant roaring, like the crash of unseen unstoppable waterfalls. Sheer rock faces seem to close in and cut off perception. Sharp escarpments surely drop away just inches from her faltering steps.

Is she in Beijing's Temple of the Eastern Peak? Or atop the highest summit of the Western Hills? Or has Cassia ascended faraway Mount Tai, passing through the First Celestial Gate, Red Gate, Mid-Sky Gate, over Cloudstep Bridge, through the Southern Gate of Heaven, and up to the iron-roofed Palace of the Verdant Clouds of Dawn?

Or has she flown to a higher realm? No matter. She is *here*. She gazes without wavering at the Sovereign's ample body, her small bland gold face. This is Cassia's chance to ask for a return to her old life. This is the Holy Mother, the Heavenly Immortal Jade Woman of Mount Tai.

Suddenly, Cassia is abashed. Our Lady gives life, she thinks. The goddess grants good fortune, and nurtures us as does the fertile earth. But how much dare I ask? The earth replaces each spring, each creature, every generation, with the next. Does it ever bring the dead year back, ever make a duckling of a duck?

She looks again at a face not unkind, but imperturbable. A face that gazes on mortality from afar, as one atop a mountain might look down unblinkingly onto the sharp rocks of a gorge, at the white bones of someone fallen long ago.

Tears fill Cassia's eyes, or what would be her eyes. How can she presume to beg the Sovereign to break the order of things, the very order the goddess upholds when she grants a baby's birth?

So Cassia—the Cassia of this moment, who is not the Cassia of an hour ago, nor the still-too-human Cassia who will burn and twist in some future hour, regretting this very swerve—Cassia offers up to the silent gold-faced one her devotion, and a different, more suitable, a *possible* request.

At the foot of the Mount Tai massif in Shandong province, the poorest pilgrims, bound for sunrise at the summit, assemble with torches and lanterns at day's end. Tonight their lights will glow like fireflies rising among the trees late on a summer eve. They will stretch along the pathways on the mountainside like a twisted unrolled bolt of glimmering white silk. At dawn—a fortunate clear dawn— the mists will part and the pilgrims will spy a fiery thread, distant in the east: the world's-edge horizon line of the sun-ignited sea.

Back in the main courtyard of Beijing's Temple of the Eastern Peak, a woman bent with calcium deficiency opens a bamboo cage. A large black bird, wings and breast blazed effulgent white, breaks free and flies away. The woman's dried lips crack as they stretch into a smile. She knows nothing of the trivial cataclysmic slap dealt by one young woman to another on just this same spot earlier today, or yesterday, or sometime last week.

In the Manchu City, in the Jins' fine home, Wintersweet and her maid Happiness weep in separate rooms. Young Master Jin is nowhere to be seen.

And in the northern chamber of the western side hall in the Upper Courtyard of the family compound of the Suns, an imperial bondservant relaxes with his concubine. He has paid his duty visit to his father; the old man's health grows worse. He complained of back pain, and difficulty passing water. Then Taiyang was dismissed.

The couple fills the evening with talk of Taiyang's plans for advancement, and her subtly offered advice. They eat well, they pour wine for one another, she plays slow melodies that fill the household with quivering tranquility. The little maid Snow banks the fire beneath the brick bed plat-form, says goodnight, and falls asleep on her pallet in the building's middle room.

Cassia, caught and drawn by the airy nothing of her passions to that same chamber, now strains against the weightless bonds that hold her there. Strains unsuccessfully. It's one thing to request a goddess grant good fortune to another person, as Cassia did for Taiyang. But it's a dif-ferent thing entirely to watch—to be unable not to watch—your lover with his love.

To hear him call her (once, a slip, and yet . . .) your old name, Biyangga, *moonlike*. To see he cherishes her for her resemblance to the wife he lost more than two years ago—and for other reasons too. To know that, thanks to the Verdant Dawncloud Sovereign, this night of love-making (its springlike bee-sting warmth, its quick tracery of flush and pleasure, its laughter glittering like reflections on pollen-tinted water, its union of male and female essences with a spark of bliss), this night will bring forth a son.

A LOTUS BLOSSOMS: 7

For a moment, the crowd of mounted guards before me parts. I catch sight of the Empress Dowager's golden-yellow palanquin entering the central portal of the Gate of Rectitude and Beauty. Harsh sunlight glares off the white paving stones and the bearers' scarlet silks. The sign overhead names the gate in Manchu, Mongol, Chinese, Uyghur, and Tibetan: Here, each of the empire's five chief languages has a place.

We have reached the Warmriver summer capital at last. And I am still uncertain about so many things.

Yura's not: She's purely happy that we're here. Protocol will still rule court ceremonials, but we're told our daily life will be less constrained. She nudges me none too gently, eager for a turn at looking out through the small opening at the front of our cart.

But now Lady Brightcloud and Lady Miao-shan lean forward; their wide Manchu headdresses block our view. Yura rolls her eyes. The cart's wheels creak. We turn to the window slits on either side and pass blindly through a lesser portal, into the shade of the imperial residence.

For seven days we've sat cross-legged on a sheepskin pad, jouncing past sun-hardened fields, past scrubby trees and pastureland: through the Long Wall's Old North Gate, up over stony ranges, down to the sheltered valley that holds the shabby country town where my friend grew up. All my life, I've heard my father describe the untamed greenness of the emperor's mountain estate, its fearless waterfowl, the herds of deer that roam at dawn and dusk. Now Father remains at work in the Forbidden City, and I am seeing it for myself.

A few minutes ago, attendants' carts and consorts' carriages alike sat unmoving in the heat while His Majesty came out to greet his mother; this year, he arrived a full day early. Yura squirmed and peered so frantically, reeled off so excitedly the names of shops—and the owner of each summer mansion, and the respectful onlookers, and a curly-tailed dog ambling down a side street—that Lady Brightcloud spoke to her quite sharply. Even sweet-tempered Lady Miao-shan patted her small hand in kind reproof.

Soon her Dowager Majesty's grand palanquin and the senior ladies' carriages are emptied and we four can crawl out onto the paving stones. The beautiful chyn my father sent me just after New Year's has made the journey without damage. Yura groaned a playful groan when she realized I intended to take it with us inside the cart, but now she grins as I cradle the long instrument underneath my arm.

The eunuchs guide us through courtyard and gate and courtyard again, and then the side gate to the walled plaza before the entrance of the Pine-Crane Haven, where we'll live till the hot season ends and autumn wanes. Inside, we pass more whitewashed square enclosures, more low buildings with roof tiles of cool ordinary gray.

It's as if a dream has taken me home to my family's compound; the place is almost familiar, half transformed, stretching mysteriously on and on. I find my small trunk deposited in a servants' building facing the Empress Dowager's Happy Longevity Hall. By the time she, and then we, are settled in, when Yura and I snatch a moment to investigate the garden courtyard behind the hall, the shadows of the pines reach long across the rock hill there.

"Look!" says Yura. She grabs my hand and points out the path to its peak, which rises higher even than the pretty two-story building beyond, at the northern end of the women's quarters. "Clarity says, from up there you can see the Frontier Lakes. If we can climb it sometime, and look the other way, maybe we'll see the rooftops back in town. Maybe even pick out my family's house." She exhales heavily.

Beijing seems as far off as the moon.

As far off as yesterday's strange conversation with the Fifteenth Prince in the woods near the last of the travel palaces. I haven't seen him since: I wouldn't risk slipping away again, even if he had asked me to. All day I've brooded, wondering if what I said might have caught his fancy, if I can make from a chance encounter the rise at court my family wishes for me, even wondering—at one weary moment—if it really took place at all.

Early this morning, Her Majesty the prince's mother told the Empress Dowager that he would ride ahead with a small company of guardsmen to give the emperor formal notice that the ladies' procession would soon arrive. Naturally, the First Consort ignored me as she chatted with Her Dowager Majesty. But a moment earlier, when she walked into the room, she sought me with her eyes.

"So there you are!"

Sharp words from Chief Bao pull me out of reverie. The Empress Dowager summons me to play for her. She wants simple music for her first evening on the estate, the eunuch says.

His voice drips respect; his features squeeze toward one another in an elaborate expression of distaste. "Well," he adds, "simple is what one's bound to get from a beginner, eh? But Her Dowager Majesty condescends to enjoy the *delightful depth of feeling* behind your touch." Chief Bao turns on his heel and walks away.

What do I care for what a eunuch thinks? Tired as I am, I'll play my best. I only wish I had more time to practice. Still, in the months since the Empress Dowager last asked me to perform, I've learned to make my fingers glide and tremble the way the piece called "Buddha-Spell" requires: She's bound to like its chantlike sound.

I understand now what my father's concubine told me, that the music can lift me above homesickness and sorrow and the hard life of a palace serving girl, the way a mountain's peak can float above a layer of clouds. I hurry to the maids' room, check the chyn's silk strings, wrap my arm around its ice-smooth wood, walk back toward Happy Longevity Hall.

The twilight thickens. A breeze strikes up, despite the walls that shelter the buildings of the women's residence. I shiver in the sudden chill.

. . . .

Did you like my present?" The Fifteenth Prince steps closer. "The name of that goddess is Mamaki. My lama-teacher told me it means *my very own*." He has shown me through the elegantly modest buildings of this aerie in the estate's hill district. Apparently it pleases him to treat me almost as a host would treat a guest. Well, then, I will fulfill my part.

I kotow silently, stand up, tell him I'd like to show my gratitude by playing for him on the small terrace off the book room. "This hall has a fine secluded beauty . . ." I choose my words with care. "But if we follow the walkway back to the terrace, the waters' melody will be all the more profound."

He takes my hand. I don't dare withdraw it, but I won't clasp his in return. "We can't see the creek from there," he says.

"Yes." I remember the subtlety with which my father's concubine instructs. "But as His Highness wishes. Shall I begin by playing 'Deer Call'?"

I free my hand and turn as if to take my chyn out of its brocade cover. I can't believe I'm acting like this, so willful and evasive, can't believe I'm here with a son of the emperor.

Nor can I fully believe Her Dowager Majesty gave her grandson quiet permission to have me brought to this First Flowering Lodge—"to play music for His Highness," Lady Brightcloud said when she came to tell me. "It seems he's heard you sometime or other, and fancies the sound of that expensive chyn your father bought."

She gave me a different sort of smile then, as if she were being introduced for the first time to some person she knew better than to trust. "Your father is a clever man," she added. "Clever, and fortunate to have such a beautiful—and such a *very* clever—daughter. And *you* are fortunate that Her Dowager Majesty thinks it best her grandsons be served by girls she knows personally."

I forget her, forget everyone else, as the prince laughs out loud. "You're nervous," he says. "You don't have to be." But when his hand reaches out to trace my arm beneath my sleeve, I see a sharper brightness in his eyes. So. He's been known since childhood, after all, as a boy who loves the hunt.

"I'll show you a place you haven't seen, instead," he says. "If you really want to go somewhere else."

I do. An unfamiliar energy fills me, despite the awkwardness of my hushed departure from the palaces, and the rough donkey ride up into the hills. I'm wearing the silken boy's clothes Lady Miao-shan handed me with no comment beyond a look of wordless understanding, and—he's right—I'm more nervous than I've ever been: I feel I could walk for miles.

More nervous, and yet calmer. I have no doubt what's going to happen between us here. I knew it when Lady Brightcloud came in with the message from Her Dowager Majesty, knew it before the eunuch-guards brought me to the gatehouse of this lodge and I saw the prince's eyes grow wide and dark at the sight of me. It's exactly what my family and I have hoped for, if I can make his interest in me last.

And suddenly, I'm certain I will know what to do and say, as my father's concubine said I would, should a chance like this one come.

The young prince seems to be relishing this brief escape from studying and the ceremonial duties that fill so much of his time. Will this small adventure's removal from his normal life be the only part that he remembers? Or will it make him care the more for me?

His Highness says a few words to the eunuchs in the next room, then leads me out to a small door in the wall that curves behind the largest building, nodding briefly at the guards who fall in behind us. We climb the slope on a long flight of stepping stones, toward a gazebo atop a knob covered with wild pear and apple trees. The air's fresh as the ferns nodding in the dampest corners of these woods. My thin clothing frees me to move easily.

"This is Fargaze Gazebo," the prince says lightly when we arrive. "Surely it's remote and, and elevated enough to suit your music!"

I bow my head. He seems contented with my silence—a good thing, as the beauty of green hills washed by yesterday's long rain has stolen all my words. Let him wonder what I'm thinking. I've never seen a place as fair and pure as this.

" 'Deer Call,' eh?" The prince reaches out as if to pinch my cheek, and the dreamlike feeling of some days ago returns: Could he, could someone, have reached toward me like that before?

Not him. Inexplicably, my eyes grow wet. I look away.

His hand falls. A flush creeps over his broad face. He grunts softly, with a tender satisfaction. "You're as full of feeling as I thought," he says, too quietly to be heard by the guards who've stopped a short way below. "Whatever some people say."

I'd never ask what that means, nor does he give me the opportunity. "Not the grandest view in the estate," he continues in a new, more polished voice,

"But one I like. The eunuchs will be bringing tea and fruit and sitting-mats in a few minutes, along with your chyn. *And* an incense burner to clear our minds. You may play for me, and afterward, if you're not tired, I'll show you a little Dragon Monarch Shrine. See the roof? Over there, among the maple trees just above the spring."

Then, as I continue gazing outward, he mutters, "You're not easily commanded, are you?"

Time to let him end the hunt. "How," I ask, "could a palace bondservant dare refuse the wishes of the Son of Heaven's son?" I turn to him at last, offer him a look that says his command's exactly what my heart desires.

By the seventh day of the seventh month, it's clear that all the Empress Dowager's servants and attendants know about my visit to First Flowering Lodge. And the ones that followed. Goldflower and the other maids treat me with a new respect—or caution. But only Yura asks me what the prince is like, for who would break the silence Her Dowager Majesty ordered with a wordless frown?

I tell my friend the only truths I can, that he is kind, and that I've no idea what will happen next. If anything. When I stop at that, she draws away, hurt by my reticence, joining the others in their careful watching. But I don't know how to express to her what I can't figure out myself. What would Yura say if I explained that the brief ardor of the Fifteenth Prince when we lie down together moves me less than does the lingering resonance of my chyn as I play "Buddha Spell?"

She'd say that was unimportant: *She* has no desire to stay at court a moment longer than she must, but I've been granted the opportunity I wanted. Then I would—I know I would—think of the knife-flash certainty of the Emperor's Muslim consort, that cold day when the old eunuch choked me and all around us failed to act. Will I hesitate and doubt, or will I go where it seems I must?

After that, I'd admit out loud the truth of Yura's words, and would confess that, really, I am not unmoved by this earnest young prince.

If pleasure were the thing that mattered, though, I'd choose the dreams that now overtake me almost daily when I lie sweating through the afternoon rest hour, or in the early part of the warmest nights, before the air cools down. But it's not at all what matters. And he is truly kind, and works hard to be as noble as a prince should be. I admire, even pity him for that. Quite aside from my duty to my family, I do sometimes long to see him—although I can't name that longing's reasons, or its source.

If people here in the north half of the women's residence know, then surely word has spread among the maids and eunuchs and the ladies-in-waiting in the lower courtyards. But it seems no one has braved mentioning to the First Consort anything about this trifling unofficial interest of her teenaged son's. From what I've heard, the emperor's decision to have the Sincere Fourth-Ranked Consort brought along to Warmriver has made for enough tension in the buildings attached to the prince's mother's Palace of Repose Achieved.

At any rate, the emperor keeps the Fifteenth Prince beside him, sometimes hunting, sometimes observing official business. And the prince tells me His Majesty has little tolerance for unsanctioned dalliance—by his sons. For my part, I remember a story of Little Auntie Tuo's, about a winehouse entertainer who drove off patrons with question after question about when they'd next visit her.

So I try not to think of him too much, or of the future. It's the senior ladies I have on my mind when the seventh of the seventh month arrives, and the First Consort hosts a holiday gathering in honor of the Weaver Star.

Yura, Clarity, Goldflower, and I follow the ladies-in-waiting clustered around Her Dowager Majesty as we make our way along a willow-shaded causeway to one of the islands in the chain of lakes. A flute strikes up, easing the ache that has gripped my head since early afternoon. Its plaintive song floats above the shallows where ragged lotuses bloom in the angled rays of the late-day sun.

When our procession approaches the southern gate building of the island's retreat, Clarity leans close to Yura and they puzzle out the sign carved in the calligraphy of His Majesty's grandfather, "Moonlight Colors and Yangzi-River Sounds." Yura adds something I can't catch, which makes Clarity giggle, till one of the eunuchs shoots her a warning look.

The whole day has had a disconcerting feel, to say nothing of the heat. For a week, Goldflower's described the enchanting Double-Seventh pageants she's seen in the East Palace theater: "Lovematch at the Celestial River," "Girls Beg the Weaver Star for Skill," and more. I looked forward to seeing some such celebration of the Weaver's annual reunion with her beloved Cattleherd star. But it turns out no plays are to be performed this year.

Moreover, not one of the emperor's daughters is here to take part in the festival, and word is that the First Consort misses the Ninth Princess, who married a Manchu nobleman named Jalantai two years ago. And surely the emperor's first lady worries about her elder girl: The Seventh Princess languishes in Beijing, too ill to travel, though her Mongol husband, Lawangdorji, will accompany His Majesty to the Mulan hunting park next month.

But worst, rumor has it, is that the emperor turned down the First Consort's invitation to join us here this evening, saying a full day hosting a tribal delegation would leave him too tired to watch the women's games. Of all the imperial ladies, only the Empress Dowager remains serene, secure, never out of sorts—how can I but admire her then?

Now, Her Dowager Majesty wishes to seek further coolness before we join the others. We circle the east side of the walled retreat, along a tree-lined sluice, admiring the rooftops and the kiosks on the leafy islands beyond.

"The First Consort must have had hopes for this evening," Goldflower says in an undertone, "since the magpies will be forming the bridge for the Cattleherd and Weaver to, you know, get together. Perhaps she thought the birds would help her through the rear door of His Majesty's bedchamber." She smiles, tight lipped. "Too bad it only opens from inside!"

"More separates them than the night sky's Silver River," says Clarity, her eyes fixed on the ground. "Maybe His Majesty has grown weary of her allknowing ways, or her petty jealousies."

Yura's head jerks around at that. Goldflower just looks sad.

After that, we're all four silent. Fall's first cricket chirps. We pass the retreat's rear gate—"A Hidden Painting of Lakes and Mountains," the sign there says—and move past the fishing jetty, turning to complete our circular promenade.

I look across the water, toward the hills; a red sun burns my eyes. The First Flowering Lodge is too far off to see, and besides, a long ridge blocks the view.

The First Consort and her fourth-ranked rival wait with their ladies on an airy lakeside loggia, bowing down to welcome their mother-in-law. Beyond them, in the square pavilion where the causeway joins the island, the flutist starts a livelier melody. Clarity and Yura start whispering to each other once again.

Soon, the food and wine arrive. Everybody's spirits rise. The heat breaks and the sky's tints deepen, blue turning to violet, the amber edges of the few thin clouds going toward coral and maroon. Her Dowager Majesty entertains the group with reminiscences of the Double Sevenths of her girlhood. Melons are placed reverently on a table near the shore, between two vases of needle-leaved cockscomb flowers. Beyond, the new moon's crescent trails in the sun's wake, hanging high in the west.

After the ladies have eaten and we maids have shared the dishes passed on to us, the smiling Empress Dowager tells us to follow the ladies-in-waiting, bowing before the temporary altar, asking the Weaver star for more skill in our needlework. Both of His Majesty's consorts have brought along spiders in tiny boxes to place beside the melons; we're sure to hear tomorrow which one wove the finer web.

A few large fireflies rise above the darkening grasses of the lakeshore. The senior ladies take up colored silks and each one threads seven needles by moonlight. Lady Miao-shan proves nimblest of them all. "Better if I had the skill Her Dowager Majesty displayed," she says in her sweet sincere way, "when she stitched that lovely tangka of Green Tara for the Yong-heh Palace Temple lamas." The other ladies chime in, agreeing. The old lady—her calm face so beautiful in the silver light!—merely nods.

At noon, we younger ones floated straws like needles on bowls of water; now the senior ladies laugh and tease us as they talk over the results. The shadow cast by Clarity's was especially thin and sharp, and at Her Dowager Majesty's command, she shows off the fine embroidery on a sash she brought along. Yura beams as though the praise were hers.

How beautifully Nurse used to sew, I think. My own straw's shadow lay thick, light splintered, on the bottom of the bowl. Now, I hear someone passing on a labored witticism about its resemblance to the chyn my father spent so much silver on.

"*This* little maid doesn't need to sew well," adds Lady Brightcloud. "She uses the silk strings of her precious chyn to weave *her* webs!" She glances slyly toward the First Consort, but the prince's mother doesn't seem to notice; she's deep in a conversation with her favorite attendant, discussing Double Seventh poems.

"I rather thought that particular shadow looked like the beads on an abacus," the Empress Dowager comments mildly. "The sign of a girl with a good head on her shoulders, I've always heard."

Naturally, Lady Brightcloud says nothing after that. I look to Yura, to share my amusement, but she seems to be off on an errand. Perhaps she's been sent to fetch something from the retreat's main hall, where they say His Majesty as a boy studied *The Book of Changes* and other classics at his grandfather's knee.

Just then, the First Consort announces the poetry competition—"for all who *wish* to take part," she says, nodding with utter graciousness in the general direction of the Fourth-Ranked Consort. "The rest are excused." Their close quarters in the Pine-Crane Haven must have revealed a lack of literary education in that daughter of the Uangs.

The verse form to be used is announced, and the First Consort recites an example, a Double-Seventh poem by a southerner named Jiang Renlan that begins, "Up in the heavens, lovers meet." The twilight it describes might be tonight's. The poet's sorrow at separation from her husband might be—well, anyone's.

Her Dowager Majesty declares that whoever wishes to go off to a quiet spot while composing may do so. The flutist will summon us back with the melody "Stars Cross the Magpies' Bridge" in the time it takes to drink two cups of tea. At her request, someone repeats the short poem twice more, so everyone can be certain of the rhythm and the line lengths we're to use. I already know the pattern well; for an instant, I see my southern poetry tutor's moonlike face, see Third Aunt as she brings a paper-bound volume closer to her gentle eyes.

More than one pair of arched brows rise when people notice me—a mere maid, and so young!—slipping off toward the dim lakeside path that leads to the fishing jetty.

Phrases are already coming to me by the time I step out on the jetty, away from the glowing lanterns that now frame the retreat's rear gate. I stare west again, into empty darkness, thinking not of the Fifteenth Prince—not really—nor of Yura's recent coolness, but of a yearning that has been with me far longer. Mama will never hear this poem, I think. Mostly, though, I'm caught by what I've seen today, and the sound of the water lapping at the nearby rocks, and the melody of the words.

The lines fall into place. I begin to repeat my poem beneath my breath. Something—a frog? a leaping fish?—splashes in the lake. Another bit of the day rises, unwanted, in my mind: the slender speechless young man who robs me of my sleep.

After the needle-shadow divination at noontime, as I lay with the other off-duty maids dozing through the worst heat of the day, I found myself again in that dream yurt on the unbroken grass of the steppelands. By now, I know well the feelings he stirs in me—I've even tried envisioning his face to mask the solemn ruddy visage of the Fifteenth Prince, so I can respond in ways that might please His Highness. But today was not like other days.

He spoke, the first time ever. He told me there was something important I had to do. *What?* my dream-self asked him. *Tell me what.*

I've been trying to all this time, he said. *Trying to speak to you.* Then he said, *No, I've let myself be snared in these distractions, haven't I? They are so sweet.* He reached toward my cheek but his gaze left me then, and seemed to focus on a memory. *But I'm trying to understand something one of the lamas told us apprentices . . .* His lithe body wavered, as if about to fade from my vision. I wanted him to stay.

His voice grew faint. And then grew strong again. *Listen!* he said. *I, we cannot stop, can we? But we* could *make of these pleasures a higher bliss. The bliss of emptiness. First, though, you have, we have, things to learn. And for your mother's sake, you must—*

At that exact moment, Goldflower nudged my shoulder with her foot, told me to hush my sleep-talk yammering, lay back down on the woven bamboo pillow at her end of the bed. I did not sleep again. Indeed, the whole dream disturbed me greatly; I had to push it from my mind.

Till now. When once more—for what else can I do?—I nudge the memory back and recite my poem again, changing a word or two. There's not much time left till jealous ears will hear the effort of a maid they think reaches much too far above herself; I must chant it flawlessly.

Another, louder splash interrupts the final line. Right below my feet: In the faint beam of the distant lanterns, I see ripples spreading out across the liquid blackness.

A third splash. The gleaming colorless head of a huge carp rises from the surface. It casts a stone into a clump of grass before me, swirls once in a twisting double loop, and disappears. A few bubbles float, then vanish, traceless.

Have I left the Frontier Lakes and entered again into a dream world? At any rate, I know with dreamlike surety that I must take up the stone. And like a dreamer, I am not at all surprised that the stone turns out to be something else.

It is a metal statue smaller than my hand. A ferocious guardian warrior, who holds a chain.

The flute rings out. I tuck the statue in my plain dark sleeve.

But this day's conundrums are not finished. I decide to return through the retreat's rear gate, using its lantern-lit galleries to reach the loggia. The first courtyard I enter is the garden: I can just make out the library building beyond the path that winds among rock hillocks and tall pines.

Then, in the unstable lantern light, I see Yura sitting on the edge of one wide porch. See her arm draped affectionately over Clarity's shoulders, see their heads leaning intimately together. Hear Clarity murmur something as she breaks away and softly laughs.

And why not? I have no claim on Yura. It's only that I feel cut off, feel that something I didn't know I treasured has been lost. The loss joins the whirl within me as I stare. Is this unhappiness affection's price?

Then Yura says something about the flute song, and while Clarity's responding I rush on noiseless feet along the opposite gallery, through side hall and library and up to where the ladies wait.

The two appear, separately, a few moments later, but by then I've wrapped myself in the composure I know can look like haughtiness. I clasp my hands, lest the guardian-warrior statue slip out.

I try to nod and look impressed by the various poems, but when at last—at very last, as fits my standing—my turn comes, my heart is pounding so that I can hardly stand. That intimacy of Clarity and Yura's has raised me to a passion more relentless than the grunting prince's dutifully counted thrustings, more sharply memorable even than the fluid playfulness of that other, unnamed, young man when he laughs and pulls me dreaming onto his naked lap.

My cheeks burn; I can feel them, hotter than today's unclouded sun at noon. It grows worse after I lower my head before the prince's mother, when I look up to catch sight of Lady Brightcloud, who stands beside the First Consort's chair and flashes a sharp look into Her Majesty's narrowed eyes.

If only the figures I faced now were compassionate Guan-yin with her attendants, or wise Manjushri, the bodhisattva whom Yura—Yura!—reveres above all. If only I were again a little girl, reciting someone else's poem to the kind encouragement of Mama, or Father, or Third Aunt.

Still, no help for it. "This is called 'A Boon Begged of the Weaver Star,'" I say, ignoring the whispers that have begun to fill the hanging silence. I bow more deeply in the direction of the Empress Dowager, and begin to chant:

> No clouds, no rain, a dry night wind.
> The Silver River cuts the sky,
>   no ford to link its banks.
> A silent room, raised windowblinds—
>   one cricket sings, and who is there to hear?
>
> Moon hangs and swells, a jadewhite hook.
> A lake of flowers: a boat slips through
>   as dampened petals part.
> The Weaver grants a single glimpse—
>   a bridge of wings, a spiderweb of words.

At first, no one says a word. Of course. It's only one more Double-Seventh poem, using the same familiar images. How many have we heard tonight?

But the First Consort's frowning, her fine-arched eyebrows drawn together. "Well," she says. "It fits the form. But—really!—rather brazen for one so young."

One of the ladies in the haze around me hisses, *jade hook! damp petals! clouds and rain! and in Her Dowager Majesty's venerable presence—shocking!* I make out beyond my heart-thumps her neighbor whispering, . . . *the sort who calls unseemly male attention to herself. Surely she knows . . .*

Then I can hear nothing until the old lady clears her throat. The crowd on the loggia falls still. "I must say, I thought it no harm for us women to indulge in a bit of poetry, to be kept strictly among ourselves, of course. But we all know the teachings about the dangers of female talent."

She pauses. Is she looking to the First Consort? I squeeze my eyes closed, lest the tears leak out, though it makes me dizzy. "Now, the girl's not to be blamed for a minor lapse of taste," Her Dowager Majesty continues. "I take the responsibility myself. She's got backbone as well as beauty, I will say that. But perhaps . . . perhaps too much."

Shame drowns all my other emotions. Fireflies, starry lovers, the sky-long Silver River whirl around, within me. I don't know whether I throw myself face down, or fall.

THE PRIVATE JOURNAL OF
JULIAN N. S. REES, MAPMAKER

Introduction to the 1996 Henry Holt Edition:

"Throughout these grounds, . . . everything seemed to be avoided which betrayed a regularity of design. Nothing was observed to be directed, unless for very short distances, by straight lines."

—Sir George Staunton, 1797

Much has been written concerning the 1793 embassy of Lord Macartney from the court of King George III of Great Britain to that of Aisin Gioro Hongli, the Qianlong emperor of the Qing. This much is certain: The delegation cost a great deal to finance, was received with courtesy despite the ambassador's refusal to perform the usual *koutou*, and did not achieve its goals—among them, establishment of a British diplomatic mission in Beijing and an opening of trade.

Nevertheless (or consequently), the experiences of Macartney and his secretary and Minister Plenipotentiary, Sir George Staunton, became a basis for future representations of the Qing rulers as arrogant, obstinate, and despotic, of those they ruled as wretched, and of both as meriting such nineteenth-century enterprises as the Opium War (1839–42).

The events of 1793 and the texts that mediate or re/create them have gener-
ated wildly differing readings of ritual practices such as the *koutou*, of the role of
"tribute" in the fluid semiotic systems of relationships among political entities, of
imperialism/s in its/their manifold historical and cultural contexts, of the construction of ethnocentrism/s and marginalization/s in subjectivities "East" and "West,"
of the landscape at Rehe (Jehol, Zhe-hol, *warm river*, also known as Chengde or
Ch'eng-teh) and its hermeneutically decoded subtexts, of the laudatory self-
descriptive monologues and dominant paradigms of both existing orders, and
of the geobody of "China" as stage upon which are enacted the privileged scripts
of power.

Which is to say, the stories told about the embassy have much to do with the
stories that the storytellers tell about, and to, themselves.

Now a new text enters the multivocal discourse. Julian Noel Sean Rees was a
civilian assistant to Lt. A. H. Levi-James, the officer charged with making mea-
surements, engineer's elevations with sectional drawings, and the like throughout
the journey; for reasons soon to be apparent, however, the civilian's efforts never
appeared in the official report.

What follows derives from a half-burnt handwritten fragment recently discovered and purchased for the Farquhar Library of Asian Cultural Studies in
Aberdeen (formerly the Division of Orientalia of H.M. Archives of the British Crown
Colony of Hong Kong). The journal's authenticity is beyond question, its value—as
the private record of one of the less-known persons among the ninety or so in
Macartney's suite—beyond reckoning. Perhaps, as we reconfigure yet again the
maps of the Central Kingdom and of the peninsula of Northwest Asia, it is fitting
that this troubled cartographer have the last eyewitness word.

· · · · · · · · · · · ·

Gene Larsson, Ph.D.
Bradley Hall, Hong Kong University
May, 1995

[Sunday, Sept. 8, 1793]

. . . & so this day, but three weeks short of a year since we sailed from
dear old England, we have completed the seven-day journey along the rugged
road from Pekin to the summer capital of Zhe-hol. Even this humble man of Sci-

ence feels a quickening of the Fancy:—what visions shall I see here at the Celestial Court?

Ah, but I must remember that my business remains impartial observation & the application of consistent scale, that I may work with Lieutenant Levi-James in transmitting on Plain Charts an impartial record of the terrain.—& not the distorted patchworks of exaggerations, blanks, & geomancers' cloudlands that in China pass for maps.

I calculate, then, that we are 117'52" East of the Prime Meridian at Greenwich, & at latitude 40'59"N, with which objective reckoning surely none can quarrel.

Late yesterday, I scrambled up a summit from which I espied the adjacent Ridges rising in parallel, sublime undulations on an enormous granite sea. The last rays of westering Sol struck a wonder of nature far to the East, a giant upright fuller's rod or pestle or inverted hammer formed by natural erosion of the stone, which I later was inform'd overlooks the Vale of Zhe-hol. A Herculean club? My pulse beat more rapidly at the sight.—

My description of this marvel brought a half-smile to the lips of our younger interpreter, Master Yuan; but as he is himself a native of the area, I took his response to be the delight any man would take in a traveler's interest in the curiosities of his home. Indeed, I continue to find Yuan a man of cultivated understanding, far more dispos'd to social intercourse than his superior, who of course must devote himself to His Excellency the Embassador.

As for the reception of His Excellency & our suite, we were met in Zhe-hol this after-noon with the courteous pomp and military honours which have been accorded us ever since our landfall at Taku harbour. To-day, in addition to the usual crowds of gaping commoners on foot, we were welcomed by a phalanx of yellow-hatted friars (or la-mas) belonging to that sect of Fo-worshippers profess'd by the Imperial family. Their sanctimonious decorum as they chanted their liturgy much resembles that of priests & monks in those European nations where the Romish Church holds sway. I admit this mummery afforded a colourful spectacle, & was in no way disagreeable to the ear.

But the aching of my head oppresses me; and I must sleep, lest I fall into gloomy agitation once again. How grateful I am for the course of chymistry prescrib'd for me by our expedition's good Doctor Gillan!

Tuesday, Sept. 10, noontime
[editor's note: The next half-sentence is indecipherable.]

. . . straining overlong upon the necessary stool. Even so, after but a day & a half, our time here in the Summer Capital already promises to be more pleasant than the five days we passed in the dusty heat of Pekin.

Nonetheless, I daresay there exists outright hostility to our party from certain factions within the Court. Hints have been received that His Imperial Majesty's second Minister, a former Viceroy of Canton, harbours a great coldness toward our interests, perhaps due to an indignation born of some trifling or imagined slight from a European trader there.

His Excellency takes care not to protect his own dignity (which being the natural superiority of the well-bred Englishman cannot, as he has remark'd, entirely be obscur'd); but only refuses that a servile abasement be required of the representative of His Britannic Majesty.

Yet I here privately unbosom myself of one observation—that the performance of the courtly prostrations and genuflections is not ungraceful, nor does it look to me to be degrading; but that is mere opinion, no more to be trusted than Yuan's assertion that the one who bows down in this manner thereby takes an equally important part in a Relation I believe he would call 'reciprocity,' had he the word.

Of such sophistical speculation, no more!

We are quarter'd on a low hill on the west bank of the broad river Wu-lieh-h'o, at the southern edge of the hovels and the mandarins' Summer mansions, which constitute the town of Zhe-hol. (The great walled imperial garden Estate & it's palaces lie just north of the town, some three English miles from here.) The site & it's prospect are pleasant; & our spacious residences are built in the Chinese manner, which prevails throughout this section of Tartary.

Certainly, Zhe-hol town, with it's unpaved crooked lanes, is no match for Pekin, where the four walls of the Forbidden City total over two miles in length; those of the entire Imperial quarter, six miles; the surrounding Tartar (or 'Manchoo') City's, fourteen; & those of the Chinese City south of the Tartars' precinct, ten.

But I have been told that the imperial Estate's enclosing wall—tho' its height (sixteen feet) be inferior to the ramparts of Pekin (those of the Tartar City rise to some forty feet)—forms a rough circle of perhaps seven miles in circumference.

Shall I be allow'd to measure it for myself? At present, I know not even whether or no I will be allow'd to join the party of gentlemen accompanying His Excellency & Sir George to court within the park. Yet Expectation stirs.—

Wednesday, Sept. 13, 9 P.M.

About those walls of the Tartar City of Pekin:—most singular it is to learn to-day from Master Yuan that, in seeing their foundations, I have seen the trace of walls built for the great Mongol conquerer Cublai Can round his second capital. Singular, because it was Samuel Purchas's description, in his *Pilgrimage*, of that same Cublai's northern capital Xamdu, or Xanadu, ("Shang-doo" says Yuan) that ingender'd my boyish desire to travel to Cathay.

I open my worn copy of that fine old book, which I have carried all these miles; & find these words: 'a stately Palace . . . with a wall, wherein are fertile meddowes, pleasant Springs, delightfull Streames . . . and in the midst thereof a sumptuous house of pleasure, which may be removed from place to place.' Exactly like the removed imperial Seat to which I am arriv'd, like the great enclosed garden of royal tents & scattered castles outside whose gate I, a pilgrim in the name of Reason and the Science of Geography, do wait.—

Now, no more idle mooncalf's allegory,—but my anodyne, & to bed.

Thursday, Sept. 12, evening

I have been much tax'd by Lieutenant Levi-James this past four days to improve my sketches & topographical surveys along the road to Zhe-hol. Our purpose here remains frustrated by bland affability & obdurate refusal, which parry his efforts at negotiation; but I here confess that the respite from the baleful influences of travel is not unwelcome to at least one member of our party.—

At table this evening, one of our Neopolitan linguists describ'd a present made by certain Roman priests in honor of a birth-day of this Emperor's mother, who died sixteen years ago, in Anno Domini 1777:—it was no less than a theatre in miniature, peopl'd by automatical musicians that play'd hourly on stages back'd by scenes cunningly painted to deceive the eye. The gift was greatly prized. Such is the charm, to those who turn from the unsullied light of Rationality, of Fancy's tricks!

Sir George then told of the sham city market street suppos'd to be set up among the garden palaces outside Pekin. He has heard that there the Eunuchs assume at times the roles of merchants—as well as taverners & haggling customers—offering odd ends of such divers sorts as old clothes & the snacks sold by wandering hucksters, that the Ladies of the *gynaeceum* may gratify their wish to taste the excitements of the Common Life from which they are debarr'd.

Just now, discussing these replicas with Master Yuan, I am inform'd that the whole of the imperial Park here at Zhe-hol is understood to be a not dissimilar Representation. It's palaces may be taken as figuring, in small, the Forbidden City in Pekin; & the adjoining lakes & islands as the riverine landscapes of the Great Kiang; whilst the prairie district north of the lakes—the Garden of a Myriad Trees—where His Imperial Majesty holds court before a large round tent after the Mongol manner to Mongol musicians' tunes, renders the Mongols' woods & grasslands; & the largest district—forested hills abounding with beasts of chase—completes this Map of the empire by shadowing forth it's vast frontier lands and Northern marches.

(As for myself, I wonder if the surrounding wall might not be taken as a facsimile of that remarkable Great Wall anciently built by the Chinese against the hordes without. So well built, & so often breach'd.)

The great arc of Fo-ist temples beyond the rivers flowing North & East of the Estate are, Yuan assures me, variously constructed after the fashions of the Mongols, the Thibetans, and the Chinese. Moreover, the joss-houses whereat are made adorations to the deified philosopher Kung-foo-tse, & such members of the Chinese (and 'Manchoo') Pantheon as Zhe-hol's tutelary Genius, & a hallowed general,—these all abide outside the Southwestern portion of the Estate's wall.

He then began a further explanation, involving the "Nine Hills and Eight Seas" (*viz.*, the chain of so-called Frontier Lakes and the artificial island-peaks among them), which I believe was meant to indicate an allegoric vision of the Estate—like unto the Hindoo or Fo-ist *mandora*, or mapping of Creation, with nine ring-shaped mountain ranges separated by eight oceans. But I may not have the conceit correctly;—such Pagan metaphysics elude this simple man of Logic!

It is my great and simple Desire merely that I may see for myself these splendors of architecture & landscape art.

Yet at these words, Despondence knocks again upon my window.—I'll have no more on't! Adieu.

After my nightly draught, a sudden thought: Is it that aforementioned Desire to see, which of late paints for me such peculiar nocturnal visions? Forbidden gardens, and palaces whose corridors might be stalked by a Minotaur—

Ah, but to mull over the random Phantasms of the sleeping Brain is to open the Pandora's box of superstition; & who c'ld assure me that any wan Creature so comforting as the Hope found by poor Pandora might also lie within for me?—

Friday, Sept. 13, after noon

The compliments of his Imperial Majesty having been delivered to His Excellency promptly upon our arrival, & various negotiations having finally been completed, the official audience is set for to-morrow. His Excellency & Sir George will be taken to court by palanquin. It turns out I am to join those who accompany them!—for His Excellency wishes both Lieutenant Levi-James and myself to observe as much as possible of the Estate. We shall set out at 4 A.M.

I must remember to tell my young friend Samuel Taylor . . . [editor's note: The next four pages of the manuscript are missing, depriving us of Rees's version of the imperial audience and subsequent formal banquet on the fourteenth, and a second meeting and the party's horseback tour (in the company of high-ranking Manchu officials) of the eastern section of the imperial estate on the fifteenth.

The account picks up with an entry that must have been dated Tuesday, September 17, 1793. We know from other sources that the ranking members of the delegation set out for court that morning at three, and paid their birthday respects to the emperor—who sat invisible behind a screen—sometime after 6 A.M. The party's tour of the estate then continued with a long ride through the hills.]

. . . Nor did our unshod mounts misstep as they climbed the rugged staircases hewn out of the living stone.

Having partaken of a fine collation of savouries & sweets, in one of the excellently situated Summer-houses scattered among the sublimity of the Hill district, a puppet show was presented for our entertainment. We saw several lively puppet jousts, & a puppet *opera bouffe* very like the farcical misadventures of England's own Punch with his wife, which His Excellency pronounced "capital."

My favourite, however, was an extraordinary morality play about a melancholic Chinese puppet damsel who strummed a kind of Chinese dulcimer, or zithern, it's sound being feigned by some sort of unseen ha'penny whistle. All at once, a gyrating female puppet clad entirely in white appeared within the splendid colours of the japanned wooden stage;—unreasonable tho' it be, the eerie sight and airy music affected me exceedingly.

Her long hair loos'd and falling to her knees, the pallid figure began to remonstrate earnestly to the maid.

'It is a Ghost,' whispered Yuan, in translation of the puppeteer's falsetto. 'The Ghost of the mother of the girl, from a locally transmitted faery tale.'

Apparently, the Ghost thereupon charged the girl with gathering up a scattered group of Idols, for the good of someone's—the daughter's or the mother's?—immortal Soul. I smiled broadly at the quaintness of the Conception, whereupon Yuan's face changed & he looked suddenly a Stranger to me, despite the European habit in which he clothed himself.

But I am weary & fretful with fourteen hours of riding & feasting & *divertissements*, & must—lay my pen aside.

later

Yuan's face: It was like that moment this after-noon, when as we approached the poorly lighted, gold-adorned Holy of Holies within the grand Potala temple north of the walled Park,—one friar hastily drew shut the curtain before the innermost shrine.

Wednesday, September 18, late

Last e'en, I recorded virtually nothing of our post-meridian visit to the magnificent pagodas, monasteries & temples outside the imperial Estate. Having written that far, I found myself in an unaccountable state of direful irritation. A witticism of His Excellency's, in which he compar'd his first official audience with the Emperor some days ago to the glory of King Solomon—as represented by a puppet show seen when His Excellency was a lad in Belfast!—kept ringing in my mind.

Fearing a return of the dismal malady of my Student years, I resorted to a larger than usual draught of my laudanum. Yet half-waking Phantasms pursu'd me thro' the night.

To-day was long as well. I had hop'd to record now the pageants & pantomimes, & other dramatical presentations perform'd this morning in continued celebration of His Imperial Majesty's birth-day, & the varied exhibitions of tumblers, palaestrians, juglers, & the excellent show of fireworks that fill'd the late after-noon & evening hours. Reasonable reflection, however, informs me that the weak & weary Flesh has it's own needs, which must be met.—I go to take my rest.

Thursday, Sept. 19, 11 A.M.

My spirits are much improv'd this Morning, despite a somewhat unpleasant conversation with Doctor Gillan after we made our breakfast.—But all is well, & to-day our party continues quietly within doors at our residence. I confess it feels something of a Holiday.

I shall continue with my account of yesterday's theatricals, before turning to work on our Report.

The Emperor, at age eighty-three by the Chinese reckoning, is a strait-back'd, spare-bodied old Gentleman, so hale one might take him to be younger by a quarter-century. We have been giv'n to understand that he is a man of frugal tastes, preferring such soldierly sport as weight-lifting or horse-races to the pomp & extravagance of celebratory processions or the more fanciful plays.

Yet even he, it seems, allows exception, when press'd by his adoring subjects, or to indulge his Ladies. Or to put in good humour the Mohammedan Kalmucks & other simple outland tributaries who are also presently at Court.

In any case, the theatres said to be so plentiful within the Pekin palaces have not been omitted from this smaller Capital. Our senior interpreter tells us one stands on the estate's Ju-eu (which means 'As You Wish') Isle. We—

O, but first, lest I should forget it, I return refresh'd now to my account to record some poetical appellations with which the hand of Man has inscrib'd itself upon the Estate:—'Morning Alpenglow upon the Western Range,' 'A Myriad

Ravines of Pinewood Wind,' 'Fragrances Remote & Beneficial Clarity,' 'Mountain-slope of Docile Deer,' 'A Limpid Fountainhead Coils over Stones,' &c. &c. &c.

From such naming of locales & buildings, according to Yuan—for we are once more on the best of terms, and he is ever glad to have new English words of me—each prospect is believ'd to be brought fully into Being. But 'tis not enough, in China, that Adam utter words unseen into the ear of Eve. No, signs must be posted, so as to form a sensible Object within the field of vision,—as tho' a descriptive Verse, or the title of a landscape painting were boldly indited above the Mists or Nebulae drifting in it's upper air.

As tho' the landscape were a Chinese painting scrawl'd with drifting, cryptic Chinese hieroglyphs.—

after-noon

I have slept and return to my subject:—we entered the Estate *via* a postern in it's South wall known as 'the Gate of Virtues Converged,' which leads directly into the closed quadrangle of the Eastern Palace. (I surmise this allows the common Actors to come and go without further access to the Park, that they may not taint the rest of the Imperial Precincts—in particular, the nearby Palace of the Ladies.)

Our small party being conducted past dressing rooms and buildings for storing stage properies, we were shewn our places amongst the Mandarins on a side verandah of the courtyard in which the ornamented three-story stage building stood. His Imperial Majesty sat atop the broad steps of a two-story building opposite; & His Excellency & Sir George were summon'd thither to attend him. An honour guard stood at attention in the pit. The Ladies beheld the stage from behind lattice screens on the floor above and behind the throne, the strict rule of Modesty being thus observ'd.

O, the plays! No music accompanied them, tho' some were sung, some spoken, & some done in recitative. I found most enchanting a love scene depicting a young woman who—Yuan said—announc'd herself as having walked thro' her pillow, *id est*, to have entered, in Reverie, a castle garden in the air. She wore a great bat-winged headdress in the Tartar style, much elaborated with artificial flowers and dangling ornaments; & minc'd upon tassel'd shoes. Her face was painted very white, her cheeks shone very fresh with pink; & black paint outlin'd her expressive eyes. Nymphea (or 'Water Lily') was her name.

This Nymphea sang a tremulous aria, revealing her pure yet impassion'd nature, as she describ'd the garden; & her great Wish to meet with her Betroth'd, one Scholar Woo, from whom she had been for long years parted by unfortunate Fate. As she concluded, the youthful scholar—or his dream-Semblance— appear'd. I render their conversation only somewhat improv'd on Yuan's fluent rendition, which did increase further my admiration for his Intellect—

> She: Who art thou, Sir?
>
> He   (taking her hand):
> I am he for whom thou longest.
> Come with me, come!
>
> She (hiding her face):
> Whither?
>
> He: Behind that tower-mount of stone
> Drawn from pellucid waters
> Of a vasty flower-strewn lake.
> And I shall loose your girdle,
> Shall take you to the vapourous Gorge-cleft
> Of the eastward-rolling River Kiang.
> There, where the ancient King made sport
> With the Mystic Mountain Goddess,
> I'll teach thee of love's dalliance
> In this Realm of Dreamt Delight.

She resisted,—he embraced her—& she resisted not; but swoon'd as he carried her offstage. At this moment, a trapdoor in the ceiling above them opened; & an Angel garb'd in all the colors of the Spectrum descended, holding a painting album of the Chinese type in her fair hands.

The Angel—who was in fact Empress of the Flowers—bemoaned in song the foolishness of the departed maiden and her lover. Some of our party had grown already restless &, like the Mandarins, convers'd among themselves. Yet I remained absorb'd, musing 'pon the mechanics of the trapdoor & the floating Actor,—most ingenious contrivances.

Then, when the Empress of the Flowers opened the album wide, to display it, I felt upon perceiving the Void of its blank pages, a sudden shock I cannot put in words.—

. . . .

There follow'd tragical scenes from History; & a rousing battle-dance by a most acrobatic Warrior Woman of the ancient Dynasty of the Tangs, clep'd Second Daughter, who defeated a monkish Serpent-monster with her sword; & part of a queerish tale about a magic mirror; &c.

But I pause now for my restorative. I must conserve my energies. The day after to-morrow, we depart for Pekin.

late night

Sleep & Work & the tumult within my Heart be d——d! Two more tales I *will* relate, here & now—

Narration of the first, perhaps, will prove a balm to the effects upon me of the second, as the former at least may be described without affront to Reason. But why the chief figure in the latter drew my attention thither, I cannot say.

I outpace myself. First, then, to the first:—the grandest of the birth-day pageants.—By means of a revolving platform, the lowest stage was quickly set to simulate a lake thick with water-lilies. Then a single giant pink lily-bud was push'd invisibly forward onto the mid-level stage. Somehow, whilst the observing eye was thus distracted, a tall conical wooden structure appear'd on the small stage of the building's uppermost floor.—'The Great-Vehicle Hall in the Universal Peace Temple,' murmured Yuan as he gestured toward it, 'It is the also the mountain at the centre of, of all the world, no, worlds.' I did not take his meaning.

A girl wandered singing along the lakeshore. Of a sudden, a light-footed actor clad in black silk sprang forth, face painted most hideously, hair caught up in two tufts like a devil's horns:—a Dragon, explained Yuan.

This black Dragon twirl'd and postur'd, long whiskers waving, rather lithe than fearsome, yet clearly possessed of pow'rs unknown to Zoology. It then pantomim'd an urgent presentation to the awe-stricken girl, who had watch'd it all the while. Finally, it plucked from thin air (or in Truth, from behind one of the stage-lilies) a bundled silken handkerchief, which the girl accepted.

That moment prepared us for the climax of the spectacle, for as Yuan inform'd us that the silken bundle contain'd likenesses of a saviour-deity call'd Ah-mi-tuo Fo & four surrounding seraphic spirits, first four impassive idols—and then a fifth and larger one—rose majestically from beneath the lower stage, as if to prove what Yuan had said. Great pots of incense being ignited, vapours wafted from the theatre-building, as the audience cried out in approbation, *'How ah, hung how ah!',* which is to say, 'Most excellent!'

Yet a final effect ensued, & all, I am certain, design'd with idolatrous signification as well as the mechanical skill which impress'd itself upon me:—for the giant lily-bud on the central level split open to reveal enthroned on its petals, a female Fo, head draped by a hood of pearl-coloured silk, holding a willow-branch. ('The Goddess of Mercy,' quoth Yuan.) A boy costum'd as a novice friar stood on a lily-pad to one side of this Fo; & the black dragon (having vanished offstage from the lake below and scrambl'd unseen upwards) took a place on t'other, thus completing the tableau.

At least, this is how I recall the pageant. But though such recollection has bred somewhat more of tranquility within me, as I prepare to write down what has transpir'd this very e'en, agitation wracks me once again.

But I have said I would. I pause only for my physic.

The second event:—this after-noon, having completed my entry in this journal, I fell asleep in my chair. It was full twilight when a furious knocking roused me—the subaltern Paull, a most reasonable man, begging my pardon and seeking permission to speak.

In brief, he took me to the front Gate of our suite of edifices, where on the granite steps stood Yuan,—with a Creature dressed in rags. A chill mist had crept along the low hillside as I slept, imparting a disheartening clamminess to the ill-lit scene, for all I knew it to be the direct effect of the rapid drop in temperature of the ambient air at sunset on an unusually humid day.

'Mr. Rees,' said Yuan. 'Allow me to present . . . *une religieuse.* A Mongol holy woman. We were children together here at Zhe-hol, her father being a bondslave, on permanent staff of His Imperial Majesty's Estate.'

Paull shrank back, as if from a dread horror. Peering more closely, I saw that the diminutive Creature was indeed a Woman, despite it's, her, roughly shaven pate, & that she might well have been about Yuan's age, a bit over thirty years. A small mole dotted the lower portion of her chin. The eyes above her broad cheekbones held a look of mysterious Power in the flickering light of Paull's torch.

'She implores me,' continued Yuan, 'to impart to you a message. Yet I believe I must first apologize for any rudeness. . . . You & I have come to be friends, have we not?'

Observing in my, yes, friend an uneasiness I took—& take—to be grounded in his one flaw of Character, a veneration of idolatry & superstition (which is, after all, but the flaw of the Nation of which he was born), I gripped his hand, as one honest John Bull grips another's.

'And friends speak as they must to friends,' quoth I. 'Besides, you speak tonight for her. Say on!'

At this, Yuan nodded, & interpreted directly for the woman, who at his behest began to make her speech.

'You British come,' she proclaimed *via* Yuan, who must have drawn upon every new word of English he had learnt in recent weeks, 'with surveyor's quadrant and three-legged staff, with planetarium, with globes celestial & terrestrial, with astronomical chronometer and meteorological devices, with engravings & Josiah Wedgwood's jasper ware, with weapons, saddles, carriages, & models of stout warships in silver & gold. With telescopes to render keen the human eye!

'Yet you bring nothing that is wanted, and insist we give you in return that to which you have no claim.'

She paused, allowing Yuan to catch up. Her voice as she continued softened, yet retained its austere clarity. 'But such I daresay is the foolishness of all Men. Tho' it's manner vary, tribe to tribe.'

Paull (who has a good bit more of the Chinese language than I ever shall) goggled as she then raised one arm in my direction. Terror-struck, he began to stammer unintelligible protests. She ignored him entirely,—as a great Lady ignores a malicious jeering urchin upon the street—and desir'd me most commandingly to ponder the pageant I have just now written down.

'You, Sirrah,' she said then, 'have fail'd especially in this:—you were born not ox, nor dog, nor demon, but a Man, and were brought by Destiny'—or so Yuan styled it—'from the farthest Kingdom of the earth. Yet you hear the Teaching and do not listen. You see the silk, but not the signs it holds. You observe the budding lily, but you do not see what lies within. You must look, and look again, before you draw your *mappemonde*.'

Her declamation concluded, she turned & left. I bade Yuan a swift Goodnight & retir'd here to my chamber, leaving Paull all of a tremble, as if seiz'd by a morbid aversion—and indeed I have heard some among his heartier fellows laugh and deem him a misogynist.—If true, he would surely be most distress'd by such a woman's well-spoken words, & by her treating him, despite his uniform and his Sex, as disregardable.

Now I have written long by candlelight. Labour & Reason have soothed me. I will think on these things no more.

Friday, Sept. 20, near dawn

Still half asleep—after a night thro' which I have not for one moment slept by more than half, despite my anodyne—I have risen, to read again that final passage. I had hop'd it would explain the dream from which I have awakened.

I was lost in a pleasure-ground of endlessly diverging & intersecting pathways, design'd with exquisite artifice. Was it—it was the Imperial Estate, as I saw it not three days ago spread out below the pavilion called 'Clouds and Hills in Four Directions,' atop the highest peak. Was and was not. Was in aspect redrawn.

So far, then, can Rationality clarify the source of Apparition.

But then this:—Clutching my surveyor's chain—or dream-chain—& phantasmal spy-glass, I tried to measure a terrain that shifted each time I scanned. I discover'd then a book;—it's blank pages suddenly bore words, as a sky empty at one glance has at the next a hint of nebulous Condensation. It said, 'this is the unstable landscape of de . . . [editor's note: Here, the fragment ends.]

DISPOSSESSIONS AND POSSESSIONS

Look around. This place where you find yourself (green or dusty, biting cold or breeze cooled or sweat hot) is a mandala. It is an altar, a sacred mansion, a healing image hidden only by your ignorance, a radiant perfected land here and now on earth.

This place is a mandala, like those you have already met with. Some are painted. Some are jeweled. Some are made of metal, or dried dough or colored sand or clay, or of fine-carved wood. Some show rings of gathered deities, and diagram the cosmos. Some map out a palace for a god.

And some are formed by learning how to see anew the inner structure—the holy landscape, the subtle geography—of your body's energies.

The sounds you hear (birds' territorial warnings, a weary cough, a pulley's squeal and clatter, water plashing onto granite, animal bleats of lust or terror, your own sleep-mutterings beneath your breath): These sounds are mantras, ritual syllables of wonder-working potency that resonate in emptiness, incantations that can link you to the essence of a deity.

Say *om mani padme hum* and the calm tenderness of Avalokiteshvara surrounds you like a six-spoked wheel of light. Recite *om muni muni mahamuni shakyamuni svaha*, and the wisdom of that great sage from the ruling family of the Shakyas, the pure mind of Siddhartha Gautama, can pour into your heart, a stream of gold.

This place is a mandala, and you have the power to see it so. After all, your empty hyperactive mind invented it. What you have created, you can transform.

This place, then, is the ground plan for a celestial dwelling. Cleanse the site, seek refuge, make the vows. Re-draw the map. Invite the deity to come within.

· · · · · · ·

That may be a little like what the lama from the Potala temple at Warmriver has in mind as he speaks with tranquil gravity to Lotus, who lies half waking in her bed. He sits cross-legged on a cushion at her side, he tries to teach, he blesses her. But his prayers and benedictions fall on sterile ground. However he explains things, she cannot understand.

Her thinking veers. Her senses all assure her that the waking world's a very different sort of place. She can't imagine undertaking all she'd have to do and learn. She moans, and turns back to her dream realm, turns away.

She remains troubled, sometimes flushed, more often pallid, dangerously ill. Weeks have passed since she fainted on the Double Seventh; afterward, the Fifteenth Prince found several chances to summon her, but now he's off with his father on the annual hunting trip. And she's had other strange attacks since then, tumbling briefly out of the semiconscious state most people think of as the real world.

Mostly, though, she simply slips longer, deeper, into slumber, day by day.

The Empress Dowager hears the lama's report. She observes the hectic patches on the young maid's pale cheeks, the spectral thinness of her body. Annoyed and worried by the possibility of harmful influence, Her Dowager Majesty nonetheless remains unwilling to let the young bondservant fade—or be sent—away.

It's not only the responsibility for dependents that comes with rank. The girl has a genuine appeal. She *does* play nicely on the chyn, and then the old lady has the interests of her cherished grandson to consider. He'll soon return from the camp at Mulan: Best not give him cause to sink sadhearted into a decline, best try to get her on her feet again, and let his infatuation run its course.

The other maids report that Lotus is most unsettled in the nighttime, though often in the rest hour after noon she writhes like someone demon ridden. So when that little Mongol girl mentions a local healer whose treatments are especially efficacious, the Empress Dowager orders that the shaman be invited to the Pine-Crane Haven.

Maybe the blacking-out and wasting-away, the visions Lotus is rumored to be having, all come of influence by a malign spirit, or some devil. Maybe she can be cured.

By evening on the day the shaman comes, Lotus has fallen into a feverish drowse. Sometimes she lifts her head and answers questions. Sometimes she can swallow the medicine that's been brewed for her—to no visible effect. But mostly she lies unmoving on her bed.

To the more experienced of those around her, she looks to be trapped in the enchanting languor that can overtake the body after coitus, that seizes the limbs with heavy weakness, and saps the vital force from mind and tongue. Is she, they wonder, in the possession of a ghost?

If so, the shaman's drum can exorcise. Her fire can purify. The words the shaman chants can draw in her mighty helpers. Half the night, a-sway in flickering half-darkness, the blind woman invokes the spirits who assist her, protectors long since dead who aided others as this woman does, when they still lived.

"O my teachers," she cries out to the almost-steady rhythm of her drumbeats as she turns her body, rolls her head. "You have given me unwritten teachings." The silent maids and serving women gathered in the room where Lotus lies watch patiently. "O my guardians," the shaman croons, "you have taught the faith not found in books."

Lotus trembles. She doesn't want to leave her vague pleasant sleep, the cosy satisfactions she finds over and over with that slim young man in the shadowy round tent. The shaman grips the leather handle of her drum, she beats it with a snakeskin-covered rod, she rattles its nine iron rings. The red silk snake tongue flicks and flicks as she beats the drum again.

Lotus's eyes fly open. The sleeves and front of the shaman's long loose dress—which fastens, unlike any normal clothing, Manchu or Han or Mongol, in the back—are hung with fluttering strips of cloth, as plumage covers a raven's breast, as pinions flare from the wings of a hawk. Feathers rise from a band across her forehead. Lotus wonders muzzily if the woman has become a bird.

"O my strong mirrors," the healer's trance voice sings. "O you who see all secret thoughts." A round mirror dangles on her chest. "O you who drive away with fear the fearsome evil powers." Small mirrors stud the belt atop her dark baggy apron, protecting her from demons, soaring devils, wandering phosphorescences, the hideous ill-willed dead.

"*Uuu, uu, uuu,*" cries Lotus, or cries someone, casting a great sound of weeping out from her red mouth. Clarity gasps, and clutches Yura's hand. Yura's eyes are wide, and fixed on empty air.

A young man's voice? Perhaps. Or it might be a mourner's wail. It might be burdened with the blind pain of lamenting its own end. It surely bears a load of hurt and grief.

The shaman beats her drum and cries out in quick time with the quickening drum skin. She rolls and rolls her head.

A small green-spotted snake eases from the corner of Lotus's mouth and flows across her cheek, onto the small hard pillow. It wrinkles. It disappears into a crack between the bed and wall.

Wu Ming, pursued by flitting wraiths of light, had no choice but to leave her. A relief, he thinks, now that he's gone, though he could not bring himself to break away. As for transmuting their shared pleasure to the sexual yoga—whether physical or envisioned—that the lama spoke of in the Beijing temple workshop: Ah, that's more than he could do.

He sighs. All that clouds-and-rain (and all unhampered by any soreness, dryness, silly slippage, by fear or time or awkwardness), all that delightful clouds-and-rain notwithstanding, he really hasn't done much to help Lotus gather up the statues, as the Lord of Mount Tai said he must.

To be sure, he's made an effort: Here, perhaps, a useful urge, and there a nudge toward silence or acquiescence. But it's been so difficult to break through the sound barrier between the realms—and through the haze born of briefly gratified, soon-renewed desire. The most Wu Ming can claim credit for is the single lovely statue of the fluid Buddha goddess Lochana that he prompted Lotus to steal last winter in the Forbidden City.

Like the appealing image of terrene Mamaki that the Fifteenth Prince gave the girl, like the lost effigy of airy Tara and that lively likeness of fiery, meditative Pandaravashini, aquaeous Lochana is undeniably a crucial figure in the first mandala ring around cosmic Vairochana. But the task is still so far from being done.

And who knows when the Lord of Mount Tai will have Wu Ming hauled back to his subterranean courtroom for an accounting? The pretty-faced artisan shakes his head.

His green-spotted head. He blinks, and shakes his head again, feels a spine-ripple run to the tip of his reptilian tail. Time to let go of *that* fleshly form. He shakes again.

Ah, immateriality. That feels better. In fact, he has gotten to rather like it: certainly more enjoyable than wedging one's wriggling body between two rough slabs of clay.

But before Wu Ming can contemplate the implications of that last thought, it comes to him that he has a problem. He's lost his essential bond to Lotus, now that the shaman has driven him away from her.

Well, then, where should he go?

Somewhere safe, yet not too far. Must he become a snake again? He, with all his artistic gifts, a creeping snake?

A snake. A dragon. A site within the imperial estate. A place he knows because Lotus has been there, a deep welcoming cleft charged in her recollection—and so in his—with the shifting–air pressure energy of impending sex.

Another blink and wrinkle. Wu Ming emerges at a mountainside grotto near First Flowering Lodge. At the little Dragon-Monarch Shrine.

And look! He's got his human form back! He's once again a slim-shouldered, smooth-cheeked youth, whose every graceful movement hints at high aspirations and noble sensitivity and deep vital strength. Joyously, he runs one palm across the nubbled surface of a stone, traces with his finger a scaly wooden claw on the long vermilion body coiled round the carved pillar at his side.

"Well? Did you mean it?"

Wu Ming jumps at the sound of the light voice in his ear. *What?* he thinks. *Mean something? When and what?*

"Did you mean it?" Amusement ripples (like the spring-fed rivulet below the shrine) across the face of the young woman now beside him, ripples, cascades, shines, and gives way to a pool of patience. "What you said to Lotus on the feastday of the Double Seventh, about getting caught up in . . . the distractions of what you do together. Have you finally seen beyond all that jolly tumbling in a tent?"

Who is this? Wu Ming stares at her dark piled-up hair, her sweetly composed face, the serpentine gold circlet on her head. Her eyes—don't they have the look of a girl from Khotan he once met? Do they in truth (she cocks her head, still smiling, waiting) flash green, like some rare pearl or a fluke of light tossed out by the setting sun?

No, no. He can't be thinking clearly. It must be dawn, not sunset, that lights his vision, after—he shudders—after the shaman's night-long vigil. And his companion . . .

Well, whoever she is, she's certainly attractive. Wu Ming makes the automatic count he's made so many times before. The wineshop owner's coy daughter, who taught him that he had a talent for beguilement. The lonely widow so easily charmed. The tempting quickly yielding fellow apprentice. The neighbor's reluctant maid, who made such an exciting scenario of all his gentle coaxing. And Lotus, all tantalizing shy readiness, once he'd reached through to her.

Can this new one, he wonders, be cajoled? Surely, a bewitching challenge. The heat and honey of seduction begin to work their way upon him. Though he believes—he actually believes—that he controls the game.

He clears his throat.

And she clears hers.

Wu Ming stops cold. Her dress, her posture: He's seen them in a religious picture somewhere! Not one of the Tibetan models back in the temple workshop, no. A simple woodblock that his mother showed him years ago. Was it with Lady Guan-yin of the Southern Sea?

"It's important, what you said," continues the young woman, "about the bliss of emptiness. Even though you were merely parroting words you don't really understand."

Now the sun clears the eastern ridge and falls forcefully through a break in the mountain foliage. The early morning chill transforms—like that!—into a foretaste of the sticky warmth to come. Wu Ming stares at her, transfixed. The silver-tongued seducer at a loss for words. The charmer, at last encharmed.

At least he listened to that powerful teaching, the Dragon Daughter tells him. At least now he can imagine something besides the fox-fire enticements of vainglory in his skillful hands and eyes, in his ability to lure others down a winsome path of artful words.

The rising sun shifts. It strikes young Wu full between his eyes.

"Would you like to know more?" his companion asks him.

Wu Ming nods.

"Sit down then. Oh, don't worry. We'll just talk. You've got a lot to learn."

Taiyang and Inkscent both realize, vaguely, that they too have things they need to know. If only they knew what.

They sit together in the Sun family's Upper Courtyard, shaded by the canopy of matting set up back at summer's start, anxious for the first foretaste of the cool months to come. Orange-pink crab shells litter the table in front of Taiyang. Inkscent dips her fingertips into a small bowl of water on which a few dried jasmine flowers float. Behind them, Old Master Sun snores, oblivious, in the stuffy shadows of his North Hall.

Taiyang picks up the new silver chopsticks he presented to his father as the steamed crabs were brought in from the kitchen, and inspects them once again. On his way home from his quarters in the Imperial City, he bought a basket of river crabs at first-of-season prices, in hopes the old man (so frail these days, so morose and thin!) would take something more nourishing than yellow wine. Old Master Sun ate one crab, told Taiyang he was a good, well-meaning son—if a bit extravagant—and retired, wincing as he leaned on Prima's arm.

Not important, Taiyang tells himself. No hint of spoiled crabmeat turned this shining silver black. Let no resentment taint my filial heart. He rolls the chopsticks idly between his thumb and palm.

Whether his father acknowledges it or not, Taiyang's pleased by his rising fortunes within the Imperial Household Department; his colleagues and the top-ranked eunuchs can see he's won the emperor's favor with his scheme to plumpen the ever-hungry Privy Purse. It looks like the new system of quiet "voluntary fines" from the most bribable—the richest— bondservant officials will indeed help pay for the palaces and temples and memorial archways with which the Qianlong emperor displays his piety, and the rightness of his reign.

Never mind (Taiyang does not quite allow this thought to form) that these secret payments make the Son of Heaven himself the corrupt beneficiary of corruption; it brings funds where funds are needed. It keeps the most venal of the bondservant elite in line.

And Taiyang gains the respect that traipses after wealth and the dread power of naming names. Does he not deserve at least that much? He has done no more than duty asks.

Yet—Taiyang slaps the poison-sensitive chopsticks back onto the tray—he's angrier than ever at those complacent aristocrats who reckon him just one more mercenary bondservant. This very morning, he was snubbed (subtly, oh, subtly and unmistakably) by a high-born government functionary with half his brains! Pride and a greed for public honor blaze up in Taiyang at the thought.

Common faults, of course, and doubtless understandable. But it's Taiyang himself who pays the price, taken over as he is by avarice for an empty coin. He begins to eat again. The savory delicacy of the crab, the fruity tartness of red vinegar and sweet tease of fine-chopped gingerroot: All are lost to him. *The man's rank was embroidered on his chest*, thinks Taiyang. *I know my place. He had no need to make a point of it.*

He forces himself to take another mouthful. *Bondservant!* Taiyang thinks. The rich yellow crab roe turns to sand.

"More wine?" Inkscent leans toward him only slightly, as if wine were all she offered. Taiyang refuses, pats her hand. Ignoring the softly talking maids waiting over on the south veranda, he lays his broad palm on her swelling belly.

"You've felt it move?" he asks.

Yes. But only once, Inkscent assures him, and she's started taking "placid-fetus" herbs. She ties the sash more tightly now, as well. She'll do all she can to prevent miscarriage. He shall have his child.

Yet she is certain Taiyang's much too worried. Except for such quick pats and trifling caresses, he hasn't touched her since he found out she's pregnant—and to tell the truth, she's come to miss his open-hearted lovemaking.

When the old man grunted and warned his son that she shouldn't eat much ginger, lest the child be born with rootlike extra toes and fingers, Taiyang nodded dutifully—and she resolved she wouldn't take a morsel, would not let it be forbidden her.

The real danger, Inkscent knows, lies elsewhere, in the rage that surges through her at the sight or sound or thought of selfish murderous Old Master Sun. Such anger could send her bodily forces spinning out of balance, bringing her a treacherous birthing, a sickly short-lived infant, or a sudden end to pregnancy in a great cramp and gush of clotted blood.

Thinking about him does me, does the child to be, does that poor dead weak-eyed widow, no good at all, Inkscent tells herself once more. She's imagined stabbing, or poison, or complaining to a magistrate. But what dreadful consequences any of those actions would bring the whole family—even Taiyang, even her daughter or her son! Her fury can't bring him to justice. Yet she knows no way to make it stop.

Save one. "Shall I play for you?" she asks Taiyang. At times her chyn allows her to transmute her rancor into a vibrant melody, a passion to be contemplated calmly: a flurry of tremors that rise up, strike the senses, end.

The longing woman brushes jasmine-scented fingers across the wrist of the brooding man. She wants now to destroy not that pathetic heap of pains in the North Hall, but her own miserable hate.

That, and all her other angers. An ice grain ignited the day a young girl learned that her father (having made her, seen her, held her) had left her and her mother without a backward glance. And despite the good new life this winehouse entertainer has so skillfully brought herself into, despite her deft navigation of the narrow channels in which a woman's life's allowed to run, deep in Inkscent that cold fire still smolders.

But Taiyang bids her rest a little longer after eating. "Besides," he adds, "it's best not to waken Father."

Inkscent folds her hands upon her lap. No music. Yesterday, her hand shook at the sound of the old man's voice, and spoilt the painting she was working on. No painting, then. No comfort in the bedroom. Precious little companionship, compared to her old life. Besides backaches, heat rash, sore breasts, and waiting, what does she have?

She sighs, as quietly as possible. Inkscent can no longer set the wish aside: She must find a lama to instruct her, soon.

A recent talk with Padma has convinced her of the urgency of this. Danger lies in the Tantric practices passed on to Inkscent without proper guidance. Padma's cautioned her: A mind attempting self-transformation yet not prepared for what it may experience may be badly hurt. At best, it will remain enmired. Can Inkscent persuade Taiyang she ought to have the money, and the bit of freedom, that the search for the right preceptor requires? He's a giving man, and yet . . . She sighs again.

Taiyang hears those quiet sighs. He turns to stare at Inkscent's moon-like face. He wants his concubine to be happy. He regards her—as might any man of his time and place—as the most precious of his possessions. And as something more.

How, he wonders, can he distract this beautiful, talented, pregnant woman from this evening's mood? He coughs, and soothes his throat with a last sip of tea gone cold.

Ah. "There's something I've been meaning to give to you," says Taiyang. "Something you'll like," (there: she's smiling, half smiling, anyway: let her know the truth: he has given this gift some thought) "even though it came to me in an odd way. Never mind that. A present for you." He calls out lightly, "Snow!"

The maid hurries over. Taiyang sends her into the side hall to fetch the box he's brought home from his quarters. When Inkscent opens it, she sees the small metal figure of a buddha seated in meditation, surrounded by four statues of bodhisattvas. His right hand reaches down and out in the boon-granting gesture. His left hand rests palm up. It holds a jewel.

"Ratnasambhava," she whispers, "who overcomes pride and avarice." In a flash, she understands why it came to this good-hearted man beside her, made so vulnerable by his insatiable need for other men's esteem. "The generous one," she says a bit more loudly, thinking, Ratnasambhava who grants the wisdom to see how all people, whatever their rank or position, are the same.

Then another understanding comes to her. Taiyang's never seen the five statues given her in Nanjing, the night they met. Yet, how strange!— Inkscent looks again at Ratnasambhava and his four attendants—the size, proportions, the fine chasing on the body, the details of the lotus petals on the thrones: The two sets seem perfect mates.

Ought she then consider why the main image the mysterious Mongol warrior gave her on that Lantern Festival night is the buddha Akshobhya, transmuter of anger and hate? Might she begin to see this man beside her, all men, herself—the flaws, the goodness—simply as they are?

She'll come to those thoughts later. For now, it's enough to take away the untruth she set long ago between herself and the man she chose to take her out of her old life.

"Will you come inside with me?" asks Inkscent. "I have something there you wanted, once, to see."

Another swollen heavy uterus, another woman's yin-charged body invaded, pushed out of equilibrium—in the eyes of those around it—by the yang force of a growing fetus: Wintersweet sits, near full-term and weary and afraid, in the coolest corner of the small courtyard that is hers, and hers alone.

Except, of course, for Happiness. The two sit together, sewing, and do not speak. If only, the young wife thinks, I knew how to tell the tale of my misery. It would give me more than the sharing of troubles. It would let me change them into something I had *made*, as the story took on its own form and found its way through the world. It might let me lay this burden down.

But (ah, such self-pity, such grasping after the pleasure of making, with never a thought for those she'd tell it to!) she still clings tightly to her suffering. "It happened again last night, didn't it?" blurts Wintersweet. "While I was over having supper with Grandmother Jin."

Happiness says nothing. She has said very little to anyone for months now.

"You know," says Wintersweet, putting down the adorable baby cap she's stitching, "I can smell him on you, afterward."

Happiness peers more closely at the little scarlet jacket crumpled on her lap. The young master just keeps after her, and won't be stopped. Of course she likes the flattering attention, likes the brief excitement, the persuasions and the pleasure. But she's as loyal to her mistress as she can be. If it weren't Happiness, it would be someone else.

"I can smell *you*."

Happiness quits her sewing. She's blinking furiously. He's not cruel. He's just a master. And she's just a maid.

"I can smell the dead stink of your mother's stinking cunt." Wintersweet says this evenly, as if she were commenting on the jadewhite early-autumn flowers on the nearby althea shrub.

Happiness grips the half-sewn jacket with both hands. A wet splotch appears on the scarlet cloth.

Wintersweet feels a similar squeezing deep inside her, the strong grip of self-loathing and regret. Yet how else can she protect herself? She is bloated and uglier than ever and can't stop her husband from doing as he wishes. If he loses interest in her permanently, if the child's a girl, if it doesn't live, she'll have nothing. She'll be alone in the Jin household, without even her maid for a friend.

Now Wintersweet does look at the translucent discs of the althea blossoms, that opened this morning only to wither in a few hours more. If the child should die . . .

Happiness suddenly kneels before her, knocks her forehead against the paving stones, begs Wintersweet's forgiveness for an offense she doesn't know how not to commit.

"Oh, get up, get up," says Wintersweet, and waits till Happiness has taken her seat again. "I know your sneaking ways. Apologies now, and bedroom business out in the gazebo later on. Well, you'll probably have an easy time of it soon enough. If I die delivering this child, he can poke at you anytime he wants."

Her mouth distorts with a sour-sweet smile that Lotus never saw on her merry cousin's pock-marked face. "Until he moves on to whoever's next."

Wintersweet shifts her awkward bulk on her hard chair, feels the hemorrhoids itch and blaze. At least she need not take the trouble to get up, walk over, and slap her maid. She has found an easier way: "You're pretty, of course. But there's plenty as pretty—and as ready to let him climb aboard—as you. And then where will you stand?"

Before she can continue, that same deep squeezing (*how can I say these awful things? and to Happiness! but oh, how can I not?*) clasps her again. More fearsomely this time.

Time. It's time. A great terror washes over her. "Happiness?" she says. "Happiness! The baby's coming early. I need help."

That's life in one realm. Here's another. Dispossessed by her daughter's thoughts of the Fifteenth Prince and her seductive connection to Wu Ming, the ghost of Cassia has followed Lotus to Warmriver at a distance. She has watched and worried. Now, a few days after the shaman's exorcism, Cassia takes a chance.

Half out of an abstracted kindness, half annoyed to see a servant girl so long idle, the Empress Dowager has ordered that the troublesome sickly maid devote herself to her music. As long as the Fifteenth Prince is taken by this fancy (the old lady decides, mulling the situation over in a sitting room scented by its handsome nanmu cedar walls) he might as well be exposed to the most elevated playing possible. And—one can never predict where a man's desires might take a woman, *she* certainly knows that—it can't hurt to pamper this young Lotus just a little, to keep the child's allegiance firmly in her own knotted hands.

So on a warm afternoon when the East Palace isn't in use, Lotus sits in one of its dusky side rooms, out of earshot of the Pine-Crane Haven, practicing her chyn as two eunuchs lounge outside in the shade, picking at their cuticles and exchanging the latest scuttlebutt. The room is not the remote refreshing site the *Chyn Handbook* calls for, but she does all she can to prepare herself properly before she plays.

She has washed her hands, she has lighted the incense the eunuchs grudgingly provided, she has placed the instrument on a table low enough to serve as a "chyn altar." She breathes evenly and tries to empty out her mind. I won't wonder what will happen when the Fifteenth Prince returns to Warmriver from the hunt, she thinks. I won't worry about what people say, or that night with the shaman, or what I can do to make Yura believe that life here's not so bad.

While Lotus plays, the incense rises. The subterranean coercion of the sense of smell begins. Her thoughts turn to her lost mother. Her eyes well, and (oh, just for a moment!) her fingers stop.

She gropes for her handbook. She will calm herself by reading again about Ou-yang Hsiou, who eight centuries before was plagued by unrelenting sadness—till he learned to play songs in autumn's minor mode. He found in them restrained delight that drove despondency away.

Instead, her eye falls on another brief history: that of Wang Jing-bo, whose chyn "Responding Soul" drew down a dead girl's spirit one moonlit night. With a shudder, she hurries on to the next anecdote, which tells how during the time of the Three Kingdoms, a ghost appeared to Hsi Kang, borrowed his famous chyn, and—draped in iron fetters—played an eerie melody.

Outside, one of the eunuchs drags his feet toward the door to see what's up. Unbearable that he should see her damp-eyed unhappiness and make of it a frivolous story in the eunuchs' quarters! Lotus bites her lip, begins to pluck, at random, a chain of pure and sorrowful notes. They float and fall in air like invisible pearls.

What happens next, however, *is* seen, and overheard. It becomes the stuff of gossip, of local legend, and eventually a puppet play to be performed for simple folk, for women and visiting foreigners: Crossing over on a bridge of passionate music, the ghost appears. Loose haired, white clad, she is able (at last!) to charge her daughter (able, at last, to hear!) with the gathering of the scattered statues, so that Cassia may be relieved of her tormentful longing.

But gossip, legend, puppet show don't tell the whole story. How Lotus will now be marked as one irredeemably haunted, and so as a vessel through which a prince might be bedeviled. How Cassia will see this written on the eunuchs' pasty faces, will realize the costly consequences of the wish that has consumed her. How she will flee before she can explain things fully, seized by regret and uncertainty, blown by anguish and good fortune northward over the imperial estate and the half-dry riverbed beyond.

Uncertainty, because ever since that moment of compassion before the Verdant Dawncloud Sovereign, when Cassia asked a boon for Taiyang—and for Inkscent—rather than herself, she has felt her world-longing begin to ease. Good fortune, because the mixed gusts of her mingled feelings carry her to someone who might help her remedy what she's done—although that action too, of course, will have its consequences.

Cassia soon finds herself on a hillside between two grand temples in the Tibetan style. Dust and fumes and workers' shouts rise above another half-built imperial sanctum, this one dedicated to the bodhisattva Manjushri.

Sagacious Manjushri: who gives the clear mind and well-spoken tongue that grasp and pass on teachings of the Buddhist Law. Enlightened Manjushri: who holds the book of Perfect Wisdom, and the flaming sword that cuts away mere eloquence and intellect. Princely Manjushri: who can take on a wrathful guise as death-slaying Yamantaka, and esoteric incarnations as Khubilai Khan or the Qianlong emperor.

Holy Manjushri, help me now! We're behind schedule, and I'm absolutely stuck! The bolt of emotion accompanying this thought strikes Cassia, fixes her attention on a stocky sweating man. He wears the uniform of an official in the Imperial Household Department. He plants his hands on his hips, surveys the octagonal pavilion in front of him.

Tegridorj tries to placate himself. The stone masons have made good progress on the lattice work for the front gate since he last dropped by. The majestic staircases on which the Son of Heaven and his blessed mother will ascend through the hillside temple complex are under way. The side buildings have started off well enough.

The great hall behind him is nearly ready for its roof of imperial-yellow tiles. But there's something distinctly wrong about the way that crucial structure looks.

And what is Tegridorj to do about this Pavilion of the Precious Image, after which the whole Manjushri-Image Temple is to be named? Its eight pillars stand firm. The carved marble base within it awaits the painted statue of Manjushri, mounted on his lion and crowned with the five transcendent buddhas, that will be the temple's final jewel. The problem is, the shelter too is out of proportion, ugly, wrong.

With the architect suddenly taken ill, *he's* responsible. The bondservant pinches his broad forehead with one sturdy hand. The hammers in the distance are driving spikes into his head. *Oh, Wise One of the Five Crest Mountains, I'd dedicate to you my only child, my Yura, if I could.*

At those two names, Cassia's drawn closer to this imperial bondservant with the Mongol name. The Five Crest Mountains are Manjushri's prime residence on earth—and the place to which the mandala must be delivered. And *Yura.* That's her daughter's little friend!

The man is to be helped then. Whatever loss of rapport the two young ones' love-adventures may have caused, Yura seems to be the one companion Lotus can truly count on. So maybe Tegridorj can give Cassia the means to reach her daughter safely, to communicate in more detail just what the girl's to do—without putting her into an even worse position in palace society.

And surely, thinks Cassia, the merit from this quest will do my daughter good. Her invisible eye sweeps over the roofless great hall, and the unfinished pavilion. She sets aside for a second time her own desire for physicality, its heat-born headaches and delicious lures. All her will's directed now toward helping Lotus out of her difficult situation and on to Five Crests—for the girl's own sake.

At that moment, Cassia's wearisome longing eases further. Why, she thinks, if I don't want it, I needn't *want* it so!

Why, she feels like a new person altogether.

A puff of dust curls skyward on the wind. A skinny old man with a long white beard walks up behind Tegridorj. "Excuse me, sir," he quavers. "If I might 'ave a word?"

The supervisor swings around, glares at the shabby gaffer. It's hot. He's covered with grit and dirt. He could be executed if the emperor's sufficiently displeased. And his head aches horribly. What next?

"Yer've a two-fold problem, 'aven't yer, sir? Double-trouble, so ter speak." The old man twirls the carpenter's ax he's holding loosely in one hand. "I mean, the main 'all *and* the pavilion. 'T'ud be nice ter kill *two* birds wi' one stone, wouldn't yer say, sir?"

Tegridorj opens his mouth, prepares to roar at the half-wit workman.

"Please, sir, don't yer be thinking that I'm dealing in duplicity," the old man says hastily. "Nor dualism, neither." He winks. "Though yer might say I'm speaking wi' two tongues!"

Tegridorj's mouth snaps shut. He gets it, at least partially. He's spent enough time with carpenters, bricklayers, masons to know the tales about their patron god Lu Ban. Now here he is, apparently, offering the solution to a construction problem in his usual way: a riddle? a pun? some sort of double-talk . . .

That's it! A *double* roof on the great hall and (he swings his solid body around) *and* the statue pavilion! Exactly what's needed to fix their proportions, and to tie the two together visually as well. Tegridorj's career, and possibly his very life, are saved. His headache vanishes. His sweaty face splits in a grin.

Then Tegridorj remembers the way the tales of Lu Ban end, with the sudden disappearance of the god. He whirls back, before the strange old man can go. "Wait!" he cries. "That is, thank you, your . . . your holiness."

The old man's still there. And now he's grinning too.

"Double roofs! A most elegant solution." Tegridorj tries to stop babbling, but he can't. "You've saved me. Thank you, Master L . . . Ah, you *are* Lu Ban, sir, aren't you?"

"Now, now." The grin widens. The ax twirls again. "Yer've heard the stories. D' yer think I'd tell yer if I were?"

Of course. "Ah. Well, thank you again, sir. Is there *any*thing I can do to show my appreciation?"

In fact, there might be, the old man says. Tegridorj oversees construction and maintenance on the Outer Temples north and east of the imperial estate, does he not? So he knows their priests and lamas, doesn't he, since some of them are under Imperial Household Department supervision, and he works with them all?

Yes, yes, Tegridorj acknowledges with pride.

The old carpenter continues, looking pleased. While the emperor's still off hunting at Mulan, Tegridorj might need to report to the Empress Dowager on the progress of the Arhat Temple being built a little west of here, mightn't he?

Yes, says Tegridorj. In fact, the new temple dedicated to the five hundred saints now awaits only consecration. He'd hoped to present formal notice to Her Dowager Majesty tomorrow. "But why—"

Again, the ax twirls. Again, Tegridorj's mouth snaps shut. "One more thing," the disguised supernatural figure says with a reassuring wink. "'Ave yer ever noticed, in one temple or another, any small bronze statues— quite small, I mean—of, say, the buddha Amitabha, or Vajra Bell or any other being 'oo might be the door guard of a little-known mandala?"

. . . .

So things begin to happen, much to Cassia's delight. In the absence of the emperor and princes, Tegridorj sends his report on the two newest temples to the Empress Dowager. As he presents it to the head eunuch of the Pine-Crane Haven staff, Tegridorj draws him aside, quietly offers information that Chief Bao could use to lighten the old lady's load of worries—and so increase his standing in her eyes.

Chief Bao, lips pursed, raises his chin as if to say, why do you make this gift to *me*? Then Tegridorj off-handedly suggests that his daughter Yura's the obvious companion for the ghost-ridden maid, should Her Dowager Majesty decide to try the cure he's recommending. "My girl's nothing special, of course," he adds, "but she knows the Outer Temples better than any of the other females. And I understand she has as good a chance as anyone of keeping His Highness the Fifteenth Prince's little, little musician from throwing one of her fits."

Ah, a doting daddy! thinks Chief Bao. I wonder if he knows his daughter also had a fit of sorts not long ago, on Clarifying Lake? The lengths these breeders will go to, simply to lay eyes on a child that's supposed to have no dealings with the world outside! And a girl, at that. Amazing, really just amazing!

Reassured by this plausible but harmless motive (for what more plausible than irrational self-indulgence, on a fellow human's part?), the eunuch passes the suggestion on. And is confirmed in his scorn for those who scorn him simply for being what he is.

The Empress Dowager's willing to make a last attempt at keeping her grandson in good spirits by trying the proposed temple-visit cure, but she certainly won't go herself. Frankly, the old lady thinks, staring at Chief Bao's pudgy back as he bustles off to carry out her wishes, she wants no more to do with the whole tiresome affair.

She's got more important worries. Before the emperor left for Mulan, he suddenly sent to Beijing for his Muslim consort, that she might join him for the hunt. Then her lama advised the old lady to avoid the weeks in camp again this year, so her son ordered his First Consort *and* that quarrelsome Fourth-Ranked Consort from the Uang clan to stay on at Warmriver and keep his mother company.

This kind of company I don't need, the Empress Dowager muses, signaling a maid to take up a peacock-feather fan and stir the air. In Beijing, each of the senior ladies could sulk in her own palace. But in their close quarters at Warmriver the two left-behinds are at one another's throats! I should have insisted he take all three, she thinks.

She taps the arm of her carved blackwood throne. Emperor he may be, but he's still her son. This is the last time she caters to any man's lustful foolishness. And that goes double for the boy.

Nonetheless, Lotus—and, yes, Yura—soon depart from the imperial estate, in the care of Lady Brightcloud and a detachment of eunuch-guards. Tegridorj awaits them on the bluff near the red wall surrounding the black-roofed Pacified Outposts Temple, his favorite, where the local horse market's held. A fine clear morning: His shadow still stretches long toward the river when he sees them on the far side, leaving the northeast gate of the estate. He watches the females being carried across the ford, then scrambles down to intercept the small party on the floodplain below the Temple of Universal Bliss.

When he lays eyes on his little girl—the first time since she entered the service in the palace, and oh, she looks almost grown-up now—Tegridorj can hardly maintain his dignity. They climb up to the temple and he can't stop smiling; he simply can't.

Universal Bliss? Is this the place to try to cure this vexatious unchaste maid? So thinks Lady Brightcloud as they enter. I liked her well enough at first—she's as smart as she is pretty, I'll grant her that—but she was so quick to cast aside her virtue! And now all this bizarre behavior.

It seems to be contagious, too—her little friend's the one who broke out with that nasty jingle about the landscape the other day. If Her Dowager Majesty would only ask, Lady Brightcloud would advise packing both girls back to their families right away. Instead, they get all this special attention. Maids being carried about in sedan chairs, as if they were ladies-in-waiting! Really, it's just too much.

The thick-set bondservant official bruskly orders the chair-bearers and the eunuch-guards to wait in the forecourt. Lady Brightcloud watches him greet three lamas come down from some other temple just for this visit, since it's too expensive to keep all the Outer Temples staffed full time. It's so silent here, so empty. She doesn't like the place.

Universal Bliss indeed! She, the two girls, and the four men ascend to the gate of the third terrace, where atop two square tiers of stone, the great Round Pavilion stands. She'll be much happier when they move on to the other temple they're to visit, Universal Peace, with its huge statue of Guan-yin. Things are so much livelier there: a large staff of lamas, a bodhisattva every Buddhist honors, and no secret deities.

Lady Brightcloud glances up past bright ceramic reliquaries, toward the mandala-shaped pavilion's conical yellow roof. There's something bothersome about the way its swollen gold finial pokes up, right on a line from the estate's Gold Mountain island, along the length of the temple's symmetrical grounds, to that lewd-looking Pestle Rock on the ridge beyond! Her neck hurts as she cranes it, looking more steeply up.

Too much double-vision here. The lady-in-waiting has heard about the protective power of this axis, how it links estate and temple and the giant life-giving stone, so that the imperial family may be blessed with vitality. She's also heard talk of the paired-bliss statue that's sheltered within the Round Pavilion, right beneath its erect finial—a merging of yin and yang, some say, of mother and father, of wisdom and compassionate action.

Well. She'd hardly criticize Their Majesties. And she certainly wishes them longevity. Yet privately she wonders if some of the Yellow Hat monks aren't simply indulging in prurience, or even lascivious deeds.

But what is this?! By now, the small group has climbed to the second tier, and circumambulated and climbed again, arriving finally at the entrance to the Round Pavilion. And Lotus is being led inside this holy of holies by the senior lama and the Mongol bondservant! With no chaperone save the other little maid, on whose arm she leans!

Lady Brightcloud rushes forward to fulfill her duty. She gets a peek at the painted wooden structure (a symmetrical four-gated palace, it looks to be) upraised on the building's central platform, beneath the elaborate golden sky-well of the conical roof. And what's that inside? A many-armed figure of some sort? Two figures? *Oh.*

In an eyeblink, the two junior lamas block the doorway. Have they grown taller, heftier, since Lady Brightcloud last looked at them? But that's impossible.

Standing shoulder to shoulder, they make it clear that she may not go in. No harm will come to the girls, says the handsome smooth-faced lama—and Lady Brightcloud blushes. Lotus and Yura have simply asked the senior lama for a bit of teaching, adds the lama with the green-flecked eyes. They'll be out soon.

In fact, it's several hours. But the long-earlobed senior lama sketches a blessing in Lady Brightcloud's direction as he emerges from the shadowy interior, and she blinks and yawns as if she'd just awakened from a peaceful sleep.

And how are the girls? Little Yura seems stunned, but not upset. Lotus does look better than she has since she collapsed while practicing her chyn the other day. She's clearly got something on her mind, but that peculiar air of bearing a desperate hopeless burden seems to have eased. Everyone's clothing is in order; the lady-in-waiting checks most carefully.

When they've walked back to the forecourt, ready to be carried north to the Temple of Universal Peace, the senior lama gestures another blessing toward Lady Brightcloud, just as Lotus is stepping into her lowered sedan chair. Naturally, the lady-in-waiting bows her head, so she's not at all sure what she does or doesn't see.

But thinking back on it later, Lady Brightcloud decides she might have glimpsed the maid tucking some metal object—something bronze, and so small it was almost hidden by the girl's hand—underneath the cushion of her chair.

FROM THE COLLECTED LETTERS
OF HEDDA SVENSDATTER

Wagons-Lits Hotel
Rue Meiji, Legation Quarter
Peiping
September 5, 1930

Cher Philippe,

I am just returned from a lovely tiffin at the Mission, in celebration of my safe return yesterday to dusty, dear Peiping—ah, but I almost wrote "Peking"!—and am charged with sending you the fond remembrances of kind Evelyn and lively Ruth, wise Donald and dashing James.

Yes, my return! I am bursting to tell you—for who can better understand my jubilation?—I have been to the former imperial summer palaces at Jehol! Could any of our little group have imagined, as we said *au revoir* up on the Manchu City wall, and someone (Peter? or perhaps Mr. Lowe?) compared the green map plotted by the trees in the innumerable walled yards below to the living maze of a Sinologue's research, that I should get the chance to lay eyes on that fabled site?

I only wish that you will have such an opportunity. When we meet again, I shall describe everything, but today I must pass on a few of my impressions, including an astounding tale related to us at the Temple of Universal Peace, where the giant statue of Kwan Yin stands. Even Papa grants that, if true, the story made the entire trip worthwhile.

Dear Papa! Indefatigable explorer though he is, he was most perturbed by a message he received not three days after your departure, from the Chinese architect engaged in creating the replica of Jehol's Golden Pavilion for the Century of Progress exposition. It urgently requested Papa's presence there again; he was to go the very moment the end of the summer rains allowed auto travel across the bridgeless rivers and rutted roads.

Yes, dear perturbed Papa! How much worse for him when the part-Norwegian daughter he never knew he had—until my arrival here with poor Mother's letter—insisted she would not be left behind a second time! No bandits had troubled them a few weeks earlier, I pointed out. I pointed out many things, and in the end, prevailed.

The circumstances of our three-day journey to Jehol much resemble those with which Papa regaled us both upon his first return to Peiping in July: the difficult driving (the very running boards of our motor-car loaded with petrol cans and camping gear), the half-tumbled watch-towers, the fields of nourishing maize or millet next to others filled with snake-stemmed poppies, a night's camp in the remains of an imperial travel lodge, the unruffled cheer of our fearless Mongol chauffeur Altani and our wondersome cook Hsi An-chi.

As we departed through the An Ting Men—do you miss the city gates' crush of camel drivers, rickshaw men, coolies, cyclists, red-capped Moslims, families in their springless carts?—Papa spoke of that over-shadowed fifth son of Ch'ien-lung (or was he the fifteenth?), the emperor Chia-ch'ing, who on a sultry August day one hundred ten years before us, left through that same gate for the mountain estate—a stout man of sixty-one with barely more than a week to live.

Philippe, do you think that ineffectual emperor died of apoplexy, or of a lightning strike from a Heaven outraged by scandalous amusements in a Jehol summer-house? Since the Chinese themselves do not agree, I shall say only that History holds more stories than it holds deaths, and that we would do well to listen to all we can. In either case, I now feel more fully the sadness of the decline into which the estate fell after that unlucky imperial demise.

In Jehol, the general now residing in the main palace accepted our courtesy call. Alas, he did not offer us a tour of the Imperial Park, as Papa had seen it so recently! I do not know who was more disappointed, I or the learned Professor Gernant, who had agreed on such short notice to accompany us as translator.

Yet I think now it was just as well: Could I have borne the sight of ruined kiosks, vines growing over foundation-stones, the deforestation of the once-cool hills, those linked lakes dried to greenish mud? Bad enough to see a red-faced warlord in a field-gray uniform seating himself on priceless brocade once touched only by the holder of the Dragon Throne!

Yes, I do remember you saying that the Manchus too had their garrison at Jehol, their four barracks and their training ground! Perhaps their soldiers were no nobler, no less rapacious, than the modern ones. Perhaps.

Fortunately, other wonderworks awaited us, and I was able to see them all. My height, my bobbed hair, and my sensible trouser costume served to convince all we met—save our good host at the Belgian Catholic Mission—that I was Papa's young male amanuensis. Indeed, the general seemed quite distracted by rumors from the headquarters of the Young Marshal, who keeps as tight a grip as ever over Jehol province.

By the way, one hears just today in Peiping that the Young Marshal would be well advised to keep an eye upon the Japanese forces, and upon that last twig on the Manchu imperial family tree, Henry P'u-i! What further depredations does the future hold for Jehol? But, hush!—enough.

Our first two days there were largely taken up by Papa's dealings with Mr. Liang at the Potala temple, which I was able to explore at leisure. I still marvel! A pious Tibetan paints a pilgrim's souvenir of the Dalai Lama's original Potala in Lhasa, a traveller brings that picture to Ch'ien-lung's court, and the great construction is begun. Did you know the very name "Potala" proclaims that both represent what the Chinese call P'u-t'uo Island, their sacred Kwan Yin's home?

And now, modern men of East and West labour to create what Papa calls "absolutely faithful replicas," in Stockholm and Chicago, of the most splendid of its pavilions! Though I do not here attempt to recreate the temple with my words, I too made at Jehol clumsy Potalas in my sketchbook. Tell me, why this human urge to copy, copy?

Why, when no likeness can ever be exact, or true? Surely I, imperfect imitation—or "knockoff," as the American dressmakers might have it!—of my father, of my mother, am living testimony to that fact.

But no more philosophizing! I shall not describe the Outer Temples' crumbling walls and leaky roofs, the gangs of unpaid soldiers and skinny lamas fending as best they could for survival in what was once a fairyland of lavish grandeur. How sad, to see a vandal-plundered temple dedicated to "universal bliss"—or one built to house an image of the divinity Manjushri—half gone to wrack and ruin!

Rather, let me tell you the remarkable story given us on our last day by an old lama at that northernmost of the Outer Temples, the Temple of Universal Peace. After the initial greetings, one toothless lama emerged from the inquisitive crowd of his threadbare fellows to be our guide. He showed us various courtyards, galleries, image halls and pagodas of red, green, black, and white. Professor Gernant translated the proclamation of emperor Ch'ien-lung carved into a memorial stone, which revealed the Mahayana Hall to be a Mount Meru. O colossal centre of the universe!

Indeed, seen from without, the building's commanding height and its five layers of successive roofs, each a bit narrower than the one below, do suggest that mythic form. The walls of red-brown wood pull the eye upward as powerfully as the cathedral stones of Chartres, while the central finial rises above the four smaller ones like a Buddha surrounded by four divine attendants.

Ah, but the design of the dim interior is even more cunningly charged with meaning: I hadn't realized the stunningly painted idol so fills the narrow heights with its two-and-twenty metres that it cannot be taken in with a single glance. Philippe, you cannot imagine the effect!

At ground level, one is a mere ant, crawling about the lotus pedestals and trailing hems of Kwan Yin and a pair of towering attendants. Climbing to the first of the two galleries, one sees the ropes of pearls, filigree bracelets, wrist-rosaries, the very navel of the idol. And one begins to examine the beautiful hands. Two of them meet as in reverential prayer before the chest, but this is a "thousand armed" Kwan Yin: The forty remaining upper limbs behind the idol's head and torso formed, I thought, a kind of many-spoked wheel, almost a halo. The old lama showed his gums and bade us take special note of them.

From the upper gallery, beneath the ceiling of vermilion, turquoise, azure, gold, one may view the Compassionate One's contemplative face, the meditating Buddha in the crown—and may realize one has lost sight of what one could see before.

We descended. We lingered in the relative coolness of the incense-cloying Hall on that warm afternoon, content to have come down from the aging scaffolding and be Kwan Yin's ants. The lama told his tale.

Once, in the days of Ch'ien-lung, three *femmes de chambre* of His Majesty's aged mother—one Chinese, one Mongol, and one Manchu of higher rank whose family had taken on Chinese ways—came to burn incense at the temple, escorted by a local palace official of Mongol ancestry. A rite was performed on their behalf, and the old lama showed us the very *pilutu*—a Manchu word, Professor Gernant said—his predecessor wore that day, taking pains to point out the repeated pictures of the cosmic Buddha Vairochana all about its brim.

What role madness plays in the following, what role autohypnosis, what role miracle, I cannot say. But the old lama assured us that, the esoteric rite completed, one supple wooden arm of the very statue that we saw before us began to move! Maintaining the occult configuration of its fingers—for just as in Deborah's photograph collection, some of the hands hold offering scarves or jewels or sacred thunderbolts, but others form cryptic *mudras*—it gestured toward the lotus pedestal on which one of the paired attendants stood.

A small shadowy niche revealed itself among the petals.

All present stared. The lamas had never seen that niche, and later it was not to be found again. *Our* lama showed us its exact location, which, when rapped, sounded no more hollow than any other portion of the carving.

The arm of living wood again drew the attention of the company to the niche, then to the Chinese girl. This being repeated several times, the Chinese, moving like a sleepwalker, took from the niche five small bronze statues. At that, the arm signed a blessing and, evidently satisfied, returned to its accustomed pose.

The statues, the lama told us, were of "Ah-mi-tuo-fo" and four attendants—the very Buddha we had just seen in Kwan Yin's crown. This became the occasion for a lamistic homily on the dangers of passion and delusion, which—he said—this Ah-mi-tuo-fo can help us transform into a discriminating wisdom that sees each being in its distinctiveness.

As the lama spoke, the roofbells hanging from the corners of the eaves outside began to tinkle in a welcome breeze. Soon, however, the allure of storytelling overcame the urge to sermonize.

There was another miracle, the lama said, sucking in his sunken cheeks. The Mongol palace official suddenly spoke out in an uncanny tone. "The girl is to keep the statues Kwan Yin's attendant has given her," he said, sounding like a spirit from another world. "And she must take one more. Look on the rear altar. At Vajra Bell, guardian of a northern gate."

There the company saw a bronze figure that indisputably matched the five the Chinese girl had already taken. Yet some of the temple staff dissented, saying that while they had no argument about the miracle of the lotus pedestal gift, they could—with their meditation-sharpened eyes—perceive that this palace official merely feigned a visionary state, wishing her to receive the sixth statue for some obscure motive of his own!

The temple's oral tradition holds that other lamas present pointed out this figure had been donated only recently, and clearly belonged with guardians of the other three directions, not by itself. (Today at the Mission, smiling Donald gently explained that debate is central to the training of an educated lama!) As the first party began to reply, the palace official drowned out the disputation with cries of "Five Crests! She must take them all to the Five Crest Mountains, to the holy seat of Manjushri!"

I could not tell what the storytelling lama believed about the authenticity of the shouting Mongol man's delirium, but he certainly believed in what happened next. For myself, I take it to have been a form of hysteria, induced in the young female Mongol by the half-trance of her Chinese companion, and the perhaps false one of her compatriot. At any rate, she began to chant softly, softly, "Five Crests." (It seems this was not the first time she'd behaved like what the Theosophists would call "a sensitive"!) Then she and the Chinese girl both crumpled to the floor.

In the end, the old lama said, the servant of the Empress Dowager was allowed to keep all six statues. He did not know what came of her after the imperial family's annual return to Peiping, but the young Mongol became a wandering holy woman, a prophetess of sorts, and lived her days out at Jehol.

Ah, but I have written until my hand cramps, and in closing will simply offer heartfelt thanks for your invaluable contributions to my understanding of this extraordinary place. Where should I be without the Sinologues?

As ever,

Hedda

P.S. Do give my regards to that most charming of Manchus, darling Princess Der Ling, and to Monsieur Pierre Menard, should he have returned from Buenos Aires. One hears from Nanking that Mrs. Buck is quietly writing another novel. Have I told you that we met once, at the Chia's, and spoke long of our respective schoolgirl days at neighboring women's colleges in Virginia?

THE OFFERING-MANDALA

And now you see (resting on an altar, or sealed in a museum case, or reproduced on paper slick with clay) a gilt brass offering-mandala—both its height and its diameter, about a foot or so. A rich design encircles the gleaming rim—flowers, words in Sanskrit, jewels enflamed, the eight-spoked Wheel of the Law. Engraved on the upper surface of its round hollow base are endlessly repeating interlocking ocean waves.

Atop that: Perfectly cast miniatures, arranged in radial symmetry. A ring of dancing deities. Others seated in prayer or adoration. The Eight Treasures. At each of the four quarters, tiny buildings stand, every brick and roof tile outlined with precision, flawless chasing indicating latticed windows and foundation stones. Your eye may linger on a placid horse, the elephant that bears the bodhisattva Samantabhadra, a reverent water buffalo.

Held aloft on golden curls of cloud, two discs float frozen in their circumambulation: a moon blazoned with the relentless lunar hare; a sun etched with its dark crow. And in the center, Mount Meru rises above all else, surmounted by a stupa and the primal syllable *om*.

Once, in eighteenth-century China, someone must have presented the exquisite artifact to a Tibetan Buddhist temple. Perhaps it was an emperor's gift to the lama he acknowledged as his teacher. Afterward, morning offerings were made in turn to it, and so to the universe it presents and represents. Look again, then, at this three-dimensional map. What can you learn from such a model of devotional cosmography?

That there is no beginning, and that this is how the world lies: in the middle of things, Mount Meru, pleasant home of gods and demigods—who linger there too long, lulled by, ah, such delights! Trees dripping gems, ambrosial scents, savory dishes heaped voluptuously on plates of gold and silver, intoxicants for ear and fingertips and eye: The gods and demigods forget that even long life ends. But they are again in time reborn again to suffer once again.

Below, four continents—with their tile-roofed, stone-based, sea-hemmed buildings—surround the towering peak. On the southernmost, our own Rose-Apple Island, we human beings huddle, labor, eat, laugh, kill, sit numb with boredom, copulate, sing, chatter, shriek in pain.

Or, we can take advantage of this rare chance—a fortunate birth below the seductive life upon Mount Meru, above the sufferings of dumb animals or hungry ghosts or gut-wrenched beings down in hell—take advantage, listen to the teachings. See the possibility of liberation. Set foot on the Way.

A LOTUS BLOSSOMS: 8

Jadewhite Lampwick, Honey Bracelets, Ashen-Egret's Wings: Nearby, my grandfather lies ill, but here in the weak sunlight of our Upper Courtyard, his chrysanthemums bloom as though a killing frost will never come. I examine each plant, idle, restless, wondering what Father and First Uncle and Aunt Gao will decide is to be done with me. I almost pick a blossom, almost begin to pull its petals off—but I am already too much in disgrace.

Here's a broad-petaled beauty called Eastern Dragon Instructing Sons. The worst thing, I think, about leaving the Empress Dowager's service was my last conversation with the Fifteenth Prince.

No. The worst thing was that I have failed my family. That I betrayed my father's aspirations, and now wonder bitterly if I was a fool in doing what I did. But second worst (for saying good-bye to Yura at Warmriver was merely sad, and her dismissal, her "sudden serious illness," exactly what she wanted), second worst was that farewell.

Just how the prince broke through the cordon of distrust and fear Lady Brightcloud raised around Yura and me after our return from the Outer

Temples, I still don't know. But he is a prince: He's used to getting most of what he wants.

He is a prince, and his grandmother took her time deciding which posed a greater danger, the supernatural disruptions plaguing me, or the frustration of his desires. Shortly after he and the emperor and all His Majesty's entourage returned from the autumn hunt at Mulan, on the day a courier brought word of an uprising in Shandong near the Grand Canal, the Fifteenth Prince proposed his father be diverted by a new musician's songs. And the Empress Dowager let me go. So while His Majesty brooded over military operations against the zealot followers of the Ancient Mother Neverborn, I went to play my chyn for him in the Commemorated Kindness Hall. I had no doubt the Fifteenth Prince would be there.

To perform before the Son of Heaven! My hands shook as the eunuchs led me from the Pine-Crane Haven to His Majesty's favorite lakeside study beyond its northern wall. Surely, at such a moment, far better musicians feel the same.

Yet when Chief Bao silently laid my chyn before me, my hands grew still and sure. I stopped worrying about the strange occurrences at the temples of Universal Bliss and Universal Peace, stopped trying vainly to understand just what I must do, and how. I thought of nothing but the music. I've never played so well.

When I struck my first notes, it was His Majesty's pleasure to pay little mind. While I played, it was his pleasure to look out absently over Scepter Lake and Lower Lake, toward the bridges and enticing islands beyond. Then it was his pleasure to send for General Shu-he-de just as I began a melody the Fifteenth Prince especially liked: I saw the prince's guarded face flush slightly at the sound of it.

When the emperor spoke, I paused. But His Majesty bade me play a little longer, and I heard him ask whose child I was. My turn, then, to feel my face warm. At least I'd given Father this much, that his daughter had pleased the emperor.

Even in that informal setting, the Fifteenth Prince would hardly approach me in his father's presence. He listened, waiting beside an elder brother—the talented Eleventh Prince, I realized, another of their father's favorites. Would I have tried to evade a life as an imperial lady, if the emperor's fifteenth son had his brother's artistic sensibilities?

I think so. I did what I did, and needn't seek for reasons beyond what happened in the temples, and the ghost's unclear charge to me—no matter that I lack faith in them now. Besides, the Fifteenth Prince is likable enough.

Better, then, if that speech of music and attentive silence had been our last. But when I was dismissed, and two eunuchs took me along the covered walkway toward the rear gate of the women's residence, the young prince followed.

"I want to talk to her a moment," he said, no longer the stolidly respectful son, or the youth deferring properly to a brother in his twenties. "In there."

I followed him into a little book room, smelling the sharp pine wind, knowing what I had to do. The eunuchs waited outside.

He whirled to face me, a quicker motion than usual for him. "My mother says you're—"

"It's true."

He frowned, perhaps as much at my discourteous directness as at what I'd said. "A ghost come back to the realm of light to rob me of my energies? I don't believe it."

Quick and easy if I lied to him, claimed to be what I am not. I couldn't. "Not that. Ghost-ridden, maybe."

"If someone's casting charms, or making effigies to cause your, your spells . . ."

I could see that, sensitive to all lapses in the respect due—not himself, but due his rank, the prince was ready to defend me against any jealous attack. To defend the maid he'd favored, the maid favored by the emperor's son.

So I told him all Her Dowager Majesty had ordered—the shaman and the release from duties and the temple visits. I described the appearance of my mother's ghost, though I didn't tell the puzzling things she'd said—surely the First Consort had passed on a more frightening version of that story. And I didn't mention the distancing from ordinary life brought me by those events and by the weeks, before them, of feverish dreams. The distancing from what, for my family's sake, I ought to want. From him.

The prince began to talk of having a forty-nine-day purification service said on my behalf. "And when we get back to Beijing," he added, "I'll see to it they burn the best incense for you at—at the Convent of Scattered Flowers, where so many noble ladies go. That should end the talk."

His face tightened. He knows how to ride and shoot, how to please his father, how to give orders when he is supposed to. This was a different matter. "Spiteful talk's the real problem, isn't it?" he said. "You don't *look* unhealthy." He stepped closer. "You—"

I had to stop him then. Or never. "Aren't we all ghosts?" I said quickly, addressing him for the first time as a familiar, and not a prince. "Don't we all just visit this human realm?"

The prince halted, shocked, a little angry now.

"Do you think my flesh, or yours, is real?" I asked. The tightness of my throat gave my speech the right edge.

I could see him thinking, *Crazy talk.* Thinking, *Or mocking me. Could a bondservant dare?*

And when I changed my voice, laughing like someone who has won a drinking game, and asked him if he really planned to defy his mother by taking me into his palace, he thought quite visibly, *Or clever. A scheming maid, of course. I would have to move her in now. If I were allowed—*

Outside, one of the eunuchs coughed a long loud cough.

"I have to go," the prince said. And for all that had raced across his face, I could hear his regret. "We'll be leaving for Beijing before ten days have passed. My father needs me beside him now, and I need to learn from what he does. Someday I—but I'll arrange to see you there." He reached his calloused finger-tips to my cheek, caught a tiny pinch of skin.

I had to make sure he wouldn't think again, wouldn't try to win Her Dowager Majesty over. Had to, whether I wanted to, or not. "No," I said, trying to make my voice cold as Aunt Gao's, sharp and undeniable as the pinewood wind. "No, I believe you won't. And I don't want you to."

Yet even as he turned away, I began to think how I might win him back.

Autumn Waters, Immortal Old Man of the Mountains, Dawn-Mist-and-Dusk-Frost: Each chrysanthemum is carefully labeled. Not, this year, in Grandfather's hand, but in Little Auntie Tuo's.

It was my father's concubine who suggested I sit out here in the courtyard, on what might be the ninth month's last warm afternoon, while she practices her chyn. She asked if I wanted Snow to keep me company, and simply nodded when I said no. Now she's playing "Journey to Widewintry Palace"; I can almost see a mystic traveler rising through the clouds, toward the Moon Lady's spacious crystalline towers.

Impossible to sit still. I walk slowly from one potted flower to the next.

Grandfather moans from his North Hall. These days, Tetra and Quinta sit always in the central room, waiting for Prima's summons. They say each trickle of bloody urine is like liquid fire to him, yet he uses his chamber pot again and again.

When I was a child, I went every morning to pay my respects to Grandfather. Then he put a stop to that, caring only for his gardening and his wine cup and his friends. Now Aunt Gao says we are to make our daily calls again, and he does not say no.

He says almost nothing. His misery is a dreadful thing to see. Pain grips his ribs and lower back as if there were a hundred tiny fractures in his bones; no doctor's remedy is strong enough to give him rest. He can hobble into his little garden with someone supporting him on either side, but he can't bear to sit there long. Snow told me he cried out once that he would rather die than live on as he must.

It's no comfort that his condition provided a face-saving reason for my return home. Father spread the tale around the palaces, making much of his gratitude for Her Dowager Majesty's act of mercy. But this suffering of his father's can only add to his unhappiness, as he endures the inquisitive looks of others in the Imperial Household Department.

Does Father even know the real reason I was treated more kindly than other maids? We've hardly spoken, and then only of Grandfather, or of unimportant things. I move on to the next flowers.

Swan Quills, Silver Tiger Claws, Sweet Pearblossom, Gold with a Thousand Flecks of Clay: If that moment with the Fifteenth Prince was the hardest, the best was Lady Miao-shan's parting gift to me.

Kind Lady Miao-shan. She persuaded the Empress Dowager it was simplest—and safe enough—to let me stay in an unused alcove in the Pine-Crane Haven's servants' hall for the short time remaining till the return to Beijing. *You need rest and seclusion,* Lady Miao-shan whispered to me. *You have a lot to think about.*

I myself cared little then for what might happen. After pushing away the Fifteenth Prince, with Yura sent home and nothing to sustain the visions I'd brought back from the temples, I slipped into a state not unlike the emptiness of heart brought me by Mama's death—or my motionless despondency after Nurse's fall from Marvel Peak and Third Aunt's unaccountable decline.

But really, it wasn't as bad as those other times, I decide, looking again at the single Swan Quills, heavy headed on its fibrous stalk: The outer petals have already crumpled. I suppose it's knowing no day can ever be as bad as those, that gives me a strength other girls don't have.

Nor were my last days in Warmriver like falling back into the consuming world within the drowsy yurt of my reveries. In spite of all I don't know, I do know I've wakened forever from those dreams. In the Round Pavilion at the Temple of Universal Bliss, the senior lama told me that the body's joy is to be used for a higher end than self-indulgence. Maybe someday I will better understand those words.

Still, lying in that alcove in the servants' hall I often felt sick with misgiving—I'd thrown away the chance a hundred girls competed for. And on what might be a useless whim: What exactly is it Mama wants of me? She vanished too quickly. I still had so much to ask her.

So I was glad to stay alone while the others went through the motions of celebrating Double-Ninth Day despite the troubles in Shandong, and made preparations for the journey to Beijing. I often thought of Yura. How happy she'd been when her father was summoned to take his daughter away, saying there was no place for haunted maids at court. I could see Yura barely keeping her pleasure off her face: She'd told me it had come to her, at the foot of the great wooden image of Guan-yin, that she had to set her life upon another course. I envy her her certainty.

Now Grandfather groans, and I do pull off a few chrysanthemum petals— but only withered ones, as he might have done, to groom an aging blossom. It's hard to understand how Yura could become so sure so easily. But she'd never wanted palace life, and knew the shaman healer would take her in and teach her. What could I do but be glad for her, and wish her well?

Sometimes, though, I thought of Yura's father. Of the grief on his face when he saw his daughter, judged *bedeviled* and cast out. Saying good-bye to my friend, I caught sight of his sorrowing eyes. And marveled at her tranquility, and wondered how my father would take the news: That glimpse of Yura's was enough to give me some idea.

And so I waited in my—what? my unhealthy sickroom? or my unlocked prison cell? By then, I truly didn't care.

At times, I tried listening only to my breathing, or reciting the syllables the senior lama taught me, or envisioning the red glow of a western sun in an empty sky. But my mind would wander. To turn it away from things that pained me, I started thinking of another person, one I'd seen only briefly and that months before: the emperor's Muslim consort.

She had returned with the Emperor from the Mulan camp, Goldflower told me one day when she brought me supper. After that, I'd lie in the alcove and picture the lady in the Imperial Garden the day the eunuch tried to strangle me, seeing again the deft flash of her life-saving knife. Goldflower reported she was staying in a separate villa within the estate—perhaps a lodge beyond the plain that held the Mongol camp. Here at Warmriver too His Majesty kept her apart, and continued her special allotments of delicacies from her homeland, the mutton she ate instead of pork.

That evening, sifting through the swirl of stories surrounding this Fourth-Ranked Consort, I caught hold of her fierce devotion to the teachings of her religion; surely, to herself as to the storytellers, she remained above all other things, a Muslim. Then surely, I could find the calm and keenness and devotion to walk the path that ghostly mother and miraculous moving wooden arm and long-eared lama had all indicated I was meant to walk.

The moment I formed that thought, a twist of wind came into the court-yard of the servants' hall, carrying the low steady notes that sound when someone swings the striking-log against a heavy temple bell. I've no reason to suppose it was a sign for me. But I resolved to think no more of how I might renew my connection with the Fifteenth Prince.

Now I pluck one more creamy petal. Above all things, a Muslim? Maybe. Maybe not. They have no love for holy statues. And does the lady hate the emperor as the conquerer of her people, or love him as the father of the child Goldflower heard she might be carrying? How can I know?

All I really understand of her, I finally decide, is mere appearance—as remembrance paints it. That, and what she said to me about the little statue hidden underneath my clothes: *If you've really stolen such a thing, if it means enough to you to do so, guard it fiercely. Guard it well.*

The rest of her? Beyond my knowing, I see now. And wonder if anyone is not.

Crimson Pine-Straw, Rinseflower Creek, Pale Crane Sleeping in the Snow: These three chrysanthemums are new to me. Perhaps they were given Grandfather after I left for the Forbidden City, to cheer him in his long descent.

Those words from that unknown Muslim woman were a gift to me—a gift that stopped me from discarding the stolen figure of clear-eyed Lochana later in the winter, when I feared discovery. But it's Lady Miao-shan's farewell present that keeps me from giving up entirely on what my ghostly mother said when I unwittingly summoned her with my chyn.

The reason's simple. The little statue Lady Miao-shan quietly pressed on me the night we returned to Her Dowager Majesty's palace in the Forbidden City completed the outermost ring of a mandala.

There is a scattered mandala of holy images, said Mama's ghost in the Eastern Palace. *For my sake, daughter, you must reassemble it, and present it to the temple for which it was made. For my sake, and, I think, your own.* One thing the senior lama in the Temple of Universal Bliss showed to me and Yura was a faded painting of a mandala we'd never seen. He made sure I knew all the deities within; I wasn't ready yet for higher initiations, he said, but he would honor our request for teaching. After talking of the buddha Amitabha, he named the four door guardians again, taking pains to point out how they might be recognized.

Useful knowledge, it turned out. For thereupon he gave me a small bronze likeness of the eastern guardian, Vajra Hook. Then, at Universal Peace, Yura's father dumbfounded the watching monks, shouting that I was to take the statue of Vajra Bell, keeper of the northern gate, from the altar in the Mahayana Hall. In that same moment, I realized who the figure was that the carp had thrown me in the starry twilight of the Double Seventh: Out of the Frontier Lakes came Vajra Shackles, western guardian of the mandala.

Finally, from Lady Miao-shan, came Vajra Noose, who secures the southern entryway.

"I bought this statue when I went on pilgrimage before I left home for Beijing," the lady-in-waiting said as I tried to refuse the gift. "To Little

Southern Five Crests, in the Jong-nan Mountains. But, Lotus, you're the one who needs a holy protector now."

I touch the slender petals of the snow-white Pale Crane flower. *Little Southern Five Crests,* I think again. Named after the great Five Crest Mountains, the very place that Yura and her father both said I ought to go. Suddenly, I shiver in the cooling air. I should put on a thicker jacket, but I won't.

The image of Tara that Padma lent to Mama has been lost for well more than a year; besides, I've only memory to suggest it might belong with the Pandaravashini my poetry tutor left hidden in the lotus lantern, with the stolen Lochana, and the statue of all-loving Mamaki from the Fifteenth Prince. And though the Amitabha and four bodhisattvas from the lotus pedestal match the others well enough, the incomplete assemblage still *might* not be part of an actual mandala.

But I can't doubt these four defenders of the four directions were made to go together—and if there's a full set of guardians, then why not those whose dwelling place they guard?

I keep turning away from certainty, but that portent of completion pulls me back again. It *must* be true that I'm meant to gather all the statues. Not the trick of a lying ghost, but my mother's behest. Not false words from a demon disguised as a long-eared lama, not some delusion of my own.

True, then, that I'm meant to go to the Five Crest Mountains, with the entire mandala, and seek its proper resting place. True that I was right to leave the imperial palaces. True that what the apparition—Mama—told me, what Yura moaned and her father shouted, is beyond disbelief. But how can I do it? And, really, why?

The Buddha's Lotus, Falling Radiance of Maple Groves: No, stop enumerating flowers for a moment, I think. Stop running through the past and count instead the statues of the mandala. The four door guardians. From Warmriver's Temple of Universal Peace, Amitabha, buddha of the west, guide for those lost in desire. And four attendant bodhisattvas: *nine.*

Oh, and here at home—of course, of course—a tenth.

Forcing myself to pass slowly through the central room of our side hall, I nod to my father's concubine and Snow, vaguely smiling my pleasure in the music, rubbing my arms to indicate I've come in for warmer clothes. No need to excite their interest.

In my room, deep in the trunk that still holds the lotus lantern's beautiful Pandaravashini, I uncover the wrapped statue the fortune-teller Mother Jia commanded me to take from Marvel Peak the day Nurse died. I was blind with grief then, and did not even wonder which buddha it might be.

Now I place the statue on my outstretched palm. It's a little taller than the rest.

The smile, unearthly. The hands, held level with the heart in the teaching gesture. Each thumb and index finger touch, to form two circles that show the turning of the dharma wheel, that leads us to enlightenment.

Vairochana. The illuminating buddha who transmutes our ignorance and delusion. The central figure of the mandala.

That's ten. And (*Mamaki, Lochana, Pandaravashini*) the three buddha goddesses make thirteen, I think, and remind myself to breathe. If I had the Tara again ... (*she'd be fourteenth*), and the buddhas of the north and east and south, wherever they are, each with four bodhisattvas (*fifteen more to find*, and weakness washes over me—it's more than I can do, more than I can conceive of doing—but I force myself to keep on with the reckoning) ... of the thirty-seven holy beings that form this mandala, I would still lack ...

Eight. The eight goddesses of the offerings.

I begin to walk (quietly! I tell myself, don't attract attention) back and forth across the bedroom: I know I've seen them, actually seen them, some-where. But if I can't remember where, what hope do I have?

A room of shadows. Eight statues lined up on an altar. Their drifting scarves. Their assured, enchanting faces. One holding incense, one a lamp, another one a wreath—

Wintersweet, too? Oh, Father, please! I have to go. I must."

My father frowns at this insistence, and I throw myself down before him, kotowing furiously, knowing that as always he will laugh and lean down from his seat on his bed platform and pull me up.

He doesn't. The weary look of his face grows sadder, heavier. But his tone is not unkind as he tells me to stop and sit on the nearby stool.

It comes to me that since he brought me home from the palaces, I haven't seen him smile.

"I've failed the family," I say, ashamed to look at him. "But I—if she's in such terrible spirits over losing her baby—you know how she always laughed when we were together. Besides, Grandfather—"

"Your cousin is with the Jin family now." *She fulfilled her elders' wishes, as a good daughter does,* my father doesn't say. Or have to. "And with all regard for my brother's, ah, unswayable filiality, this is not the time of year to head into those mountains. No matter how much they rush the preparations, it will be well into the eleventh month before they get back to Beijing." He coughs. "It's hard to see why such a venture would do you *or* Father any good, whatever my sister-in-law thinks."

But the autumn has been mild, and Lady Ding has convinced Aunt Gao—and so, my First Uncle—that a pilgrimage in chancy weather will show greater faith and reverence. With greater results. I'm about to say all that when Little Auntie Tuo catches my eye. I fold my hands and bow my head.

"They say spring's more treacherous than winter, at Five Crests." Lifting the teapot, the concubine moves gracefully as ever, despite the largeness of her belly underneath her padded gown. "Perhaps the journey had best be put off till summer, then. If—the Jins' poor little grandson may not have long to live, Madame Gao said, but I'm sure our Old Master still has many years before him. His will is strong."

Father presses his lips together and says nothing.

Little Auntie Tuo finishes refilling Father's cup. "Your daughter's innocent devotion to her grandfather is bound to bring him blessings, when she goes. And homage to Manjushri and Guan-yin might free her of, whatever's been troubling her. Lady Ding's hardly the only one who's benefited from a pilgrimage to the Five Crest Mountains—think of all who travel so much farther, and through truly dangerous territory!" With one slim finger, she traces the teapot's handle, down and up again. "Still, it's only nine or ten months till the best weather comes."

Nine or ten months! Can Grandfather possibly live that long? Can he stand that much pain? And I know Wintersweet has hardly left her bed in the weeks since she bore a tiny girl, except for the perfunctory rites a few days later, after the sickly infant died. Must she lie until next year's seventh month—weeping, eating almost nothing—in a lightless room?

After a moment, Little Auntie Tuo adds that although by postponing the trip we lose the chance to have me ask Guan-yin that *her* child be a boy, by summer perhaps she herself could join the travelers.

My father clears his throat, and turns to look directly at his concubine. "Boy or girl, I believe it was decided months ago," he says. Then he makes half a smile, at least. "Don't think I don't know what you're trying to do. But if it might ease Father . . ."

He looks at me with the new thoughtful look he's given me several times of late. I can see some of the strain lift from him. "All right," he says. "Even Her Dowager Majesty has traveled safely among the five peaks, and the last time she was in her seventieth year. The road from here is safe enough these days. And my brother can't be stopped in any case. It could do you some good, daughter—you might as well go along." And now he really smiles.

The next day, after Father hurries back to the Forbidden City, his concubine invites me into their room for tea. When I first see Little Auntie Tuo I catch my breath: Her hair's fixed differently today, and she looks so much like Mama.

A book of poems open on my desk, I'd fallen to wondering what it must have been like in the Upper Courtyard before I was born, when not only Third Aunt, but Third Uncle and Grandmother and Grandfather's last concubine all lived here, when baby Wintersweet and her brother would be brought in from the West Courtyard—before war and the smallpox goddess and anger and coughed-up blood took so many of them away. When Mama was the family's pregnant young daughter-in-law, pregnant with that stillborn boy, or me.

Now, fresh tea poured, and the two of us warmed by the heated bricks beneath us, I mention to Little Auntie Tuo how different the family compound seems these days.

"Perhaps it's you that's changed," she says.

I look to see if she's laughing at me, or chiding, but the smile on her lips rests easily, approving. I smile too.

"You're a better musician," she adds. "I could hear that right after you . . . came home. And not as good at painting, I expect—no, no, of course you wouldn't have had a chance to lift a brush. I'm not blaming you. Maids in the palace aren't given time for such things, I know. But that's not what I meant."

She knows what happened with the Fifteenth Prince, I think, knows I broke with chastity, yet wasn't given a position in his household. I hang my head. Of course. No one's mentioned it, but what one eunuch hears and sees, the other eunuchs know. And Father has friends among them. He's been told everything. What *will* become of me?

A muffled groan emerges from the North Hall.

The little auntie breaks the silence, telling Snow to go ask Cook to stew some persimmons. "I'm eating all kinds of peculiar things," she says lightly, and adds that Snow should also tell Cook to brown some flour and make a bowl of hot sugary *musi* broth for each of us.

The southerner has learned some Manchu, I think. And remembers what I like to eat. I recall how I hoped to see her wincing as she walked up Marvel Peak on her lily feet. Again, I'm too ashamed to look up.

"I wasn't talking about His Highness," she says after Snow has left. "You did no wrong—you could hardly refuse the desires of a prince. It's a pity no more came of it, but who knows better than I do how easily most men move from one woman to the next? And it's natural that this house looks small and plain after all you've seen. But there's something else that's new about you . . ."

I'm tired of worrying alone. Her gentle matter-of-factness loosens my tongue, and in a rush I tell her it wasn't that the prince lost interest in me, or even my mysterious fits that caused my dismissal, but mostly what I said to him after the charge given me by my mother's ghost. Then I have to tell about the statues I've kept secret for so long. "But I don't know why," I say. "Mama said the mandala should be donated to some particular temple. For her sake, she said."

Eyes full, I look at Little Auntie Tuo, to see if she thinks I'm lying, or that my mind's been taken over by some crazed spirit. But her gaze is level, steady, pure attention.

"If my mother's caught in the ghost realm, I'll do whatever I have to, to give her peace. But I don't—Five Crests has so many temples! Even if I did know which one they're to go to, there are still fifteen statues to find, besides the Tara. And then there's getting hold of the eight offering-goddesses!"

She only nods. But I have more to say, now I have begun. "Even if I did all that, would Grandfather be cured? Would the donation help Wintersweet too? Do you think it's really the answer to Mama's plight?"

"The lama and the great Guan-yin in the Warmriver temple and your friend—Yura?—didn't tell you exactly why you're to do this either, did they?" The concubine pauses. "Perhaps this chance for you to cheer your poor cousin *is* part of the reason. That's why I thought your father ought to let you go." She sips her tea, reflecting, and once again I absorb something of her tranquility.

"But if there's another purpose to this pilgrimage, I suppose you're meant to reach understanding by yourself," she says. "Meanwhile, I think I can help in the matter of the statues." She puts a hand on my arm. "In fact, I know I can. My apologies—your father had me look for something in your trunk and I saw the Pandaravashini. It's an exact match."

"A match? For what?"

She has Akshobhya and Ratnasambhava, she tells me, the buddhas of the east and south, and their eight bodhisattvas, leaving only Amoghasiddhi with his attendants to be sought for. And the lost Tara. She says she'll gladly give me her ten statues, and that the stories of how she—and Father!—received them will prove to me there's some strange design at work. "But first," she says, "before Snow returns, I think we ought to speak of something else."

Dispassionate though it is, her voice frightens me. I want to leave the room but cannot move. "Young Mistress," she says, "do you know the real reason your Third Aunt died?"

Dull smells hang in the stale air of Wintersweet's overheated room. Her hair falls tangled around a pox-roughened face untouched by rouge or powder. The embroidery crumpled on one corner of the bed platform looks to be a half-finished picture of Child-Sending Guanyin. Happiness sets a teapot, cups, and a plate of cakes on the low table between the two of us, nods wordlessly when I thank her, scurries out the door.

"So I did ask Mother Ding about giving you the eight goddesses," my cousin says, continuing what she'd broken off when Happiness entered the room with her tray. "But I knew she'd say no. If your note had given me some reason . . ."

She waves a hand, as if to brush her words away. "I'm sorry, Lotus. It wasn't your fault. You can't imagine how glad I am that you can come along to Five Crests. I just . . . failed you. I suppose that's no surprise." She pushes the cake plate toward me, pours the tea herself.

In the old days, Happiness would have stayed. In the old days, Wintersweet would have been altogether different. I don't know whether to slap her or take her in my arms as Nurse would when I'd fallen and banged my knee. Finally, I reach across the table, wriggling my fingers as if about to tickle her into merriment. She responds with a wan smile.

"Listen to me!" she says. "How can you keep from laughing out loud at such woeful talk? But I can't seem to . . ." Another wave. "Anyway, thanks to my good mother-in-law's convictions, you and I will soon have weeks together."

She shakes her head. Her loose hair sways. "Just seeing you today makes such a difference, Lotus. I've been so tired. Exhausted. This is the first time since . . ."

She stops again. "Let's not talk of it just yet. And maybe Mother Ding is right. Maybe Manjushri will help Little Treasure recover his strength. He's a dear child, and if I can't—Please." Wintersweet breaks a cake in half, waving the larger part beneath my nose as if she were nine years old again. "*Mmmm. Smell the wine and jujubes?*"

The sweet, eggy cake is too rich for my taste. I start persuading her to let me fix her hair so we can join the others for the send-off party in Old Lady Jin's apartments. Her husband's grandmother may have excused her, I say lightheartedly as I can, but *I* will not.

"She's giving us a fine farewell, Wintersweet. With a ballad singer *and* a sacred-story recitation! You really should take part—what if someone decides you aren't up to leaving for the mountains tomorrow?"

"Oh, the more who pray for Little Treasure, the better. And there's still hope I might bear a son, a healthy one—we'll be asking Guan-yin and Manjushri for that too, of course. They'll let me go." Her laugh has an edge to it, but at least she laughs.

"But the ballad singer," I say as I get up and tug her toward her dressing table. "She's one we've never had in *our* house. Your sisters-in-law said she's good, but I won't go without you."

That works. Wintersweet has always loved the long tales in rhyme, and the way the women who chant them change their voices to become each character in turn while they strum their lively tunes.

As I ease the comb through her snarls, I try to tell my cousin all I couldn't put in my brief note. Or most of it: I say little about Grandfather, and nothing—not now—of Third Aunt. Nor do I bring up the puzzle of what holds Mama in her terrible life that is no life.

Wintersweet is darkening her eyebrows by the time I finish reciting the list of holy statues I already have. Once she interrupts, cautioning me to lower my voice: "Or that sneaking chit of a maid might overhear and make trouble somehow." In that moment, her face is acid with jealousy. But I'm so pleased to see her returning to something like her old manner that I say nothing in defense of Happiness.

"In a way," I conclude, "I suppose it makes sense that it's the images of the All-Accomplisher and his bodhisattvas that I'm missing. Since he's the buddha who can grant us fearlessness—and Wintersweet, I'm afraid. I don't see how I can *do* anything. Scary miracles and confusing ghostly messages and teachings I don't understand . . ."

Blinking fast, I look away, but don't dare stop talking. "Or maybe it's because of my, my pettiness that those particular statues haven't come to me. Maybe I was too envious of the success of others who've served in the palaces, instead of . . ."

My cousin's staring quizzically at me, as if it's only now that I've really awakened her attention. "Amoghasiddhi?" she says. "It's the buddha of the double thunderbolt you need? Who holds his right hand up, palm outward?"

Yes, I say without a word. She sees it.

"Then, right now, before we go to Grandmother Jin's, I've got to show you something. In Grandfather Jin's Lodge of the Immortals' Isles. His study, in the garden."

Her face lights up, just for a moment, with her old glee and daring, as insecurity and spite and paralyzing sadness fall away. "You'll see why when we get there, Lotus," she says. "And then somehow maybe we can find a way to make Mother Ding and the Old Master give them all to you."

THE FEMALE SCHOLAR'S DESTINY

TRANSLATORS' INTRODUCTION

What can we surmise about the anonymous author of this late Qianlong-era *tanci* (literally, "words for strumming") or ballad?

Its language reveals that the poem was composed by someone who grew up in or near Beijing. Although many such metrical narratives were undoubtedly the work of semiliterate professional singers, "The Female Scholar's Destiny" gives evidence of some literary education. Moreover, its brevity suggests the effort of an amateur.

We can speculate that the author was a woman: There's a high proportion of female authors among those tanci ascribed to known individuals. Some scholars believe these works often mingle autobiography with their obviously fantastic elements. This ballad's heroine "Jessamyn" (literally, "Winter Jasmine") may be, then, a reflection of the writer, her life transformed by reverie.

"The Female Scholar's Destiny" has features typical of these romances, from the passive male who "legitimizes" a homoerotically charged female bonding, to pairings of characters that create pseudo-twins or doppelgängers. While one scene draws on the tropes of literary erotica, the story finally disavows the overt transgression of gender-role boundaries, in favor of a secure social hierarchy. Debate continues: Do such fantasies inscribe an accommodation to the existing order by sublimating subversive impulses, or resist it by constructing woman-centered utopias?

The heptasyllabic form of the tanci (4 + 3 syllables, with a midline pause) has been rendered in this very free, abridged translation by the familiar meter of the English ballad. We have not reproduced the original's end-stopped rhyme. To the modern reader who protests the many implausible features of "The Female Scholar's Destiny"—or any such product of the imagination—we ask if plausibility is indeed the *summum bonum* of a fictive world.

Saul & Jannie Loneseer
Oberlin, O. / Iowa City, Ia.

Come hear this song of a noble girl
   named sweet Jessamyn,
How she assisted her true love
   —and made herself his wife.
Now, Jessamyn was her grandsire's pet;
   he loved her like a boy.
When she was but a pretty child,
   he betrothed her to Young Jin.
The astrologer cast their horoscopes,
   and month and day and hour
Were each one in exact accord—
   a potent harmony!
Through poems exchanged, both lad and lass
   began to share their hearts.
A passion pure, predestined, strong,
   took root, and grew, and bloomed.

"O Jessamyn, my granddaughter,
   with your talents heavensent,
Be ever faithful—be true till death—
   now your troth is pledged."
"O Grandfather, I promise you
   Young Jin shall be my mate,
The grandson of your own dear friend—
   or I'll wed no man at all!"

Alas, the course of destiny
    is not an easy road.
A widow-woman in that house,
    still young, and comely too,
Fell under a seducer's spell.
    The scandalous tale spread far.
Jessamyn hung her head, ashamed
    by the blot on her family name.
"A dreadful dowry it would be
    to bring such ill repute.
I cannot wed, I will not wed—
    no, I shall run away!"

The maiden tucked black clouds of hair
    beneath a student's cap,
And with cotton wool, stuffed heavy boots
    to hide her lovely feet.
By dark of night, in her mannish guise,
    she crept toward the household wall:
To win great glory, she'd steal forth;
    her honor she'd redeem.

But Jessamyn's clever serving maid
    caught her by the sleeve.
"O Lady mine," said Little Joy,
    "you need not go alone.
If you were a man, if I were a man,
    ah, then what might we do!
But since we're not, dressed as a groom,
    I'll guard your chastity."

Bold Jessamyn and Little Joy,
    on the road through winds and frosts,
They traveled to the capital,
    taking temple-lodgings there.

"I'm a humble orphan, Scholar Sun.
   I've come here to Beijing
To undertake the great exams
    that the emperor's decreed.
On th' appointed day at the Testing Hall,
    they'll seal me in a room;
May the poems and essays I write then
    earn laurels for my clan!"

How firm, the rule of karma's law
    that intertwines two lives:
To that same temple in Beijing
    another hopeful came.
He was no other than Young Jin,
    Jessamyn's own true love.
The two young men—or so 'twas thought—
    met, and talked, and found
A remarkable affinity,
    and soon swore brotherhood.
Yet Young Jin's face showed sorrow deep
    as at a hidden woe.
"Pray tell me, Elder Brother Jin,
    what troubles do you bear?"
"Ah, one is secret, but one I'll tell
    the brother I cherish so:
I am no scholar. I lack the skill
    to pass the great exams.
Yet I dare not fail my family,
    and know not what to do!"

Soon Scholar Sun brought forth a scheme:
    he'd give his name as Jin,
And take the tests in his brother's place
    for sake of brothers' love.
Young Jin agreed. The plans were laid.
    But on the night before,

Jessamyn lay sleepless, worried
   about Jin's other woe.
"He said he had two troubles, yet
   he only told me one.
Can it be he loves another girl,
   forgetting his Jessamyn?"

Jessamyn spoke with Little Joy,
   the groom, the clever maid,
And ordered her to test Young Jin
   while Sun took the exams.
For three days, Scholar Sun was gone,
   and when the first night came,
The slim groom crept into the bed
   where Young Jin lay asleep.
"O, sir, I am no stableboy,
   come, feel my body's signs!
I am the orphan step-sister
   of your own Brother Sun.
For all this time, in boyish guise,
   I've watched you, and I've loved!
I beg of you, this very night,
   let us be as man and wife."

Her eyes were bright as caltrop flowers,
   her skin, as smooth as jade.
Her slender fingers, gleaming, pale,
   like scallions in the spring.
And every feature Young Jin saw
   resembled Jessamyn's.
But he refused. The second night,
   he turned her back again.
On the third night, she offered him
   a friendship pledge instead.
With sweet hot wine she plied Young Jin—
   and joined him in his bed.

The clouds, they gushed, the rain, it spilled;
    two phoenixes took flight.
How tenderly he plucked the flower!
    How red the virgin's blood!
Till dawn they sported, duck and drake,
    within the gauzy drapes:
A goddess like a rainbow mist,
    a besotted mortal man.

The day the Passing List went up
    at the imperial gate,
Behold! the very name Young Jin
    appeared above the rest.
Fame and praises now were his,
    and an official's cap,
Yet when the emperor summoned him,
    the brothers quaked with fear.

The truth must out: our gracious sovereign
    praised the *faux* Young Jin,
Who then admitted, "I'm Scholar Sun—
    and the daughter of my house!"
His Majesty saw she'd meant no harm;
    he acclaimed her loyal love.
"Alas, that gifted womankind
    cannot serve the state.
This maiden's talents We have seen;
    We see her worthy heart.
If the real Young Jin inspires such love,
    he deserves a rich reward!"
Young Jin was given a high post;
    the wedding day was set.
Returning to her family home
    and proper modesty,
Our Jessamyn saw her love no more

till the wedding procession came
To fetch her with gongs and flags and drums,
    till he lifted her red veil.

That night, at last Young Jin confessed
    his second secret woe.
"When you disappeared, my mother came
    and bade me take a wife.
I swore I'd wed no other, but
    my lineage has no heir.
I knew my duty to my house—
    so I chose a concubine."
Jessamyn smiled, and took his hands,
    and said, "'Tis better so.
And you shall take my serving maid
    as Second Concubine.
Yes, twice you did refuse her,
    'twas wine that made you yield—
We all shall live in amity,
    and each will have her place."

And so it was: in happiness
    and peace, the four did dwell.
Modest Crimson, First Concubine,
    gave birth to three strong boys.
Clever, lusty Little Joy,
    now Second Concubine,
Stayed by the mistress she so loved—
    and each bore a fine son.
Young Jin became Grand Minister;
    his fame spread far and wide.
The grateful populace never knew
    his wise decisions' source!
And pure, upstanding Jessamyn
    with five lads at her knee

Tutored them, and all did pass
   the Imperial Exams.
Each loved her as his mother dear;
   each rose up to great heights.
So fivefold glory came to her,
   and honor, all her days.

JOURNEYS

A traveler gazes toward the five great crests of the mountains called in Chinese "Wutai shan." They rise, five grassy earthen terraces like natural altars, among the lesser summits, above dark pines and bleak eroded slopes.

Over the centuries, so many have looked upward to those distant peaks! So many have wondered what divine play of light and color might manifest itself before them there, what indigo mist or lightning flash or iridescent cloud. Soon, two cousins—who resemble one another as much as sisters might, yet in the end seem not at all alike—will enter the foothills, having journeyed with their companions southward from Beijing. One will carry a mandala of statues, carefully protected yet still incomplete. Both will peer toward the unknown terrain ahead.

Already weary with days of travel, when they reach the narrow river valley that forms the eastern entryway to this hundred-square-mile realm, they will see forbidding clouds roll in to block the view. At the temple where they'll stay that night, the party's seniors will decide to take the monks' advice: *Circle around the sacred precincts' southern edge while the bad weather passes, then take the northward road past Buddha-Radiance Temple, enter from west and work your way back here.*

So the cousins will have to wait a little longer to find what comes of their looking, of the trek they are about to hazard among cliffs and tors and hills. Hearing of the new route, Lotus will think how it's like going around to enter a walled garden—or a palace—by another gate.

So many others have made this pil-grimage, by so many routes. Each one following a different map, each enters different highlands. Each brings together and lays out—however carefully they try to follow their predecessors' teachings, the rules that govern form and space—a different scattered mandala.

The first visitors find mountain spirits, dragon ponds. They discover marvelous signs of Taoist transcendents already dwelling here. The spring waters well up clear and cleansing; sometimes the catchpools reveal palaces in their depths. The air wafts fragrant with life-enhancing herbs, with flowers that bloom all winter long: Sweetgrass, Jade Sylphs, Gold Hibiscus, Heavenhemp, Bodhisattva-threads, Hundred Harmonies.

In the violent years after the Han dynasty's demise, over a hundred families flee to this fastness far from the cities and the battlegrounds. It's said the smoke of their untroubled cooking fires still sometimes floats above a ridge.

Later wayfarers search for that secret refuge among the foggy dells. The dogs and roosters can be heard, far off, but no one finds the way there and returns to tell of it.

On the mountaintop called Central Terrace, a fourth-century emperor presses his footprints into a rock. His horse does the same. These traces remain—along with stone monuments and monasteries—to show those who come after the reverent power of this Buddhist overlord.

During the glorious Tang, from India and Central Asia, from Japan and Korea and the great peninsula to China's south, Buddhists of many schools come to obtain scriptures, and other sources of illumination. A hundred temples and cloisters guard manuscripts and grottos, offering priceless teachings to those prepared to learn. Lone monks and nuns meditate in hidden caverns, pursuing with the fiercest of dispassions their individual pathways to enlightenment.

In the years of Mongol rule, imperial patrons from Khubilai on encourage Tibetan teachers to establish more centers for worship and learning—and divine protection of the empire—in accord with the Thunderbolt Way. Ocean of Vistas, Ten Thousand Saints Guard the Nation, South Mountain, Sea-Gaze, Clearcool: These are among the temples founded during the Yuan.

Tibetans, Mongols, Han Chinese, all make the demanding journey throughout those years and the Ming and Qing—and even in the next, appallingly disordered, century. With the ruling family's aid, human constructs prosper. In leaner times, the Five Crest Mountains abide, a place for vision, cold and pure.

So many travelers: Right now, just before the midpoint of the Qing and just before their departure from Beijing, those same two cousins, harboring secret smiles, join a group of women and girls at a farewell gathering. Old Lady Jin, anxious to buoy the pilgrims against treacherous or simply unpleasant weather, has arranged the most inspiriting sendoff she can. Age and frailty keep her home, but like her daughter-in-law Lady Ding, she knows the power of a vow to Manjushri. And her youngest great-grandson (once so plump and rosy, and so listless now!) is the darling of her heart.

The two latecomers apologize for their impoliteness; the kind-eyed welcomes they receive suggest that some at least of Wintersweet's insecurity has been of her own making. A blind entertainer twangs her samisen and begins the ballad the matriarch has requested. Her mobile face transforms itself as she becomes first one character and then the next.

Wintersweet listens with something like her old intensity. To judge from her looks, thinks Lotus, my cousin finds as much sorrow as amusement in the adventures of the ballad's daring heroine. But if it saddens Wintersweet to think she'll never do such unlikely things, the story also seems to offer her a kind of balm.

Lotus herself is grateful that Euphonia and Constance are distracted by the music and the tale: The two have not yet had enough descriptions of palace life. Especially not of Lotus's own circumstances, and the exact reasons for her early release from service. They're terribly sorry to hear of Old Master Sun's painful state, of course (haven't they said so, more than once?) but they suspect there was something else afoot. They want the whole story, straight and clear.

Aunt Gao and Lady Ding and Old Lady Jin are more involved with Wintersweet's two sweet-faced older stepsons. Just after Lotus went off to Wintersweet's apartment, their younger brother, Little Treasure, was brought in to lisp his gratitude to the pilgrims for the exertions they will make on his behalf. But he was deemed too ill for these excitements, and his wet-nurse quickly carried him away.

Looking toward the maids clustered near the door, Lotus sees that Happiness has quietly joined the others. In fact, she's found a place next to Little Auntie Padma—who sits on a stool in her usual territory between the servants and the wives and daughters—and appears to be catching up on news from her old home. The concubine maintains her unreadable quietude: Surely she's pleased to be allowed to add her petitions for Old Master Sun to those of the others, since it means a chance to worship at the Five Crest Mountains; surely she's reluctant to leave her chubby toddling daughter in Beijing for several weeks in only a nursemaid's care.

The ballad ends. A meal is served, and Wintersweet jumps up to wait on the senior ladies, determinedly cheerful, her depression pushed aside. Lotus must devote all her attention to Euphonia and Constance. So she's especially pleased when the nun is ushered in.

The story reciter's head is shaved. Her robes are somber gray. She leans on a walking stick as an old woman might, yet Lotus observes a youthful spring to her step. After greetings and tea and pleasantries, the nun unwraps her book and shows the frontispiece, in the manner usual for any of her sisters who visit the women's quarters with pious narratives that also entertain.

But when her eyes—her perfectly normal, curiously familiar eyes—lock for an instant onto Lotus's, do they not spark green?

Lotus can't be sure. Later, she will review that instant more than once. On cold mornings, looking up toward the faraway peaks, or waiting, shivering, at evening while her quilts are being spread out on the bed platform of a flea-ridden inn, she'll try hard to remember when she saw—when she might perhaps have seen—the nun before.

But at the moment, it's no more than a flicker in Lotus's awareness. After the group prayer and the lighting of incense, the nun's voice swells as she chants her brief invocation to Guan-yin. She keeps time by beating on a hollow wooden fish. She begins the opening poem:

> "A lotus-flower in a tiny sea:
> a burning altar lamp.

So the light of faith casts beams in hell,
to save—with Guan-yin's aid."

The narrative itself relates an inspiring life story like so many of these popular *precious volumes*—certainly a suitable entertainment on the eve of a pilgrimage. Yet as the details mount up, Wintersweet and her two sisters-in-law begin to steal glances toward Lotus.

"I will go on," the nun is saying, "to tell how, having been summoned by the emperor's heir for sake of her talent and intelligence and yet having refused to become a future imperial concubine, our Miao-lian began the spiritual practice that would allow her to achieve enlightenment. Since her birth into this world of red dust, Miao-lian had forgotten her original nature, her vision remaining clouded by ignorance and delusion . . ."

By this point, Aunt Gao and Lady Ding and Old Lady Jin, and more than one among the maids, are staring. Only Padma and Happiness, distracted by their whispered conversation, seem unaffected. Only Padma and Happiness and Lotus herself, who simply listens, oblivious, absorbed in the tale.

In the silence after the recitation ends, quick-witted Wintersweet calls for hot water, and hurries to refresh the older ladies' tea. This gives her the chance for a few quiet words with her grandmother-in-law, concerning Lotus and two sets of bronze statues.

Old Lady Jin (still amazed, still wondering just what sort of person this Lotus might turn out to be) is quick to respond: If Wintersweet really thinks allowing her cousin to donate a few small statues to a Five Crests temple might aid Little Treasure, she'll have a word with her husband about the images of Amoghasiddhi and his attendants. And surely Lady Ding . . .

Oh yes, of course, murmurs the old lady's daughter-in-law. She'll gladly allow the girl to have her set of offering goddesses. She cuts her eyes at the quiet girl with the passionate face, glad now her son has the wife he does, and not this other daughter of the Suns.

Precisely what the nun's tale means is anybody's guess. But from that moment on, all present participate in the unspoken—and unsettling—agreement that their pilgrimage has yet another goal, even if it's not clear what. And all treat Lotus more than ever as one somehow set apart.

JEANNE LARSEN

. . . .

FROM " 'A LOTUS-FLOWER IN A TINY
SEA': MYTHOPOEIC DISCOURSE AND
ICONIC POWER IN *THE PRECIOUS
VOLUME CONCERNING MIAO-LIAN,
DIVINE WOMAN OF THE
WUTAI MOUNTAINS*"

. . . .

Lureen Joana Seesnil
Tunghai University

*(draft version for presentation at the 1997 Annual Meeting of
the Modern Language Association not to be cited or
reproduced)*

... Recently discovered in a temple library on Putuo Island in Zhejiang province, this *baojuan* ("precious volume") presents itself as a story from the Qianlong reign period. But—in yet another duplicity—aspects of both style and content suggest a later date of composition.

The text revels in its intertextuality. The heroine's bloodless birth from the flower bud of a cassia tree is but one of many bald-faced appropriations of tropes well known to readers of popular Chinese religious materials. And the encoding of "Taoist," "Confucian," and "heterodox" language into a syncretic but predominantly "Buddhist" discourse exemplifies the semiotic system within which this and other baojuan are inscribed. Even the story's unusual Tantric flavor has roots in writings about incarnations of Guan-yin dating as far back as the Song dynasty.*

The devout surface of *"Miao-lian"* (literally "Marvelous Lotus"—the very name of that floating signifier, the virtuous protagonist, signals Buddhist piety) may be deconstructed to reveal resistance and subversion. This baojuan, like so many, speaks to the concerns of women as well as men, especially those not born

---

* I owe what small understanding I have gained of these matters to the guidance of my Tibetan friend Nen-rje 'Alensa, and here express my gratitude.

into the aristocracy. Nor is it the only baojuan to suggest—over against the circumscriptions of Chinese culture—that a woman's refusal to marry might not be morally wrong.

Furthermore, the text proclaims a genealogy of transgression. It states that enlightenment is to be achieved by realization of the buddha nature within, an intertextual gesture evoking the writings of a Ming dynasty sectarian leader who authored five highly influential—and suppressed—baojuan.

Yet perhaps of greatest interest to the modern Westerner are the reminders in the text itself of the ritual force of any performance of this "talismanic" verbal artifact. As Professor Nadeau has pointed out, the very acts of reading, copying, or financially supporting the printing of a baojuan were understood to have religious merit "independent of the semantic meaning"—a pleasant thought for this translator, her publisher, and anyone who buys a copy of my rendition of Miao-lian's story!

Like the reminders of artifice inherent in the text's mixed form (prose *and* poetry, diegetic *and* mimetic narrative), this insistent self-referentiality forms a discourse on discourse, even as the playful interplay of words, the self-creating chatter, paradoxically invokes the silence—the emptiness—before, after, and between the lines.

The author is anonymous; the text proclaims its power . . .

$\int$o many travelers looking to the Five Crest Mountains. Who has left a written trail?

Among others, two medieval Chinese monks and a ninth-century priest from Kyoto. A progressive statesman—and student of Zen, and visionary—during the Northern Song. A Ming scholar who resisted till his death the conquerors calling themselves the Qing. Compilers of local histories in government gazetteers. In the tense mid-1930s, a Scottish artist and her Ohio-born companion. Two men whose book was published in Tokyo during the Pacific War, when Japanese forces held the mountains and the surrounding land. More recently, scholars and tourist-industry workers from Beijing and the provincial capital, and an adventurous Ivy League academic, traveling by bus, by jeep, on foot.

So many writers. So many, too, who travel as their eyes pursue a track of ink: The encyclopedia officially published by the Qianlong emperor's father includes some eighty poems on sites within these mountains, poems read how many times? How many more were written later? How many have been lost?

You and I now follow after them. And might we, as we travel on, find words that Lotus wrote? Or has that pathway disappeared among the others, true and false? Is it vanished like a byroad in a heavy fog, like the missing Tara statue of the mandala?

The morning before the party reaches the Buddha-Radiance Temple, Wintersweet awakens. She can make out the shape of Happiness still drowsing at the far end of the bed platform. Out in the yard, the others are talking themselves awake, discussing the change in weather: still cool, but clearing, it seems. Apparently, her mother-in-law has excused Wintersweet from morning duties.

Travel has tired the young wife, but only physically. She and Lotus have talked together to their hearts' content. Her cousin seems so much older now—her calm words are comforting and, yes, often wise. And such secrets she has told! Her strange dream about the Queen of the Flowers, for one: Wintersweet would like, someday, to write that story down.

The pure air and exercise, and the stimulus of new scenes, have righted the balance within her body. Call it a matter of yin and yang or postnatal hormones, a shift in the Five Elements or in her brain chemistry as mourning works itself toward its end: She feels better than she has since her poor sick baby was born and died. No, better than since those first giddy weeks right after she was married.

Wintersweet exhales, long and deep. Her baby. After the brief lift that came of helping Lotus gain possession of the statues, she could sense the ashen cloud settling down on her again, the morning they left Beijing. She knows that many babies die, knows she should expect loss as other women learn to do. But she won't forget that unnamed child.

Yet somehow, in coming to the Five Crest Mountains, to the moist vistas of the foothills and their dustless atmosphere, it's as if Wintersweet herself has been reborn.

It's partly that we're all together, she thinks. Mother and Lotus and the others from my old life *and* the women I'll live among for the rest of my days. I've even had long talks with Papa. Some of us seek aid for Grandfather, and some for Little Treasure, but I am snugly in the middle: I'm dedicating prayers to both. I don't care about what Euphonia said to Constance, that Mother's too eager to strengthen the connection between our two families. Why shouldn't she? It means we can see each other more.

Now Wintersweet yawns. Someday her sisters-in-law will marry—it can't be put off too much longer. Then perhaps they'll look at things from a different point of view!

And may they get the husbands they deserve. But in the dimness of the room, Wintersweet blushes at the unkind thought, and hurries to revise it: *May they find ways to be happy with whatever husbands they get.*

A week ago, she still burned at the notion of her own husband and his concubine Redgirl left alone together in Beijing. But what does that matter, really? *She* is the boys' official mother: They'll care for her to the end of her days, and then they'll provide for her soul. She's not a concubine; she's the wife—someday she'll have her own daughters-in-law, her own household to run. Someday, with luck, she'll be as respected as Old Lady Jin.

Remember the women in the ballad at our send-off party, she tells herself. How easily they got along. How deep the bond between the mistress and the maid. Foolish to squabble, when you might have that instead. For a moment, Wintersweet drifts toward her favorite daydream: living out—or failing that, then writing—such a romance herself.

Yet her thoughts soon turn more serious. Looking back over the past year, Wintersweet realizes it was when she didn't seek him out that her husband was most eager for her company. *If I don't worry, if I don't waste myself on envy, then I'm not afraid. And when I'm not afraid of where I stand in the eyes of the household . . . then I have my old energy! The energy to think and act and live.*

She blinks. *To see the world for what it is.*

The understanding comes to her like that: an electric discharge in a shattered second—so bright it blasts away the dragging build of obscuring clouds. A neural flash. A transforming diamond bolt from the buddha

Amoghasiddhi. Lightning that dispels the low-pressure anxiety of dull thunderheads. She laughs aloud.

"Mistress?" Happiness sits up and leans tentatively toward Wintersweet from her place at the other end of the bed platform. "Mistress, are you all right?"

"I'm fine," she says. "I'm absolutely fine. Except . . . I'm a little chilly. Come here, won't you, and get under the quilts with me?" And so these two travelers turn onto a new path.

FROM *RECORD OF A JOURNEY TO THE FIVE CREST MOUNTAINS*

You Shi-wo [1750?–1849?] *(Neal Rae Ninesoule, S. J., transl.)*

The Five Crest Mountains, also known as the Clearcool Range, lie in Five Crest County in Shanxi province. Emperors and their sainted mothers having been among the pilgrims who throng from all the world to burn incense in these numinous grounds, I too went to pay my respects.

It is a landscape that resonates with spirit realms, where the earthly matches the divine, where it is possible to catch sight of what cannot commonly be seen. Hidden watercourses link one tarn to the next; caves contain crystal chambers filled with jewel trees, golden towers, and wondrous musical instruments. Holy texts brushed on slips of sandalwood have been discovered in occult crannies among the hills.

The pathways among the Five Crest Mountains branch, and one must choose one's route. Even in summer, one must be wary of thick fogs and sudden storms. Yet while moving from temple to temple, the traveler may find several types of people worth watching.

On the entry roads in the summer season, beggars, tea sellers, amulet vendors, hawkers of tiger claws and medicinal herbs—these approach all who pass them by. Some have faces sharpened by hunger or avarice. Some seem dull with stupidity or want.

In a temple courtyard guarded by two iron lions, fierce dancers drive away demons while lamas in yellow hats blow conch-shell trumpets. A man in a heavy mask sways and spins, warding off devils that would harm the Buddhist Law. Some of the red-robed monks chant without stopping; others keep time on stretched hide and wood, or bone.

A sickly gray-haired woman is carried up a rocky path on the back of a strong young farmer, perhaps her grandson. He pauses for a moment in the shade of a bent pine tree, wipes his forehead, marches on.

Near the great white round pagoda, a Mongol merchant clutches his guide-book, having made his way at last to the place he wishes someday to be buried. His red-dark face shows the weariness of long travel; his eyes blaze with joy. Flags flutter, inscribed with sacred words.

A noisy crowd of village women ride donkeys, making a great show of the paper buddha images on their heads, their dark-blue eye shields, and the bunches of incense wrapped in handkerchiefs they carry on their backs. The two old dames who appear to be the organizers of this pilgrim club pat their purses, looking pleased.

A lady of good family peeps modestly from her sedan chair. Her son or brother steadfastly scrutinizes a cliffside pocked with caves, the sublime peaks beyond.

In a hidden cave, a traveler of a different sort, solitary, lean, obtains at last a vision of the Lord of Speech astride the courageous lion of his enlightenment. Or perhaps powerful Ekhadashamukra, eleven-faced Guan-yin.

The flames of a hundred lamp-buddhas illuminate a temple's painted ceiling, while the teachings written in a thousand sutras revolve on a carved repository cylinder. A lone man in an official's cap leaves off studying the inscription carved into a stele and runs his hand along a row of prayer wheels. He sets them spinning for the salvation of all who journey through all the worlds.

Of course, many travelers never wrote accounts of what they saw. Yet there are other ways to shape human experience. The Buddha-Radiance Temple, for example, seems designed to ensure the visitor will undergo a series of architectural maskings and disclosures, tantilizing as slow zigzags of a plot.

Wintersweet and Happiness and Lotus, and the others who are riding or being carried in mule litters up the long trail to the temple, can see nothing of its ancient structures till they pass through the veiling evergreens. There—like the reader who encounters a revelation at chapter's end—they find themselves, abruptly, at the foot of the front wall.

The pilgrims mount the twisting entrance ramp and soon proceed to a twelfth-century building off the first courtyard. They stop to offer incense to Manjushri, the heavenly architect. Then they climb to the second level, where their vision's channeled forward, onward, by two plain residential cloisters that flank the open square.

Yet they still can see no more before them than another high protective rampart—and, beyond the steep stairs leading upward, the beckoning roof tiles of the ninth-century main hall. Their view of the ascending interweave of wooden bracketing that supports those welcoming eaves, their culminating vision of five haloed golden buddhas and their round-limbed clay attendants, is delayed, controlled, held off.

Even when they get there, the supplicants will not yet have discovered the hexagonal whitewashed tomb behind the hall. It holds the remains of the mystical Tang dynasty devotee of Manjushri who lived and taught at Buddha-Radiance for forty years. It waits against the sheer slope behind the complex, a denouement startling as the one that waits at a lifetime's end, a conclusion obvious in retrospect at least, like the moral of a tale.

Then is not art—the builder's or the narrator's, the poet's or the metalsmith's—a skillful means to help us on the path? That's what the long-armed abbot says the next morning, to Lotus and Padma and several of the others.

The party has divided for the day: Despite the lingering threat of rain, First Uncle and Aunt Gao—along with Lady Ding and her two robust daughters—have gone off on a side trip to a nearby cliff known for its hermit grottos. The cousins and Padma, accompanied by their maids and two older married serving women, are staying back at Buddha-Radiance to rest a bit: Tomorrow, if it clears, they'll all move on, into the territory's heart.

Wintersweet and Happiness sit close together, smiling. Lotus remains abstracted, a traveler still unsure of both road and destination, wrapped in an otherworldly air. Then she asks for ink and paper. The peculiar looking abbot obliges, with a cheery wink.

WRITTEN ON THE WALL OF THE
BUDDHA-RADIANCE TEMPLE

Here near the end of the trail from the dusty world,
Temple banners mark a Dharma-realm.

At daybreak, clouds hang thin around the peaks,
While pearls of light burst through above the pines.

Noontime drizzle blocks the pallid sun,
Yet gold lamps flash amid the late day rain.

A path leads upward through the grass and mists:
Lose your way, and who will guide you on?

A few hours after the arm-waving abbot's talk, Padma and Lotus slip out of the Sun family's room in the little cluster of women's lodgings attached to a corner of the temple complex. The other stay-behinds evidently remain sunken in afternoon sleep, but the light rain has stopped and the two are tired of huddling indoors. They stroll to the far edge of the entrance ramp and look down over the ravine.

"Do you think that's true," asks Lotus. "What the abbot said?"

Padma, at ease in Aunt Gao's absence, has more to say than usual. She reminds Lotus that the body of a buddha can appear in whatever form we need: a tiger, a preacher wandering northern India, a golden bridge suspended in midair, the inky word that one day leaps off the page to glow within the mind. "Think," she says, "of all the languages different people speak! Yet we each hear the holy syllables in a form we can understand. Why shouldn't an enlightened one appear to us as building stones, or paint?"

"Or bronze, I suppose," murmurs Lotus, eyes fixed on the scene unfolding as the rainclouds lift and melt away.

At those words, another traveler draws near: a ghostly young man with a pretty face. Yet revelation's not such an easy thing, at least not till the moment when it *is*. Wu Ming doesn't break his silence, and neither gazer sees anything more than a slight shimmer in the new-washed air. Still, Lotus's attention drifts away from the conversation, out toward two cranes wheeling above the treetops far below.

"Bronze, too," says Padma after a few moments' silence. "You know, I should tell you something. Do you remember the little statue of Tara that I lent your mother? The one that . . . disappeared?"

In that instant Lotus is blinded to trees and parting clouds and the long-legged birds now settling in the shallows of a creek. And yet, she sees so clearly, without doubt or hesitation, what is about to happen. Padma found the statue, she will say, perhaps not in the West Courtyard carp pond where the hand warmer was, but somewhere Mother Jia and her apprentice Jadewhite Rosary passed by that day.

Exactly so: It turns out that some months ago, Padma spied a dark gleam at the bottom of the family's other pond, the one in the Front Courtyard where the lotuses grow. Soon she found her chance, and quietly fished the small statue out. "You were gone by then, Young Mistress," she says. "Or I'd have told you right away. But I haven't thought to mention it since you came home from the palace."

The concubine hesitates. "Or at least, I'm telling you now. So you don't worry about it anymore."

Padma has grown in confidence since she proved her fertility with her daughter—and since Aunt Gao's grudging acceptance of her presence in the household. But seeing the anguish on Lotus's face, she withdraws into the near invisibility that has so often kept her safe.

As for Lotus, she scrapes the plain cloth sole of her shoe back and forth over the fitted stones of the entrance ramp. *The one statue needed to complete the mandala!* Why didn't she think to ask Padma if she knew anything about it, before they left Beijing? How simple that would have been.

Now the final figure of the mandala has been left behind. Tears well, and the wet stones blur.

Padma misreads the averted face, the tight-pressed lips. "Don't be angry, Young Mistress!" she says. "I did think about telling you after the send-off party, when people said the one in the nun's precious-volume story might be you. But, begging your pardon, that didn't seem possible to me, seeing as how such stories are about things that have already happened. And I wanted—"

Lotus waves away confession. She's opening her mouth to tell Padma about the bronze figures in her baggage—thirty-six parts of a mandala composed of thirty-seven!—when the round-faced woman touches her hand, then continues speaking.

"When I found out we were coming here, I decided I ought to have it blessed," says Padma. "After all that time in the mud. It's just over in our room, actually, Young Mistress. Shall we go have a look at it?"

Before dawn, my eyes fly open. The roomful of women in our temple lodgings slumber on. I lie unmoving between Aunt Gao and Padma, trying to remember every detail of my dream.

Father once explained that there are many kinds of dreams: Some tell the future quite directly, some hint at it and must be interpreted, a few reveal a truth from the past. I learned myself that others allow us journeys into another realm.

But Father told me most are the fruit of the thoughts and wishes we have when we're awake. Just as strong emotions—hate or fear or longing—can make us ill, he said, so they can give rise to certain dreams.

Was the dream I've just had one of the last kind? I can't be sure. Perhaps the value of any dream is that it teaches us uncertainty about what we call real.

I rub my eyes. *This* dream didn't seem like a visit from Mama's actual ghost. Yet it felt more immediate than the soft snores and heavy quilts that now persuade me I've returned to the crowded room where I fell asleep.

Last night Padma let me pack the statue of lovely Tara carefully among the others: The mandala is complete at last. Wondering exactly where in all these mountains I am to present it, I drifted off. Now I stare into the darkness and try to take myself back to the dream's beginning, try to remember everything.

I sit tucked like a child between Mama and my grandmother at a Sun family party in the North Hall at the start of spring. Yes, Grandmother. The solemn face I know from her portrait smiles at me. Yet I am full grown, and

Wintersweet is bustling about and pouring fresh hot tea as if she were our family's daughter-in-law.

My two aunts chat pleasantly with one another. How young they look! I stare at Third Aunt, at the freshness of her beautiful high forehead above the plain widow's clothes. No one mentions Father's concubine—it must be that she does not yet live with us. Little Auntie Wei, the concubine of Grandfather's I remember best, sits fidgeting by the door.

Grandfather himself is somewhere else, but when Father and First Uncle come in to pay their respects to Grandmother, she tells them they must join us for a while. "We're all family here," she says. "Let's not stand on etiquette today."

From the warmth of the bed platform, I look out at the windborne petals of the flowering plum. Yet beyond their flurry I see the pink frills and ripples of the apricot tree already rushing into bloom. At first, I am happy, free of worry or sadness. But it comes to me that something is wrong.

No one will speak of whatever it is. I start to call for Nurse, then decide I shouldn't, though I can't quite think why. My stomach tightens.

The others begin to play some kind of game; those who fail must drink a penalty cup. They talk, laugh lightly. Grandmother's face is flushed. She cackles at a joke of Wintersweet's, then starts to cough. I catch Father's eye and the look he gives me tells me he too knows the secret: Mama is with us now, but she is already dead.

She is dead, so she must leave us. Father seems to nod, silently, almost invisibly, in acknowledgment of my realization. I turn to look at her. The paleness of her skin strikes me like a weak slap—not horrid, but unnatural, all its subtle colors gone. Now it is Mama's eyes that meet mine, bright, too bright, as they were in her last days.

Shadows surround that face: She looks thinner, more delicate than ever, as though even her bones have shrunk. Fear and worry begin to well up within the shadows' embrace. She too knows it's time for her to go. But she wants to live.

Outside the room, apricot petals scatter. I see them from the corner of my eye. The heavy-headed peonies in the vase on the table nod, their clear crimson darkened by dry old age. The season's not the plum-blossom start of spring, after all, and not its apricot-petaled height, but the beginning of spring's end.

The chatter and clinking of the party fades to a low murmur, sifting around the two of us. Now all I see, can see, or want to, is my mama. I pull her close to me, as if I were the mother, and she the child. I couldn't say whether she has shrunk or I have grown even taller, but when I put my arms around her fragile frame, she fits easily within their circle, and her head falls naturally, lightly, on my chest.

"It's all right," I murmur. "You can rest now." The words come without thought.

The look in her eyes eases. Her bleached face relaxes. She breathes out, free now from dread and the sorrow of departure. I hold her as the sight of her dims, as she dissipates like wisps of scented smoke, shifting into nothingness within the circle of my arms.

That is when I woke. There, in my dream, I too felt solace, and knew that what I said to her was true. But now that I've returned to the cold and dark of this room for travelers, tears sting. My throat aches—the first time in so long! I bite my lips, half comforted, still longing, half unsure.

So the girl could have *retrieved* the Tara statue from her family's *lotus pond*? She must have walked *past* it three hundred times before she left for the palace!" The Lord of Mount Tai shakes his green squarish head. "They *miss* so much, don't they?"

The Chief Secretary of the Joint Ministries of Baubles, Babble, and Extraneous Narratives purses his lips, looking rather as if he were both sad and wise. "Well, my friend, that's the way they are. And one does hear . . ." He looks toward the prismatic clouds surrounding the celestial gazebo where the two have met, sees no one. "One hears that despite all that woe and agony and so forth, they do have the chance to learn, ah, a thing or two. A chance that *we* don't . . ."

But what use, or interest, is such talk? The Lord of Mount Tai sketches a kind of midair Möbius strip and smiles a toothy smile. "Shall we play? I'm afraid I've grown rather *rusty*, but your kind invitation has quite *whetted* my appetite for a game." He indicates the go board laid out on the cumulus table between the two. "And *such* an attractive set you've brought along!"

The Chief Secretary inclines his head. An old one, he murmurs, presented to His Divinity the Jade Emperor long ago. "I took the liberty of borrowing it from the treasure house when His Majesty suggested that I arrange to, ah, have a chat with you." One of the Chief Secretary's gray eyebrows rises, indicating that more will be revealed in due time. "I'm sure His Majesty would be pleased to hear that his principal aide finds pleasure in the thing. Look!"

He whisks off the lids of the two bowls that hold the go stones. But they're not the usual rounded pebbles—a set of white for one player, black for the opponent. Instead, they're gleaming heaps of carefully matched pearls, one soft nacreous ebony, the other a rainbow of oyster-shell pastels.

The Lord of Mount Tai squints as if beset by a half-remembered dream, a twist of déjà vu. But never mind: He remembers how to play the game. He considers how he might best begin to claim territory on the board, and places his first pearl.

Soon the neat crisscross scoring on the rhinoceros-horn board is overlaid with pearly lines and loops resembling a tangle of broken garlands, or scattered rosaries. The Lord of Mount Tai squints again. A bit abruptly, he inquires after the Jade Emperor's health.

Fine, just fine, the Chief Secretary replies, and takes the hint. It seems His Divinity has become curious, he explains, about certain souls associated with the very case they were just now discussing. Certain, ah, departed souls. The girl Lotus's garrulous nurse, for one.

The magistrate of the underworld knits his brows. "The *nurse*," he sighs. "I see so *many* . . . Ah. Proud of being a Beijinger, right? Plump, *gossipy*, rather good at managing *others*, but *far* too fond of doing so?"

The Chief Secretary nods.

"Yes, the *nurse*! Rather interesting, really, though I *don't* wish to *shock* His Divinity . . ." In the hanging silence, the Lord of Mount Tai fiddles with his bowl of pearls, then plunges on. "*Well*. In view of her good *heart*, and the arguably *noble* manner of her demise, she was to be *allowed* to be reborn *male*. Virtue rewarded with upward *mobility*, that sort of thing."

Another approving nod from his companion.

"*But*. She actually *refused*. Or—they can't *do* that of course, but she made such a *fuss* that in the end it was *simplest* to send her packing. Into the *next* body ready to emerge. She's a well-to-do bannerman's *daughter* now. And I understand the God of *Literature* has started keeping an eye on her. All that *natter* and *nosey-parker-ing*, you know. She's too *vulgar* to write real poetry, of course. But odds are, she'll grow up to be a playwright. Or . . . or a *novelist.*" The divine judge rolls his eyes. "Re*mark*able. Why, if she'd gone along with being born *male*, she could have been a famous *critic!*"

The Chief Secretary of the Joint Ministries of Baubles, Babble, and Extraneous Narratives opens his mouth, pauses, shuts it, and tactfully clucks his tongue. "And the girl's Third Aunt?"

A difficult situation, his companion replies, the go game languishing forgotten now. Virtuous widow, or culpable suicide? Victim or heroic martyr or self-murderer? He settles back in his cirrus chair, enjoying the telling of the tale. "*Now.* Her *father-in-law* has yet to come before my bench. But he's already paying the *first* installment on *his* karmic debt."

The Lord of Mount Tai leans forward to whisper the name of a certain affliction into the ear of the Chief Secretary, who shudders and crosses his legs. "A *long* dying, too," he continues. "But then, male or female, they *all* suffer so! And I must *admit*, as a sort of retribution it struck me as rather *neat.*"

The expression on the face of the listening celestial bureaucrat remains grim. The storyteller hurries on.

"*So.* It finally worked out this way: As a suicide, the aunt must remain in *limbo* a few years longer. Rules *are* rules. Then, when her niece finally bears a *healthy* baby . . ."

Two gray eyebrows fly upward in surprise.

But it turns out it's the other niece that's meant. ". . . the one called *Wintersweet.* Well now, the aunt will have an *extremely* long and pleasant lifetime as that family's most successful *son*, despite the wars and such to come. Government *official*, wealth, scholarly *recognition*, everything one could want. Good thing for her, er, *his* mother, too, of course—a nicely *orthodox* balance for that Wintersweet's happy scribblings in her . . ." He swallows. "Her *Jade Terrace* studio by the Sun family's lotus pond."

"*But.*" The magistrate rubs a pearl between his forefinger and his thumb. "There's still all that *rage* the poor aunt's soul has yet to come to *terms* with. And not without good *reason*. So most likely in the *next* go-round—well, we both know China's due for some extremely *interesting* times."

Now it's the Chief Secretary who leans close to his companion. "Revolutionary?" he murmurs.

The Lord of Mount Tai's stately head bobs wryly. "And *free love* advocate. A sharp-eyed Shanghainese who laughs at pain, and *unbinds* her feet."

Three days after Wintersweet makes peace with Happiness, somewhere in the sudden fog that descends onto a long hillside between Clearcool Temple and the Gold Pavilion, the party of travelers loses its way. In the space of a few moments, it becomes impossible even to judge which way is uphill, which way down.

Lotus is the last to notice. She's been riding head down, worrying, thinking about her recent dream, trying not to weep. *I thought I was through with grief:* The words run through her mind again and again. *I thought if I could gather all the statues, I'd find peace. But I can't be certain I've helped Mama until my task is done.*

Not for the first time, she wonders if she should have presented the mandala at Buddha-Radiance, or perhaps the temple where they stayed last night. Her thoughts move to Gold Pavilion and what some travelers have seen there: an airy aureate bridgeway leading to gilded towers and colonnades of light. *Will I be granted a sign?*

Her donkey stumbles, comes to a dead halt. Her head jerks up. She sees only a few stones in the dirt, some tufts of grass, a white wall up ahead. Featureless white walls on both sides. She whirls in her saddle: soft unyielding white behind. Lost in a nebulous paper-colored maze.

"Blessed Guan-yin help me!" Lotus murmurs, clutching the reins. Which way to go? Impossible to discern the trail, and the donkey shows no inclination to move at all. She shivers in the dampness. When she thinks to call out—more loudly—for human aid, the only reply is an eerily toneless echo that might have come from anywhere.

No, wait. Is that not another voice? Perhaps a familiar one?

As Lotus stares, a slender young man steps out of the heavy vapors.

Or perhaps he's formed from the mist itself—she can't be sure, and anyway, at the sight of him, her mind flies to other things.

"You," she says. "Have *you* been sent by one of the holy bodhisattvas?"

Certainly, any pilgrim of her day lost in the Five Crest Mountains and coming upon such a figure—whether youth or aged monk riding on an elephant or man who holds aloft a jewel lamp—would expect a divine guide. But Lotus remains wary. That tender face, those lean and languorous shoulders: This is the one who held her fast in the sandshift of her passions, in the dangerously pleasant shelter of a nomad tent no other living person could touch or see.

He smiles with genuine, if newfound, modesty. "Sent only by a bodhisattva's attendant, I'm afraid. I'm to guide you to meet the others at Gold Pavilion, so you can pray together before its great image of Thousand-Armed Guan-yin. Then I have to go."

Lotus remembers that slow smile. And something he once said to her: *We could make of such delusions a higher bliss. The bliss of emptiness.* "Do you know," she asks quickly, "that sometimes I imagined your face—"

"When you were with the Fifteenth Prince?" As she looks away and nods, he urges her to learn more about that kind of vision. "If you can learn to see . . . not mortal bodies, your flesh, his flesh, the deceitful apparition you might call *a man*, but to see yourself a buddha, to see two buddhas joined . . ."

For an instant, he wraps his right hand around the forefinger of his left. "Then you'll see the unity of form and emptiness." He drops his hands. "That's all it takes."

Those are almost the last words Lotus hears from Wu Ming. He clucks to her donkey, leads her through the low-lying cloudbank, toward Gold Pavilion. Shortly before they reach the temple gate, she catches a muted shout: First Uncle.

She answers, but her voice doesn't seem to carry. Before she can call again, the fog brightens, thins, and falls away. The donkey breaks through into the angled sunshine of late afternoon.

Lotus sees the stocky figure of her uncle standing on a boulder up ahead, peering anxiously into the whiteness below. Despite the light streaming from behind him, she can make out the huge grin of affection and relief that paints itself across his face as he runs—literally runs—in her direction. "Niece!" he shouts, and stops to catch his cap, to wipe one hand across the shaven front section of his scalp and on back toward his hanging queue. "Niece! Oh, excellent! After we were separated, blessed Manjushri sent a monk to lead us here—or holy Pilgrim Lad, your aunt says it was."

He trots toward Lotus, still shouting. "We all feared—well now, here you are, safe and sound! But how?"

At that same moment, Wu Ming, who has fallen a pace or two behind the donkey, says quietly, "Now have done with weeping: It is no help to those you mourn for. Tomorrow, you should present my, present the mandala to the temple at Bodhisattva Crown. At the altar where you look upon the face of death." He sighs a short, sharp sigh. "She only needed for you to let her go. And now, farewell."

When she turns toward his voice, Lotus sees nothing but a valley filled with fog. Fog and the long rays cast from beyond the temple. Fog and a wide white marvelous arc of light tinted reddish orange at its outer edge, blue-green within.

FROM *THE PRECIOUS VOLUME CONCERNING MIAO-LIAN, DIVINE WOMAN OF THE WUTAI MOUNTAINS*

. . . And so you have heard how having refused marriage despite the urgent pleadings of her family, Miao-lian was cast out of her home by her grandfather, and after great hardship made her way in the company of her female paternal senior cousin to the Wutai Mountains, where she received secret instruction at the temple called Gold Pavilion.

Hail to One who hears this world's cries!
Hail to blessed Guan-yin's holy name!

Journeying then to the high valley at the heart of Wutai where the Great White Stupa stands, she paid homage to the lock of hair from wise Manjushri within it. She made her circumambulations, she spun the prayer wheels, she prostrated herself upon one of the praying boards at the stupa's base.

In like manner, Miao-lian made her devotions at the other temples clustered thereabouts. Finally, she slipped away from her cousin and the party of pilgrims they had been traveling with, and climbed the hundred and eight steps to the Cloister of the True Countenance atop the hill called Bodhisattva Crown. There she gazed upon horrific Yamantaka, Conqueror of Mortality, whose nine wrathful faces bear the frightening aspect of Death itself. There in the center of a great ring of peaks, in the palace of the god, she presented the offering she had carried for so long.

The room stood empty, except for her. From the next courtyard, two long demon-mouthed trumpets wailed. Cymbals clashed, drums echoed, and the sound of chanting rose. As Miao-lian placed the statues on the altar, she looked unblinkingly at Yamantaka's strong blue body and the enraged bull buffalo head with its diadem of skulls. At last she knew no doubt or fear or sorrow. Her task was done.

Just then, Miao-lian's cousin ran up to the doorway of the room. She saw a mist of indigo arriving from the direction of Dragon Spring Temple across the valley; it wrapped itself around Miao-lian's body and carried her off toward the south.

Tears sprang to the cousin's eyes. She knew she had seen a miracle, and that Miao-lian had fulfilled her destiny. But she was sad at the loss of her companion, until looking once more toward Dragon Spring Temple, where the sun had just dipped below the horizon, she observed a bank of lustrous clouds such as she had never seen. They resembled the beads of a beautiful rosary, iridescent with turquoise and violet and kingfisher green, like the scales of a moon-colored carp or the mother-of-pearl within an oyster shell. Seeing this divine manifestation, the cousin shrank in awe, and yet felt greatly comforted.

Up in the Five Crest Mountains,
at Bodhisattva Crown,
the faithful girl has persevered
and made her offering.
The Wise One takes the form of Death,
and Death is overcome.
A cloud from heaven's edge,
like Guan-yin's chain of pearls:
she's carried off to Guan-yin Cave

on the slope of Southern Hill.
In that dark cleft with its sweet spring,
she starts her vision quest.
Like one who sees a mandala,
and rainbows born of white,
she looks beyond the magic show
the Body of mere Form.
She seeks to see the glorious,
the Body of Shared Joy.
I keep time on a fish of wood;
I tell of miracles.
I praise the Bodhisattva Guan-yin,
Great Compassionate One.

You mean that's *it*?" asks the Lord of Mount Tai, slapping one green palm in amazement on the arm of his scarlet throne. "The girl *finally* delivers those statues . . . and then she runs away from her *relatives* and devotes her *life* to seeking a vision of the, ah, holy bodhisattva?"

"Yessir," says Wu Ming, careful to maintain a respectful distance from the courtroom bench. "But surely . . . that is to say, I just heard in your waiting room that her father's concubine is scheduled to bear four sons in the next few years, so the family's future is taken care of." Hastily he adds, "Very kind of you and your daughter, sir, I daresay."

But then he can't resist adding one more thing. "So surely what she's doing is not as foolish as what I wanted. To smear my name all over some—"

"*Yes*, yes. Some silly work of *art*. Hardly *that* bad, I'll grant." He snorts. "Don't you know that your precious *mandala* will be melted down before the dynasty's end? Even before the *looting* of the Forbidden City's splendid *treasures*, the foreigners' *destruction* of the gardens and villas outside Beijing, before rowdy soldiers start *pulling down* pillars at those fancy—and *ruinously* expensive, you know, literally *ruinous*—those palaces and such at Warmriver? Immortality in*deed*!"

Then the judge of the underworld waves the ghost of the young man closer. He glares around the shadowy room. His tactful bailiff noiselessly steps away. "But what of the, ah, Tantric *sexual* practice? Wasn't she destined to become a *teacher*, to use desire as a, what do you call it?"

The bailiff's lips move. Wu Ming can't hear what he says.

"*That's* right," says the Lord of Mount Tai. "A *skillful means* for reaching spiritual ends?"

Wu Ming, stunned by the news of the mandala's future, only shakes his head to indicate he can't talk about what he doesn't know. Or doesn't yet understand. The judge of the underworld falls to brooding. The silence drags.

"Please, sir," Wu Ming finally croaks, still crestfallen. "I realize that none of us can go back to our old lives. Nor would I want to, now. But I'd like another chance. Please, sir, may I be reborn?"

Sometimes, when no visitor has disturbed me and I have fasted till I no longer need to fast, my thoughts turn to my mother. By this time, she has long since made her way through the dreadful darkness and into a new life. When I feel the pain of longing for her, or anyone, when I feel any such grief for any traveler through the grief-riddled world, I look at those feelings, breathing slowly, until a fresh wind sweeps across the sky, and my lips form an easy upward curve.

I know now that death can be overcome. By going through it.

More than that I can't explain, not even to myself. I can only move forward, toward the center of the hidden pure land, the walled garden palace, the mandala that unfolds itself around me. Into the banks of clouds above the peaks.

You mean that's *it*?" asks Pilgrim Lad. His eyes pop. His long soft earlobes quiver. "No heart-rending farewell in a freezing rain, no dissolving rainbow body, no Zenlike breakthrough of the—woof!—a-rational, no exhortation to compassionate action, no revelation of a scripture or a mantra-charm?"

The Dragon Daughter shrugs. "Oh, you can tell yourself all those things happened if you want them to," she says.

"All that coincidence swallowed, all that incredulity suspended, all our troublesome interventions . . ." His shrill voice cracks. "Why, you didn't even get the movements of imperial personages on the dates their annals record. And one *could* point out, that particular mandala was an odd choice for that time and place. Besides, it wasn't consecrated!"

Nearby, violet shadows waver. A cool breeze rustles through the bamboo grove. The surface of the lotus pond before them trembles as the huge bewhiskered carp rises to take in a gulp of air. Pilgrim Lad stops sputtering, and—quite visibly—collects himself.

"Right," he says. "Flawed, but offered with . . . with some *smattering* of good intentions. Along with the usual baser motives." He shakes his shaven head. "What more can one expect?"

At that, the Dragon Daughter smiles at him. Nearby, the brilliant-dark cascade of water splashes onto the mossy stones. Its deep rush and liquid tintinnabulation become a temple drum and bell, become a single voice forming perfect chords as it chants a mantra of great power.

The white parrot at long last stops circling overhead and perches on a willow branch above the diamond boulder where Guan-yin sits. "Look," says the bodhisattva to her attendants. "There, next to the lotus that's just coming into bloom."

From the waters of the pond, the carp rises up again. In its mouth, it holds a glimmering rosary of pearls, unbroken, untouched by mud.